THAT
NAIROBI
AFFAIR

By *Betty Leslie-Melville* with *Jock Leslie-Melville*

ELEPHANT HAVE RIGHT OF WAY
THERE'S A RHINO IN THE ROSEBED, MOTHER

THAT
NAIROBI
AFFAIR

———

Betty Leslie-Melville

DOUBLEDAY & COMPANY, INC.
GARDEN CITY, NEW YORK
1975

Library of Congress Cataloging in Publication Data

Leslie-Melville, Betty.
That Nairobi affair.

I. Title.
PZ4.L6374Th   [PS3562.E83]   813'.5'4
ISBN 0-385-01185-7
Library of Congress Catalog Card Number 75–6158

To Jock, of course

Acknowledgments

To Jock, my friend and husband, without whom this book would have been started, but without whose enthusiastic and endless encouragement, it would not have been finished.

To Lisa Drew, my friend and editor, who so cheerfully held my hand both through the long pregnancy and the birth of this first novel, and made it not only painless, but fun.

THAT
NAIROBI
AFFAIR

Hallit *remembered Lysbeth saying once that she had taken al-gebra at night school to find out what X equaled, and he won-dered if she had ever found out. Even now, even at this last moment, he could not help wondering if they would ever find out about this particular X and if they did not, it would surely not be for want of trying or for lack of interest. Violent death among celebrities has always generated morbid fascination, and the killing of Otis and the subsequent trial had provided months of headlines and juicy speculation over dinner from New York to Nairobi, where it happened, and everywhere in between:*

LEADING HEART SURGEON SHOT IN HEAD
Peer Film Maker Charged.

———————

LORD LINDSEY ON TRIAL
Jealousy motive in heart surgeon murder.

Jesus, he thought, so corny. I'd never dream of producing it as a movie . . . "dream of" . . . "movie" . . . they say that if you drown, your whole life passes before you like a dream-cum-movie, but I'll be damned if I'm going to jump into that freezing Thames for the sake of that. Anyway, where would the movie of my life begin? Not simply with childhood, he thought, or youth, or even his first movie success. He'd begin when he was born, which was when he was forty-six years old. There he'd be, fresh from the womb, a 6' 3" 165-pound baby boy.

His emotional life before then—before Lys—hadn't been even noteworthy. Nothing had mattered, really, until almost three years ago—in fact, nothing seemed to have existed before that. His relations with people had not been beautiful or ugly or ecstatic or

1

painful—just a flat gray plain of not much of anything. For every mountain you form you have to form a valley, and it was she who took him up to the pinnacles of joy and down to murky depths of despair. If he had a choice, would he go for the emotional ups and downs of mountainous country, or would he prefer to remain bored in the plains?

Lysbeth would not hesitate at all—she'd opt for the contrasts. But he thought now with hindsight that if he had it all to do over again, he'd be a plains dweller. If he hadn't gone to the top, he reflected, he wouldn't be sitting here now with a gun about to shoot himself, for Christ's sake. If he had to do it again, would he even choose to meet her? For the choice would be to live, or merely to exist. The moment he saw her was the moment he gasped his first real breath—she was the doctor who had spanked him into life.

Hallit and Lysbeth

Lord Hallit Lindsey, the Eighth Earl of Lindsey, looked the lanky aristocratic skeleton that he was as he leaned on the rail of the ship gazing down at the presailing frenzy on the wharf. It wasn't his features that made him so compelling to look at—the perceptive eyes were just vaguely blue, his mouth looked like a mouth and was neither sensuous nor hard nor slack nor mean, although it did perhaps reveal laconic humor. His forehead looked as if it was crossed with car tracks over which fell a thick straight shock of hair-colored hair, and one would say he had a "fine" nose. No, it wasn't the features that made him outstanding, it was the shape of him and his bearing. His head was a beautifully sculpted skull with the skin drawn tightly over it accentuating high cheekbones, and his face was outlined in masses of elegantly cut hair. The impression was that of a white American Indian Chief, were there such a being. He was too thin, but the way he moved erased that impression and made others around him look fat and awkward. If one word could be used to describe him, it would be "intelligent," and while meaningless as a physical description that adjective nevertheless would convey the overriding impression, for he looked like the genius he, in fact, was.

Among the great film makers in the world, there was Bergman in Sweden, Bertolucci in Italy, Altman in America, and Lindsey in London. People knew his name, indeed film buffs mentally genu-flected to it, but few recognized him, or indeed any of the great directors because their faces were seldom publicized. He wore none of the usual props movie people wear to advertise their occu-pation—he had no beard, no sunglasses, no neck scarf, no suede jacket. In fact, the only clue that he might be other than a rich and elegant gentleman of leisure was that he wore a tiny gold earring

5

pierced through his left earlobe—and of course no true gentleman would wear a thing like that.

Lord Lindsey, in jeans and an open-neck blue shirt, was leaning over the rail of the S.S. *Victoria* in his princelike way, and with little interest was watching the other passengers board at Southampton for their voyage to Africa.

He didn't care at all who his fellow passengers might be because he had no intention of speaking to any of them during the twenty-day journey. Instead, he planned to lock himself away in his stateroom while he worked on his next movie, which he was on his way to Kenya to film. In fact, that was the only reason he was sailing—he was buying the time away from telephones and interruptions, not the trip.

And then he saw her.

He had seen many women more beautiful than she, but she exuded a quality to which men reacted like opium. It was that characteristic, that essence, which drifted up from the bottom of the gangplank and made him first notice her, and he instantly wanted to rip her clothes off, throw her on the deck, and rape her. He also wanted to hit the man standing next to him for thinking the same thing. How extraordinary, he thought, I've never before had a desire to commit rape or to hit anyone. And why do I feel I want to protect her? And against what, for Christ sake? She was climbing the gangplank now, and she moved more like a kitten than a cat—lithe, yet playful. She had turned to wave to friends, and it was a bubbly wave—a childlike gesture—and from the back she excited him even more—small, firm, and tilted buttocks seemed to wave at him as she waved, and the wind blew her skirt and exposed long, strong, stockingless, suntanned legs. Moving up the gangplank again, her straight blond hair was churning like a windmill around her small face which was delicate but alert and alive—like a sparkling Christmas tree light. As she reached the deck she glanced around to see which way she should go—their eyes met, and she looked at him, not with interest or flirtatiously, but simply with candor. Feminine as she was, there was a little-boy quality about her too, and he realized that his original impression of her being catlike was quite close, for now he could see that she was in fact, a young lioness. Her hair was the same color as a lion—blond and beige and golden and tawny hues all mixed together. But it was her eyes that sealed the feline analogy. To say that they were amber and shaped like a lion's would not be wholly accurate because they were more than that—they possessed, as well, a warm, hypnotic quality. He felt as if he were on safari again and a lion cub was staring up at him; yet there was an elusive element too, of complexity—or anxiety—just beneath the surface of the eyes which the sparkle of warmth and fun could not completely hide.

As she went toward the bow he followed her. Looking to the right and left down the passageway for her stateroom, her hair swung back and forth in rhythm with her step, and by the time she got to her cabin he had decided on the subtle approach, so just as she was opening the door he tapped her on the shoulder and said, "Will you marry me?"

Looking up at him with amber eyes too big for her face, she said, "Why not?" laughed, and went into her cabin closing the door softly.

"Sorry, we can't give out the names of passengers," the chief steward said automatically without looking up from his desk, and then, glancing up he corrected himself, "Oh, Lord Lindsey, I *am* sorry, I didn't know it was . . . let's see, I'm sure it's all right for you, but you do understand our regulations—I just didn't see it was you . . ." he stammered accepting the five-pound note.

The card the steward handed him read: "Ms. Lysbeth Long. American. New York, N.Y." He returned to his stateroom and dialed her cabin. "Hello," she said. It was electrifying.

"Do you think we should meet now to make the plans for the wedding, or should we simply get the captain to marry us right away and discuss everything afterward?"

With a twinkle in her voice she answered, "Either way, dahling, it really doesn't matter. Why *do* you bother me with these details?"

Approving of her quick retort he continued, "Well, since the captain is frightfully busy right now, starting the boat and driving it away and all of that, and with the traffic in Southampton at this hour, let's meet for a drink first. In five minutes in the pub on deck B?"

She hesitated. For the second time within the space of fifteen minutes, he was aware of feelings that normally never assailed him. If she replied no, it would seriously upset him. Even her hesi-

7

tation had him in a dither that he hadn't felt since he was a school boy.

"Fine," she said, and hung up.

At a specially selected corner table in the pub he sat facing the door waiting eagerly for her, and when she walked in his heart began to pound. I'll be breaking out in acne any minute now, he chided himself. Then continuing the game, he pulled out a chair for her and said, "We've got to stop meeting like this. That's why I'm so glad we're getting married today. Do you, Lysbeth, take this man to be your . . ."

"How do you know my name?" she interrupted, smiling, but then not waiting for an answer, she asked, "What's your name? I wouldn't ask, but since it's about to become mine . . ."

"Rufus."

"Just Rufus?"

"Yes."

"Just like the orphaned rhino in Tsavo Park—don't you have a surname either?"

"No," he said.

"That's good because then I can keep my own. I really don't see why women should take their husband's name, do you? They don't in Ethiopia. Not that I'm big on women's lib but . . ."

Just then the waiter arrived and said, "Your order Lord Lindsey?"

"A martini and . . . ?"

"Lord Lindsey! Ah, so . . . Rufus Lindsey—Rufus H. Lindsey —what's the H for?" and turning to the waiter, "a whiskey sour, please, straight up."

This was the first time in years that someone hadn't made obvious remarks upon meeting him—either how exquisite such and such a movie was, how they admired his films, and what was the next one going to be?—or if they disliked his work, snide queries about whether the last film was serious or a joke?

No one had ever just asked, "What's the H for?"

"Horseshit," he answered.

"How pretty!—and what a coincidence that your mother named you after my favorite saint—St. Horseshit. . . . But you are messing up my test question quiz. In fact, you're very close to failing it before I've even given it to you."

"I'm terribly sorry."

"Well, I guess it isn't all your fault. You'll just have to answer me outright. Promise you'll tell the truth?"

"Yes, indeed, and by the way, would you mind telling me what we're talking about?" he said as the waiter put the drinks on the table.

"Whenever I meet new people—on airplanes, or at dinner—any-place—I have three test questions which saves an enormous amount of time because by their answers I can determine a whole series of other things about the person, and then I know if I want to be their friend or not. I'm always delighted when people fail because I have too many friends now and I really don't have room for any more—I've put some people on a waiting list for when one dies, but if they don't pass the test, they don't even get on the list. Not that there are any rights or wrongs about the answers—it's just that for people to enjoy one another they have to have the same standards and values. They simply have to be on the same wavelength. So if you like football games, it would be a waste of both our time to be friends because you'd want to go to the games and I wouldn't so one of us would have to sacrifice—and life's too short for that. . . ."

"You mean our entire future is based on football games? That's the most absurd thing I've ever heard. A football game takes an hour—two hours a week. Why can't I go to the game alone and see you the other one hundred sixty-six hours of the week?"

"I don't only mean football games—that was just an example. I don't even have sports in my test questions. Perhaps I should, though, because I don't like any sports—I just could never really care if Army beat Navy. Anyway, my first question is always about the movies—it sounds really stupid on the surface because I say, 'Seen any good movies lately?' Just that dumb. Then I wait for people's answers, and they'll expose themselves every time. For example, if someone says, 'Nothing lately, but I saw *The Sound of Music* four times,' that's the end of that. I don't even go to question number two because I couldn't like anybody whose zenith is *The Sound of Mucous* as Christopher Plummer called it. But if I get an answer like "Bertolucci's latest, or Fellini's," I race, pleased, right to question number two. That's why you have ruined my whole test—because you *must* be biased, and I wouldn't even know how to interpret your answers about movies."

"I saw *Sound of Music* six times—wasn't it wonderful?"

9

Lysbeth smiled and continued, "It's much easier to make people cry than laugh. There aren't many funny movies—for me anyway. Usually I go to the movies and everyone else in the whole theater is laughing but me. I don't think most hilarious films have one funny thing in them, and everyone else falls out of his seat laughing.

"I also think humor—having the same sense of humor—is perhaps the most important ingredient for friendship. I don't want a friend who is going to drag me to see *The Computer Wore Tennis Shoes*—and it has nothing to do with a film's being good. I like a lot of garbage—dreadful films really, but if they're *good* garbage, I adore them. I want to laugh or cry in a movie, or to have a revelation—I guess everyone does—it just depends on what makes you laugh or cry—back to standards and values—you see?"

"Ummm—go on."

"Well, if you pass the rest of the test, I guess we'll be talking about movies a lot, so we'll skip them now and go on to the second question which is about God."

"Who?" he asked leaning closer to her and frowning.

"God."

"Oh, her."

"You passed!" she exclaimed.

"To answer your question more fully, Lysbeth, I shall tell you a true story about myself. During World War II, I was going to have to go into the Army because I was eighteen. The thought appalled me, especially the thought of dying. I did a lot of research and learned that, pro-rata, more lieutenants got killed than anyone else, and they wanted *me* for officer training. I insisted that I be either a private soldier—an 'enlisted man' you Americans call them—or a general. 'It would be most difficult,' they informed me, 'to make you, an eighteen-year-old who has no knowledge or interest in the Army, a general,' 'Fair enough,' I said, 'then I'll be a private soldier—one or the other.'

"It wasn't easy for me to avoid becoming an officer, but through sheer perversion and perseverance, I managed it. Oh, if I could have avoided the entire thing I would have—I would have stabbed my eyes out if it would have done me any good—but in the British Army they'd have given me a rifle and a seeing-eye dog. So, there I was—a private in the Army—and what did they make me—me—a self-acclaimed atheist? A chaplain's assistant! I went to—

can't even remember the name of the camp now—Ft. Nothing—reported in, and told the chaplain, 'I don't go to church.' He said that since I was assigned as his assistant, I *would* go to church. 'No,' I told him again, 'I just don't go to church.' 'I order you to go to church,' said he, the captain chaplain. 'No,' I said nicely, but firmly. 'Then you'll clean latrines.' 'No, I don't clean latrines. That's for peasants—that's for people who clean latrines—I'm a goddamn genius.' What's your third question?"

"No, first I want to know what happened in the Army?" said Lysbeth laughing.

"Well, actually the chaplain turned out to be all right—once he recognized my genius. He wanted to know in what field I excelled, and I told him in many, but the one they could best benefit from right then was my film genius. The Army was using the most antiquated system of teaching—so anyway, I made instruction films for the Army. That's all. Next question."

"Did you like Nixon before you knew anything about Watergate?"

"It would have been a toss up whether I liked Nixon or Hitler better."

"With flying colors! Phyllis Diller always said she had a test question too. Hers was, 'I beg your pardon, but could you tell me what time it is?' And just by the way the person told her the time, she could tell if he was smart, efficient, capable—everything. So on her first plane flight, she was very nervous and wanted to ask the pilot her question, so she waited for him, and when she saw him sauntering toward the plane, she ran up to him and said, 'I beg your pardon, but could you tell me what time it is?' and he looked at his watch and answered, 'Ummm, the big hand is on the six.'" He laughed, and Lysbeth went on, "You're going to ask me to have dinner with you, aren't you?"

"Well, I didn't really want to, but since we're getting married, perhaps I should. Are you going to South Africa or—where?"

"Mombasa," she answered.

"I too. And why, may I ask, are you *sailing* to Mombasa—it's terribly Victorian of you in these days of flying machines."

"I have six reasons . . ."

"The first four will do."

"I never miss a war if I can help it, and I think there's going to be a good one soon in Uganda . . ."

"You don't look like a mercenary."

"I'm a journalist and photographer. When there are no wars, I write about anything. My first assignment in East Africa this time isn't until a month after we arrive—then I go to Ruanda to do a story on the gorillas. . . ."

"Was it you who did that spread in the *American Geographic* on baboons?"

"Mmmmm," sipping on her drink, "last year. I spent quite a bit of time in Africa. Have you been often or is this your first trip?"

"Heaven's no—I've been vacationing there ever since I was a child, and I have a farm in the Rift Valley—but this is the first time I've worked there."

"Work—what are you going to do?"

"Make a film."

"Oh, that's not work—work is selling shoes from nine to five or being a banker. Are you a Muslim?"

"I thought we had the question of religion settled."

"This isn't about religion, this is about marriage—are you married?"

"No, not currently, are you?"

"How could I have accepted your proposal if I were—that's why I thought perhaps you were a Muslim, so you could have four wives."

"Oh, I've had four wives, but linearly, not all at once."

"You've been married *four* times already?"

"Yes, all my other wives left screaming, but I'm sure you won't—you're different. Every time I get a divorce my lawyer says, 'You are now free to make the same mistake again.' And I do."

"I just got my first divorce, which is the third reason I'm sailing—to sort of gather myself together and rearrange myself. I'm not sailing for the sea, I'm sailing for the privacy. Do you know what I mean?"

"Of course I know what you mean. That's why I'm sailing too—look how we've ruined each other's plans. Are you upset about your divorce?"

"No, if I didn't want it I'd still be married. It wasn't an ugly divorce—he's very nice—we're just different tribes. And it wasn't any question of failure—I didn't fail, I just changed—you know?"

"Of course. Any children?"

"No."

12

"Would you like another drink?" he asked.

"Not for me thank you—I should go look around the ship and unpack . . ."

"You will do no such thing. There is absolutely nothing to see on this ship, and you do not have to unpack—how dreary—are you always so dreary? You will sit here with me while I drink."

"Do you drink a lot?"

"What a rude question. Yes I do. But I'm not an alcoholic. I'm a drunk. I have always made sure that I'm the latter because the difference between alcoholics and drunks is that drunks don't have to go to meetings . . ."

"In the States the difference between getting drunk or being tight depends on your social position. Taxi drivers get drunk and chairmen of boards get tight. Why do you wear that earring?"

"It's an affectation."

"Lords would never get drunk—they probably wouldn't even get tight. Do you like being a Lord?" asked Lysbeth seriously.

"What do you mean, do I 'like' being a Lord? How do I know?—I've never been anything else. It is a completely meaningless decadent English custom which will end with me because I have no children. No boy children—I do have a few girls—two or three of them."

"Do you see them often?"

"Never. I don't particularly like them. They've never done one interesting thing. If and when they do, I'll pay some attention and perhaps I'll grow fond of them, but they're only about twelve or sixteen now, and totally inane."

The ship's bell sounded and she wanted to watch their departure so he went with her and stood at the rail enjoying everything vicariously for an hour or so—he would never have thought that he could get so much delight out of someone else's pleasure. They watched an unspectacular sunset—unfair, he said, considering the circumstances, and then he went below to arrange a lonely, romantic table for them for dinner.

"Since the ship is so crowded it may have to be the boiler room," he told her. "I will fetch you in fifteen minutes, for I can wait no longer."

Fifteen minutes later he was at her cabin door. She was all beige—her hair, a full-length suede skirt, and a beige cashmere sweater. He noticed the room had four different large bouquets of

13

flowers with white cards hanging from them, and he walked up to one and opened the card. Scrawled on it was, "I love you, Jujubee."

"Who's Jujubee?" he asked her.

"My friend. I'm starved . . . let's go . . ."

"We're going back to the pub," he told her, "because we are going to have dinner brought there, so we won't have to go into that awful dining room where all those *people* eat."

"Marvelous," she said and they went back to the cozy little cocktail bar on deck B, to their intimate table in the corner.

After he ordered drinks and dinner and wine, he asked, "Which part of the States are you from?"

"New York."

"A real aborigine?"

"No, I was born in Philadelphia . . ."

"Wasn't that where W. C. Fields was born? . . . And on his tombstone doesn't it say, 'All in all, I'd even rather be in Philadelphia!'?"

Nodding in agreement she said, "People are always rude about Philadelphia, but I love it. Not as much as New York, though. I was born in Philadelphia and lived there and worked there, and then my husband—ex-husband—was transferred to New York just a year ago. He's a stock broker."

"Have you always worked in journalism?"

"No, I modeled first. It was such a mindless job. I loved it. The first day I worked in a big fashion show one of the girls put on a hat just before she went out on the runway, and the fashion co-ordinator hollered at her, 'Take that hat off—it looks like hell on you.' I felt sorry for the model and said, 'I think it looks great,' and the co-ordinator turned on me and said, 'You're not being paid to think,' and I thought, that's right, that's absolutely right, so for four years I never had another thought. I'd have worn men's clothes if they had told me to. Modeling certainly does free your mind, I'll say that for it. Then just before I went on my first trip to Africa one of the fashion photographers I worked for showed me how to use a camera, so I took pictures on the safari, and that's how I got into this. . . . Do you like New York?"

"I absolutely adore New York."

"What a relief—you know so many foreigners hate New York— they all love San Francisco. But I am in love with New York—I

14

feel absolutely sensual about it. It is such an electrifying city. I bounce around in the streets of plenty just overflowing with joy. New York is a world, not a city. It has nothing to do with the rest of the States. It is such a feast . . . that is, if you're a cultural consumer like me. It's also a city of winners. There're losers in New York too, but they're there only to mug the winners. It's the best and worst of everything. It's all black or white, there're no grays in New York—and I like that.

"And New Yorkers—do I love New Yorkers! Not only the people who were born there but the people who chose to live there. 'You're running away from little ole Macon, sonny,' the folks would scold, but they weren't running *away*—they were running *to* something. There is the best cartoon—you know how everyone says, 'New York's a great place to visit but I wouldn't want to live there?' Well, in this cartoon, this Texan is walking around New York with his cowboy hat and camera, and two obvious New Yorkers are looking at him and one of them says to the other, 'New York's a great place for him to visit, but I wouldn't want him to live here.' And it's so competitive. I like competitive, or at least committed people. And it's the most private city in the world, and so funny—the city makes me laugh. One day, I saw a wrought-iron Volkswagen—an entire car of wrought-iron curlicues going down Fifth Avenue and the passengers were sticking their hands out through the roof and doors and waving at everyone. It's the important things like that that makes me really love the city."

"Do you always talk so much?"

"Hmmm."

And all through dinner they talked about different places around the world, and during coffee she wondered why so few people were in the pub for brandy or after dinner liqueurs. Aware that neither of them wore a watch, she asked the waiter what time it was.

"Later than it's ever been," Lindsey answered her.

"Two A.M.," the waiter told her.

"Two A.M.!—I thought it was about eleven."

"See how fascinated you are with me?"

"I'm exhausted, I'm going to bed. Right now."

"You mean, you are *not* fascinated with me?"

"You have fascinated me, Rufus . . . but I don't want to call you 'Rufus'—"

"My other name is Hallit," he said unconsciously as he signed the check, "and that's what I'm sometimes called."

"Liar—you told me it was Horseshit, and that was the *only* reason I was fascinated with you. Now it's all over. . . ."

He walked her to her cabin, they smiled good night at one another and she was gone. . . .

He had much work to do and he picked up his typewriter but he couldn't write, so he smoked and then went out and walked around the deck and wanted to awaken her. Instead he went back to his stateroom and drank brandy and tried unsuccessfully to concentrate on his script. But the only thing he could think about was her eyes, all amber, and her hair churning like a windmill, and who was Jujubee? So he forced his mind to Africa, but there he saw a lion that was her all over again—beige and tawny and golden—so finally he gave up trying to write and went to bed, but he was so full of her that it wasn't until dawn that he drifted off to sleep.

At 11 A.M. he awakened and reached for his phone, but there was no answer from her cabin. Without ordering breakfast, not even coffee, he hurriedly dressed and raced about the ship looking for her everywhere. Where was she? She's probably fallen overboard, he dramatized, and while he was having a mental funeral for her he found her all wrapped up on the sunless sun deck, struggling to write with gloves on. "What *are* you doing?" he asked her, sounding like a father who has lost his little girl in a department store and is so worried that he is angry at her when he does find her. If she noticed his concern, she didn't show it at all.

"I'm making a list of all my friends and categorizing them."

"A list! I have three friends in the world and I despise them all."

"I have sixty-eight—I just counted them, and thirty-four think they're my best friends because I tell them they are—because they usually *are* at the moment I'm telling them . . . even my plastic friends. Sometimes I need plastic friends to satisfy my plastic side, but my first-team friends all over the world are writers or editors or film critics or artists—I don't have one friend who's 'in ball bearings,' do you?"

Standing next to her chair, he said, "No, but I wish you did so I could convince you to get rid of him and then there'd be space for me. Haven't you got any friends on the critical list? Or any whom I could poison and put there? Let's go and have a cup of coffee

16

and decide which one of your friends is going to go." He pulled her up from the chair and led her by the arm to the pub.

Unbundling herself, then sitting at the table with her nose all red from the wind she looked like a little girl to him. "What are you going to be when you grow up?" he asked her.

"Everything," she answered with a shiny smile. "You know one of my friends in Nairobi may be moving to Italy—perhaps I could fit you in there. But you ought to get some friends—don't you think you need more than three?"

"You know, if I hadn't read your article on the baboons and man's superiority over animals, I'd think you were dumb as hell. You haven't said one intelligent thing since we've met. It's hard to believe that it's you who stood up against the animal fadists. Did you actually write that article or did you plagiarize it?"

"I wrote it because I truly believe that man is the only animal that can change his environment *because* his brain can break down territorial imperatives. But you see, I only *write* intelligent things, then I put my mind in a cage and cover it over like a parrot and spend the rest of the time feeling."

"You are one hundred per cent wrong, and you know it as well as I—that 'feelings' come from your mind. Where else could they come from?—outer space? And you also know that the greatest pleasures come from man's mind. What about his creativeness? Look how his mind has transformed the world. I marvel at it constantly. If it weren't for man's mind, there wouldn't be a New York, we wouldn't be on this ship—I couldn't build this ship, could you?"

"That is perhaps the greatest difference between man and animal—only man can accumulate knowledge. . . ."

"Do you love Jujubee?" he interrupted suddenly.

Looking slightly startled she said, "Yes, of course I do," perfectly openly and directly.

Hallit just looked at her in despair.

"Why shouldn't I love her?"

"Her? HER?"

"Yes, she's *very* nice—you don't even know her," she said.

"Don't look all defensive and loyal—I thought she was a man. What the hell kind of name is 'Jujubee' anyway?"

"It's just a nickname—she used to eat those little round all-colored candies called jujubes—the same things Churchill used to eat—that's why they call her Jujubee."

"Because she looks like Churchill? Do you two go around writing and telling each other you love each other all the time?"

"Of course. Don't you think it's nice to tell people you love them if you do? Don't you like to hear someone say 'I love you'? I like it even if the person doesn't mean it, even if it isn't true. I remember once an Italian I had just met in an Alitalia office chased me all round the elevator, telling me how much he craved my body and adored me and couldn't live without me and all of that, and my husband, who was waiting for me outside in the car, got furious when I told him how enjoyable it was. He said, 'Do you want me to give you all that Italian bullshit?' and I told him, 'Of course I do.' It may be nicer when it's true, but it's nice even if it isn't. Don't you agree?"

"No."

"Why not?"

Answering seriously he said, "Because nothing is nice that isn't true. What's it all about if we don't know the truth? You will say there are many truths. All right, then, tell the many truths—the whole truth. But you must start with a truthful premise. Look, I really wonder why some people ever do anything because most people—two thirds of the world—go to bed hungry every night and we know that they will be hungry for the rest of their lives. They have little or no joy and no way of achieving it, and death is the only thing they have to look forward to. Why do they prolong the torture? It can only be that the masses think in concrete terms and not abstract thought, and therefore never think . . . conceive . . . realize . . . how wretched their lives are and how futile, because if they pondered about it they'd all commit suicide."

"Or do what they do instead—invent a belief in the hereafter to make death less final."

"You can't invent a belief," insisted Hallit.

"You're right. But they pretend to believe it. The masses are asses."

"Which proves my point about the truth. That if they faced the facts, the truth, then perhaps they would say, 'This is a miserable existence. I will try to improve it.' But to do this one has to learn truths—life is too short to cope with the distractions of lies.

18

Therefore, I have never told anyone I loved them—because I haven't."

"Not even your wives?"

"Not even my wife—I was teasing you, I've only had one wife."

"Then what's all this truth bullshit?" she asked peeved.

"It's different when I do it," he grinned happily.

"Bastard!" She smiled. "I always tell everyone I love them because I usually do. But then we have to define 'love' or else we'll have all sorts of semantic problems. Do you want to hear my theory on love?"

Gesturing for more coffee he grinned, "I hope it's better than your other theories."

"Ready? O.K.—I'm convinced that love is all there is and there is no substitute for it. But what does love mean? What does it mean when someone says, 'I love you'? There's hardly anyone who doesn't love his mother, his dog, beauty, laughter, Coca-Cola, as well as his romantic interest. Now you can't feel the same about Coca-Cola and your fiancé, yet you say you love them both. So, I thought about it a long time and decided there are four parts of love: the mental, the emotional, the physical and—for the lack of a better word—the spiritual.

"The mental is obvious—it is the *liking* of someone or something, and when it is extreme, it may indeed be love. One can certainly love a friend, music, baseball.

"The emotional is the being *in* love. It's the flutter of the heart and the feeling of one's stomach getting up and marching around just at the sight of one's beloved. It's the romantic aspect that everyone sings about, writes poetry about, and swoons about. This has nothing to do with loving a person or even liking him, this is pure romance.

"The physical is obvious—the sexual desire, which is a necessary part for the total love because without it you might just as well live with your brother whom you like, or love.

"The fourth—the 'spiritual'—is the admiration you have for a person, and this must be included with the other three aspects if you are going to have the all-consuming love. I may like—meaning enjoy—a thief, but I won't admire or respect him. I may admire his ability, but that has nothing to do with him as a person. Or the reverse situation may arise. I may respect the Pope's sincerity, may even admire his good will and intentions, but I may not like him or enjoy him as a person.

"And of course there are all the different combinations of the four. It's possible to love someone and not like him. You may love your mother or your sister but not like—enjoy—them. It's possible to be in love with someone and not love them. I've been in love with people I've loathed—dreadful people—yet, there I was, madly in love. And the opposite can be true because you can love someone and not be in love with them—such as one's child. There is no doubt that that is love, but there is also no doubt that you're not *in* love with your baby. You can certainly be physically attracted to someone you're not in love with, whom you may even dislike. It's possible that you may want to go to bed with a blonde with an I.Q. of 32—someone you feel nothing for other than a sexual attraction. Right? Right.

"You may be *in* love with someone, like someone, crave them sexually, or admire them, but until you get all four parts together, you don't have the big I LOVE YOU. I love everybody and everything, yet I don't think I've ever really *loved*. So when Jujubee and I say 'I love you,' it means we like each other so much it has exaggerated itself into 'love.' "

Throughout this soliloquy, Hallit just sat there and stared at Lysbeth, listening to her wispy voice telling him her theories, all of which he had discovered when he was eighteen years old but most people never learned. Then he said, "Yes, the majority of people go through life thinking they love, and all they actually feel is lust—not that there's anything wrong with lust—it's just that it should be recognized for what it is. As everything should—back to truth again. Without love of some kind life would be impossible. I love my work which encompasses many things—ideas, creativity, and so forth, but I've never come close to loving a person, or even being in love."

Lysbeth looked astonished and said, "You've never been *in* love? I like being *in* love best of all. I fell in love the first time when I was eleven, the second time when I was eleven, and the third time—in fact, that whole summer I wanted to elope with each new Good Humor man. I suspect that I am so addicted to romance and hate the vacuum so much that I fill the emptiness with anyone. I just hate not being in love—everything is so dead and so earnest when you're not in love—you only hear music

20

through your ears, not through your heart, and it's the only way to lose weight—my stomach disappears when I fall in love. Do you know what I'm talking about?"

"Of course I *know* what you're talking about, I just haven't experienced it. Does that make it any less valid? Do I have to be a child molester to be able to make a film about a child molester?"

"Do you see the steward's watch? Do you realize that we've been sitting here for three hours talking?"

"Let's sit for three more, and eat eggs Benedict."

"Beautiful," she said enthusiastically as he called the steward and said to him, "My mistress and I each want eggs Benedict."

Lys smiled but the steward didn't, and she continued, "You see, this is where you have an unfair advantage—because you are you, and I have seen your films. I know that, for me, each one is a revelation, so you have the advantage that I already admired and respected you before I met you. Also, fame is very sexy. Power and fame are the two strongest aphrodisiacs I can think of, and that isn't fair either—because are you attractive because you're attractive or because you're famous?"

"Both."

As they ate she asked him, "What would you rather be other than a film maker?"

"Dead," he answered. "I just cannot imagine life without making films. At the age of two I made up my mind to be a film maker—the minute I saw *Snow White,* and I never deviated once. I spent my entire life in movie theaters and insisted on going to Eton instead of Harrow because films were more accessible there —the town was closer. At fourteen I got a 16mm. Bolex for my birthday—the only thing I had wanted since I was two—and made my first film, which I edited myself and forced my mother and father and friends to watch. Everyone hated it and spent the summer trying to avoid me and it, and subsequent films, but I knew then—at fourteen—that criticism, as well as praise, has to be judged from its source, and everyone who had seen my films was a cretin. Oh, my mother patted me on the head and said sweet Mother things, but they were invalid.

"Then one weekend my family had some guests—one of whom was John Farrant, the drama critic. At the lunch table I stated obnoxiously that I'd like to show Mr. Farrant my films—much to the horror of my mother and father, of course, but he was very polite

21

and said he'd actually love to see them. Perhaps he preferred an hour of bad films to the lack of my parents' interest in all films. I never did work out why he came for the weekend—he probably didn't either—unless it was for the salmon. Anyway, I set everything up and I dragged him into the darkened library and showed him what I thought was my best effort. After the first hour-long film, I saw him change from a patronizing and kindly man to an interested one. He asked if I had another to show him—no other comment. I showed him another, and again he asked if I had yet another. Three hours later my mother knocked on the door and said it was tea time. Could he possibly have tea sent in, he asked her, he would like to talk to me about films. I'll never forget how I felt. Since I had no sound equipment, I had had to talk throughout the films explaining what would have been said if there had been sound, what music I would have used, and so on. It must have been a wretched experience for him, but he was the first one to recognize my genius and he gave me a tremendous amount of encouragement.

"That was when I first experienced the joy of recognition by someone I admired. He explained to my parents that I must be given sound equipment because I did have a large talent. So, at eighteen I sold my first short, then went into the Army and wasted two years of my life, and then from twenty to twenty-five I did nothing but make films. At twenty-five I had my first big success. I've never really had a financial success in the terms of what films *can* make moneywise, but I'm not interested in making money—the filthy lucre has never motivated me, though I admit it's useful to have. Films, to me, are an art form encompassing all the arts, not a commercial venture aimed at a specific common denominator for box-office appeal—not that I don't enjoy seeing entertaining films—it's just that I couldn't set out to make one. As you know, there are few actors who can work with me or with whom I can work because I cannot stand anyone with an idea—it has to be all me. I will not compromise. Everyone criticizes me for it, but I am right and they are wrong. Take a painting—can you imagine an artist letting the man who makes the frames add a little something of his own on the canvas? Can you imagine a composer allowing his sister to write a few bars for the middle of his concerto? Yet in films everyone, especially actors and actresses, seem to want to add some of their own 'interpretations or personality.'"

22

"What do you say when an actress says she would like to inject some of her taste or personality into a scene?"

"I just tell her the truth—I tell her she has no taste or personality."

"Is that kind?"

"No, but I'm not dealing with kindnesses, I'm dealing with truths. That is all that concerns me. The only thing that makes me cry is discovery—discovery of another truth, whether it's a philosopher's or a film maker's or a writer's or mine. You probably never sacrifice kindness for truth. Well, you will with me. I don't care how ugly, how complicated, how painful or hurtful it may be to you or to me, truth is what you will give me."

"For the whole twenty days till Mombasa?"

"For the rest of your life," he answered, looking at her seriously.

"That's going to be very difficult for me because I lie a lot. But here's a true statement—I must go now to my cabin and write. I have an article I must mail off when we get to Tangiers and it isn't finished."

"I'll pick you up at five-thirty for dinner."

"Who's ever heard of dinner at five-thirty?"

"We did—just now. Unless you prefer five?"

With a wave and a laugh she was off.

I'm drunk on her, he thought. He tried to write in his stateroom but he could get no further than describing the heroine in his film who was like a young lioness—amber eyes too large for her delicate face, with hair like a lion's mane—who talked of total love—how to really love you must have all four parts.

And at five-thirty he was knocking on her door and she called, "Come in, it's open," and there she was in a long coffee-colored sweater dress with a tortoise-shell belt and bracelet. Her jewelry was always seeds or leather or tortoise or brass—never gold or diamonds or emeralds or shiny things. They went back to their table and he ordered a whiskey sour straight up for her and a martini for himself. While they were talking and waiting for their drinks they heard music, so they got up and followed the sound to the ballroom where everyone on board was dancing: "It's a tea dance," she said as they hid on a balcony and peeked through a heavy velvet curtain. "They're 'getting to know' one another!"

"I always feel like a Martian in these circumstances. I just can't

23

imagine going to a tea dance. What kind of people enjoy meeting strangers?"

"What do you think most of these people do?" asked Lysbeth.

"Revolting things—the mind boggles . . ."

As they went back to their pub she said how she'd hate to be a man. "It would be terrible for lots of reasons, but one at the top of the list would be that it is so limiting. For a man dancing and sex are so similar . . ."

"Yes," he interrupted, "I've never been able to tell them apart."

"Oh, not similar to each other, but each time you dance it is practically the same as the last time you danced. It may be slightly better or worse depending upon your partner's ability, but it's still within the same framework. For a woman, dancing with five different men in one evening can be five different things ranging from terrible to excellent—but each time it is definitely different. How do you know if you're a good or a bad dancer? You have nothing to compare it to. You don't dance with other men, you see? Same in sex . . . only even more so. Really, the difference in men making love is as different as eating steak or a fudge sundae. It's all eating food, but very different. And it's a field that you poor men are absolutely deprived of. How do you know the different ways men make love—how could you possibly know the difference? Unless you're a homosexual. You're not a homosexual, are you?" He shook his head. She continued, "Then every time you make love it has to be similar—there may be a few variations depending on the woman you're with, but as in dancing the woman can only be as good as her partner. She is limited by him. Maybe that's why women talk about whom they go to bed with and if he's any good and so forth more than men because for a woman it's more than a personal experience she is discussing—it's also an observed art, a technique, a skill . . . where a man would be only involved in a personal discussion. Women have told me some extraordinary things—one man roars just like a lion every time he has an orgasm, and another cries 'Mother!' each time—I promise you it's true. Now, perhaps those men think all men roar or call Mother when they're having an orgasm. . . . You look astonished, Hallit! Well, that just proves my point—women know that men perform differently, but you don't. Dancing produces some good and some bad partners, even some rhythmless ones;

24

and the same in sex, some partners never hear the music either. . . ."

"What an unpleasant theory. I shall dismiss it at once lest it prey upon my mind that I am being typecast and graded each time I indulge."

There was a Bogdanovitch film they both wanted to see, so at six-thirty they went to the early showing and by eight-thirty they were back at their table in the pub, discussing the film, other films, talking about nothing and everything, laughing, and eating, and when she finally insisted on an early night he walked her back to her cabin. They smiled good night and he was back in his stateroom in worse shape than the night before.

He picked up his phone and dialed her cabin.

"Brunch at eleven?" he said. "I can't go on another hysterical treasure hunt like this morning's looking for you. Meet me in the pub at eleven, and oh, incidently, I'm in love with you," and he hung up without waiting for her to answer.

What schmaltz—how trite and insipid. I've always derided these things yet here am I, the gormless hero in the soap opera experiencing sloppy sentiment firsthand. He lay there hoping that his new movie would not turn out to be as saccharin as the way he was feeling. But, sure enough, his emotions flowed through from his fingers into his typewriter and he had to stop. Yet I haven't even tried to kiss her. He remembered having read somewhere that love was a combination of fear and desire, and while the desire part had always been very clear to him, the fear was strange indeed. But for the first time in his life he was afraid—afraid of offending her or of failing to please her—or was it really of being rejected?

Once again he didn't sleep until dawn.

They had brunch together but neither said anything about his having told her he was in love with her. In the afternoon the ship docked in Tangiers and they walked in the old part of the town through narrow and evil-looking streets, and he bought useless Arab things for her, and they ate exotic looking food in a grundgy cafe, and they laughed at everything as they strolled arm-in-arm—just as any two lovers would. He wondered if he'd have the courage to take her in his arms later on, and when they got back to the ship it was late and they were sweetly tired and they stood at a secluded part by the ship's rail and watched the lights of Tangiers fade, then disappear as the ship sailed out to sea—ten days now before they'd see land again. He looked down at her hair all ruffled in the wind and he turned her to him and took her head in his long hands and held her hair back from her delicate face which he tilted up to him, and amber eyes looked wide at him and he looked back at them very seriously, and slowly, slowly, he bent down, looking into her eyes all the time, and still holding her head in his hands, his lips reached hers, and they touched, their lips, ever so gently, and his eyes automatically closed. Then he opened them again, and raised his lips from hers softly and looked into her eyes which had gone all misty now, but just for a second, for then he let go of her and roughly gathered her in his arms as he opened his mouth and brought it down on hers, hungrily this time and her hair churned like a golden windmill around two heads kissing and kissing and eating each other's lips, and they clung to each other and he kept saying, "Oh, Lysbeth, oh, Lysbeth," and she kept saying, "Oh, Hallit," and they kissed and clung and pressed themselves into each other.

Then he put his arm around her shoulder and led her to his stateroom, and they said nothing. They were all feeling now—brilliant feelings he had never known before—and he opened the door to his cabin and the minute they were inside he folded her to him again and kissed her and put his tongue inside her mouth and kissed her more and she kissed him back with her tongue and he touched her breasts and whispered, "I'm so in love with you." And she took hold of his hands and pulled him over to his bed, and they sat on its edge side by side and she turned, and facing him, she looked up and said, "I think I'm falling in love with you too—the moment I saw you at the top of the gangplank something happened to me and it gets more minute by minute." And the whole while she was tracing his mouth with her fingers and touching his cheekbones and when her fingers got to his eyebrows she reached up to them with her mouth, and kneeling now on the bed close to him, she kissed his eyebrows and ran her tongue over them and nibbled on them with her teeth, and he grabbed her hard against him and pressed his lips to her neck, and she ran her fingers through his mass of hair-colored hair and he pushed her gently down onto the bed and they kissed and clung more and more because they couldn't get enough of each other.

Lying half on top of her, their legs still dangling off the bed onto the floor, he pulled her fully onto the bed, and he sat up beside her, and looking down at her he gently kneaded her hair with his elongated fingers and said, "Your hair is like cobwebs and I've never been in love before. This is a discovery, a new truth for me. I've felt sexual desires for women—strong aggressive feelings—but I've been unaware of women other than sexually. For you I feel such tenderness, I actually worry you'll catch cold or something ridiculous like that. I no longer know myself, but I do know I am hopelessly in love with you." And he leaned over her and kissed her again, and as he did he unbuttoned her shirt and put his hand on her bare breasts. He felt her tremble, but it wasn't a tremble of joy . . . what was it? he wondered. Suddenly she sat up on the bed and pulled her blouse together and her knees up, and with her arms wrapped around them and her chin resting on them she said, "I really think I'm in love with you, I respect you and admire you, and I even like you—but I don't want to go to bed with you."

"Why not?" he asked incredulously.

"Because I want to think about what's happened so far. Because I want to feel just this . . . this brilliance, and I don't want it changed into something else, and I couldn't stand any more joy. I want to preserve this—just this, for tonight."

So in tacit consent he lay next to her on the bed and they kissed and talked and clung and kissed, and his hands would naturally find her breasts but she would stop him, yet at that moment he didn't really care because the perfection he was feeling was so new and so much greater than sex, so much greater than anything he had ever known. They were ecstatic in their discovery of each other and he wanted at least to hold her all night in his arms, and when at three A.M. she said, no, she wanted to go back to her cabin and sleep, he was disappointed but not for long, for how can disappointment survive in bliss? And he kissed her all sleepy at her door and didn't even try to write when he got back to his stateroom, he just lay there and reconstructed everything that had happened and admitted to himself that he was so insanely in love that his judgment must be impaired. But she seemed to be almost as much in love with him as he was with her—yet she didn't want to make love. Why? He couldn't imagine—if she felt even half of what he was feeling. Why would any woman not want to go to bed with someone? he asked himself. He could think of three reasons.

27

Firstly, because she was not attracted to the man—but that was ruled out—Lysbeth had told him not only was she attracted to him but that she was falling in love with him. Secondly, because she was a lesbian and was not attracted to any man—well, that was out. Thirdly, because she was in love with someone else—that was out, too. Well, she'll just have to tell me, he decided. Funny, though, if I'd been with any other woman tonight I would have insisted on knowing, I would have banged on the table and shouted, and she would have told me. Yet instinctively I feel I can't do that with Lysbeth—I have this mental picture of her running and hiding in a lifeboat for three days if I do. He saw the dawn break, then he drifted off to sleep, dreaming the same beautiful things of her over and over again.

At ten A.M. he rang her. "I'm still in love with you. Come here right away," and in five minutes she arrived with a thermos of coffee and a scrapbook under her arm, and fully dressed climbed into his bed. They smiled and touched each other's lips, and when he said, "I want you so much," and started to undo her shirt, she answered, "First you have to look at this," and jumped out of bed and got the scrapbook, "and I never make love on an empty stomach—eggs Benedict?" As he ordered them he wondered if he should find out right then what this avoidance of making love was all about, but decided he should let it go for the moment and see if she would reveal it herself.

Sitting up beside him in his bed she poured coffee and showed him her book. Nothing in his forty-six years would have bored him more previously, yet now he was intrigued—it was just as absorbing as looking at his own baby pictures. Here was a snapshot of her sitting on her father's lap—she still looked almost identical, only slightly bigger. Here was her mother, their house, and all of it looked just like everybody else's mother and father and house, yet it was such a different experience for Hallit that he actually found himself gazing at photos of a three-year-old Lysbeth on a beach with a bucket and being very touched. His own children had never affected him this way. He spent more time over the pictures than she wanted him to, pausing over each one and even asking the details about them, until impatiently she hurried him on toward the end of the album. "There!" she exclaimed, "who does that remind you of?" Hallit had to agree that that picture of Lysbeth's father did look remarkably like himself.

28

"So, you have an Electra complex about me."

"Look at him in this one!" she cried with glee, "that could *be* you."

"If I had a top to my bathing suit . . . I'll have one stitched on immediately—so you'll let me make love to you," he said gently, and with a smile, smoothing her hair with his great long hands while she continued with the book.

She ignored his remark and went on, "Here's Jujubee." He saw a very interesting-looking woman whom he guessed to be in her late twenties staring out at him with a big contagious grin—yet something about her expression carried a hint of cynicism.

"Is she cynical?"

"She's a sentimental cynic."

"Is that her husband?" asked Hallit pointing to the man with her in another photograph.

"That's her 'part-time husband' as she calls him. He spends most of the time in Paris or Dubrovnik or Capetown, and she spends most of her time in Philadelphia.

"She looks familiar . . ."

"She's a portrait painter . . . Baroness Leda Boucher."

"Of course! I know the name well, and I've seen her work in New York—you never told me who Jujubee was. Yes, she's married to that French baron . . ." said Hallit as he looked more closely at this picture.

"She was married before to her brother . . . look at this—my first modeling picture . . ."

"Married to her brother?"

"Mmmmm . . . look at this . . ."

"No, you're going to have to tell me first about Jujubee's being married to her brother."

"Well, she and her brother were orphaned when she was just a few months old—parents killed in a car crash and no relatives—something like that. Anyway, they were sent to an orphanage in North Carolina, probably run as she claims all orphanages are, by 'religious dykes.' Later she was adopted but her brother wasn't. She was only about two and didn't really know she had a brother. She grew up in Norfolk, Virginia, with her adopted parents, and years later—when she was about seventeen—she had a blind date with a sailor and they liked each other at once and saw each other constantly for a few weeks until his ship left. They

29

wrote to each other and on his next leave they got married—she was eighteen or nineteen then. Soon afterward the Navy sent him to a base overseas and she needed a passport to join him. Although she knew she was adopted, she had never known her real name. To get her passport she needed her birth certificate, and when she got that she found that her real name was the same as her married name. She says she didn't think too much about it because she had always assumed her adopted parents got her from an orphanage in Virginia, where they lived—she didn't know she had been brought there from North Carolina, though she knew her husband had been raised in an orphanage there. But her husband, who was four years older than she, remembered he had had a sister and began investigating—and eventually he told her they were brother and sister."

"Christ, what a hideous debacle! Then what happened?"

"They had the marriage annulled, or it wasn't legal anyway—I don't remember exactly how, but they didn't stay married. She doesn't talk much about it."

"It would make a good film . . . who's this?" he asked, pointing to a picture of a very handsome priest in the scrapbook.

"That's a priest I know."

"Tell me about him."

"Not unless you tell me about all your women."

"I'll be glad to tell you, but you'll be bored to death. However, you are going to tell me every single thing about yourself, and you're not going to leave out one little bit, because I *have* to know. I *must* know every last thing about you."

"It may be impossible for me to tell you the whole truth because, as I told you, I lie so much."

"I don't care how difficult it is and I don't care *what* it is so long as it is truthful. If you let a pig screw you, that is beautiful to me because it's truthful. I know it will be difficult for you—it is for anybody at the beginning—but you'll grow to value—even enjoy —it. Let's start practicing with your priest."

"Well . . . um . . . there I was screwing this pig, and this priest came along and said, 'It is against God's word to screw a pig,' and I said, 'God never said a word to *me* about it,' and the priest said, 'Honest?' and I said 'Injun,' so he took down his pants and he screwed the pig too—and that's how we met. And every day for two years we met there and took turns with the pig. Then one day

30

he said, 'Think I could do the same to you?' and I said, 'Well, I ain't never thunk about that . . ."

"Come on, Lysbeth," said Hallit impatiently, but smiling at her hillbilly accent despite himself.

"If you don't believe that, you'll *never* believe what I'm going to tell you."

"Try me."

"O.K., but first you have to tell me about someone you were in love with."

"How can I be in love with a blackmailer? I keep telling you I've never been in love before you—"

"What about your wife—you must have been in love with her."

"I never loved my wife or told her so. Nor was I ever 'in love' with her. I married her because it seemed easier to marry her than not to. I liked her—she was perfectly O.K., she was good in bed, and what else was there? For me, there wasn't any more. My heart was captured by my work, and no woman ever interested me one-sixteenth as much as films. But marriage, I reasoned, would stop her from asking me when we were going to get married, it would stop my having to go through the mating dance of getting someone else in bed with me when she was out trying to make me jealous, and I hate going to prostitutes, so marriage would be sexually convenient, and I wouldn't have to take my clothes to the cleaners, which I loathe, and the buttons would always be on my shirts, and I wouldn't have to worry if there was enough wine and grapes for my cook to make the lobster sauce if I had a party. Marriage would *free* me—free me from petty inconveniences, and then I could concentrate solely on my films. And so it did. She kept a beautiful house, arranged elegant dinner parties with people she knew I liked—never those I didn't. She understood why I was away so much of the time and never complained. Oh, occasionally in her horsy way she made British noises and neighed a bit about my 'indifference,' with which I agreed totally. We never fought; I was always polite to her—as I am 'to all my servants' she later told the judge. But I could never remember her name. Sometimes, I'd go to introduce her to someone and say, 'I'd like you to meet . . . ummmm . . .' and I'd just have to say 'my wife.' It was dreadful of me, but I just could *not* remember because, for me, she didn't really exist.

"Then one year she told me she was pregnant even though she

had agreed not to have children—perhaps she thought it would get my attention—but it interested me not at all. She had the baby, which interested me even less. I was away when the second one was born, but I saw them once or twice over the years when she insisted. One night, fifteen years later she said, 'Rufus, I want to know what you really think of me.' It was the first time I remembered her saying anything personal to me since we were married.

" 'I don't really think of you,' I answered truthfully.

" 'Do you care about me at all?'

" 'No,' I said, but gently.

" 'Do you care about Annie and Georgie?'

" 'Oh, our daughters . . .'

" 'Do you care about them?'

" 'Not really.'

" 'Do you care about anything other than your films?'

" 'No. Nothing at all.' But now I must write to her and tell her that it's no longer true—that I care . . . and for the first time . . . about someone named Lysbeth. Anyway, that evening she announced dramatically that she was going to get a divorce, and I told her sincerely that she should have done so much sooner, that she deserved someone much nicer than I. She stormed out of the room and my life, and I've never seen her since. I think someone told me she's remarried. I told you my story would bore you to death—there just couldn't have been a more dull or uneventful marriage. She was an empty box."

"She should have married my ex-husband—they sound as if they deserve each other."

"Why did you marry him?"

"That's what I kept asking myself over and over again fifteen times every day for years. He wanted me to marry him and he was pleasant, and I kept thinking I should marry him because he'd 'make such a good husband'—whatever that means. I was hesitant, and he told me I must have the courage of my convictions. I told him it wasn't the courage I lacked but the convictions, but he didn't understand that. You see, at the time I was madly in love with a married man much older than myself—a practicing Roman Catholic with six kids. So I led myself to think of my life as beautifully doomed anyway and settled for comfort—at the age of twenty-one—whew! I remember walking up the aisle in a long white wedding dress with only one thought in my mind—was Wilson, the married man I loved so desperately, at the wedding? and looking from side to side to see if he were there."

"Was he?"

"Yes. See, I was really stupid, but I smartened up quickly because six months later we were together again. I tried being faithful for six whole months—which I considered a sterling effort—and then I gave up. 'If at first you don't succeed, give up' I always say. But those six months were torture. I decided right then that if that was virtue, I didn't want any part of it."

"Why didn't you get a divorce?"

"Because that does take courage—it really does—it's much easier just to cheat. That way you don't upset your husband or your father or your Aunt Sophie . . . How long were you married?—*fifteen years?*"

" 'Habit is stronger than love or hate,' " quoted Hallit.

"Didn't you have affairs when you were married?"

"Only once. I was not interested in women or romance, and my sex life was medicinal but satisfactory. I never felt the desire for another woman—except once when I proceeded to fling myself into this love affair in Corsica. So we made love on the rocks all day and I had to work all night—it was exhausting. But I mind unfaithfulness and dishonesty . . ."

"Probably because you're Anglo-Saxon . . ." said Lysbeth.

"Or perhaps it's what Shakespeare said, 'Weakness makes waste of my potentials.' "

"Weakness makes waste of everyone's potentials."

"No, because most people have no potential."

Nodding in agreement, he leaned out of bed and poured more coffee from the thermos for both of them. "The dishonesty bothered me so much that I actually telephoned my wife in London to confess. When she heard my voice on the phone she was thrilled to think I had called her. 'Oh, darling, how nice of you to call—what have you been doing?' 'Screwing a Corsican woman three times every day' was my answer."

"Jesus," said Lysbeth, "you are terrible—just to relieve your own Anglo-Saxon conscience. How can I like you? I like nice people, sensitive people. You're so sensitive in your films, how can you be such a shit in real life?"

33

"Because my films are—were, my life; it was my *real* life which didn't exist. Can you understand that?"

"Yes I can. Did your wife ever have an affair?"

"I certainly hope so—for her sake."

"Would you have cared?"

"Cared? Of course not. Would you have cared if your husband had an affair?"

"Oh, very much! I didn't want him, but I didn't want anyone else to have him either," she said emphatically.

"That's kind and nice."

A knock on the door interrupted them. Their breakfast was brought in and Lysbeth lay flat under the covers with the blankets pulled over her head to hide from the waiter who said, "Top of the morning to you, M'Lord. Going to see that new musical flick showing today?"

"Most likely, thank you."

When the waiter had left, Lysbeth came out from under the covers and Hallit laughed at her and she explained, "I'm a puritanical American. What's the name of the musical?"

"I haven't got a clue. The only musical I ever liked was *Hair*—did you see it?"

"Ummmm, I saw the play in London—right after it opened. I knew nothing about it—I had just arrived from Nairobi that very day, and I volunteered to take my god-daughter, who was just twelve, with me. Afterwards we went to the Great American Disaster for hamburgers and milk shakes, and she asked me what 'fellatio' was . . . she remembered the word from the song. So I figured, well, she's twelve, and if she doesn't know by now, she'll find out within a year. So I told her."

"What did she say?"

"All she did was make a terrible face and say, '*yuk.*'"

"You must not have told her very well."

Lysbeth laughed and sat down at the small round table the waiter had wheeled in. Hallit asked, "Are you really so puritanical—not wanting the waiter to see you in my bed?"

"Not really, but I do have a big hang-over from Sunday school—I never knew which color to color Jesus, and right from the beginning I never believed anything they told me, but something must have rubbed off. Did you go to Sunday school?"

"Heaven's no. My family's far too intelligent and decadent for

34

that. At the age of six—or perhaps it was seven—I said to my father, 'Is there a God?' 'No,' he answered, not even bothering to look up from his newspaper for such a ridiculous question. 'Three of my friends go to church—may I?' I asked him. 'If you want to waste your time,' was his answer. So, not wanting to waste my time, I never went.

"Tell me about your family," he said watching her pour more coffee.

"There's not much to tell really. They were a typical middle-class American happy family. My mother died when I was three, and I don't really remember her. My father raised me—he was a newspaperman—I don't think they called them 'journalists' in those days. He worked at night and took care of me during the day. He only slept when I took a nap—or went to school. He worshipped me and I him. But he died when I was ten."

It was the first time Hallit had seen her look sad. She was quiet, too, and had withdrawn into herself momentarily becoming just the opposite of what she had always been before. It intrigued him, and it pleased him to learn that she could be quiet—even sad; a constantly happy person is exhausting and often irritating. He watched her closely as she stared at her eggs. She didn't seem to notice the silence. "You loved your father very much, didn't you?"

"Ummm—very much," she said raising her eyes, "I hardly remember anything at all until after he died—in fact, I remember no one but him in my life—until he was—gone."

"And then what did you do?"

Looking down at her plate again she continued, "I couldn't believe it when I was told he was dead. I remember the feeling though—the actual physical pain that started at my head and went right through every part of me. Then I screamed and threw myself about on the floor and cried. I was distraught for days. And right after the funeral I used to talk to him every night when I'd get in bed. It would be dark and I couldn't see him, but I knew he was there. He used to come into my room and stand at the foot of my bed and say, 'Lolly'—he always called me Lolly because I loved lollipops. Everyday when he came home from the paper he'd swing me around in the air and then give me a lollipop—we always played that game." She looked up in Hallit's eyes and said, "I've never told anyone that before." She rearranged her eggs on her plate with her fork and continued, "As far as my daytime life went, I decided I'd go it alone. No more putting all my eggs in one basket—it's too painful when your basket goes. I decided I'd never need any one person again. And I never have. Oh, I've wanted people, but not needed them. I guess I've never totally loved anyone since then. Except myself."

As if to bring herself away from being ten, she took a bite of egg, pushed her chair back and ran to him and sat on his lap and kissed him with egg all over her chin, saying, "And now I love you."

"Watch it," he said, "you may be *in* love with me, but it will take a while for you to *love* me. Not long, because I am very lovable but . . ."

"You don't love me?"

"Not yet, but I think I may by next week—"

" 'Not yet'—what a dreadful thing to say . . ."

"No, it's good because it's true, and just think how much it will mean when I do say I love you—because you'll know it will be true. And it'll give you something to look forward to. Love takes time—you told me so yesterday. I've only known you three days and already I'm *in* love with you, which is a miracle for me. Do you expect a miracle every day?"

"Yes."

"Good, for another miracle is about to happen—we are going to make love."

He stood her up, then stood up himself and casually took off his robe and gathered her in his arms and gently, very gently, unbuttoned her blouse. She just stood there in jeans and nothing else, and as he looked at her a smile crossed his face because her full but small breasts, which he had just bared, matched her nose in their tilt and they seemed to be looking up at him like daisies. He eased her onto the bed and kissed them softly as he slid her jeans off. And let them fall to the floor.

As he looked at her nakedness, he noticed that quick shudder again, and he felt he had a little featherless bird in his care, so slowly and carefully, he lowered himself onto her. He heard a whimper, an almost inhuman moan, and looking at her he saw the ravaged face of an animal trapped and recoiling in terror, and then suddenly like a wild beast in a desperate final bid for life she sprang at him, no longer fragile, but desperately fighting him off.

36

He quickly let her go and she leaped to the floor and crouched by the wall as if he was going to strike her. "Lysbeth, Lysbeth, what is it? I'm not going to hurt you—please tell me—what's the matter?" He knew he couldn't advance toward her, so he remained sitting on the bed and said, "I won't touch you." Slowly, as if wakening from a nightmare, she became calmer and speaking gently, he kept repeating, "You know I won't hurt you." Wrapping a towel round himself he walked slowly toward her with his bathrobe and covered her with it. Putting his hand on her shoulder he led her back to the bed and sat next to her on the edge, "What is it Lysbeth? Please tell me." He put his arm around her.

"I'm sorry," she whispered, her body and voice still trembling as if she were coming out of an epileptic fit, "I can't . . . talk about it."

He stroked her head and said nothing for a minute. "You must. You know you must talk about it. Things left unsaid fester inside and become worse than they really are. You know that."

Lysbeth bit her thumb. Silence. Then, staring at her lap she said, "I can't."

Gently he stroked her hair. "Let me help you—let me guess—ummm, you don't want me to make love to you because then I'll find out you're a boy. Right?" A slight smile crossed her face. "Or I'll find out you have clap or crabs?"

"All three—how'd you guess?" she said weakly.

He lit each of them a cigarette and persisted, "What is it you're afraid of?" Because she didn't answer, and still holding her hand, he repeated, "What . . . ?"

"Men," she answered, still staring at her lap.

"All men? Me?"

"All men, least of all you. I know how you hate physical force and violence—you say so in all your films."

"So that's it," he said very sadly.

"Probably not—probably not what you're thinking—I was never raped. It's . . . I just don't know how to tell you—it's a long ugly story—one I've never told anyone before—not even Philip, my ex-husband. I can't . . ."

"Yes, you must tell me. I know it's painful for you, but you can't keep fears penned up inside—talking about them will release them—it's the only way I can help you. Tell Dr. Lindsey . . ."

They settled back on the bed and he put his arm around her

37

shoulder and after more coaxing she finally began. "It's not any one thing really—but then you don't commit suicide for one reason, do you? There must be a whole series of reasons, don't you imagine?"

"Yes, I would think so—it's the last drop that overflows the cup, not the biggest, and so forth. Go on, my love, you must tell me."

Taking a deep breath, visibly upset, she forced herself to talk. "Well, there are a whole series of unpleasant incidents that left me with this terrible fear of men. My first introduction to sex was when I was about eleven years old—I knew nothing about sex then. I had a friend named Elsie Schneider whose house I used to go to and I frequently spent the night there. Her father was a peculiar-looking man—he had no hair at all and big watery poppy eyes—he looked like some terrible fish. I hated the way he looked, but other than that I didn't pay any attention to him. One night I was sleeping there and Elsie's bedroom was on the second floor of the cottage—the type of house that has two bedrooms upstairs but no bathroom—that's downstairs with the other two bedrooms. Well, about midnight—we had been talking and talking—I went downstairs to go to the bathroom before we went to sleep. I was in my short nightdress and when I got to the hall, the bedroom door opened and her father came out—her mother was away at the time—and . . ." Lysbeth reached for the pack of cigarettes and tried to light one from the stub of the one she had, but her hand was shaking so, Hallit lit it for her. She took a deep drag and continued, "I said 'Hi' as I walked by him, but he grabbed me and pushed me against the wall and held me there while he fumbled around in his pajamas and the next thing I felt him rubbing himself up and down my leg. It was ghastly. I was so shocked by it. I was appalled and scared, and I wanted to scream and kick him and claw him, but I was afraid to make any noise because I didn't want Elsie to know. I pushed him away and ran upstairs shaking and I thought I was going to be sick all over the bed. I told Elsie that I felt suddenly terrible—something I ate, I muttered—and just lay there all night trembling and waiting for him to leave for work. Needless to say, I never spent the night there again—I never told her why, I just kept making up excuses why she had to come to my house instead.

"And then Elsie and I took a picnic lunch on our bicycles in the summer of the same year and went riding through this wooded

38

area near where we lived—it had paths for horses and bikes—a huge sort of park—and a river. Well, we had stopped our bikes in a deserted place and were sitting under a tree by a narrow gorge eating our lunch when a fat, round, man, all soft and white and pudgy looking like a grape, came along the path on the other side of the gorge. He stopped, lowered his pants, and looking at us, stood there masturbating. Both of us were just sort of frozen to the spot for a few seconds, and then we got on our bikes and pedaled away as fast as we could—leaving our entire lunch behind. That was my second experience with sex and it upset me far more than it did Elsie. She seemed rather intrigued and curious—I just felt sick. 'I've never seen one before—have you?' What could I say? 'Only her father's'?"

Lysbeth stubbed out her cigarette and began to bite her nails. She had started to shake again. "This is just to show you what a good start I was off to and to give you the background to the really ugly events. When I was twelve I fell madly in love with the boy next door who ignored me totally—he must have been seventeen and I was just the ugly, skinny twelve-year-old next door. One day I came out of the corner grocery store and he was passing by so he walked home with me and I secretly committed myself to him forever. I found out what time he went by the store every day, and I would make a point of being in there—buying something like one Coke at a time instead of a six-pack, and taking hours to pick out *which* Coke bottle—and when I'd see him coming down the street I'd leave just in time to bump into him accidentally. My whole life centered around this two-block walk home every day. About the fifth time, we got talking about being ticklish and I told him I was ticklish, and he said he could cure me. 'How?' I asked. 'Well, you just come here,' and he led me down an alley into someone's empty garage and said, 'Lie down with your arms out to your sides and close your eyes tight.' I would have lain down on the train tracks if he had wanted me to, so naturally I did what he suggested. I lay there, eyes and fists clenched, and the next thing I felt was his hands going up my skirt, ripping my underpants aside and shoving his finger hard inside me and holding me down. It hurt terribly, but I didn't notice the physical pain—I remember the fighting and the struggle and my running away from him and feeling the same sickness all the way home I had felt after my other two encounters with sex. It was too terrible to talk about—to anyone—to my aunt with whom I lived after my father died—or my girl friends. So I never said anything, and after that I hid every time the boy next door went out of his house. I went away with my aunt for the summer and when we got back he had moved.

"That fall, when I started finding out everything about sex from my peers, I at least understood what had happened on those three previous occasions. All my girl friends were so anxious to have sex, but it was the last thing I wanted. I listened but I never said much. I had no desire to go to bed with a man—only a revulsion against it—and on nights when I was out with boys who would try despite my protestations, it was Mr. Schneider and the fat grape man all over again.

"My sex life really seems to be accident prone. One night when I was about seventeen and still a virgin—and still with no desire to be otherwise—I had a date with a man about ten years older than I. He was huge and very bellicose and it turned out, very drunk. We were at the beach and we had gone to a bar where you could also dance to a juke box, and coming home he parked the car and grabbed me and kissed me. As usual he wanted to go to bed with me, and as usual I was fighting him off with lies and saying no and stopping his hands. Usually it worked but . . ." And suddenly Lysbeth stopped and couldn't continue. Hallit didn't hurry her. He chatted about nothing for a few minutes and fixed each of them another cup of coffee before gently coaxing her to go on.

"You must, you know you must, my love."

Lysbeth lit a cigarette. "He pinned my hands behind my back, straddled me and beat me . . . he . . . he put his cigarette out on my chin . . . see the scar?" and she turned to Hallit to show him and as he touched it gently with his fingers he knew he had never felt such tenderness in his life for anyone or such rage against a stranger. He held her head as she buried it into his chest so that he could hardly hear her saying, "So he beat me and beat me—mostly in my face—and I got hysterical which I'd never been before—but I couldn't move—I was pinned under him my arms behind my back and he was sitting on me, hitting me and hitting me." And then she started to cry and Hallit held her and let her cry it all out. Between the sobs she told him that she had finally scrambled out of the car and run to a nearby trailer camp. She hid among the trailers, and cowering behind one she saw his car driving up and

40

down between the rows of trailers looking for her. Then she went almost rigid as she had been before when she had crouched against the wall.

"What is it, Lysbeth? What is it?"

"The monster's eyes," she choked.

"What monster?" but she didn't answer. "Lysbeth, Lysbeth!" and he shook her ever so gently by the arm and she began rocking back and forth and said,

"I think the lights are the black monster's eyes. You see, I seem to panic and then things fade away into a—monster of some kind. I know it's my imagination, but it seems very real at times. Especially at night. I dream about it frequently—too frequently—and then I sit up in bed and scream, and it is very embarrassing to have to explain you screamed because the black monster with the electric eyes was holding you down. I'm not four years old any more. And today when you started to get on top of me you turned into the monster. I'm so sorry. Oh, Hallit . . . I really am sorry because I know you would never hurt me, but it isn't a rational thing at all. I should have told you first I suppose, but I'm always hoping it'll go away—that I'll be over it."

"How long has it been? How did you get over it with your husband?"

"Oh, I haven't been to bed with anyone since it happened—"

"But you were seventeen then! What about . . ."

"Oh, no, that incident isn't what created the monster—just its eyes, which are the headlights searching for me. No, I haven't told you the really bad thing that happened two years ago . . . do I have to tell you about it now?" It was a pathetic plea.

"Yes, my love, you do. Then we can work it out and get rid of it."

"You see, if I had had a good sexual relationship just once it might have negated some of the horror stories, but I've *never* had a good relationship with a man . . ."

"What about your husband?"

"Oh, he was very gentle—it wasn't frightening—I told him when we got married that I had a fear of being held down, so he never held me down, but he never asked why or anything. Of course, I wasn't about to tell him anyway—I had never talked to anyone about it—really never until today. Sex with Philip was all very antiseptic and unvaried—silent and dark and boring—not what every-

41

one tells me it can be like. And it must have been just as boring for him too, because gradually we made love less and less, and finally, for the last two years, hardly at all. The few times he tried in the last year, *I* refused because of . . . what I haven't told you yet—so it wasn't all his fault."

"How about the married man you were in love with when you got married—you told me you were back together in six months. Was that a satisfactory sexual relationship?"

"Oh, I never went to *bed* with him!"

"You never went to *bed* with him!" exclaimed Hallit. "Some affair . . ."

"That's just what Jujubee said when I told her."

"How about since you've been divorced—haven't you had an affair? Haven't you been to bed with anyone?"

"Oh, I thought I was in love a number of times, and I tried going to bed once, but the same thing happened that happened today when he wanted to make love to me. I panicked and never went to bed with him—I swear I am telling you the truth. I'm psychotic—you've got a real nut on your hands."

"Oh, my poor baby—look, hurry and tell me this last thing so we can get it all over with and start to make things better."

For some minutes he coaxed her and finally she began again. "One night I was at home alone—I've never been able to stay alone since—and I was really badly beaten up—ended up in the hospital—just two years ago . . . that priest . . ."

Looking haunted and hunted, smoking one cigarette after the other and her voice and body shuddering as she relived the terror, aided all the while by Hallit's gentle questions, Lys dragged the details of that horrendous night from the inner caverns of her memory where she had unsuccessfully tried to bury them. Later, when it was all over Hallit said quietly, "We will work this out . . . it won't be too difficult . . . I will make love to you very slowly and you will tell me everything you are feeling and seeing and imagining, and I'll hold you safe every night, and soon you'll be all right."

Lys wanted to believe it, but didn't.

Hallit believed it, but shouldn't have.

Relieved that the ordeal of telling him was over, and feeling ten pounds lighter because it was all out in the open and because

Hallit understood and would help her, she suddenly felt ravenously hungry. "I'm starved," she said.

"Starved? Every day you get hungry—what a nuisance you are. But come on, I'm starved for a martini." He sat in a chair and put on his shoes, and she went to him and kneeled on the floor and buckled his shoes for him and he lifted her up to him and kissed her and she kissed him back and her fingers went up and down his spine and he said, "Jesus," in her hair and broke away and pulled her up and said, "Come on, or I'll be the next one to molest you. She stepped into her clothes, and they made their way to the pub."

"I want three cheeseburgers—with onions."

Hallit ordered, "Three cheeseburgers with onions. And three martinis, also with onions, please."

For the next week with much self-control, he worked with Lysbeth and helped her in a way one would help a child to walk. He talked, he listened, he made her tell him things, he let her rage or cry—she even screamed—and through it all he held her softly and safely, and little by little, day by day, she became less frightened of his physical self. She still could not let him make love to her, but after another week of "therapy," as Lysbeth called it, she said that she wanted to try.

Wishing that he could turn himself into a midget so small that it would be impossible for her to fear him, he drew her to him so that they lay on their sides face to face because he reasoned that in this position she would not feel trapped as she would were he on top of her. Very gently, very tenderly, he made love to her. He felt as if he were making love to a virgin, and it aroused him in a way he hadn't experienced since he was fourteen.

He soared, calling, "Lysbeth, Lysbeth," over and over again, and when he was able to open his eyes, he looked at her and saw her sad. "What is it?" he asked gently.

"Nothing. It was very beautiful," she smiled softly, and ran her fingers through the hair on his chest and twirled it around. "I had a nice orgasm."

For the first time she saw him angry, and she hated it—and hated herself for making him this way. Eyes blazing, he grabbed her arm and shook it and said, "I was serious when I told you not to lie to me," and gritting his teeth, he said between them, "don't you *ever* lie to me again. I know you didn't have an orgasm, and I know

43

you lied to please me, but it doesn't please me if it isn't true. I *mean* it when I say you're going to tell me the truth, do you hear me, do you understand?"

She nodded, eyes wide, and he, getting angrier still, said, "Don't you ever lie to me again. I not only know you didn't have an orgasm, I know *why* you didn't. And I also know you shall. There is no problem—but there will be one if you lie."

"I love you."

"Christ," he said searching her face with his eyes, "I think I love you too." And then he kissed her softly and held her gently and whispered, "See, you have such enormous power over me that it is impossible to be in your presence without experiencing your spell—I can't stay angry with you."

They lay quietly close together and then he said, "You're not worried that you'll never have an orgasm are you? Just because you've never experienced it with anyone doesn't mean that you won't—you know that don't you?"

"Oh, I know that—I've had orgasms with . . ."

"You told me you hadn't!" said Hallit sitting up with a start and getting angry and upset again.

"I told you I hadn't with *men,* but I've had lots with Jujubee," said Lysbeth lightly.

"Jujubee!" Hallit said aghast.

"Now, don't act as if it's important—it isn't, and wasn't then. It was casual and unemotional—I could never kiss her or anything like that. It was sheer sex devoid of emotion. I liked it because I had no fear—no fear at all, and she liked it because, well, Jujubee would like sex with anyone at anytime—regardless of which sex, although she prefers men." Lysbeth said it as nonchalantly as if she were saying she and Jujubee had often gone to the A&P together, although Jujubee preferred Gristede's. "Neither of us attached any importance to it—it was great sex, but nothing more. At one stage I did begin to feel guilty, I guess, because I thought that's how I should feel, but I soon had an instant cure with the unwitting help of Father Ryan—that's why I had asked him to come to my house that night when I was alone—don't you remember I told you something was bothering me and I wanted to talk to him about it? Yes? Well, that's what was bothering me, but you can imagine how insignificant it seemed afterward."

"Did your affair with Jujubee go on for long?" asked Hallit.

44

"Affair?" laughed Lysbeth. "It was no affair—it was pure mechanical, clinical sex—and it didn't happen often or last long. In fact, every time I've seen Jujubee for the last year, nothing at all has happened. Haven't you ever had a homosexual relationship?"

"No. I have no objection to homosexuals, but I'm just very heterosexual."

"I didn't realize you were so abnormal," she teased. "I'm so in love with you I am really beginning to love you, and I've never felt this for anyone before—not even half. Thank you for filling my desert."

A couple days before the ship was to dock in Mombasa, Lys and Hallit were in their pub when he said, "Durrell once wrote, 'A city becomes a world if you love one of its inhabitants.' Well, for me this ship is a universe. Let's sail 'round and 'round Africa and never get off. O.K.? I just can't get enough of you—I love the things you look, the things you do. You make life seem more exciting than it really is. You make every minute seem important, and that is the greatest compliment I can pay anyone. Before, my work was important but no one in my life was. The idea of your not being in my life now is totally impossible. Will you marry me?"

"I think you're getting senile," said Lysbeth with a big grin on her face, "you're so repetitive—you already asked me to marry you—that first day, and I already *told* you yes—'twas the first word I spoke to you, remember?"

"Why do you want to marry me?"

"Because I want to be a 'Lady,' because I like your aristocratic eyebrows and the way you say 'raspberries'—'ros-burries.' But most of all so my initials will be L.L.L.L.—Lady Lysbeth Long Lindsey."

"They're the best reasons I've ever heard. When shall we be married? Today? Should I call the captain?"

"It's too corny to get married on the ship and also illegal. Ships' captains can no longer marry people. But if we wait until Nairobi, I'll have to invite my sixty-eight friends. Why don't we get married in Mombasa when the ship docks?"

"Fine," answered Hallit, "I'll cable for my car to be sent to Mombasa and then we'll drive up to Nairobi through Tsavo and spend a night or two there. Game parks are like Rome—you have to be in love to enjoy them. I detest game parks normally, but I can hardly wait to spend two days in one with you. See what you do to me—you ruin my impeccable taste. We'll get married in Mombasa—it'll take a few days to get the license—then we'll go to Tsavo. So, one week after we dock we should be in Nairobi. We can go to the farm then for two weeks, and I'll have the script ready when the crew comes in—"

"Fine, but . . ." Lysbeth asked hesitantly, "do you expect me to stay at the farm while you go to Nairobi? I'm afraid I'm going to be a terrible burden to you because I won't stay alone. My only phobia left—I hope I don't have to go through your trying to cure that too."

"I wouldn't expect you to stay alone—you'd decay up there even if you weren't psychotic," he teased. "It's a nice place for working or a holiday—but you have to have a vacation *from* something. We'll work it out—we'll get a house in Nairobi!"

"I don't mind being in a hotel, but I just can't stay in a *house* alone. This is going to be so tedious for you isn't it?"

"No, not for me, because I want you to be with me every single minute, but I can see the situation arising where I'm going to have to go to London for a production meeting, and you're going to be involved covering the Organization for African Unity or something at the same time . . . we just can't live at the Norfolk Hotel. How about if we get you a baby sitter?"

"Jujubee!" squealed Lysbeth with delight. "She used to stay with me lots in Philadelphia when Philip had to go away. Jujubee would love to come here—she can paint and—oh, Hallit, what a wonderful idea—you'll love Jujubee! She won't be a nuisance to us because when you're free we can go to the farm—just the two of us and leave her in Nairobi. She wouldn't mind at all. Or if you're in Nairobi working and can come home every night she can flit around Europe having exhibitions." Hallit agreed that the suggestion had merit, though he experienced a passing qualm that their physical relationship might start up again—after all, he had only just heard about it. "Oh, let's telephone her the minute we get to Mombasa—I just can't wait to tell her. I wrote to her just a few days after I met you and told her about you—I mailed it in Tangiers. I also told her we hadn't made love yet—I said it was because we couldn't find any place to do so—I led her to believe we each were sharing cabins with other people. And I got a letter from her in Durban." She jumped out of bed and rummaged in her purse till she found a crinkled note scrawled on a Pan Am vomit bag, and she read from it, "If you can't find a place to make love, then you're too dumb to be my friend. Ever think of the lifeboat, the fan room, the ladies' room after hours, the men's room before hours, the pool at night, the anchor chain, the captain's table? You . . ."

Hallit interrupted, "Why did you 'lead her to believe'—you use such nice euphemisms for 'lie'—that we were sharing cabins with others . . . ?"

"Well, I don't know, it's just that Jujubee thinks I'm so peculiar about not going to bed with men—she doesn't know about my . . . problem. I so hate to talk about it that I never told anyone. I was always making excuses to her why I didn't go to bed with men. I can hardly wait to tell her about us."

She threw her arms around him and said, "Oh, Hallit—our life will be filled with so much happily ever after—we'll never get a divorce will we?"

"Never say never," Hallit said rather sadly and quietly.

"You sound sad," Lysbeth said turning on her stomach and looking down at him.

"Not sad, my sweet one, just aware of the facts. You see, for you, life is to be lived at the peak of one's spirits and at the top of one's voice. You may grow . . . not bored with me, but you may come to need another . . . peak. You are continuously celebrating the pleasures of living, and a new pleasure may arise. You would react to it with warmth, merriment, and commitment—because you have spontaneous joy in your heart. You would not accept the limitations put on you by 'fidelity,' and I know all this, yet I would like to join you in your never-ending celebration—for now at any rate."

"My joy is yellow and orange—what color is yours?" asked Lysbeth, fearing what he had said to be too true to deny. He knew that she was evading his statement, so ignoring her frivolous question, he continued,

"You see, you are a hero. There aren't many heroes nowadays. I have never been interested in people, only in their ideas, their work, their performances—what people face and if and how they overcome it. You, Lysbeth, have faced a lot, but you have fought and persevered to overcome it, and through it all you've found joy.

47

You have not claimed yourself a victim and wallowed in self-pity. You have fought—you have won. What a rarity you are these days. Everyone else blames society—'I'm a victim of society,' they say—Jesus! Did you ever read R. H. Gardner's *The Splintered Stage?* He says that today the sick is substituted for the noble, the grotesque for the beautiful, the obscure for the significant, and the sensational for the sublime—and he is right."

Lysbeth reached on the floor for the *Herald Guardian* she had thrown there the night before when she had finished reading it, turned the pages and said, "Here it is—I meant to read it to you last night. It's Gardner. You and he must have some kind of mutual worship club going. He says, 'Lord Lindsey is known for his keen intelligence and his moral standards in film making. Life to him is a search for meaning in his own life and for order and purpose in the universe—that is his genius . . . when he makes a discovery he must express it. To do this, to externalize it, he makes a film. It is to perceive this form and to understand the meaning it represents that people go to films. The emotions aroused by Lindsey's perception, by his discovery, are far more profound than those aroused by escape or superficial and momentary entertainment.'"

Hallit kissed her on her nose and said, "You will never see a film of mine that has a comedian walking through a screen door, or a sheriff riding into town on his horse, or an entertainer tap dancing in puddles. This is not to say that some of these aren't well done and that entertaining films have no value—some are as you describe them—'good garbage,' and I myself *enjoy* many films in that class, but that doesn't make them good. I think today's films should be classified into two main categories and should be distributed either as entertainment or art form—though, of course, the two are not always mutually exclusive."

Lysbeth reached for another paper saying, "Have you read what they said about you in here—it's marvelous!" Hallit took the paper from her and threw it on the floor and kissed her again. She broke away and asked, "Have you read it?"

"No," he said. "I have no interest in reading that or anything written about me or my films by someone I don't value. I don't care what most people think about them. I know they are great—all that matters to me is the greatness, not whether it is recognized. Most people won't recognize it—just a few, like Gardner, will. I know my own value, so does he—and so do you," he said gathering her up in his arms.

The ship docked in Mombasa and they checked into a beach hotel and telephoned Jujubee who reacted with unrestrained delight and wanted to know all about their marriage and promised to come to Nairobi whenever she was needed. Then Hallit left to get the marriage license and returned in an hour saying he had had to get a special license because by Kenya law you have to wait three weeks—unless you were pregnant. "So," he told her, "tomorrow you will be pregnant—but not the next day or the next or the . . . did I ever tell you I hate children? You don't want any do you?"

"Well, yes . . . I actually would like children . . . but I'm used not to having them. I guess I don't really care one way or the other . . ."

"Well, I do. The thought of some mindless wet rubbery bundle limiting and interfering with our freedom and happiness is outrageous . . ."

"But they develop a mind."

"I couldn't wait that long. Look what I bought you—your wedding ring!" He handed her a ring box and gleefully she opened it. It was an earring identical to his own. "Everyone wears a wedding ring on his finger—you'll wear yours in your ear."

"Sure you don't want it through my nose?"

As he pierced her ear, he told her how the Romany gypsies had done the same to him. He had lived with them for six months before he did his film on them, and they honored him when he left by giving him the earring and making him one of them. "I've also been around Cape Horn under sail—the only other entitlement to a single gold earring—unless of course you're my wife."

The next morning, at a brief civil ceremony in the District Commissioner's office they were married, and when the proceedings reached the moment calling for the ring Hallit solemnly put it through Lysbeth's ear and the D.C., though he looked astounded and made as if to protest, must have decided it was not his business and let it pass without comment. They both wore white and blue—white shirts and blue jeans—and when they had signed the register they kissed and ran down the stairs from the D.C.'s office, and they kissed again under the elephant tusks on Kilindini Road. Then they walked through the streets of Mombasa to the "shady"

49

part of town in the Arab quarter near the old Mombasa harbor, and there, in a dingy little cafe, they bought the best samosas and kebabs in the world, and they bought lots of Lamu mangoes from an open market place, and with a bottle of ice-cold Dom Pérignon and a jar of Baluga caviar which Hallit had brought from the ship, they sat under the world's largest Baobab tree, which overlooks the entrance to the harbor, and watched the ships come and go. They feasted on their wedding banquet and drank the champagne and soon they saw what they had been waiting for—the S.S. *Victoria*—their ship, their universe—and as it nosed its way out into the Indian Ocean their eyes filled with tears and they waved and watched it disappear. It was a very special ship.

Three hours later they were in the orange glow of Tsavo Park, Africa's largest game park. The rosy hue of the setting sun glanced off the red tie-dyed earth and the dry brown grass and bush combined to suffuse their whole world with a warm, burnt-orange tone that would have been rejected by a photographic laboratory as being overdone and unreal. Twenty majestic elephant were drinking at a water hole about thirty feet from their car. Then they saw that on the other side of them a male lion, perfectly camouflaged in the long golden grass, was staring at them. "He looks enough like you to be your brother," said Hallit. And as they drove slowly forward a herd of about four hundred buffalo crossed the road just in front of their car. Again Hallit spoke, "It is so beautiful it is hard to believe it is real. How many people bring their wives to Eden for a honeymoon?" And instead of going to the fancy lodge with its tourist-crowded Hilton version of an African bar and dining room, they went to the old group of *bandas* which had only thatched roofs and no electricity and where an African cooked their food over a fire outside. Hallit had booked all six *bandas* so they would be completely alone, and they sat outside on a log and watched the sun disappear and the moon come up and elephant come to drink from the water hole there, and they laughed at two baby elephant playing and rolling in the mud and spraying each other with their trunks. It was, Lysbeth said, the best wedding dinner in the world. The music was also good they agreed, for the sound was the orchestra of the African bush—the trumpeting of elephant, the snorting of rhino, the sawing cough of the leopard. And then a hyena laughed, for he was happy too. . . .

Hallit picked Lysbeth up and carried her into their *banda* and by candlelight they took a bath together, and then he watched the flame from the candles dancing shadows all over her naked body as she lay on the bed. And he kissed her softly from her forehead to her feet, running his tongue in between her toes and working his way back up to her lips. Then he turned her on her side and entered her, and for the first time—the very first time for Lys—making love was almost what it should be. This night it was a symphony, a symphony in slow motion with both of them falling up and up into fluffy white clouds, into a hazy brilliance, and gentle smiles shining through serene faces and hair falling up in slow motion, and their bodies feeling like the sound of a cello, getting louder, and now one note in a steady force lifting them even higher, falling up-up-up with smiles smiling now into frowns of the agony of pleasure and eyes clenched in ecstasy and clouds exploding and puffing higher and higher—a bomb of bliss bursting in silent slow motion and subsiding gently into quiet.

When they returned to earth Hallit said, "You weren't afraid that time," and she smiled at him as if she were a two-year-old who had just succeeded in tying her shoes for the first time. Then she sprang from the bed and grabbed the rest of the champagne and they drank from the bottle and toasted the herd of elephant they could see from their bed and laughed at the trumpet they received in return. They lay close to each other, naked, and watched the geckos run up and down the walls and listened to the sounds of Africa, and he kissed her on the nose, and they fell asleep in each other's arms.

In the morning he slid out of bed quietly and put his pillow over her naked back so she would think he was still holding her and would continue to sleep, and after lowering the mosquito net over her again he sat on the terrace and watched the morning break and the zebra run and the impala jump, and he had never been happier nor had he ever known such beauty both inside and outside of himself. At seven the cook arrived with tea and hearing their voices, Lysbeth called, "Hallit?" And he kissed her awake and they made beautiful sleepy morning love. By the time they poured the tea it was cold, but they didn't care.

Later, outside on their terrace, they ate bacon and eggs and had coffee and then they went on a game run and saw giraffe loping through the bush and water buck and lesser kudu and gerenuk and Grants gazelle and dik dik and wart hog. They drove to Mzima

51

Springs and looked at the hippo and the crocs and went down into the little glass house under water and watched the hippo swim by surrounded by thousands of tilapia. When they walked back to their car it looked as if it had sprouted monkeys for they were sitting all over it, and they laughed at the bright blue testicles of the males. Then they drove to Lugard Falls and walked down the river a way on the rocks and ate a picnic lunch at the water's edge under a doum palm and watched a pride of lion playing on a sandbar on the far side of the river. And driving to the tented camp farther downstream where they were to spend that night, they saw two ostrich making love so Hallit and Lysbeth made love too, right in the car alongside the ostrich. And at dusk, all hot and dirty and wonderfully tired, they arrived at the tented camp and Lys suggested they bathe in the river. So they stripped, and with towels wrapped around them ran to the river which was no deeper than their knees but flowed swiftly, so Hallit sat in front of her to keep her from being washed downstream. Sitting tucked behind him with her arms wrapped around him, she kissed his back, and in the river they watched the sun go down. Just as it disappeared she asked, "Do you feel that sudden current of warm water?"

"Yes, as a matter of fact I do . . ." he answered puzzled.

"That's because I'm peeing on you," and she got up and ran and he chased her naked all through the river and up and down and over rocks. Then they put on their towels and went back to their tent. After fixing two drinks, and still in their towels, they sat in deck chairs and made wishes on the falling stars until their supper was cooked on the open fire. Famished, they ate at a small table outside their tent, and with their coffee in tin mugs they walked down to the river and sat on a large rock in the moonlight and watched six elephant drink at the other side. Then two buffalo arrived and everything was silent—even the falling stars were silent as they fell. "The sound of silence . . . I hear silence more than sound," said Lysbeth, finally breaking the spell.

"How do animals cry?" she asked as they walked arm in arm to their tent.

At seven the next morning they drove off and arrived in Nairobi in time for a marvelous curry lunch at the Norfolk. Hallit bought a newspaper and during the meal, as they penciled circles round the houses for rent or sale which they wanted to see in the afternoon,

Lysbeth's eyes suddenly filled with tears. "What's wrong?" asked Hallit both concerned and astonished.

"That little girl over there is eating a lollipop . . . I know it's silly . . . but lollipops make me cry . . ." said Lysbeth trying to smile.

"Jesus! Whoever thought I could love someone, much less be married to someone, who cries over lollipops!" But he patted her on her knee under the table and was surprised at himself for being moved by it. "I want something obscene for dessert. Do you?"

"No, I couldn't eat any more."

". . . until you see mine."

Hallit turned to the waiter and said, "Bring me a piece of lemon meringue pie—with two straws."

After lunch they drove to Muthaiga and looked at four houses, but they both felt Muthaiga was too suburban. "I can't tell it from Philadelphia," claimed Lys. So they drove to Langata on the west of Nairobi, and as they crunched in the gravel driveway of the third house on their list, Lys and Hallit both knew it was what they were looking for. Lys called it a "big little house" since it actually looked grander than it was because of the large upstairs ballustraded terraces. But it was not massive enough to be 'spooky' Lys said. There was an entrance hall with marble floors. The enormous living room had a fireplace at one end and a few alcoves which made it interesting architecturally. The dining room was splendid, and off it was a terrace with lots of arches—a place that would be beautiful for lunch enthused Lys. The swimming pool was beyond the terrace—a perfect rectangle with a Roman pillar at each corner. Upstairs were four bedrooms and three baths, and two of the bedrooms opened onto the terraces. "I love it—I love it as much as I love you! There's only one problem— there's no study for you—unless we make one of the bedrooms your study?"

"Lysbeth, I really think we ought to have separate bedrooms anyway. I work from midnight to six every morning, and I'd drive you mad pacing around and typing. I'll come to bed with you most nights, but then I'll get up about midnight and go to my room and write. You see, I work until about three, but then I lie down, and when I think of something I get up and write. I jump up and down until about six—and then I sleep soundly until nine. Why don't you take the bedroom opening onto this terrace and I'll take the one on the other terrace and you can have a cord by your bed which will ring in my room, all right?"

"Fine, then your study can be the bedroom there, mine here, we each have our own bathroom, and Jujubee's room can be there—sharing the bath with the guest bedroom—perfect!"

The grounds were beautiful. There were sixteen acres of which part had been developed into a formal garden with a grotto and a fish pond, and part had been cleared to create the impression of a park. The remaining seven acres of virgin African forest helped give the property the feeling of being miles from civilization. The house itself was well situated on a little knoll and commanded a fantastic view of the Ngong Hills.

The owners were going back to England and selling some good antiques. Everything seemed to fall into place including the fact that the servants, who were about to be signed off, declared that they would like to stay on for the Lindseys.

All evening they talked about the house and how they were going to decorate it. "I've never been happier," they said simultaneously at one point, then burst out laughing.

The next morning they set out on the spectacular drive to Hallit's farm. They stopped to admire a breath-taking view of the Great Rift Valley and he pointed out his farm way over on the far side of it. Farther on they passed Lake Naivasha and decided that it and the hills behind looked more like a bad backdrop for a stage play than a real panorama. From there they went on to Lake Nakuru to look at the three million flamingo around its shores. Then on again into the golden plains, and it was here that they passed the occassional Maasai standing on one foot just as the pink flamingos had stood, but giving off a darker hue of red as they leaned on their spears. The wind blew and exposed their chiseled bodies, sensual as a leopard's, and the Citroën sped along throwing up clouds of dust in its wake that formed into a giant brown plume like an ostrich feather sprouting continually from the tail of the moving car. Halfway across the Rift Valley Hallit turned into a road with a sign that read, "Private. Lindsey."

"How many acres do you have here?" asked Lysbeth after they had been going for what seemed like endless miles up his driveway.

"Not very many—fifty thousand . . ."

"Fifty thousand! That's more than I've ever even thought about!"

"It's really nothing compared to some estates here." Then Lys saw the house. It was a single story of white stone which rambled everywhere snuggling into a green hill. It had a great sweeping wood-shingle roof, with masses of pink and purple bougainvillia growing over it. Inside it was charming with a huge open fireplace big enough to accommodate half a tree at one end of the drawing room, and there were dark-brick floors and lots of comfortable sink-down-into-furniture.

"Why did you buy such a big place?" asked Lys.

"For my four wives."

Every room had beautiful Persian carpets thrown over the brick floors which ran throughout the house. There were some exquisite antiques, the drawing room seemed to be walled with bookcases, and there were many big leather chairs. Not just the drawing room and the dining room, but each bedroom, too, had a huge stone fireplace, and the whole house had a heavy masculine yet elegant feeling about it.

"Whatever you don't like, just throw away," smiled Hallit.

"It's a masterpiece and you know it. I don't have to ask who decorated it—I know you did—it says 'you.' One of your genius fields?"

He smiled and kissed her and then took her into the kitchen to meet Njeroge, his cook. *"Habari zako?"* asked Lysbeth.

"Mzuri, memsahib. Unataka chakula sasa hivi?" (Would you like lunch right away?)

"Chakula, kitakpokuwa tayari, tulete," answered Lysbeth. (Just bring it when it's ready.)

"My God," exclaimed Hallit, "you speak perfect Swahili."

"One of *my* genius fields."

The week at the farm was idyllic.

Every day in the yellow sunshine they walked and ate and talked and laughed and worked and bathed and made love, and Lysbeth said that yellow was her favorite color because it was happy and never complained. And every night after supper on trays in front of the fire, he would take her upstairs and put her to bed just as if she were a child. She would read a while before dropping off to sleep and he always looked in at her two or three times to make sure she was all right—asleep and properly covered. Eventually he would crawl into the bed with her, but it usually wasn't until dawn. She told him he worked too hard and suggested he get a script writer to help him.

"No one could ever help me. I am much too vain for that. Every detail must be mine—the writing, the direction, the editing. If it weren't all mine—pure—I would not let it be produced. I told you that about me."

"I just think it is so selfless of you to give so much of yourself to this film."

"It is the most *selfish* thing. Don't you see that?"

She was aware that there was something bigger than she was really able to comprehend, but she did understand that she owned every part of him that was able to be owned . . . but what of that other part . . . ?

On their way back to Nairobi she asked if he didn't think it would be nice to give one big party so she could have all her friends at once. "Otherwise," she told him, "we'd have to have two people for dinner every night in a row for over a month."

"Christ, if you have to do either, have one party."

"Why don't we set the date for the party one month from today—whatever today is—because then I'll have the Langata house ready."

And the month, too, was idyllic. Lysbeth busied herself with decorating the house, and she did a bewitching job of mixing beautiful antiques with modern lucite and contemporary paintings. Each room had an elegant yet light and happy look about it. The living room was in earth colors of browns and mustards and beiges and was textured in raw silks, corduroy's and suedes. Thick silk draperies hung to the floor, and tortoise-shell lamps and stone tables were mixed with lucite ones, and dry heather was in huge bunches everywhere. The room was comfortably masculine, as so many rooms decorated by women are not—she used no gold leaf or light blue velvet or pinks. One of the alcoves she turned into a bar, and the other into a library—simply by lining the walls with books from floor to ceiling and installing a stand with a huge eighteenth-century lexicon on it. The terrace Lys made all white—white-brick floors, white-bamboo furniture, white walls, white wrought-iron table and chairs, white cushions. Only the masses of green ferns strayed from the single non-color. Around the pool, which was an extension of the terrace, were many lounge chairs and tables with a few umbrellas. Again everything was white except for the cushions and umbrellas which were paisley greens and blues to blend with the water, trees, and shrubs. Lys allowed no other colored flowers to intrude on the tones near the pool, but there were great beds of white daisies and huge clumps of blue agapanthas, but no red, or purple bougainvillia or orange golden shower. Lys had many things sent to her from New York, among them five of Jujubee's paintings. Hallit adored everything Lys had chosen and arranged, and especially the lucite grandfather's clock. But most of all he loved Jujubee's paintings and was anxious to meet her, he said. As the month came to an end the house came alive—it sang of Lysbeth and Hallit and their love for each other. It was truly elegant, altogether beautifully balanced with an atmosphere that was totally individual.

Everyone the Lindseys invited to their dinner party accepted—even the three friends of Hallit whom he despised—for it wasn't every day that people in Nairobi were invited to dinner by a famous film director and his beautiful wife. The party was everything it should be—gay and festive. To accommodate the sixty-eight guests, Lysbeth had arranged small round tables for four all over the terrace and around the pool and allowed everyone to choose his own dinner partners. The atmosphere engendered was one of sophisticated elegance rather than drunken revelry, but even so the last guest did not leave until nearly four A.M.

The year that followed was every beautiful thing it should have been. Hallit went with Lys to Ruanda while she did her gorilla story, and she went to London with him twice during the year. But when his film was nearing completion and he was traveling back and forth from London more frequently—a schedule that conflicted with her assignments—they decided the time had come to get Jujubee to baby sit.

Lysbeth wrote to Jujubee and explained that the arrangement would not interfere at all with her life of painting and exhibitions and teaching and that she would still be able to skip around the globe doing whatever she wanted.

At the same time Lys took care to reassure Hallit that with Jujubee pursuing her own life for much of the time, the two of them would be able to be alone for weeks, months even, without Jujubee. But in any case, she said, he and Jujubee would be crazy about each other—they'd be thrilled to find another genius mind—wasn't it lonely out there sometime? she teased. In fact, she said, he'd soon have a fourth friend. And she was right.

The night before Jujubee's arrival in Kenya, Lysbeth said to Hallit while he was reading the paper, "You know, any other husband would be apprehensive about the arrival of a person into our lives who I used to enjoy sex with."

"With *whom* you used to enjoy sex," he corrected her without even looking up.

"Aren't you the slightest bit jealous or worried?"

"Not the slightest."

"What if I want to go to bed with her?"

"You won't," answered Hallit with such confidence that he still didn't stop reading.

"Put the paper down and pretend you're jealous anyway—it's insulting that you're so sure of my love for you. . . ."

Lowering the paper and looking at her he said with a smile, "Why it's not insulting at all. It's a compliment to you because your taste has improved—anyone else but me would have bored you by now. Before you felt incomplete, and you are way too vain to want to be anything but 'total woman.' So there's no chance of your wishing to go to bed with Jujubee or any woman ever again. No one is more basically heterosexual than you. No one is more fully woman, nor is there a woman who is more drawn to men in every way, nor one who not only reacts to them but needs them because they make you feel like a woman. Therefore, without men, *you* wouldn't exist. Do you understand that?"

"Better than you do, smartass," said Lysbeth lunging at him playfully and climbing on his lap. "You are *so* conceited."

"I am not conceited. I simply know my own value. I just face the facts and see that I am always right—and so do you."

She pulled his hair and kissed him hard on his lips.

Jujubee arrived late the next afternoon and Hallit and Lysbeth were at the airport to greet her. She projected such a great sense of aliveness as she came through customs that Hallit said to Lysbeth, "It's more than that mane of red hair that makes her stand out in the crowd—she has a glow that infuses the room with a vibrant orange."

Jujubee and Lys hugged, then she turned to Hallit and said,

"'Hallit' . . . sounds like a fish, but I like your earring," and immediately he adored her, and she him, and Lysbeth was delighted.

As they walked into their house Jujubee looked around and said, "What's a terrible girl like me doing in a nice place like this? What atrociously good taste." While she unpacked she told Lys how she loved Hallit and every room and every inch of garden, and how she loved the prospect of being there with them. At dinner Jujubee said to Hallit, "I just saw your latest landmark in film making, *The Sound of Silence*. Every time I see a film of yours I'm afraid you may fall off your pedestal, but you keep going up higher."

"Yes," said Hallit matter-of-factly. "Where did you see it, New York?"

"No, London. I always do my laundry in London—that's why I go there—but while I was waiting for it to dry I went to see the film. What's your new one going to be about?"

"It's about all the things no one wants to know about in life; but I'm going to tell them anyway."

"The One Hundred Associated Grocers from East Jesus, Missouri, won't enjoy *that*."

"Jujubee," asked Lys, "what plans do you have—what are you going to do while you're here?"

"Exploit the white man—by selling them a few of my trinkets —and then when you go see the gorillas again, I'll join you and do gorilla portraits. I love apes. Then I'll hang them in the stuffy Philadelphia Racquets Club over a brass plaque engraved 'Founder.'"

"The Philadelphia Racquets Club?" asked Hallit.

"Oh, no one plays racquets—you can only go there if your name is 'Kiki' or 'Binksey' and if you talk through clenched teeth and say, 'It's so *cute* of you to come to the funeral . . .' Would you mind if I brought a gorilla back here with me to share my room? A big, oversexed gorilla—after all, I don't know many men here."

Lysbeth said, "We've been pimping for you Jujubee—there's a very forlorn looking Turkish artist in town you'd probably adore . . ."

"I can arrange my own perversities, thank you."

When the first course was cleared Jujubee lit a cigarette and offered them one saying, "Have an inter-course cigarette?" When the servants brought the second course, Hallit began to eat right away, not waiting for the other two, but simply saying, "I won't wait—I always display appalling upper-class bad manners."

"Remember that time I was in Saudi Arabia with that American boy friend—what was his name Lys? Well, it doesn't matter—he was a professor—the one who looked like an intellectual cockroach. Anyway, we were invited to a Sheik's tent for dinner—all very fancy. The banquet started with a roasted sheep, and with the great pomp and ceremony of Arabs, the Sheik offered me, the honored guest, the sheep's eye. I just could not handle it, but I knew it would offend them terribly and be a dreadful breach of protocol to refuse unless I could think of a very good reason. Fortunately, an excuse did come to me quickly and I said, 'I am not deserving of your most gracious gift; but my distinguished friend, a professor of great learning, would be most worthy and honored.' He got the eye and I never saw him again. Speaking of boy friends, I hope you don't have anything planned for me for the weekend because I plan to spend it in a hotel, in bed, with a man."

"Anyone you know?" asked Lysbeth.

"Not really. I know his wife—we were friends before I poached him. You know her, that famous Philadelphia bore, Colleen Black."

"Colleen . . . what's she look like?"

"She's got straight pubic hair. Anyway, he's here on safari—don't you remember him? He's English. They were at that big party of mine—you were there. He's very tidy and anal—inner chaos, outward order and all that—probably a hangover from British public schools, five years of constipation, and buggery at an impressionable age. . . ."

"Jesus," laughed Hallit, "do women always talk this way? It's much worse than any locker room conversation."

"Oh much worse," both women agreed.

"Stick around us, honey," laughed Jujubee, "you'll learn a lot. From us you can get a script that the Associated Grocers would love."

"But sex is only one aspect of life, and not nearly as interesting as the others . . ."

"Yes, but what an exquisite compensator it is. If it weren't for sex, I'd kill myself . . ."

And suddenly Lysbeth remembered the first time she had heard Jujubee say that, almost three years ago.

Jujubee

Jujubee knew the word for "fuck" in thirty-six languages; she also knew the Greek word for "doing it in a wheel chair." Jujubee was a very intelligent woman. She would do anything as long as it wasn't conventional, including marrying her brother—that is, if you consider incest unconventional. Someone had said she was "pruned in the wrong direction." She was a well-known modern portrait painter and a "Jewish Christian atheist."

"What's a Jewish Christian atheist?" Lysbeth asked the first time they met.

"Well, I'm Jewish by birth, Christian in attitude, and atheist in religious beliefs—which is the best of all combinations. The Jews are the cleverest, the Christians the kindest, and the atheists the most intelligent. A benevolent atheist has to be the best kind of 'Christian' because he performs selflessly with no hope of reward nor fear of punishment. If there were a God, He would like me very much. And then, for good measure, I'm Jewish—well, half Jewish. My mother was Jewish—sort of my mother—I never knew her. And now I'm married to a Jew—well, sort of married—he's my part-time husband—I don't see much of him. Fortunately."

Jujubee and Lysbeth were having dinner together at the Sea Horse, Philadelphia's well-known restaurant on a tug boat in the harbor, at Jujubee's invitation because there had been an article about Lambaréné in the Philadelphia *Inquirer* by Lysbeth and a picture of her in Gabon. Jujubee had telephoned her saying that although they had never met, she too had been in Gabon and had painted Albert Schweitzer before the great man had died—and perhaps they could get together and reminisce. Lysbeth had agreed and now they sat at a table overlooking the harbor and ordered drinks while she studied Jujubee, noticing that the out-

63

standing thing about her was her mass of heavy Titian hair. Freckles usually went with this coloring, but Jujubee had few.

No one would call her beautiful or pretty or even feminine, thought Lysbeth, but she was handsome—an extremely handsome woman in her mid-twenties. Her long straight Roman nose divided her long straight face precisely in two. Her green eyes were slightly slanted and small but very sharp and alert, and they were so far apart she could "see if her own ears were dirty," as she was to say later on. Her body matched her face in angles and straightness— she had few curves, and even her breasts were small and nearly flat, which later she also told Lysbeth she liked because "anything over a mouthful is a waste." Tall and lean and angular, her mane of deep red hair falling about her shoulders was a contradiction —it just didn't seem to fit the rest of her. Her mouth was straight, too, which belied her passionate nature, for if a single word description were to be given to Jujubee, it would have to be "passionate"; though perhaps "sexual" would be more accurate for Jujubee adored sex even if it were passionless. She was not only preoccupied with sex but thoroughly occupied with it as well. That first night they were having dinner, as she ordered her third martini she told Lysbeth, "If it weren't for sex and booze, I'd kill myself. But I do like to drink, and I love sex."

"Do you like Africa?" asked Lysbeth.

"As long as there's sex and booze," she grinned—a tremendous grin that always made Lys and everyone else feel silly for taking anything in life too seriously. She continued, "It just doesn't matter to me where I am really. I paint to wile away the time in between the debauchery. It's no good being drunk all day—then you have nothing to look forward to each night. Who was it who said he hated not to drink because he knew when he woke up in the morning that would be as good as he would feel all day? It must be depressing as hell, I suppose—I've never experienced it myself. But I must admit I do prefer being hung over in Africa to being hung over in Philadelphia—there is something magical in Africa."

"It's so good to hear you say that—I didn't think there was anyone in Philadelphia who understood Africa's pull. It's like a magnet, isn't it? When I came back from this last trip, I realized that Philadelphia hasn't changed, but *I* have. I feel like a displaced person here. I was so delighted when you called. Everyone I know is so sick of hearing about my African adventures, they run in the opposite direction now when they see me coming—my husband particularly. Now when I say I want to go to Africa and ask him if that's all right with him, he says fine—as long as I don't tell him about it when I get back. He refuses to go. What about your husband?"

"He's there, in Kenya, now," answered Jujubee. "I could be there too, but it would have meant going with him, and I don't like him. . . . Oh, he's very sweet, but unbearable. He's French—he probably married me for my American passport so that he can come in and out of the States and work here occasionally without having to get a special visa. I certainly married him for his passport—and his studio apartments . . ."

"What's he doing in Africa?"

"Playing polo and drinking. That's all he ever seems to do. I really worry about him—I worry he'll fall off his horse and hurt himself and never be able to play again, and that would mean he'd stay at home instead of traveling all the time—and I couldn't stand that. We have a flat in Paris and one here, so I make sure to arrange my life so that I zig when he zags—when he arrives in Philadelphia, I go off to Paris. And so it goes. Louie thinks he's Yves Montand, but he looks and acts more like a gumdrop. His heart's in his pocketbook, and he'd rather ride a horse than screw. You can see how charming he is."

"Why don't you divorce him?"

"I like the free apartments, and one day I'll inherit some of his money—when I kill him," grinned Jujubee. "What about your husband, Lys? Is he one of the typical Philadelphia Racquets Club boys—the usual forty-watt bulb?"

"Yes, I suppose he is. He's very nice and rather boring," answered Lys with some discomfort and changed the subject because she always felt disloyal talking about Philip in a negative way.

Her naïveté came through immediately, and although Lys was a year or two older, Jujubee recognized at once that she was far more versed in the ways of the evil world than Lys. Their soft-shell crabs arrived and all through dinner they talked of Africa, and over coffee Lys said she would like to see Jujubee's portrait of Schweitzer.

"Well, it's in the museum in Gabon—but I have some of the sketches for it here, and some photographs of the painting—when do you want to come over and see them? Now?"

"No, it's late now. Let's see, Philip has a dinner meeting to-morrow night—how about then?"

"Fine. Come to my apartment—I'll give you something to eat. How about six? Here's my address . . ."

At six the next night Lysbeth was in the elevator of an elegant downtown apartment house on Rittenhouse Square, going up to Jujubee's penthouse. Jujubee answered the door in jeans, a big sweater, and tennis shoes, with paint all over everything—even her ear lobes.

The apartment was one enormous, two-storied, very white, very modern room. Even the floors were tiled white blocks which turned and went halfway up the wall, giving one the feeling of being in the bottom of an empty swimming pool. In the middle of the room was a huge rotating lucite triangle filled with New York garbage. Modern works of art hung from the ceiling in the center of the room on invisible wires. There were no curtains on the twelve-foot windows, and the electric view of Philadelphia flowed in. There were no chairs, just a tiled window seat running the length of one wall and huge brightly colored pillows tossed in clumps on the floor. In one corner was a water bed with a paisley Indian spread over it and all different patterns of paisley pillows on that.

Glass cubes, no higher than a foot, were on the floor by the water bed, and a huge, low glass table surrounded by pillows was on one side of the room. Large green plants almost as big as trees were placed here and there, and hidden spotlights gave off soft il-lumination, while music flowed everywhere through concealed speakers. Rising out of one corner of the room was a white iron spiral staircase leading to the balcony which was the studio as well as the bedroom.

Lys told Jujubee what a delightful apartment it was as they walked about it with their drinks, and in the studio she enthused about Jujubee's work. Her portraits were different from any style Lys had ever seen. Some faces had no mouths, some heads were at the bottom of the canvas instead of centered—yet there was still a classical quality—like classical jazz.

After another drink in the studio, where Lys had insisted on seeing all the paintings, Jujubee said, "Come on down—let's eat." The dining table was the large, square glass one, and as Lys sank into a floor cushion, Jujubee disappeared into the kitchen and returned with a cart loaded with food. All through dinner Lys asked Jujubee about her paintings, where she had studied and exhibited, and after dinner, settled on the water bed with their coffee, Jujubee concluded, ". . . so some of the time I paint in Paris, and the rest of the time in Philadelphia—it's close enough to the market place to sell my wares."

"You mean New York?" interrupted Lys.

"Yes, but who is rich enough to live there? I can always buy the luxuries in life, it's the necessities I can't afford. And besides, New York is too stimulating for me—I'd never paint—there is too much else to do and I'd be constantly distracted. Here it is so dull that I paint to keep sane—but at least I accomplish something. I end up with paintings. And Louie is closer to the polo grounds here. He hates New York, of course—all foreigners do. Christ, I love it . . . do you?"

"It's my favorite place in the world, but Philip doesn't like it either."

"How long have you been married to Philip?" asked Jujubee.

"Forever—a thousand years. Well, at least five, anyway."

"First marriage?"

"Yes," answered Lys, "how about you?"

"Second."

And so Jujubee told her the story of how she had been orphaned, adopted, and unwittingly married into incest.

Lys declared it was the most astonishing thing she had ever heard and asked how long they had been married.

"Two years," Jujubee replied, "before it was finally annulled, but don't look so heart stricken—I had lots of other men. He was at sea most of the time, and when he was away . . . well, lovers are a hobby of mine. You look astonished—*he* was at sea, I wasn't. In those two years I seduced many a husband. I have one moral code, though—I never poach my best friend's husband—the minute I feel the desire to do that, she immediately stops being my best friend," and she grinned that grin that made Lysbeth, and indeed anyone on the receiving end of it, just laugh.

"Currently I am going to bed with five men, but I don't *like* any of them really—how about you?"

"I've never been to bed with anyone other than Philip . . ."

"You've never been to bed with anyone other than Philip?" asked Jujubee, sitting bolt upright. "How old are you—I thought

you were about twenty-seven? You must be thirteen . . .
twelve . . . ?"

"How many men have you been to bed with?" asked Lys.

"How many? Christ, I don't know. I got to eighty-nine once
and lost count—but I don't call that many. You mean you're so
much in love with whatshisname—your husband—that you've
never . . . ?"

"No, I'm afraid I'm not really even in love with him anymore,
but . . ."

"Is he *that* good in bed that you've no curiosity or desire
to . . . ?"

"No—he's *terrible* in bed—we hardly ever make love."

"Do you hate sex or something?"

"No, but . . ."

"Jesus. I have to have another drink—what about you?" and
calling from the kitchen as she made two more drinks, *"How* long
have you been married? Five years? And hardly any sex? Whew—
what's he say about it? Is he gay? Are you?"

Back on the bed with the drinks, Lys told her, "No. But we
don't talk about it. I've tried to once or twice, but he clams up.
Philip's a stuffy stockbroker—the more I keep going to Africa, the
more embarrassing it is for him—so difficult to explain to his col-
leagues and everyone. I think I've become such an embarrassment
to him that I . . . no longer arouse him sexually, which makes me
go to Africa more, which makes him withdraw more, which makes
me go to Africa—and so on. We share the same cage—that's about
all."

From that night Jujubee and Lysbeth became inseparable
friends. During the next four months Philip had to go to New
York more and more on business and Jujubee would sleep in their
house when he was away because Lysbeth didn't like staying
alone. Both of them loved horses and during the days they would
sometimes ride from the Hunt Club, and in the evenings they
would frequently go to the theater or the movies. Afterward they
would sit for hours and discuss what they had seen. They read the
same books and talked about those, too, with Jujubee always leading the conversation—and Lys—into her way of thinking. Jujubee
had a strong influence on Lys for she had a highly intelligent and
keen mind in addition to being well educated. Lys was neither that
clever nor that well schooled, but she listened to what Jujubee

68

said, understood immediately, and learned quickly. Shame at not having much knowledge never occurred to Lys, only delight that she had found someone to teach her. "Oh, Jujubee, you're so smart," she would say. And for Jujubee's part, it was both flattering and curiously heart warming to find herself in the role of a tutor to someone she liked so much.

Lys also began to learn about honesty. Jujubee was so honest she was unacceptable by most people's standards, but Lys found her both exciting and refreshing because of it. Perhaps "frank" would be a better word than "honest," for Jujubee was far from being incapable of deceit. "I am pointedly blunt," she would say of herself. Lys also found herself laughing more with Jujubee than she ever had before, and much that she had thought to be earnest and important she now saw to be shallow or contrived, and with the new revelations she gained a perspective that she had wholly lacked.

In the past, and as Philip's wife particularly, it had been Lysbeth's role to "entertain" people—she was lively and enthusiastic and told anecdotes well, so it was she who fed others on a superficial level. Philip would sit back and let her "carry the ball" (one of his typically irritating expressions), and it often drained her, but now with Jujubee it was the other way around. Jujubee filled her not only with ideas and laughter but there were many actual examples of Jujubee's behavior and attitudes which Lys had not previously encountered firsthand among her friends. For instance, once Lysbeth had to go to Washington, D.C., to see the *American Geographic* staff and Jujubee drove with her. Lys and Philip had a friend, Victor Anderson, an architect who lived in Washington and he invited the girls to lunch at his new house in Georgetown. He had not met Jujubee before but seemed to be amused by her. After the meal Lys said she'd have to skip coffee or she'd be late for her appointment, and did Jujubee want to go with her or wait with Victor and be picked up in an hour? She waited. When Lys collected her, her first question was, "How did you like Victor?"

"Oh, I liked him—but he's not all that good in bed."

Oddly, Philip liked Jujubee and didn't mind having her around. "Probably because I'm a Baroness," said Jujubee. One evening she telephoned Lys and said, "Oh, Christ, Screwy Louie's arriving tomorrow, but I have an idea—why don't you bring 'Fillup' "—as

69

she called him—"and come here for dinner so I don't have to talk to Louie. Fillup and Louie will adore each other as well as deserve each other." She was right. The husbands discussed polo and investments for hours, and Jujubee and Lys ignored them. "It's beautiful," said Jujubee afterward. "The four of us are perfect candidates for playing switches and living up to the main-line orgy rumors—only it should be Fillup with Louie, and you with me."

During the day Lys started to drop in at Jujubee's instead of driving all the way to her Haverford house in between fashion shows, which she still did occasionally. Sometimes they wouldn't speak for hours—Lys might work on an article or read a book while Jujubee painted. Then they'd have a few drinks and talk—they talked a lot about sex. Lys confessed to Jujubee how frustrated she was, but how the situation had gone too far with Philip—"beyond the point of no return." Then every evening she would go home to dinner with Philip and Jujubee would go to bed with one of her different men, and the next day Jujubee would tell Lys all about her escapades of the night before.

Once Jujubee read a poem in the paper by a thirty-four-year-old man who was in a wheel chair, paralyzed from polio. "Here's his picture," she showed Lys the next day, "right here above his poem. Look at him—isn't he beautiful? He's like Beethoven. Anyway, I saw this article after you left last night, and his was the face in the crowd I just had to meet, so I telephoned him and we talked a long time. Intelligent, he is. At five this morning I woke up and called him again and said I was coming over—right then. 'Why?' he asked incredulously. 'Why?' I repeated—'and I thought you were intelligent. I'm coming over for a good-night fuck—what else?' "

"You are so subtle," said Lys.

"It was rather interesting—have you ever been to bed with someone who's crippled—other than Philip?" she added with a grin.

Her romance with the poet lasted several months, bringing to a total of six the men she was sleeping with on a regular basis.

As a result of the trip to Washington Lys received an assignment from the *American Geographic* to do a piece on the Emperor of Ethiopia and she was very excited at the prospect of flying to Addis Ababa. Jujubee decided that she would like to go to Ethiopia too, to paint the Emperor, and unbeknownst to Lys, she had written to him to seek his agreement. A week before Lys was due to leave Jujubee received a reply confirming the commission, and she immediately called Philip at the brokerage firm, explaining to him that she wanted to travel with Lys but not to tell her—that she would simply surprise her by boarding the same plane. Philip thought it was a splendid joke and helped Jujubee book the same flight to Rome where Lys was going to spend a night before flying on to Addis. When the day came he even took Jujubee's suitcase to the airport and checked it in before the girls arrived so that Lys wouldn't suspect that Jujubee was doing anything more than seeing her off. Having gone directly from his office to the airport, he was waiting for the girls when they arrived, and the moment the flight was called Jujubee said that she had a date and would say good-by right there instead of going to the departure lounge with Lys. After an elaborate farewell she ducked into the ladies room, opened her tote bag, and quickly donned a gray wig, an old lady's hat, and a grandmother coat which reached to her ankles. Completing the disguise with steel-rimmed spectacles and puffing out her cheeks with putty, she boarded the plane a few paces behind Lys, and even Philip, who was waving Lys off, had to look twice before recognizing her.

The flight was almost empty and Lys was delighted to find that she was alone on her row and would be able to tilt up the arm rests of the other two seats and lie down to sleep. She was dismayed, therefore, when a silly old lady shuffled toward her and croaked, "May I sit next to you, honey? You see, I haven't flown before and I'm just sort of nervous . . ." Appalled, but too polite to say no, she smiled feebly and turned to look out of the window, but the old lady tugged at her sleeve, a gesture which always irritated her. Keeping her head down, so that Lys couldn't get too close a look, Jujubee fumbled with some rosary beads and said, "I'm going to see the Pope. Where are you going, honey?" As Lys answered, "Rome," barely able to conceal her annoyance, Jujubee continued, "As soon as I get me hat off, I'm going to show you me grandchildren's pictures—they live in Rome . . ." She took her awful hat off, and then she pulled off her hair and Lysbeth couldn't believe it!—she just couldn't believe it. "Jujubee—oh, Jujubee!" and they laughed and laughed. "All the way to Ethiopia! What a terrific surprise!" They ordered drinks and for the next half hour they laughed more and talked about it all—yes, she was

71

going to paint the Emperor; yes, he had agreed to sit for her; yes, Philip knew . . . They toasted each other and their trip, and Lys asked, "What are you going to do with your orthopedic clothes? You look just like my grandmother . . ."

They ordered another drink while they talked and then Lys asked, "Did Philip tell you who I'm having dinner with tonight in Rome?"

"He muttered something about a priest—I hope I misheard him."

"You didn't. Father Ryan—remember that story I did on the leprosarium in Kenya—well, he was head of the African missions at that time—before he was sent to Rome—and he helped me set it up. Nice guy—we became friends—you'll like him."

"What makes you think I'd even consider having dinner with a priest? No way . . ."

"You will when you see this one. He looks like a ravaged truck driver—not priestlike at all—he doesn't act like one either."

After the undelicious meal they both slept the rest of the way to Rome. As they came out of customs, Jujubee saw a huge man in jeans and a sweater waving at them from the other side of the glass. "Is that The Partially Reverend Ryan?"

"Yes," answered Lys waving back to him.

"Mmmmm," said Jujubee with much interest, "this might be the first weekend in his life he won't bore God to death . . ."

"Oh, Christ . . ." smiled Lys shaking her head.

Father Ryan and Lys shook hands enthusiastically, and then she introduced Jujubee. "What do you do?" he asked her as they walked toward the car. "Wait, don't tell me, let me guess—are you a newscaster on television or . . . you're familiar . . ."

"I'm a sexual pervert. And you're a God biggy—practically the same thing . . . we should get along well," said Jujubee with her grin at full blast.

"Would you like to go to your hotel first or eat or . . ."

"Let's have the Last Supper first," said Jujubee. "I'm starved," and she climbed in the middle of the front seat. Looking up at him she continued, "I refuse to call you 'Father'—you're far too gorgeous—I do not think of you in any way as 'father.' "

Father Ryan said, "I don't mind—just call me Ryan—but most people who have trouble with that have a father complex. What about you and your father?"

"He ran a dry-cleaning establishment and did abortions and

72

told fortunes on the side,"—she grinned—"right across from the Catholic church. He taught us always to keep the doors locked—with all those Catholics around."

Father Ryan had to smile because it was just so ridiculous, and Lys saw at once that he, too, was entertained by Jujubee. In the ladies room at Alfredo's Jujubee combed her golden red mane and told Lys, "I crave his lower lip. I would like to kiss it."

"You'd like to kiss a gorilla."

"I sure would! I thought all priests had brains like bananas, but this one is full of smarts."

As the girls walked up to the table where Father Ryan waited for them, Jujubee saw it was laden with martinis and a bottle of champagne, so she said, loud enough for the Americans sitting next to them to hear, "Why, darling, there's enough booze here to knock over a Roman Catholic priest!" She sat down and looked at Father Ryan and went on, "I want to say the same thing to you that Sir Richard Burton said to David Livingstone when he first met him—'I can't share your enthusiasm for God, but I can His for you.' That is," added Jujubee, "if there were a God."

"If you're going to talk to me about God, I won't be able to get through dinner," answered Father Ryan—always ready with a quick riposte.

"Then let's talk about sex," said Jujubee, not to be outdone.

Dinner went off very well—they had a delicious meal, good conversation, and much laughter, and after coffee Father Ryan suggested a liqueur, but Lys declined, "I have to get some sleep. Let's go back to the hotel then I can go to bed and you two can stay up and drink all night."

Lys bid them both good night in the lobby and was soon asleep, but a few hours later she was awakened by scuffling noises. Peering out from under the covers she saw the amazing sight of Jujubee struggling to get up from under Father Ryan who was holding her down on the bed. Every time she nearly succeeded, he would grab her and shove her down again, trying to kiss her and pulling at her blouse as he did. Lys was embarrassed and uncertain whether to intervene, but because Ryan was so drunk Jujubee soon did manage to get away from him, and as she did so, he passed out face down on her bed. "Christ," muttered Jujubee rearranging her clothes . . .

73

"Are you all right?" whispered Lys coming out from under the sheet.

"Yeah . . ."

"What shall we do with him? Give him some coffee?"

"Hell no, then we'll only have a wide awake drunk." Jujubee prodded him and shook him, and finally managed to get him up and shove him out of the door.

"Whew, something strange about that Ryan. I've been out with many drunks, but this one is really sick. After you left the first thing I got was an invitation to go view Rome from his room through our feet. But sloppy drunks really turn me off, so believe it or not, I declined. And he's been grabbing at me ever since . . . but it's as if his passion stems from hate instead of love. I sense he wants to hit me with chains. I've met that kind before—bad news. Maybe he hates women so much because they trouble him sexually and he can't satisfy . . . Oh hell, I don't know—but I do know that if you give me a drunk, you give me the true man—and that man is mentally ill." Calling from the bathroom as she brushed her teeth she shouted, "If Jesus ever met him, He'd puke," and as she came back into the room, "Christ I'm tired—talk to you in the morning. 'Night."

Over coffee in bed next morning Lys and Jujubee were discussing Father Ryan when the phone rang. "Pronto," Jujubee answered, then covering the receiver with her hand she gestured and whispered to Lys, "It's he himself—in his priest voice—sounds very gloomy." Then always ready to forget if not forgive, she said cheerfully into the phone, "Want to borrow my rose-colored glasses?" Pause. Then, "Oh, all right—just a minute," and handing the phone to Lys, "he wants to speak to you. Prick."

"Good morning," said Lys cheerfully. Long pause. "Why is that?" Longer pause. Then in her formal voice, "All right. Fine. See you . . . next time, good-by."

"What was all that about?" asked Jujubee.

"Damned if I know. A big sermon about how he is tormented and suffering."

"What did he say when you asked why?"

"He said, God must love him very much."

"Christ," exclaimed Jujubee, "he *is* sick. Did he say anything about me?"

"No, he just said how nice it was to see me again and that he would be back in Philadelphia soon and hoped to see me then. He was full of virtue."

"That's what he tells himself, too. He'll delude himself into thinking he is full of integrity, which is a substitute for his ego since he is a failure at seducing women—he has to be virtuous at least—see?"

"I'm not sure—tell me again when we get on the plane—Come on, we have to leave for the airport in twenty minutes."

In Ethiopia, Jujubee, working very fast in the limited sittings granted by the Emperor ("a short Abraham Lincoln," she described him) got enough on canvas to be able to finish the portrait later in her studio. Lysbeth did an excellent story with photographs and had sufficient material left over for a second piece too. In addition to the work, they had time for shopping in the market places and returned home laden with Coptic crosses and hand-woven rugs, and were aware that their shared experiences had further cemented their friendship into something of value for each of them.

Just a few weeks after they were back, Jujubee telephoned Lys at three A.M. one morning, and apologizing for the hour said, "Our friendship is strong enough for laughter—do you think it can stand tears? Although I don't often tell anyone my troubles, because half of them don't give a damn and the other half are glad of it, I am forced to make an exception. I have this terrible pain in my side."

She had telephoned her doctor, she said, but got no answer, and she simply didn't know what to do because she was unable to drive herself to the hospital. In half an hour, Lys arrived in the studio penthouse, got Jujubee into her car and took her to the hospital. Lys was still there at seven A.M. when Jujubee came out of the operating room minus a kidney. For the next two weeks Lys was at the hospital every day and sometimes when Jujubee was in a lot of pain, twice a day. She was given morphine for the pain and told Lys she hoped she would have to have her other kidney out so she could get some more morphine. Then when she felt better and was eating, Lys made her a cheesecake which Jujubee said was almost as good as the morphine; so Lys made another, and when Jujubee was discharged Lys was there to take her to her house—she insisted Jujubee should not go to her apartment alone. "Who would bring you chicken broth and cheesecake?"

"And morphine?"

Although Jujubee thanked Lys effusively for all she had done, she didn't reveal the true extent to which the kindness had affected her. She had never, in fact, been so deeply touched before. No one had ever cared that much; no one had ever cared at all, really. Louie had telephoned her in the hospital after his polo game in California, then flown right back to Paris. Boy friends had stopped in at the hospital once or twice to pay the expected call, as had other acquaintances, but Lys was the only one who had really cared.

Jujubee's adoptive mother kept coming into Jujubee's thoughts. After vainly trying to have a baby her mother had resorted to adopting Jujubee because, "as soon as you adopt a child you get pregnant." And sure enough, "ten months later to the very day" —as she was fond of saying—"little Wally was born," and she dismissed Jujubee from then on. How Jujubee loathed little Wally. Oh, everyone said how marvelous her mother was to raise the two children so equally—just as if they were both her "own flesh and blood." True, she spent time with both children, but that was only because the adored Wally was one of them and she could hardly send Jujubee back to the orphanage. You can be with a child twenty-four hours a day and ignore it. She ignored Jujubee. Not the shoes, of course, or the piano lessons or the toys, but the holding in her arms and the hugs. Her mother never kissed her, not even good night, not once, after Wally was born. All the love was for Wally, and Jujubee's loathing for him increased day by day. She kept remembering how, when he was ten years old, he was taken to the hospital with scarlet fever and how her mother had practically lived at the hospital and cried and cried. When Jujubee had come down with it the day Wally was brought home from the hospital, she was glad because now Mother would worry about her too. But it wasn't that way. Mother had to stay home and nurse poor Wally. She didn't come to the hospital to see her—not once. She remembered lying in bed picturing herself dying and imagining her mother's grief and despair. She created her funeral over and over and rejoiced when her mother sobbed uncontrollably by the graveside, crying because she realized too late that she had

76

cared, really cared for her. But instead of dying, Jujubee got better and went home. Her polite but insignificant father had come to see her for a mandatory five minutes each day, and it was he who collected her and drove her home, saying stiffly that he was glad she was coming back, but she knew he didn't mean it because he was never glad or sad about anything. He didn't really love Wally either—he was incapable of feeling much of anything.

When she got home she considered killing little Wally, but then reasoned it wasn't his fault he was loved, so she decided to ignore him, which attitude she had successfully maintained.

For the next three years Jujubee tried everything she could think of to capture her mother's affection. She tried pleasing her and annoying her, but nothing she did mattered—her mother's reaction whether polite or critical, amounted in the end to no more than indifference. At thirteen, Jujubee came to the conclusion that her choice in life was to be miserable or to concentrate on something else. She chose the latter, and the something else was boys. No more empty years—she filled the time with sex and tried to erase her mother from her mind. She succeeded very well, for when her mother died ten years later she received the news with the same indifference her mother had always had for her. Both Wally and her father were still in Norfolk, but all they had was a Christmas card relationship.

Although for years she had not thought about her mother, when she was coming out of the anesthesia, she had imagined it was her mother who was holding her hand and putting cold washcloths on her forehead and saying comforting things in a soft voice. She was surprised when she realized it was Lysbeth.

A few weeks after her recovery Jujubee had an exhibition in New York and Lys was as excited about it as if it were her own. "Of course I'm going," she said to Jujubee. "What do you mean *am* I going?" And all through the exhibition when someone bought a painting Lys was as pleased as if she had sold it herself. She raced out for the reviews and was ecstatic at the praise Jujubee got.

"Why do you care so much about this exhibition?" Jujubee asked Lys.

"Because I care about you—I want you to be happy."

"Why? Why do you care about me?"

77

"Because I *love* you," said Lys astonished that Jujubee had asked such a question.

"What are you talking about?"

"Of course I love you. I'd love my sister if I had one, I love all my friends—and you most of all because you're my closest friend, and you'd better love me too," Lys said openly, like a child.

From that moment Jujubee admitted to herself that she loved Lysbeth, but she didn't tell her so because she knew that what she felt for Lys was more important than what Lys felt for her.

As the months went by, Jujubee found herself thinking every day, wait till I tell Lys this, wait till I show her that, and the feeling grew until she found a whole day's happiness depended on whether she would see Lys or not. She truly wondered if she enjoyed the actuality of her sexual escapades with her men as much as she enjoyed telling Lys the details afterward. She also wondered how healthy her feelings were toward Lys.

Jujubee had a fellowship to teach at the Sorbonne for six weeks. The idea of leaving Lys for that long upset her, but she had to go. Lys took her to the airport and waved good-by. She got her first letter from Jujubee exactly one week later.

"Dearly Beloved,

Well here I am—American Art Biggy in Paris. Teaching at the Sorbonne. I'm supposed to be setting all kinds of examples, which of course I am very good at—except they are all bad. Like falling in love with one of my students which I suppose isn't cricket—especially since he's Louie's nephew—but then who the hell knows how to play cricket? My new love looks just like a giraffe and suddenly I want to go to bed with a giraffe more than anything, and I look at him in class and imagine it all, and then I cannot remember what I'm saying. He sits and watches me as if he knows exactly what I'm thinking. I am mad for him, even though he is a little old for me—he's nineteen. I can think of nothing but making love to him, which I will not do unless I get really drunk, which of course means any time now. It is an impossible situation with this idiotic close family of Louie's, but if there's any way, I'll work it out, as you know. I'm going to write a note to him now and suggest he meet Louie and me for a drink after class.

I'm five days late and I'm not pregnant, so I must have cancer. Good-by trusted friend. Give my eyes to the bank and you may have my pressed wild-flower collection.

Adieu,
Camille"

The next day Lys got Jujubee's second letter:

"Dear One,

I don't have cancer after all but I wish I did because it would be nicer than this—I am painfully in love. He came to the cafe as a result of the note I left for him which read, 'Meet us after class at the Cul de Sac' signed 'Louie and Jujubee.' So he came for one of three reasons: to see Louie, to see me, or to have someone to drink with. I could feel the electrodes sparking back and forth between us, but unfortunately I think Louie felt them too. After we got home I plied Louie with more liquor—which is as difficult to do as to ply a three-year-old kid with bubble gum—and he passed out, saying, 'You're attracted to that little nephew of mine, aren't you, my sweet bitch?' or some such endearing thing. As I have told you—give me a drunk and I'll give you the true man every time. He cares not what I do in Philadelphia—or almost anywhere else on the globe—but in Paris, I not only have to be the Virgin Mary, I have to wash his feet six times a day in front of his mother to prove that I worship him. He is a very sick polo-playing alcoholic cretin. Anyway, he passed out, as he does every night, and when I was sure he was out cold I telephoned François at his flat, and let him beg me to come over. It was one A.M.—I debated: yes, no, it's crazy, insane, ridiculous, and went. We played mental tiddly-winks, and you will not believe this, but alas it is true: I did *not* go to bed with him. Instead, he told me he 'respects' me, which I will have to correct—and soon. But it was marvelous and reminiscent of teen-age romances again where you didn't just hop in the hay immediately.

Tee-hee,
Shirley Temple"

Three days later a note arrived:

"I am rid of this sophisticated woman who is Jujubee and am a silly girl once more. I feel all self-conscious again—but if we don't go to bed soon I fear this romance will burn itself out quickly. But, Christ, right now I love this man. (Man?) But I love you more. There are parts of you I find not perfect, but perhaps your association with me will make them so.

Chicken Licken"

Two days later, another note:

"Still haven't been to bed with him. It's too 'important,' he says. Still haven't heard from you. Write. Remember, Hell hath no fury like a Jujubee scorned."

Four days later, another letter:

"Dear Heart and Gentle Person,

Christ, I write a lot of letters for someone who doesn't write letters. I received your 300-page note—write regular, hon.

François and I swing in the park on swings and he tells me he loves me every five minutes, but there are still those reservations as if he were afraid of something. Maybe it's Screwy Louie and his Mafiaesque family. But nothing matters, because François loves me. Yesterday was an Elvira Madigan afternoon, soft sunlight and butterflies, and we ran through the golden sunlight in fields of tall grass and chased the butterflies and he kissed me and told me over and over again how much he loves me. So another Indian bites the dust, and here I am picking the dust out of his teeth. I want to mother him and hope dearly he refuses to be mothered. At times when I say 'no' and he says 'yes' I cannot tell you the thrill I get. And when he bosses me and treats me like an erring child, I am in seventh heaven. I guess I do have a mother, or father, complex—probably both. I am a very sick girl. I am also madly in love with this lad even though I know it wouldn't work in a million years. I guess that is why I love him. Louie went to Berne to play polo for the day, which is what created this sinful and desirable state with François. But now Louie is back and everything he does irritates me and I cannot stand any physical contact with him whatsoever unless I am so falling down drunk I am not even aware of who's screwing me.

It is much more fun being in love when I can share it with you. I miss you dreadfully but will suffer through until November. The world will little note, nor long remember what I say here, unless you forget to swallow these letters.

Love you,
Jujubee, the Hopeful Whore"

Inside this letter was folded another which had written on it, "Read second."

"Dear Friend,

The letter you just read was also read by Louie. Yep—he was snooping around and found what he was looking for. You can imagine the trauma. Christ, I wish you were here—you could at least help me keep my lies straight. Louie screams and hollers and carries on and says he is leaving me, but I know he will not go . . . he prefers to stay and torment me. It is all very unbeautiful,

80

and it is making me very unhappy. Suddenly he is madly in love with me and tells me he has thought all along that I have been faithful to him. You can see how well he knows me. He says François broke up our marriage but of course it started eighty-nine people ago, long before François, but how can I explain this to Louie? He says he is going to name François as co-respondent, which is very ugly especially since he is not guilty. Of course, Louie does not believe that, and even I find it very difficult to believe myself, but alas it is true. Wouldn't you know I'd get caught when I'm innocent—sexually innocent at any rate, which is all that seems to concern Louie. I don't mind being guilty—I'm so used to that and comfortable with guilt that I know how to react, but being innocent is terrible and confusing and very uncomfortable. Anyway, Louie made me promise I wouldn't see François ever again, and I had to telephone François with Louie listening and tell him not to call me, which he hasn't done, and which really pisses me off—he should know that really means that I *need* him to call me. So Louie and I sit in silence and stare at the TV until he can think of something else horrible to say about my recent demise, while I sit and wait for the phone to ring and it doesn't and I am most unhappy and I really think this episode with Louie has scared François off. I shall retire to a warm bath and slit my wrists.

Love anyway,
Ophelia"

Two days later yet another letter arrived:

"This is Associated Crap bringing you the latest developments in the world of sports:

Although I said I thought François was scared off, I didn't really think so, and I fully expected to go running into his arms on some lonesome beach—but all I get are the sea nettles and the sand. He did not call for three days and I was insane, so I gave Louie more booze than ever and when he finally passed out, I called François and gave him hell for not calling me. His excuse was that he understood we were not to contact each other again because I had said we were not to contact each other again. How dumb can you get? Now he says he will call, but what the hell good is getting a call if you have to dial the number for the idiot? So he just called—but he is hesitant and seems afraid to meet me for fear he will be caught and tarred and feathered. If he really loved me he would want to be tarred and feathered. I wish he would tell me to go to hell—it would be so much easier. Louie continues to chastise me, and for gratification I eat all the time. My hips swell.

After this part of my life is over I hope to become a lesbian and start hating men. If not, I will join the circus as the fat lady.

> Your obedient master,
> George"

A week passed before Lys heard any more. Then:

"Well, it appears to be all over with François and me, and I make believe it doesn't matter, and it works out very well because I've had so much trauma before this that I'm all out of miseries. Right now I am most unhappy that there isn't somebody—anybody—to be upset about. I just hate not being in love. My newest project is just what you think, but I shall not put myself in the position of self-incrimination again. You will just have to wait to hear about it, that is, if I can remember by the time I get back. By then I will have started things to forget things that I started to forget something that I started to forget . . . You can see that I am going to the dogs without you. Or is it the nut house? I am thinking of auditioning for a mental institution in Philadelphia as soon as I return. Sure could do with a girlie day with you—it's been a thousand years—but only seven hundred more to go.

> xxxxxxxxx's
> J. P. Morgan"

Then:

"Dear Lys,

Louie will never divorce me—it would be such a disgrace to his French aristocratic family—but I don't really care, just as long as I don't have to see him. Maybe I'll enter a convent. I can hardly wait to get back—next Tuesday Pan Am's flight 100. Is our meaningful relationship still full of meaning? I hope it is for you because it sure is for me. I say nice things behind your back and miss you and love you. We deserve to live in the same forest for we are such beautiful people. Must hang up now and go teach my class. Needless to say, I am minus one student.

> Sister Ryan"

Lys was at the airport waiting for Jujubee. They were overjoyed to see one another and went at once to Jujubee's apartment where they had drinks and talked while Jujubee unpacked. She had brought one of her paintings with her from Paris and as Lys carried it up the spiral stairway for her to unwrap, Jujubee ran up behind her and playfully put her hands on Lys's waist, laughing, "I told you I'm going to be a lesbian, so you'd better watch out for me." Lys laughed too, as she unwrapped the painting, and then she saw it was a superb portrait of herself capturing all her vitality and warmth and was one of the best of the excellent works that Jujubee so consistently produced. Lys squealed with joy and hugged her friend as she thanked her.

The two of them talked until three A.M. when Lys said she'd have to go home. Jujubee asked if she wanted to spend the night, but she said she had to make Philip's breakfast in the mornings— he no longer cared what time she got in just as long as she had his breakfast ready. Lysbeth insisted on taking the painting with her, saying she wanted to put it by her bed so she could see it when she woke up. As always, Jujubee made Lys call her to say she had arrived home safely. "I wish you'd either get killed on the highway or stay all night so I could stop worrying."

The following month Lys and Philip gave Jujubee a party—featuring the painting. About seventy-five people were there, and in the midst of it all Jujubee came up to Lys and whispered surreptitiously, "Who's that over there by the clock—didn't I go to bed with him?"

"Jesus, Jujubee, can't you even remember . . . in Washington that day—it's Victor Anderson—we had lunch . . ."

"Victor, darling . . ." said Jujubee swooping toward him.

The morning after the party Jujubee telephoned Lys and said, "It was very drunk out last night . . . a great party—what I remember. I saw double on the way home and didn't know which road to take, but I found that if I held my hand over one eye I stopped seeing double—but then my other hand kept slipping off the steering wheel. Whew! My mouth tastes like the bottom of a parrot's cage. How are you?"

That afternoon Lys took Jujubee an eye patch for her to keep in the glove compartment of the car in preparation for any similar trips home in the future, and they agreed that there was little doubt that it would be very useful. Later that week Jujubee telephoned Lys and said, "The lake is frozen over. Come on down and we'll go ice skating."

"Ice skating!" said Lys. "I'm way too sophisticated for that."

"You mean you're not sophisticated *enough*," answered Jujubee.

"Besides, tomorrow is New Year's Eve!" said Lys.

"Whoopie shit," said Jujubee flatly.

"Come to dinner with Philip and me—he'll never go out on New Year's Eve . . ."

"I don't blame him—too many amateur drunks."

During dinner the following night the phone rang—it was Paris calling for Jujubee. "How nice of Louie to call you and wish you a Happy New Year," said Philip naïvely. But it wasn't Louie, it was Louie's mother summoning Jujubee back to Paris. Louie was in the hospital—a small operation, nothing serious, but a "wife's place is with her husband." Jujubee returned from the phone and said, "I've got to go to Paris—Louie's having a hysterectomy or something, and protocol and his mother demand I sit by his bedside and receive his visitors so everyone will think he has a good wife and that I care about him. I don't want to go to Paris. I loathe his mother—she looks like an albino turtle, has indescribably bad breath, is permanently suicidal, and the only thing she enjoys is a constant state of bad health. And I certainly don't want to see Louie—I may have to be with him for weeks. If I'm lucky, maybe he'll die and I could get back here in a few days . . ." Lysbeth laughed and Philip looked uncomfortable—when Jujubee talked like this he never knew if she was serious or kidding.

Reluctantly, Jujubee went off to Paris the next day, and just a week after she had gone, Lys got an urgent call from the editor of the Philadelphia *Inquirer* saying the correspondent who was going to Kenya to do the story on the total eclipse of the sun had just broken his leg and would be in traction for a month, and could she, Lys, possibly go to Africa in two weeks time to cover the phenomenon? Of course she could! Lys wrote a Special Delivery letter to Jujubee to tell her of this piece of luck and asked if she could spend the night with her in Paris on the way through, and if so, would Jujubee like her to bring a cheesecake? Lys also asked if Jujubee would meet the plane, and as a forlorn hope she asked if there was any possibility that Jujubee could take a week off from Louie's bedside and travel to Kenya with her? Three days later she received a cable from Paris which simply read, "Yes."

Jujubee was at Orly to meet her. "Are you really coming to Kenya with me?" asked Lys the minute they were together.

"Why not? Of course I am, but that's tomorrow—right now you are about to meet François."

84

"François?" exclaimed Lys. "I thought that was over. Are you still in love with him? What about Louie?"

"Louie? Oh, him—he's better. Yesterday he went to a polo tournament at Midhurst in England." As they walked to the car she continued, "No, I'm not in love with François anymore, but I've been drinking stingers at his house all night and he's expecting us back for more with the cheesecake—did you bring it? I've brought my eye patch. Here's his car. O.K.?"

"Fine with me—it's only seven P.M. my time—it's one A.M. yours, though, but that's your problem. Why aren't you in love with him any more?"

"Because I *talked* to him. He's a cretin, too—I told you it runs in the family—and he is a real Miss Nancy as well—the type who goes to the dentist every three months. But he's a gorgeous cretin and good in bed, so finally I've reached a normal, healthy relationship with him. Where's the cheesecake?"

When they got to the door of a fourth-floor walk-up on the Left Bank, a very pretty boy answered the bell and smiled an empty smile which matched his empty beauty, but Lys could see where his type of looks could appeal to some. She herself preferred an interesting face, even an ugly face if it were full of character, but she nevertheless appreciated François as a work of art. They drank stingers and ate the cheesecake and after only the second drink, Lys said, "Flying must do something to my metabolism. I really feel quite drunk."

"Of course it's the flying and not the stingers," said Jujubee who looked very drunk herself. François passed some potato chips and Jujubee said, "No thank you, they're too heavy." Afraid Jujubee might pass out, Lys pulled her to her feet, put on some good music, and the two girls got very silly and started to dance by themselves, then sing. When François joined in, the next door neighbor called—thus ending the party. As the three of them went to the car, singing all the way down the stairs, François said to Jujubee, "You're too drunk to sing, you'll have to drive." Jujubee donned her eye patch, and François sat in the middle of the front seat between the girls and when Jujubee parked the Citroën in front of her own flat, François grabbed her and kissed her passionately and then turned to Lys and gave her a long passionate kiss too. He drove off, and when the girls got inside—a huge one-room studio with two sofa beds already made up—Lys collapsed on one

85

and flipped her shoes off. As she did so she slipped down so that her torso was flat on the bed and her legs dangled over the side. Jujubee sprawled next to her and asked, "What do you think of François?"

"He sure can kiss!" answered Lys. Jujubee began describing François's talents in bed, and finally Lys interrupted her and said, "Stop talking about it, will you, Jujubee—it's making me horny—I might even rape you . . ."

"Promises, promises—nothing but promises. You know *I'm* ready for anything—but you, you—if I so much as did this to you"—and she brushed her hand softly back and forth over Lys's breasts—". . . you'd run away screaming." But Lys didn't run away at all. The only thing that even moved were her eyes which glazed over, then closed. Jujubee continued her stroking and said, "Come on, Lys."

Lys suddenly sat up and with drunken levity said, "O.K. Why not? I've always wanted to try going to bed with a woman—but first I need a drink—for courage and all that. Want one?"

"Ever heard me say no to a drink?" asked Jujubee, and they were in the kitchen laughing and giggling and talking about what they were about to do just as if they were two school girls discussing their high school prom. Their attitude was light, excited, and full of giggles as they carried their drinks to the bed, but soon the laughter stopped. An hour later they were out in the kitchen making their second round of drinks before their second round in bed.

To Lys it was a novel and highly satisfying sexual experience, but it meant no more to her than the discovery of a fine new restaurant or an exciting book. It was something good and something different, but that was as far as it went.

To Jujubee it was as important as anything that had ever happened to her.

The sun rose and still they had not slept. Finally Lys said, "Oh, no more, Jujubee, I must sleep."

"All right. I suppose I must go, anyway, and organize my air ticket. I'll telephone you later on so that you can get ready to leave."

At noon the telephone rang and as Lys reached for it and mumbled, "Hello," Jujubee said, "Jesus."

"That's just what I was going to say. Whew! Well, so be it—it was great sex. What are the plans?" she yawned.

86

Lys had dismissed the episode with the same lightness as she had experienced it because for her it had been pure mechanical sex with no emotions involved. Therefore she felt no guilt. Her thoughts of it had died with her last shudder of passion.

But to Jujubee it had been infinitely more than the sexual gratification she experienced with men. She was emotionally transfixed by what had happened and was tuned up by it to concert pitch. Never before had she felt so involved with anybody, but despite the tremendous impact of it upon her a sixth sense warned her that if Lys knew what she really felt it would frighten her. So she decided, for the present at least, to pretend that it had been no more than sex for her either.

"Our plane leaves in two hours. Get ready, I'll be back in half an hour—have some coffee going—we'll eat on the plane."

Two very striking and very hung-over females boarded Pan Am's flight for Nairobi and tilted their seats back as soon as the seat-belt sign went off. The stewardess asked if they would like a cocktail, and Jujubee said she would like six bloody marys. Lys ordered a bloody shame, to Jujubee's horror. "How can you possibly drink a non-alcoholic drink? Aren't you as hung over as I am?" Lys decided she might as well change her order to a bloody mary too, and as they were drinking them she said, "I'm beginning to think the only solution to the whole problem is to get rid of men."

"Problem . . . what problem?" asked Jujubee.

"Oh—being in love—all that pain—all that suffering that you went through with François and I went through with everyone I thought I was in love with since I was eleven. It never balances out, the pain is always greater than the joy. Pain is sadder than joy is gladder . . . it's unfair as hell, but true. But with emotions *not* being involved, sex is very good and liberating—during the day your mind is free to concentrate on whatever it wants to concentrate on, and your heart isn't getting in the way. The few men I've been involved with have either been lousy or I've just been too much in love to relax and enjoy the sex part—but I sure was relaxed last night."

"The word is 'drunk,'" said Jujubee.

"No it isn't. I've been drunk before, but sex was never like that." She spoke in the same tone and attached the same importance quotient as she gave to her next sentence: "You know those marvelous blue eye drops you have in your medicine cabinet? Well I stole them and brought them with me—they're terrific, but after you use them you blow your nose blue—ever notice that?" The night before was over. Eye drops were the subject now.

The hostess gave them earphones, but Jujubee returned hers saying they made her feel as if someone were picking her up with ice tongs. They both slept the remaining five hours to Nairobi. It was after midnight in Kenya when they arrived and by the time they got through customs and checked into the Norfolk Hotel and had a bath it was two A.M. Lys climbed into bed, tucked in the mosquito net, and was asleep in a few seconds, but Jujubee, who had had no sleep at all the night before, lay awake smoking and thinking.

Tea was brought to them the next morning at seven, and they sat up in bed drinking it and complaining that it wasn't coffee. They dressed in bush clothes and had a light breakfast in the hotel's marvelous old high-ceilinged Colonial dining room, where Hemingway, Isak Dinesen, and Ruark had sat before them.

Although Jujubee had never been to Kenya before, Lys knew her way around from her previous visits, and in a couple of hours they had stocked up with food and hired a Land-Rover, a tent and sleeping bags. After a quick cup of coffee at the Thorn Tree, Nairobi's famous sidewalk restaurant, they drove north to Tree-tops, the unique game-viewing lodge built in a tree, deep in the Aberdare Forest, where they spent the night. Early the next morning they were on their way again through beautiful farm lands on the western slopes of Mt. Kenya where the scenery was more reminiscent of Kentucky than what people imagine Africa to be. They crossed the Equator, and as they got closer to their viewing site for the total eclipse of the sun—the longest of the century— they bumped through clouds of dust into hot rugged terrain populated sparsely with nomads who wander through the arid scrub with their camels and great herds of cattle in search of water. Lys said she loved camels—they were so romantic.

They had chosen to watch the phenomenon at Laisamis where the umbra, or path of totality, cut right across, making day become night and night become day again in four minutes.

When the edge of the moon started to impinge on the sun at three P.M. the light grew very strange—not like a cloudy day, not like before a storm, not even like twilight or dawn—but eerily different from anything ever seen before. "Like a dream sequence in an early Bergman movie," someone had described it. Slowly, for an hour, it grew darker and darker and the temperature started to drop noticeably. Insects stopped their noise, birds flew to their nests, donkeys and cattle made their way to their *manyattas,* and suddenly—like the snuffing out of a candle or the click of a switch—it went as dark as a moonlit night but in quite a different way. The stars shone, but not like stars—like clear electric light bulbs hanging in the sky—and the corona, the fiery ring of the sun visible around the rim of the moon, shone with jagged electric edges. It was unearthly, unbelievable, and in an odd way unnerving too, even to the two modern sophisticated Western women. It was the never-to-be-forgotten once-in-a-lifetime experience they had been told it would be, and Lys and Jujubee, who had yelled and pointed and laughed with delight and awe during the totality, suddenly fell silent when it was over.

After the eclipse they drove back the way they had come for about an hour, and then they stopped and put up their tent under a tree and made a fire, cooking corned beef hash, scrambled eggs, and fried bananas. Afterward they sat on a log by the fire drinking coffee and discussing how the eclipse had proved, among other things, that birds respond not to time but to light intensity, for they had stopped singing and had flown to their nests during the eclipse. They drank more coffee and listened to lion roar in the distance, and while preparing for bed, Lys brushed her teeth in Zinc Ointment which she mistook for the toothpaste tube in the darkness. As she was about to climb into her sleeping bag she caught sight of a centipede about five inches long. She made Jujubee keep the flashlight trained on it while she grabbed the bread knife, and with a well aimed slash she chopped it neatly in half—and then there were two. Both halves of the insect scrabbled off in different directions and the girls shrieked, while they desperately tried to remember which was the dangerous end with the sting in the tail so that they could keep the light on it. They spent a nervous five minutes until they had tracked down both bits, and finally they were in their camp beds ready to sleep.

"I like my bath with hot water and Arpège bath oil, but I'll give it up for this anytime," said Lys. In a second she was sound asleep.

But Jujubee lay there wide awake and relived every detail of the night in Paris. She had been unable to stop thinking about it for even one minute, and she realized it was becoming more important to her each day. Yet Lys acted as if the whole thing had never happened. Still awake after an hour or so, Jujubee decided to slip outside to go to the bathroom. Lys, awakening at the sound of the tent being unzipped, asked, "Where are you going?"

"I'm going to the loo," answered Jujubee.

"Don't you want the flashlight?"

"Whatever for? I know where my pussy is," said Jujubee, and when she got back into the tent she too fell asleep.

It was a long drive back to Nairobi the next day and they had four flat tires in three hours, having inadvertently driven over the fallen branch of a thorn tree as they left their camp site, which caused slow punctures in each wheel. They stopped for an elegant buffet Sunday lunch at the beautiful Mt. Kenya Safari Club. "'Kere Nyaga' is what the Kikuyu people call the mountain," explained Lys, "it means 'Mountain of Mystery,'" but she added that she had always felt that Mt. Kilimanjaro was possessed of more mystery, and certainly more majesty.

Kilimanjaro was to be the backdrop for the next of Lys's projects—a photographic article about the Maasai.

When they arrived at the Norfolk, exhausted and dusty, they bathed first of all. Then Lys had to mail her film and report off to the States. Afterward they had a drink and a bite of supper in the Lord Delamere Bar and decided on an early night.

Just after they had turned off the light, Jujubee said from her bed, "I wish there were savage men in the streets."

"Shut up and go to sleep. You'll never be able to get up at six tomorrow morning if you don't—I'm going to sleep right now."

By eight o'clock next morning they were driving south toward Mt. Kilimanjaro, a hundred and fifty miles away. Soon after they entered Maasailand a young warrior, a Morani, flagged them down so they stopped and picked him up. He climbed into the back of the Land-Rover and Lys said, "Soba."

"Soba," he replied, his startling white teeth showing even whiter than they probably were against his dark red skin. One pigtail hung down the center of his forehead, the remaining long strands of twisted red ochred hair being tied back in a "George." He was naked except for a cloak thrown over one shoulder, and he clutched his spear as he sat upright in the back seat and said something to them in Maasai.

"I really irritate myself," complained Lys, "I don't understand one word he's saying. All I know is *'Soba'* which I can say right off, and then of course they think I can speak Maasai, so off they go, and I'm still left at 'Hello.'" She turned around to the warrior as she drove and said, *"Mimi siwezi kusema Maasai. Unajua Kiswahili?"*

"Ndio."

"Where did you learn to speak Swahili so fluently?" Jujubee asked Lys.

"In Philadelphia—I took a course at night school."

"Does he speak English?" asked Jujubee.

"I doubt it. *Unasema Kingereza?"*

"La," shaking his head.

"Then I will teach you," said Jujubee, smiling sweetly at him. "I would like to go to bed with you, would you like to go to bed with me?"

Big smile from the warrior, but no words.

"Say 'fuck,'" said Jujubee enunciating slowly, and gesturing to him to say the same thing she repeated, "Fuck, fuck off . . ."

"Fooky," said the warrior.

"When he tells one of the tribal elders to 'fuck off,' you're going to walk funny with that spear of his up your ass," said Lys.

"Don't the Maasai believe in free love?" asked Jujubee. "Isn't one of their customs to give their wives to visitors?"

"I think so . . . why? Oh yes, you'd like to have a Maasai's wife, wouldn't you?"

"Ha, ha. Very funny."

"I don't really know too much about them. There are so many myths, including one which I find hard to believe—when the boys are circumcised, which is between the ages of thirteen and seventeen, *immediately* after the ceremony they must have intercourse with a hole in the ground—*successfully*—or they don't become Morani.

Jujubee turned to the Morani and asked, "So, how was it with the ground?"

Big smile.

"Bet you'd like me better, honey."

91

"Alisema nini?" he said, asking Lys what she had said.

"Sijui—I don't know," lied Lys.

The Namanga River Inn was just round the corner, where the girls had planned to have lunch. Not that they had much of a choice—it was the *only* place since leaving Nairobi one hundred miles back, but they had decided against a picnic in favor of the charming old inn with the enormous thatched roof.

The Morani said good-by, thanking them, and they watched the striking picture he made as he strode off across the plains. The Maasai fulfilled everyone's preconceived ideas of Africa's "noble savages" and Jujubee and Lys were no exceptions in their admiration of the proud, almost theatrically arrogant and indifferent people.

"What I have to do for this article is to find out more about their social system," said Lys. "There are several stages in their lives—three for males: boys, warriors, and elders. They become an 'elder' at about the age of twenty-seven and then lead a life of 'ease mixed with drunkenness' . . ."

"Highly intelligent they must be too," added Jujubee.

"After they've been circumcised they become warriors for about ten years, and a man is not allowed to marry until he becomes a junior elder and has completed his warrior training. They don't live with their parents but in separate kraals with the immature unmarried girls, called *'ditos,'* with whom they are allowed to cohabit freely, but they're not allowed to marry. When the girls reach puberty, they return to their mothers . . ."

Jujubee interrupted again, "It all sounds so sensible. Just at the time when you are really curious about sex—when you want to know what it's all about—there you are—out doing it. Marvelous. Why can't all societies be as logical?"

As they left the Namanga River Inn a terribly disfigured and tattered African dwarf came up to the car begging for money. "Christ, the poor soul has leprosy, too," said Lys, upset. They gave him some shillings and as they drove off Jujubee quoted bitterly, "God must love him very much."

They arrived at the *manyatta* just at dusk and the orangy sunset cast an added glow over the red earth and the red people and the red blankets they wore—even their red huts. The Maasai give this impression of redness, even though they are black like other Africans, because they decorate themselves with red ochre mixed with earth and cow dung. They would be colorful subjects for Jujubee.

"What are their houses made of?" asked Jujubee.

"It's a framework of sticks, plastered all over with a mixture of mud and cow dung. They are crazy about cow dung—as you'll see."

The minute they stopped the Land-Rover the Olaiguenani, a highly respected junior elder who had served as a warrior and had been selected by the elders to lead the other warriors into elderhood, greeted them. He would be their interpreter from Maasai into Swahili to give them the information they wanted.

The first thing he did was to show them to the hut they were to share, and as they stooped down to enter it, Jujubee asked, "What about the goats—do we sleep with them too?"

"Do they turn you on as well?" asked Lys with a smile.

"This is nothing but an igloo—a cow-shit igloo! There's no window—look at that bed—it's made of sticks."

They threw their two rucksacks filled with blankets and clothes on the bed, put the third one containing tinned food on the floor, and then went outside to talk to their host. Sitting on a log in front of a fire with many people crowding around just staring at them, Jujubee sketched quickly and Lys asked the Olaiguenani first of all about taboos—just to make sure they wouldn't commit one. They were told that the Maasai must never count their cattle, the names of the dead should not be mentioned, and a man should not reveal his name directly. As he spoke, all the Maasai—men, women, and children—stopped talking and listened to him with great respect. Jujubee said, "Ask him how he and the other Olaiguenani are chosen—how do they obtain the honorable position?"

There were five definite rules. Lys wrote on her pad as he told her the first, which was that he must not be left-handed or ambidextrous. Lys laughed as she translated, because Jujubee was not only left-handed, but ambidextrous, sexually speaking, too. "I'll probably be speared in the night," said Jujubee, "God must love me very much."

Rule number two was that he must not be impotent; three, that he must be good-natured and even-tempered; four, that he must not have committed murder; and five, that his parents must be pure Maasai. In that order. "In that order?" exclaimed Jujubee.

"Murder next to last. Well, first things first. What do they do about murder?"

"The fine for the murder of a man is forty-nine cattle, but there is no fixed fine for the murder of a woman because we Maasai traditionally never murder women. A man would be invoking ill luck on himself and he would become a social disgrace should he murder a woman."

Jujubee said, "So I live!"

Lys went on to her next question, "After murder, what is your next serious crime?"

The Olgaiguenani said, "Oh, murder is not our most serious crime. Cattle theft is the worst offense. There is no fixed penalty for this, but whatever the fine, it must include the number nine because "nine" is the number of orifices in a man's body." Jujubee was silent, mentally counting the number of orifices in a man's body.

"What of marriage?" asked Lysbeth.

Lys continued to translate everything to Jujubee as she wrote the answers on her pad. "When a man meets a girl he likes, they are married, and the wife may sleep with and have children by any man of her choice belonging to her husband's age group . . ." Lys interrupted him to translate the good news to Jujubee.

"How do I become a Maasai?" Jujubee wanted to know.

"Although the women may have children with any man, all the children are regarded as belonging to the husband—the one who was engaged to her and who later married her. Any woman may marry as long as she is circumcised . . ."

Lys wondered if the Olaiguenani caught the smile that crossed her face as she translated this latest bit of information for Jujubee's benefit.

"Circumcised?"

"Yes, a clitorectomy."

That finished Jujubee. She stopped sketching and just sat there looking zapped. The Olaiguenani continued, "An uncircumcised girl does not decorate her ears or wear a loin cloth, and this distinguishes her from the married women." When Jujubee heard this, she pulled her gold-loop earrings off and got up and walked toward the hut. "Where are you going?" laughed Lys.

"I'm going to get my bottle of gin and drink it all—lest I get circumcised for being left-handed." She reappeared in a few minutes

94

with her gin bottle and a cup, and having no takers for offers she sat and drank alone and listened as Lysbeth continued with the Olaiguenani.

"What kind of games are played?"

"In the morning while the cattle are resting after milking, the children hurl dry cow dung at each other, and in the evening they practice high jumping."

Jujubee said, "We can introduce this in New York when we get back—every morning people can hurl the dog shit at one another."

Lysbeth asked about legends or proverbs, and the Olaiguenani's face brightened and he said he would ask them some Maasai riddles. "Why are you so clever and yet you cannot distinguish your cattle from others when they are together grazing?"

Lysbeth translated this to Jujubee and after a few minutes thought they both gave up and asked what the answer was.

"Cow dung!"

"Cow dung?" repeated Lys incredulously.

"Yes, 'cow dung,' " said the Olaiguenani, delighted.

Jujubee simply could not believe it, then her face lit up and she said, "He must mean 'bull shit.' "

"How about some proverbs?" asked Lys.

" 'Lies make the sun set.' "

" 'Lies make the sun set'—um, uh," said Lys, still translating to Jujubee and writing it down. "Any more?"

"Oh, yes," said the Olaiguenani proudly, "many more. 'The lion went to the jungle because it ate a deaf ear.' "

"Did you say, 'The lion went to the jungle because it ate a deaf ear'?" asked Lys, feeling very stupid when she translated it.

"Dummy, if you ate a deaf ear, where would *you* go?" asked Jujubee.

The next proverb was, "God does not eat mankind," to which Jujubee muttered, "Lies make the sun set."

Lys thanked him very much for all his information, and said since it was late they would go to bed. He asked if they would like something to eat, but Lysbeth told him they had their own food, thanked him again, and said good night.

Once inside the hut, they made their bed, ate beans out of a can, bread, tinned butter, tinned lychees, and boiled water for coffee over a little gas stove they had brought with them.

95

"What the hell am I doing here?" said Jujubee. "It's a crazy man's place."

They got in bed and said good night, and Lys turned over facing the wall, while Jujubee lay there thinking still about the night, five nights ago now, in Paris. She could concentrate on little else. For the first time ever, she really cared about someone—and then the other night to see her in ecstasy . . . just thinking about it made her desire Lys so much that finally she said, "Are you asleep?"

"No," answered Lys, turning toward Jujubee. "I was just thinking I sure could do with another night like the one in Paris."

Just like that.

In the morning Lys awakened first. Going out of the hut she called, "Jujubee, Jujubee—look!"

Jujubee staggered out in time to see two little Maasai children taking a warming shower by standing under a urinating cow.

"Want a warm shower too?" called Lys, as she clicked away with her Nikon. "Put some coffee on—O.K.?"

Jujubee reflected on Shakespeare's adage that appetite increases by what it is fed upon. After last night—their second time together—she was even more involved with Lys than she had been after Paris, yet Lysbeth seemed as casual and indifferent as ever.

Nevertheless, it was not another five days before it happened again.

Nor did it stop when they returned to Philadelphia.

Two months after their return to the States, when Jujubee was off for her six weeks of teaching in Paris again, Philip announced to Lysbeth that he had been transferred to New York. When Lys told Jujubee, she tried to accept the news of the move in her usual light and flippant manner, but inside she despaired.

When Lys and Philip were settled in their new apartment Jujubee frequently went to New York for weekends, but it wasn't the same. Jujubee decided that what she needed was time with Lys. She needed the intermingling of their lives that they had had in Philadelphia so that the two of them seemed almost one—an extension, or the "other side" of each other. It had been this merging of their two selves that had made Lys feel that going to bed with Jujubee was little more than masturbating, whereas now, with so little time together, they were separated and Lys withdrew—not from friendship or love, but from sex.

Jujubee had this much figured out, but she couldn't decide what to do about it. It was bothering her so much that finally she went to a psychiatrist. She told Lys she was going because she was so unhappy about Louie, but right after her first appointment, she called Lys and told her, "It was of no use. The shrink was a real nothing. Furthermore, he was only about twenty-nine years old so what the hell could he tell *me* about life? A waste of fifty dollars. But never again. As they say, 'Screw me once, it's your fault. Screw me twice, it's mine.' Anyway, I am beyond psychiatric help."

Lysbeth told Jujubee all about a tenor she had met in New York—the week before at a dinner party and had seen every day since. She was mad for him, she said, but she hadn't gone to bed with him. "Here we go again," exclaimed Jujubee. "Is he homosexual?"

"No. But I am, I guess," answered Lys.

Jujubee's heart quickened—this was the first time Lys had ever talked about what she felt sexually for Jujubee. Was Lys now going to tell her that she was significant to her after all?

"I don't know, Jujubee. Maybe I ought to go see your shrink. I really care about Frank, but I just can't go to bed with him. It's not that I'm indifferent—I really *don't want to*. If only I could feel for him physically what I feel with you—or even half of what I feel with you. But I don't want to go to bed with you any more because I'm not involved with you emotionally, and with you and me there could never be anything but sex. Exquisite as it is, I have learned that it's not enough for me. I'm an incurable romantic. I'm also frightened that if I keep it up with you, I may dilute my chances of ever feeling anything sexually for a man. If I ever succeed is another matter. But I am going to try—I have to find out. If I just stayed with you now, I'd sit around the rest of my life wondering if I could have found total satisfaction with a man."

Then she changed suddenly, and visibly shaken, lighting a cigarette with a trembling hand, she continued, "When you were in Paris this last time, something happened that upset me terribly. I haven't told you because I hate talking about it . . . it's nothing to do with you, but with Father Ryan . . ."

Just then the doorbell rang, and it was Frank. When Lys saw him her mood changed back again quickly from anxious despondency to delight, and she introduced him to Jujubee proudly. The three of them—Philip was away—had dinner and went to the theater and to a party afterward. When they got back to Lysbeth's apartment, Jujubee fell exhausted into bed, but Lys stayed up with Frank, and when Jujubee awoke in the morning he was back again, so she never did have a chance to ask Lys what it was she had started to tell her about Father Ryan. Two weekends later when Jujubee came to New York again, she did ask about it, but Lys dismissed it, saying, "I don't want to talk about it now. I don't even want to think about it, but what I do want to talk to you about is that I think I am going to tell Philip about Frank. I can't stand the dishonesty any longer."

"Christ, don't be so stupid, and don't be so selfish, either. To ease your rotten guilty conscience you're willing to hurt Philip? He won't be able to understand about Frank, and you can't go around telling people more than they are capable of understanding. Sometimes dishonesty is kinder than the truth."

"I guess you're right . . . but I think I'm going to get a divorce—for my sake and Philip's. I am beginning to hate him because he makes me feel guilty. Our marriage is a farce, and the only honorable thing to do is to admit it and end it, giving us both a chance for happiness somewhere else."

"That's probably inevitable. How are you coming along with your sex program with Frank?"

"It's a total flop. So far nothing. It's amazing how he puts up with me. I think he really loves me—he's asked me to marry him."

"Are you going to?"

"No. I like him, but I don't love him. But I will get a divorce, and then I'm going to sail, for twenty-eight beautiful days from London to Mombasa."

"Great—I'll come with you."

Lys shook her head and said, "No, Jujubee—oh, you know there's nothing I'd like better, but I really think I have to get away from everything so I can look at it all and try to analyze it. I can't see the ground I'm standing on and all of that. Perhaps if I can get far enough away, and alone, I might get myself straightened out. Can you understand that?"

Of course Jujubee understood that.

And so her world began to crumble. She knew that whatever she and Lys had it would never be valid this way—it would never be total but always a half measure. Jujubee wanted all, but she knew Lysbeth would have to decide what she wanted herself. She would not try to stop her leaving or persuade her to try life with her because it would be no good that way. Lys would have to come to Jujubee because she wanted to and only after she had satisfied herself that nothing else would be as good. To reach this decision Lys would have to try on many men for size to see if any of them fit, and when they didn't she knew she would come back to her. She understood it was a risk, but one she'd have to take. Reduced to simple terms, which meant more to Lysbeth—romance or sex? Though the element of romance in her friendship with Jujubee was zero, this was offset by the fact that sex as a factor in her contacts with men rated equally low. Perhaps Lys could learn to like sex with men, but Jujubee doubted it. She did not delude herself that Lys would ever become romantically involved with her, but she set much store in the fact that their friendship was solid and that Lys got great pleasure from her in bed. Perhaps, finally, this would be enough to persuade Lys to spend the rest of her life with her—and if she wanted little romances with men, Jujubee would just have to accept it.

A few months later when Lys had her divorce and had ended her relationship with Frank, Jujubee said good-by to her as she sailed off to South America for a six-week cruise. From there she planned to fly to London before taking another ship to Africa. Standing on the deck at the last minute before the gangplank was removed both girls cried and said, "I love you," at the same time.

It was three months later that Jujubee received a letter from Lys that was different in tone from the light and newsy notes that she had scribbled from South America and London. She had met *the* Lord Rufus Lindsey on board the ship to Mombasa and thought she was falling in love with him. This was followed shortly by a telephone call from Lys in Mombasa telling her they were getting married the next day and also suggesting that Jujubee think about coming to keep Lys company when Hallit had to be away filming.

During the year that followed, Lysbeth's letters to Jujubee were filled with enthusiastic descriptions about her new life, her happiness with Hallit, and reflections upon her unaccustomed contentment. In due course came a letter not simply asking Jujubee to stay while Hallit was away on work but suggesting that she should actually move in and live with them, planning her art exhibitions and teaching stints for the months that Hallit knew he would be at home. Jujubee decided, as she packed her life to go, that it could mean one of two things: either Lys had worked out her problems and was truly happy with her new husband and simply wanted Jujubee there as a friend so that she wouldn't be alone, or she had failed to find sexual gratification with Hallit, or any other man, and wanted Jujubee for that.

From the moment Jujubee and Hallit met they had liked one another.

Lysbeth's first opportunity to be alone with Jujubee was the following morning, and when she heard Jujubee ring her bell for coffee she went in and sat on the foot of her bed and said, "It's soooo good to have you here."

"I'd say it's so good to be here too, but I should think of a more original way to say it. Hallit is everything I thought he'd be—more. Got any nail polish remover?" asked Jujubee looking at her nails.

"Yes, but you shouldn't drink it this early in the morning."

"Got an Air Mail form too?" she called to Lys who was on her way to her own room to get the nail polish remover. "I have to write Screwy Louie a letter filled with empty promises."

"You're not still going through that with Louie, are you?" said Lys as she came back. "Hasn't he got another woman yet?"

"Another woman after me? Never!"

"He must love you very much."

"It has nothing whatever to do with love—he has a pathological attachment for me—that's all." The coffee arrived and they both drank a cup.

"Will you ever divorce him?"

"I can't think why. I'd have to pay a lot more for my keep than what it costs to write an Air Mail form a month. That's all he wants. That, and to see me about one week a year . . . so he can say, 'Oh, yes, that new painting of my wife's is devastating, isn't it?' Anyway, it'd be hard for me to leave him now—he's had a sandwich named after him—'The Baron Boucher'—and I think that's pretty good. We ought to work on a 'Grilled Lord Lindsey' or a 'Lord Lindsey Club'—Hallit really is a remarkable genius, and he's just everything personally I imagined he would be too."

"More," stated Lys. "I'm so lucky, Jujubee . . ."

"You're goddamn right," interrupted Hallit, poking his head around the door. "Hey, Jujubee, we've got a dinner partner for you

100

tonight. Sir William Fitzpatrick is coming down from Molo and he's spending the night—he might even arrive in time for lunch. He's head of Flying Surgeons, you know."

"I've heard of him—he's famous," said Jujubee.

"That's right," said Lys, "and very stuffy. I've only met him once—terribly British—but he wants to see Hallit about something—probably about becoming a vanilla gorilla."

"A vanilla gorilla? What the hell's that?"

"A citizen—a white citizen. That's what the Africans call us behind our backs. Want to ride before lunch?"

So Lys on her Arabian horse, and Jujubee on another borrowed from a neighbor, rode off into the Ngong hills.

Hallit had planned a surprise for both Lysbeth and Jujubee and he had wanted to make sure they would be there at lunch time—his surprise was a horse for Jujubee. He knew both girls loved riding and although he had already given Lysbeth a horse they had had to go to some trouble to borrow another mount in preparation for Jujubee's arrival, and it was then that the idea of the gift had occurred to him. He left to arrange the collection of the new horse and when he got back Lysbeth and Jujubee were still out riding, but Sir William had already arrived. The girls soon returned, and over lunch, much to their astonishment, Hallit and Lys detected an attraction between their two guests.

After the meal, Hallit sprang his surprise. Both Jujubee and Lys were ecstatic and rode off immediately to try out the mare.

"Well," said Hallit to William, "I hate to ruin your good time, but I must go into town—I have a meeting with my crew. The girls will be back soon."

As Lys got back the phone was ringing—it was Hallit. "Aren't you coming into town this afternoon? Didn't you tell me you were going to film Amin for your African Heads of State collection? I thought so. Well, listen, darling, I was just reading the paper and saw a notice in it that today is the deadline for the firearms regulation—all guns must be turned in to the Firearms Bureau no later than today or they hang you or something? Well, anyway, reading it just now reminded me that, Christ, I do still have one gun at home—remember last year when we had that panga gang scare and I kept that loaded pistol in my beside table? Then you and I left suddenly for London—remember? Well, I didn't have time to hand it in then, so I just hid it upstairs in the attic in that big trunk that

101

has all our winter clothes—you know the one I mean. Of course I forgot all about it until this morning when I read the paper, so look, darling, get the damn thing, will you, and drop it off at the Central Firearms Bureau. Don't fool with it. I don't think it's loaded, but I'm not sure—just give it in. Is Jujubee coming with you?"

"No," answered Lys adding in a sing-song voice, "She wants to stay here with William. Can you imagine it? I mean, if we looked all over the world, we could not have found two more dissimilar people, but they do seem to be attracted to each other."

"Preposterous."

"I think she's as pleased with William as she is with the horse."

"Yes, but which will prove to be the better mount?" asked Hallit. "O.K., darling, I must run, don't forget the gun. I won't be back until almost eight—hope I make it before the guests. Have fun filming Big Daddy."

Lys had already told Jujubee about her project, so now she explained to William that although she really only liked still photography, Hallit had given her a 16mm. Bolex and was encouraging her to try films. As a result, she had started collecting footage of all the African heads of state who came to Nairobi and was off to cover the arrival of Uganda's General Amin at State House. "Sure you won't come with me Jujubee?"

"No, I'm going to stay here with *my* big daddy . . ."

So Lys went up into the attic, found the gun and slipped it into her camera bag, but by the time she got in town the Firearms Bureau had closed, so she slid the gun under the foam-rubber padding in the bottom of the film bag, and forgot all about it.

At eight-thirty as the dinner guests were about to arrive, Lys took Jujubee aside and said, "Look at this, Jujubee." On the bar were bottles with colored ribbons tied around them. "Our bartender is really the gardener, but sometimes when we're having a large crowd we let him tend bar for extra money. There's only one problem—he can't read. Last time we told him which bottle was which, but he got mixed up and gave everyone scotch and tonic, or gin and soda, so now I've tied these ribbons on the bottles and when people tell us what they want, we relay it to him, a red and soda, a blue and tonic, a yellow and water, and so forth."

The dinner party was one of their usual successes and Jujubee flirted so successfully with William that he spent the night with her. Next morning when he came down to breakfast alone, he looked very sheepish. Hallit, just to make things more difficult for him—which was his way of showing affection—asked him if he had slept well and whether his bed was comfortable. Just then Jujubee appeared and announced she was going to "let the cat out of the bag." Poor William looked aghast, and then Jujubee opened a large paper bag she had been holding behind her back and dumped the Lindsey's cat out onto the floor; they all laughed. A year later they were all still laughing.

It had been a beautiful year despite the fact that the Lindseys' first separation had been very painful for both of them. Lysbeth had felt amputated without Hallit and had telephoned him every day—she had even got a call through from remote Lamu where she had gone to do a picture story. The three weeks seemed endless to both of them and their reunion had been a form of rebirth. But occasional separations notwithstanding, the year was idyllic. Hallit's film had been acclaimed as another landmark in film making and he and Lysbeth had gone to London for the premiere. Also, having Jujubee with them had worked out extremely well. Hallit had known that Lysbeth would never want to go to bed with Jujubee again—that she was over that phase of her life—but what he did not know at the beginning was whether Jujubee would still feel a desire for Lysbeth. But now, after she had been with them on and off for twelve months, he knew Jujubee to be a remarkable person. Despite her facade of amorality she had great integrity, and try as she might to conceal it she was incapable of being what she thought was two faced; and she would have thought it wrong to go to bed with Lysbeth in the circumstances of accepting Hallit's hospitality, friendship, and trust. Also, Jujubee loved Lysbeth too much to hurt her, and although Jujubee might still occasionally physically yearn for her, she knew it would now be a very serious thing for Lysbeth to do—it could not be undertaken lightly as in the days when Lys was married to Philip. Because Jujubee loved Lysbeth and knew she was happy, she wouldn't do anything to change that—of this Hallit was sure.

Furthermore, Jujubee was very involved with William. Although they had seemed such an unlikely pair on the surface, exposure to one another over a period of time had had the effect of blending them and balancing them out. Hallit had never known

103

William to laugh and be as free as he was now—Jujubee had raised him from pompous ass to delightful human being, while he had turned her into a calmer and more reasonable woman. He was probably the first man ever to really care about her—he was the father she had never had. She even liked the discipline he enforced on her and she once told the Lindseys, "He doesn't put up with my crap." In fact, Hallit bet Lysbeth that William and Jujubee would marry before too long.

Toward the end of that year, at a dinner party the Lindseys gave one night, William—'Sir Billy,' as Jujubee had taken to calling him affectionately—asked if anyone remembered seeing the cover story in *Time* six months earlier about a Dr. Otis in South Africa who had made a major break-through in overcoming rejection problems following heart transplants and who had attracted world-wide attention to his techniques in a series of daring operations performed in Russia. His latest project was the development of a treadmill machine that accurately measured and recorded the strain imposed on the heart as the subject "walked" on it. Some of the dinner guests remembered, others, including Lys, didn't, so William continued, "Apparently most people throughout the world can work the machine for about fifteen minutes before slight strain begins to register, but the Maasai and their cousin tribes, and some remote nomads in Ethiopia can keep walking for hours without recording anything other than a normal rate of heartbeat. Anyway," he explained, "Dr. Otis is going to join us at Flying Surgeons for a year to operate and do heart research among pastoral people."

Lysbeth said it might make a good story—she was always on the lookout for that kind of thing—and William confessed with a wry smile that that was why he had brought up the subject. The publicity resulting from a story would be followed by donations which the Flying Surgeons always needed. Why didn't she make an appointment to talk to Dr. Otis about it? She agreed, and as he left he reminded her again, "I'll tell Dr. Otis to be expecting a call from you."

Two days later, right after Jujubee had left for her six weeks in Paris, Lys made an appointment with Otis' secretary to see him at three o'clock in his office at the hospital.

Alexis Otis

A very tall, overgrown, brawny man in his mid-thirties with black curly hair, black shiny gypsy eyes, and a rough chiseled face looked up from his desk as Lys walked in, and right then, that very instant, she was transformed into another person. It was as if her whole being had been invaded by an outside force and had been conquered.

He stood and greeted her, this big Greek god with the Brandoesque nose and smile, and although for the next fifteen minutes she got through all the verbal formalities mechanically and asked the proper questions, physically her body was reacting differently. Lighting one cigarette after another she felt herself moving like a cat whenever she crossed her legs or uncrossed them. Her body was suddenly aware of itself and projected itself independently of her as if she had no control over it at all—as if it had its own mind. She wanted to ask him if she could run her toes through his hair, through those black ringlets, so she said, "Then I am to come to the staff meeting Monday at three o'clock?"

"Yes, that will be our next step," he replied as he stood and extended his hand, indicating the conclusion of their meeting. Tingling as she stood, she shook his hand, indicating the beginning of her new life.

She left the hospital a totally different person from the one who had walked in. In a stupor, propelled by the exuberant emotions, she played games with herself: Dr. Otis, do you feel this? Are you thinking of me now? Are you moving mechanically around the operating room as stunned as I am? If I get to the corner before the light changes, it means you are feeling this too, and that you are thinking of me now . . . I don't even know your first name. I

107

don't know if you're intelligent, stupid, kind, witty—if there is a Mrs. Otis and six little Otises; but I don't care.

She was electrified, and showed it. It was not an unpleasant sensation, nor was it unfamiliar to her—it had just been a long time. "Hello again," she whispered to the magical feelings, with excitement, but with apprehension too, because she knew how dangerous they could be. Yes, she knew the danger, but she didn't care.

But why him? God knows he's gorgeous, but I've met a dozen men just as handsome in the last two years and barely noticed them. Why him and not one of the others? Why not Hallit? For she *loved* Hallit more than all the rest put together, but he had never stirred her to anywhere near this extent.

Walking aimlessly through the streets, going nowhere, she pictured Otis—his eyes, his hair, his mouth—she saw his head on everyone's shoulders, and she smiled at people she passed. A beggar who had always irritated her and whom she had snapped at on her way to the hospital approached her again, and this time she smiled and gave him five shillings. Bewildered he stared at her and she wanted to dump the contents of her change purse in his grotty hand.

For an hour she walked in circles, accomplishing none of the chores she had thought she had to do; they were unimportant now.

Hallit picked her up in the usual place at the usual time, and she wondered if he would notice she was not the usual person—that she was no longer Lysbeth but an impostor.

He didn't notice anything.

By rote she got through the evening, carrying on all the called for conversation just as if she were in control. Why is Jujubee away? I've got to tell her, I've got to talk about it, she thought, and feigning fatigue, she went to bed early and stayed awake late, smoking and thinking of him, fantasizing about him, and finally—plotting. It's ridiculous being in love with a Dr. Otis. I've got to find out more about him. After a night of disrupted sleep she telephoned William early in the morning to ask him to lunch for no other reason than to learn more about this man who was driving her insane, for indeed she already recognized it as a form of insanity. She thought lunch time would never come and that Monday seemed light years away.

Lunch time finally did arrive and with it William. After asking what he had heard from Jujubee and trying to listen to the seemingly endless answers, she finally said, trying to sound as casual as possible, "Well, I met your Dr. Otis yesterday and we have a story in motion."

"Good," was all William said.

"What do you know about him?" she asked, trying to sound disinterested.

"Why, I really don't know much. All I actually know of him is his reputation as a heart surgeon. I met him at Sugar's in New York—he was interested in Flying Surgeons, so she got us together."

Stifling a fake yawn, she asked, "Is he here with his family for the usual two-year stint?"

"Two-year stint, yes. Family no. I think he's separated from his wife. I think Sugar was a girl friend," William answered matter-of-factly. But then becoming more enthusiastic, "That Sugar is a remarkably open woman—she talks about her affairs as if she was talking about having her tonsils out. There's no guilt or bragging about her—she is simply stating facts. You know she is about to get married again . . ."

"Against whom? Oh, that steel biggy from . . ."

And that was the end of that. She still didn't even know his first name. If it had been someone she didn't care about, she would not have hesitated to ask what his name was, but it was too important to her and she was afraid she wouldn't be able to conceal her feelings.

This is the longest day of my life, she exaggerated to herself the following day, and although she had chatted to Hallit and they had gone to a movie in the afternoon and made love in the evening, nothing of that had broken through to her—she had been with Dr. Otis in an imaginary world. Reality had been pushed aside by her emotions so that she really wasn't reasoning or thinking in terms of possible consequences. There was no thought, What of Hallit? There was only Dr. Otis.

Sunday gave her the excitement of its being tomorrow-I-will-see-him day, and also of being able to reach Sugar in New York. When the overseas operator put her through she congratulated Sugar on her new marriage, spoke to her for a minute about a film chore she had invented for her to do and which she used as the excuse for the call, and then added casually, "Guess who I'm doing a story on?—your friend Dr. Otis."

109

"Oh, he's divine in bed, darling—Jewish—have you ever been to bed with a Jew?"

Lysbeth had to think a moment. Philip was a Methodist—he even went to church. Hallit was a Church of England atheist. Frank, and he didn't really count, was an agnostic. No one was Jewish . . . wait a minute, though, Jujubee was Jewish, but she could hardly explain that to Sugar. "No, I've never been to bed with a Jewish man," she replied accurately.

"Well, darling, you must—it's an experience, I tell you, they're marvelous. Better than Chinese even, although the Yugoslavs claim they're best—the Jews *are* the best, and particularly Alexis. You owe it to yourself."

Alexis. So that's his name, she thought and asked Sugar if he'd ever been married.

"Yes, twice I think. Divorced now." Aware of the cost of international calls and the fact that it was Lys's nickel, Sugar brought the conversation to an end. "O.K., I'll get that film off to you today. Write to me. Good-by."

Lysbeth spent the rest of Sunday waiting for Monday, totally absorbed in this new world of hers, yet instinctively cunning enough to appear normal for Hallit's benefit.

Monday. Looking calm and cool in a yellow silk blouse and yellow linen slacks she glided into the staff room at the hospital, her demeanor revealing nothing of her excitement. The five men stood up, aware of her femininity and warmth, but she looked only at William who was at the head of the table and walked straight to him and shook his hand. He said, "You know everyone here I think," and as she glanced sideways at the table, she could see *him* out of the corner of her eye seated on the left side, so she turned and walked to the right, smiling softly at both men on either side of her as she sat between them. Then she looked directly across from her and faced him. He raised his head from the papers he was studying and their eyes met. He nodded formally, without a smile, but kept looking at her. She thought she was going to faint. He was even more beautiful than she remembered, and the magic feelings were greater even than in her daydreams.

Does he feel it? . . . he must feel it . . . do the others feel it? . . . it fills the room. She managed to look as if she was absorbed in what William was saying without really hearing anything. When Alexis spoke he looked at the others, not at her. A good sign, she thought, he's avoiding looking at me when he is trying to concentrate on what he's saying, hopefully because if he looks at me he won't be able to concentrate. . . .

William picked up an idea Alexis had touched upon and said, "Very good point, and furthermore . . ." As he elaborated, Lysbeth stole another glance at Alexis . . . he was staring at her, then he quickly looked away. Another good sign, she thought.

She asked a few questions which she hoped seemed intelligent. Finally the meeting was broken up by William, who explained that he was already five minutes late for an operation, kissed her on both cheeks, and hurriedly left with the others. And then it happened—Alexis came up to her and asked if she would come to his office for a minute? She followed him across the hall and in the outer office he asked his secretary to type the names and addresses of the people it had been decided she was to interview in Ethiopia. Then he gestured her into his private office.

"Must I call you Dr. Otis? You British are so formal. Or do you consider yourself a South African?"

"My name is Alexis. And I would stop calling you Lady Lindsey if I knew your Christian name."

"Lysbeth. How long have you been in Kenya?" she asked, trying to keep the conversation onto a personal instead of a business level.

Seated now, and leaning over his desk, he offered her a cigarette which she took, hoping he would notice the long artistic hands everyone told her she had and not their trembling. He answered, "Two weeks. And I'm neither British nor South African. I'm Jewish."

"But I don't say, 'I'm not an American, I'm Protestant.'"

"But I wasn't even born in South Africa or England. I was born in Germany, but went to England when I was five and then to South Africa."

"Oh?" she asked.

"My father and mother were put in Hitler's gas chambers just after I was born. I never knew them. I had one older brother and when I was about two years old he took me to neighbors who didn't want me but didn't know how to tell him they didn't, so they kept me for a while. Then my brother went off—I never knew where or why—and they gave me to another neighbor, and so I was passed around like a chain letter—from one unwanting person to another. The first thing I ever remember feeling really was when I was five and a boy about thirteen appeared and told me he was my brother. I'll never forget that sense of belonging—it lasted three days—I've never had it since."

"Why not?" she stammered shaken with his story and the fact that he had told it dispassionately as a simple response to her question.

Continuing matter-of-factly, with no emotion in his voice he said, "Three days later the Nazis loaded my brother and me into a truck and drove us to the gas chambers. At that particular prison camp the Germans had a rule not to throw anyone under thirteen in the incinerator. My brother was just thirteen, so they took him. I've never wished so hard for anything in my life as I wished to be thirteen that day, but they wrenched me away from my brother and drove me back and dumped me on the same street as they had found me. Later on that evening a woman who was trying to escape from Germany decided she might have an easier time of it if she had a child with her—more sympathy for food and all of that. So she took me off the curb—where I was just sitting trying to figure out what happened to my brother and waiting for him to come back yet knowing he wouldn't—and took me to England with her. When we got there she left me in the first orphanage we passed, and that's where I stayed until I was nine when some kindly couple took pity on me and took me to South Africa. I just left out my last name—therefore Alexis Otis alias Alexis Otis Meyerhoff. And that's the story of my life. What's yours?"

"How dreadful," was all she managed to choke out before the secretary interrupted handing him the letter and reminding him of an appointment with a patient at three o'clock.

"Christ, I'd forgotten all about that," he said glancing at his watch. "Come on, I'll walk you to the door."

When he put his hand on her back to guide her through the door, she was aware of it with her entire body. With a wave, but no smile, he was gone. She was worse than before. She was completely shattered by him.

Whatever she did the rest of that day had nothing to do with her. Where was *she* at the party that night when she sat talking to both her dinner partners about the common market and Uganda? Where was *she* when she talked to Hallit as they drove home? She was with Alexis. They were staring in each other's eyes . . . he was leaning forward and his lips were touching hers . . . his arms pulling her to him. . . .

From the airport the next morning she telephoned him.

"Dr. Otis here."

"Lysbeth Lindsey here."

His voice sounded pleased—she wondered if he were smiling—though he never seemed to smile. "Well—I thought you were in Addis?"

"I'm just about to leap on the plane now. Can you come to dinner Friday when I get back?"

"Yes," he answered without hesitation, "I don't leave until Tuesday."

"Leave—where are you going?" she asked trying not to sound as if he were deserting her.

"I have to go on a three-month 'familiarization' tour, as you Americans call it, of West and Central Africa, then back to South Africa to close down there."

"Oh, well, then," she said trying to sound as if he were merely going on a picnic, "I'm glad we can get you before you leave. Eight o'clock? You know where we live?"

"Yes."

That was all.

Three months! How was she going to be able to stand his being away for three whole months? But she would see him Friday. . . .

The working days in Addis were noteworthy to her only for their boredom, but evenings gave her the gifts of privacy and time—to think of Alexis and his effect on her life. She declined all invitations, ordering her dinner sent to her hotel room, and debated with herself:

"All right. Question number one: 'Do you, Lysbeth Lindsey, love Alexis Otis?' "

"How the hell do I know? To love someone you have to care for them, you have to be concerned with their well being. You can only do that by knowing the person. I mean, I don't know if I *like* Alexis, much less love him. For all I know, he may be a religious fanatic or a rabid fascist who likes cocktail parties and cricket matches. How could I love everything I hate?"

"Right."

"Therefore, it is impossible for me to like or to love him now. I may grow to like him, even to love or hate him, but right now because of the lack of knowledge, I do not love him."

"Established. Question number two: Are you *in* love with him?"

"I am madly, wildly, insanely in love with him."

"Do you realize this is irrational and defies all reason?"

"Yes, but that doesn't make it go away."

"Have you no control over your emotions?"

"None at all."

"Is your mind that weak?"

"Evidently."

"Do you realize that you have been living in a fantasy world?"

"I not only realize it—I prefer it to reality, if reality is gray and cockroaches and telephone bills. I've avoided those things all my life, and besides, I cope with everything I must in the real world—I function."

Even her opposing side had to admit that, but she continued with herself: "Do you think most people feel this strongly without reason? Or, in other words, do you think most people would be this obsessed with someone they didn't even know?"

"No, I don't suppose they would," she answered herself.

"Oh, so you imagine yourself capable of greater feelings than other people?"

"Yes, as a matter of fact, in a way, I do. Let me explain—first of all I do believe that when most people get so emotionally involved as I am now, they do have more justifiable reasons, or healthier—if you like—feelings. But I think this is because sex is mixed up in it. Everyone would understand what I am feeling if I had a sexual desire for him too. Everyone understands sexual attraction which may not make it right, but it certainly makes it understandable. But I think it is *because* of this lack of sexual desire with me that I feel more emotionally. Listen, I am in love from the waist up because my fear of men paralyzes me from the waist down. I am blocked, or blind you might say, in that area. Could it be like other blindness—that the loss of one sense increases the others? If you're blind, your hearing gets better. So, since I'm sexually blind, perhaps my emotional capacity has enlarged."

"Sexually blind—what bullshit . . . have you ever thought you're nuts—just plain nuts?"

114

She had pondered about that, too, but preferred not to believe it. It was more attractive to envision herself as overflowing with love rather than being less than normal—whatever that means.

At any rate, analyze it as she might, the fact remained that she was wildly, insanely in love, and the fact that it wasn't rational did nothing to make it any less.

But what was she going to do about it? And what about Hallit?

For a while she developed the line of thought that it had nothing to do with Hallit, that it in no way changed or diluted what she felt about him. After all, if you have a baby and then you have another, the love for the first one is not lessened because of it. She loved Hallit just as much, liked him just as much—in fact possibly more because now she was more alive and attuned to feel. And she wanted her life with Hallit to continue in all its aspects, but she wanted the additive of Alexis, too, to give a further dimension—but it still didn't mean that she felt less for Hallit. Now wasn't that reasonable? Of course it was, but would Hallit understand it? Certainly he would understand, but he couldn't *accept* it—that was why he must never find out.

Yet she had to satisfy this longing for Alexis. Perhaps he was the new peak that Hallit had warned her about soon after they met. If so, she had to do what she had to do; as an incurable romantic she wanted to run through the meadows, ride on the merry-go-rounds, and romp on the beach with him—but she would settle for his simply taking her in his arms and kissing her. Was that asking too much? She hadn't kissed a soul but Hallit for two whole years! How she wished it were Hallit with whom she wished to chase the butterflies—but it wasn't and she couldn't invent a desire. Equally, it would be criminal to ignore this new feeling, to allow this beautiful something, this part of her, to die.

Even as she convinced herself, duped herself with stretched rationalizations, she knew that if he "took her in his arms and kissed her" that would not be the end—she would only want more. Besides, there was just a chance, however slight, that when he did kiss her she would feel a sexual stirring in her loins that she had never known before except with Jujubee. After all, for two years now with Hallit she had been making love without fear—a good *Reader's Digest* title she smiled to herself—and on a scale from one to ten her sex life with him rated around seven which was pretty good for her—practically a miracle, considering. Perhaps this miracle could spill over and extend to another man. Perhaps she was "cured."

And so, with curiosity now added to her emotional state of being, she plotted how to be alone with Alexis. After all, she couldn't just grab him and kiss him as he walked into her house on Friday, nor in the hospital, nor a restaurant. Besides, he had to want *her,* he had to kiss *her,* and she had to arrange an opportunity where he could.

Friday morning, high on the prospect of seeing him that night, she arrived back in Kenya and spent the day going over the dinner menu, checking to see how the table was set, arranging flowers and all those things she usually did mechanically and without real interest. But today it was different.

At eight he arrived simultaneously with two other couples and greeted her formally, still with no smile, but with his eyes boring through her, and again she feared she would faint . . . his actuality was more powerful than her imaginings. He turned from her immediately to shake hands with Hallit, then she had to greet the other guests, and he stood chatting with a little group. As hostess, she could only stop with him for a few minutes at a time, and the first thing she said was, "All went well in Addis, but must I tell you about it now? If you don't mind, could I come to the hospital on Monday?"

"Of course, call me Monday morning about ten?"

Someone interrupted them, and she wandered off among other guests, but every few minutes she could look at him while pretending to be listening to someone else. I'm even in love with the way he stands, she thought.

The Lindseys' parties were excellent and this was no exception. There were sixteen for dinner, a smorgasbord of people all of whom were individuals. While some of them might not have liked each other, it was unlikely that anyone present would be bored by his companions. It would have been too obvious to seat Otis next to her, she thought, and besides, the task of playing the charming casual hostess with him in the same room was Herculean enough without having the added distraction of having him sitting next to her. After dinner she heard someone playing the piano. It was Alexis. He played beautifully—by ear, he claimed. Lysbeth liked watching his hands even more than listening to the notes for she loved hands and his were exquisite—long strong surgeon's hands.

Intrigued, most of the guests stood around the piano until midnight, then Alexis and Jack and Doria Reddy lingered on after the others had departed and the five of them sat collapsed in chairs with their feet up on the big coffee table and had a post mortem of the evening. Lysbeth's enthusiasm for life and her love of it shone through the conversation. Alexis just listened to everyone attentively but said nothing until Lys asked him, "What do you think of life?"

"'Life is nothing more than an unpleasant interruption in an otherwise idyllic state of existence,'" quoted Alexis.

"Is that really what you think?" she asked.

"Unfortunately, yes."

"Don't you get a great deal of pleasure from some one thing—say, your work or art?"

"My work satisfies me I guess, but it doesn't give me 'pleasure'; art escapes me—I suppose I play the piano for pleasure. . . ."

"Well, what about sex? Isn't sex pleasure, Alexis?" asked Doria.

"Sex is always good or better," he answered with a smile.

Lys thought he seemed trivial, she hadn't decided if he were intelligent or not. Most doctors she had found, were not. Once they stopped talking about kidneys, they seemed to have little else to say. Surgeons were simply skilled laborers. However, it wouldn't have mattered to Lysbeth if Alexis had been an orderly—what she felt for him was nothing to do with his—or her—mind.

"Do you know what happened to me the other day at my dentist's?" continued Doria. "Well, he just got furious with me. He's adorable and when I was leaving his office he kissed me good-by—not a little peck of affection—it was quite a romantic kiss on the lips—which I enjoyed tremendously . . ."

"Disgusting," her husband interrupted with a smile.

"Well, I merely said, 'Good-by' after he let me go, and he was livid! I couldn't understand why and he, in his very French enraged way said, 'But if a woman kisses a man on the lips, this means she will go to bed with him; if she turns her cheek to him, it means she won't. You let me kiss you on the lips, and now you are not going to bed with me. It is unfair.' I tried to explain how I had never even heard this theory before, but he didn't believe me. Have you ever heard of this?" she asked the group.

"No," answered Jack, "but what a marvelous idea—an excellent code."

117

Lys said slowly, "I see your point—I hadn't heard of it either—but there are lots of people I'd love to kiss on the lips but not go to bed with."

They all disagreed with her, saying that if you wanted to kiss someone on the lips, it followed that you would like to go to bed with them too.

How nice it would be to be normal, thought Lys and switched the subject. "Do you like New York?" she asked Alexis.

"What I know of it, I do. I've really only been through it on my way to the Mayo Clinic or Johns Hopkins."

Jack said it was late and they must leave, and Alexis departed with them thanking Hallit and Lys for the evening and saying to her, "I'll talk to you Monday morning at ten then."

"What do you think of Alexis Otis?" Lys asked Hallit.

"He's quite unremarkable," answered Hallit dismissing him.

At ten on Monday Alexis' phone rang and it was Lys with a cheerful "Good morning."

"What time can you come in?" he asked in what she sensed was an urgent tone.

"Well, that's up to you. I can make it any time. What about William?"

"There's no need for Sir William to be here, I'll pass all the information on to him. Can you come in at eleven—let's see—that's in an hour?"

"Fine," she agreed. "Oh, by the way, you mentioned last week at the board meeting that you wanted to see Olitipoti, the Maasai chief. I meant to tell you then," she lied, "but somehow I forgot about it until today when I looked in my date book and was reminded that a month ago I had made an appointment with him for this evening—I'm photographing him for an *American Geographic* story—and I thought perhaps you might like to come along. Hallit has a director's meeting, so I'd like the company if you'd care to come."

"What time?"

"He couldn't make it before six," she continued remembering how on Friday afternoon she had driven up to Ngong and begged Olitipoti to please make it at six o'clock instead of ten in the morning, as he had preferred, because she knew Alexis couldn't

118

leave the hospital before five, and how finally the great Maasai had consented. She knew she would be safe and would never be caught in her lie because Alexis spoke no Swahili and Olitipoti no English, so neither would ever know. "I'll be in town and leaving for Ngong about five-thirty."

"Yes," was all he said.

"See you in an hour first?"

"Yes," and he hung up.

Her heart was racing as she walked into his office and tossed the Addis pictures on his desk. Ignoring them he looked that look of his right into her eyes and said, "I don't quite know how to say this, but I truly enjoyed your dinner party—at least I truly enjoyed you. Do you have a sister?"

Surprised she muttered, "No . . . why?"

"Because I'd like to find someone just like you—with your warmth and zest for life. I've only been in love once and that was with an American girl—for two years I was in love with her . . ." He talked on, but she couldn't absorb what he was saying, why he was telling her all these things, what was it he had just said about her? As much as she enjoyed the idea of this intimacy, had wished for it, fantasized it many times over—now that it was actually happening she was unable to absorb it. ". . . but I lived in Russia for nearly five years transplanting hearts in dogs and baboons and trying to overcome the rejection problems. She was an American citizen and there were difficulties about her staying in Russia and the choice became her or medicine, so I chose medicine. Then I married a Russian girl—convenience I guess—but that didn't work out well."

"Was that the only time you were married?" asked Lys.

"Yes, just that once—no children. I'd like to show you Russia one day—that is, if you could get away."

All she managed to say was, "I've never been."

The secretary interrupted and reminded him of his next appointment, and they hadn't even mentioned Addis. Her mind spinning she left saying, "See you outside at five-thirty."

He came out of the building promptly at 5:30 and they went through an elaborate nonsense about whose car they would go in—he insisting she follow him to his hotel where she would leave her car. She didn't even wonder if leaving it at the hotel might be a ploy—she would have followed him over a cliff—but she tailed him through the streets of Nairobi to a small hotel on the outskirts of the city, which she had passed many times before without really noticing, and parked her car next to his under a large tree. "I'm just going inside a minute," he called, "get into my car—I'll be right with you."

He was back almost at once and as he pulled out into Ngong Road he said, "What are you doing for dinner afterward?"

"Going to the Reddy's in Muthaiga at eight-thirty."

"Wouldn't it be nice if you broke that and had dinner with me?"

"It would be, but I can't," she answered truthfully because she was meeting Hallit there.

Then, he simply reached over and put his hand on hers. She had not expected this; she had imagined they would talk, perhaps even about personal things through the evening, and at the end maybe, just maybe, he might kiss her good night. But this early gesture threw her completely. No one had touched her romantically like that for two years, and certainly nobody had ever electrified her in this way. She could hear her heart throbbing in her ears, and not knowing how to handle the situation she withdrew her hand from his and rambled on about everything—about nothing. After a few minutes of her inane chatter he interrupted her, "Why did you take your hand away from mine? Why are you so jumpy because I touched you?"

This only produced more stammering from her—she could hear herself making no sense whatsoever, and he, ignoring the traffic behind them as well as what she was saying, slowed the car almost to a stop and with those black Gypsy eyes blazing into hers said, "I am completely intoxicated with you."

Stunned, almost delirious and unable to answer, she just stared at him.

He stared back. "Did you really have that appointment with Olitipoti a month ago, or did you just make it?"

She looked him straight in the eyes and answered, "I just made it," half pretending to herself it was her honesty that made her say that.

He swung the car down a lonely dirt lane, stopped it, took her in his arms, and crushed her to him. Kissing her, kissing him, kissing together, eating each other's lips, clinging, holding, not talking, kissing, clinging more. Touching eyes, touching noses, touching tongues, and hair; smiling softly now, still no words, feeling, all feelings, savoring every sensation, more and more. Kissing and clinging and wishing it would never end, annihilation, perfection, more. Laughing softly now, devouring each other with their eyes, nibbling lips, ears, more ecstasy, rapture, unequaled joy, magic, unknown beauty, exhilaration, enchantment, exquisite bliss, paradise—so this is what those words mean. He was sitting in the driver's seat and she was lying across him facing him; how she got there, she had no idea.

"I feel like a bulldozer with you," he whispered in her hair.

"I've never been kissed so gently."

More.

Incoherently her feelings began to spill out in words, little words which told him about the magic she had felt the very moment she had seen him, how she had been obsessed by him ever since their first meeting, and all the while they were kissing, and she touched his eyebrows and ran her fingers through his black curly hair, and over his face, touching, touching, and telling him everything she felt, everything, because the very first kiss had been a commitment for her, a total commitment. She would not have kissed him if it had not been all-important to her, and there was not an ounce of frivolity in it, for it involved her very core. Did he realize the significance of her gift?—a much rarer one than just her body.

"The first minute I saw you I wanted to run my toes through your hair," she said lying back in his arms and touching his hair.

"Why didn't you?" he asked and kissed her on the forehead, a velvet kiss.

"The first time I suspected you felt anything about me at all was when you wouldn't look at me at the board meeting."

Holding her in his arms, touching her face with his fingers, kissing her now softly on the nose, he said—without removing his lips from her nose—"I don't mind showing you what I feel, but I can't show everyone else."

"What do you feel?"

"I can't explain it, and when you can't explain it, you know it's important."

Lying in his arms, nibbling at his lips, running her tongue across his teeth, her words echoed in his mouth as she said, "If heroin made you feel like this, I'd become a junkie tomorrow. I don't

121

know whether to thank you for making me feel alive or hit you in the teeth for screwing up my tranquillity."

Laughing gently, then more feelings, no more words, gentle kisses, soft ones, stronger now, annihilation, arms clinging, hands under sweater, on bare skin now, reading her back in braille, searching for signs of love, music blasting in ears—no music in car—hand still searching for love, lips reading lips, lips in search of love, "feed me love" cry his lips and hands, hungry hands now on breasts, pow—pow, Lys was brought back to reality and the taste of fear. She realized immediately that she wasn't "cured," that although the terror was gone with Hallit, it was still very much there with others—that she would not be able to swoop into bed with him easily. Yet she must not panic with him—she must tell him the truth, explain to him. Perhaps her fear wouldn't be as difficult to conquer with him as it had been with Hallit. . . .

Remembering the conversation they had had with Doria she whispered, "Will you be angry with me if I don't go to bed with you—even though we kissed on the lips?"

"No," he answered simply and gently.

Because she had made a total commitment to him it must be total, she thought—she must tell him why—so as much as she loathed not only talking about it but thinking about it—two years had passed since she had even mentioned the subject—she began, "I must tell you something. I have something I must tell you . . ." and unconsciously she took his hand and put it to her face. With great difficulty she continued, "I know I appear to be sophisticated, but I'm not really—in fact the only two men I've ever been in bed with are my two husbands," and then in an effort to reduce the tension she could feel rising, she added jokingly, "and if you ever tell anyone I'll swear you're lying. It's not that I'm a puritanical American with morals or anything like that, it's because . . ." how can I tell him it's because of the black monster, she thought, I can't think how to say it, yet there's so little time and I must. She stumbled on, "Ummm, well, once when I was about seventeen a man beat me because I didn't want to go to bed with him—he pinned my hands behind my back and straddled me and he put his cigarette out on my chin and beat me, hitting me across my face back and forth—I got hysterical . . ." As she spoke of it she started almost to feel the blows, to sink in the swimming blackness, to be pinned, trapped, held down, unable to move, screaming silent screams, and fighting to escape. Seizing Alexis' hand she stuck one of his fingers in her mouth and as if she were trying to suck strength from it she rocked back and forth—she had to keep moving when the black monster threatened to appear. I must go on, I must finish quickly, no need for the whole horror story, and taking a deep breath, she continued, ". . . I was hysterical, but I'm not the hysterical type, I don't scream when I see a mouse or anything . . ." She stopped again, still unable really to go on, but because she felt she owed him an explanation she was possessed at the same time by a terrible urgency to tell him why she wasn't able to leap right in bed with him. ". . . So I finally got out of the car . . ." but again she couldn't finish because she saw the searching lights of the monster's electric eyes—without pupils—coming out of the darkness, weaving around and around in the sand searching for her, searching, as she crouched hidden behind trailers, hiding, bleeding, swollen, tasting blood, cowering. Finally she managed to snap back and continue, "Anyway, he didn't find me—I walked—crawled—miles home. It took weeks for my face to heal."

Then without a pause and continuing as if there were no break in the subject matter she went on, "But the main thing I must tell you—I knew a priest . . ." and yet again she had to stop and rock back and forth, holding Alexis' fingers and pressing his hand to her face. "Well, ummm, well . . . one evening I had wanted to tell him something I was very upset about—I needed his help, and since I was alone, I asked him to come to my house, and as I started to tell him about it, I began to cry, which is something else I don't usually do, and I got up to get a handkerchief in my purse and he got up also and came to me and put his arms around me in what I thought was a fatherly gesture, and I put my head on his chest, and he tilted my chin up to his face, and I thought he was going to give me an affectionate little kiss on my forehead—we had known each other well and for a long time—but I guess he went crazy or something—he had been drinking—many martinis—it was his afternoon off and he hadn't wanted to come to my house but I had insisted. Anyway, as his lips came down they didn't stop at my forehead but went right to my lips hard, and I pushed him away—anyway, things got very forceful . . ." and right then she felt the black clerical robes and the hulk of a two-hundred-pound man inside them, and she hadn't thought he was a man before, she had thought he was a priest, but she felt him hard against her,

123

hard . . . and right then in Alexis' arms the moment re-created itself and she began to sink, to drown in the black robes, to scream silent screams, but she forced herself to go on . . . "He got very physical, and because he had never had a woman in his life I guess he went berserk. Anyway, he got desperate and picked me up and carried me into my bedroom and threw me on the bed. Then he threw himself on top of me and held me down and tried to rape me . . ." her voice was trembling and she tried unsuccessfully to block out black robes flying above her like bats, black knees on her chest, holding her down, forcing her down, unable to get up, fighting, hitting back, eyes swollen and cut, mouth swollen and cut—both cut on his ring—kiss my ring and genuflect, genuflect to the black monster, the two-hundred-pound black bat, flying at her, flying. Body aching, then no pain, no pain at all, beyond pain, animal fears, the smell of fear, fighting off, must get up, get up, held down, sinking, drowning . . . drowning in Elsie Schneider's grapes . . . come back Lysbeth, you're with Alexis, now, Alexis. She spoke again and was astonished at how normal she sounded, "Do you know that it's impossible for a man to rape a woman unless he knocks her unconscious or holds a knife at her throat?"

"Ummmm . . . go on."

"Well, that's all really," she lied, realizing as she said it that she had not articulated the whole ghastly incident even though she herself had lived through it again in tortured recollection while attempting to tell him. "So I ended up in the hospital—this time for four days, and I told everyone that I had fallen down the cellar steps. Well, my body healed quickly, but my mind didn't—still hasn't completely I'm afraid. I was left with a stupid fear of men sexually, especially of being held down. I thought perhaps I was over it, but I guess I'm not . . ." She didn't want to talk about it or think about it any more. The pain of telling him was over, and she was glad she had told him the truth—at least the bones of the truth—instead of making up ridiculous excuses, as she had done so many times in the past to so many people. Because he was really special to her he had to know, and now he knew.

Holding her quietly and tenderly he said, "That makes me very sad," and then for a few moments he continued to hold her like a child, and said nothing. The joy flowed into her again. He kissed her gently, then sat up and started the car.

"Where are we going?"

"To the hotel."

"What about Olitipoti—we're late for him already."

"Screw Olitipoti."

Pole vaulted into the beauty again, she laughed and agreed, "It's terrible of us, but I'll work it out with him tomorrow."

"Speaking of screwing," he said to her as he drove off, "I do a lot of it, but it's just that—an ugly word and an ugly act—empty too. But I have no desire to screw you—I want to make love to you."

How glad she was that she had told him because now he knew why she could go to his room with him and yet not go to bed with him—she could go with him because she wanted to be with him, the more important reason anyway, and he would understand. Lighting a cigarette for both of them as they drove along she said, "Am I glad you're leaving tomorrow—I can't take any more of this. Do you realize what you've done to me? First time in two years I've even kissed anyone other than Hallit. This turning myself inside out is more than I can bear, and it's all your fault," and she poked him playfully on the arm.

"I'm glad I'm leaving too. But you'll have to meet me somewhere—I can't wait three months to see you again."

Touching his hair, the back of his neck, leaning over kissing his cheek as he drove, she said he smelled like watermelons and they talked and recalled all their feelings and laughed at the thought of Sir William's seeing them now.

She knew even then that for the rest of her life, this night would be top of her list of "magical evenings."

Inside his room, arms wrapped around each other, clinging to each other, standing, fitting perfectly into each other, pressing into one another, flowing into one and another, looking into one another's eyes, eating each other with their eyes, kissing again, and again, and again. More.

"Come into the bedroom with me and lie on the bed. It'll be more comfortable there," he said as he took her hand and led her into his bedroom. "Take your sweater off. I want to feel your skin."

Trusting him completely, she did as he wished. Then he took off his shirt and bare skin melted into bare skin. After a few embraces he slid his trousers off and asked her to do the same. She felt the warmth of his bare legs wrapped around her and their bodies entwined like naked pretzels. This was romantic—for her it still hadn't crossed the line into sex. Where's the line she asked herself, the underwear? How stupid. But that seems to be the case for me —as long as I have underwear on, it has nothing to do with sex. Jesus, she scolded herself.

Again he said, "I really don't want to screw you—I want to make love to you—something I haven't felt for anyone else," and he reached to undo her bra. More surprised than shocked she thought, maybe he really didn't understand after all. Maybe he doesn't believe I am unable to distinguish between screwing and making love—that to me they're the same—horrible, frightening, impossible.

Stopping him she lit a cigarette and lay back looking at him. She said, "The only person I've ever felt a sexual desire for is a woman. I have been to bed many times with a woman."

"Did you enjoy it?" he asked matter-of-factly, taking her cigarette and smoking it, too.

"Very much. That is, the sex part. So much, in fact, I began to feel guilty about it. That's how I ended up being such a nut—you see, when I began to feel guilty about going to bed with this woman I wanted to talk to someone about it, and the only person whom I knew well enough and who knew her too and who would be capable of understanding—if not approving of—my relationship with her, was that priest. What I didn't know was that he was not strong enough to overcome his own weaknesses. I suspected he was violent, but I thought he had it all safely suppressed. I was wrong. But it certainly cured my guilt—perhaps because the anger at him filled me so totally that there was no room for guilt."

"Most people don't admit their homosexual tendencies, but I certainly have them too."

"Have you ever been to bed with a man?"

"No."

"You should, if you really have a desire to."

"You are what I desire now," and he took her hand and put it on him, and suddenly she thought how unfair she was being. The fact that she felt no sexual desire for him—or any man—did not make him feel none for her. It was very difficult, she told herself, for him to concentrate on anything but sex when she was in bed with him in only her bra and pants; and having her hand on his

126

penis wasn't the best way to get his mind off sex. She asked herself if he had been indifferent to her sexually, would she have really liked that, and the answer was no, because she wanted him to want her—and he did. So now that sex has reared it's ugly head, what are you going to do about it? she wondered, and concluded that there was only one way to go back to the sexless bliss of Ngong Road, to be rid of the possible intrusion of the black monster holding her down, so she lowered her face to his stomach, ran her tongue wet around his navel, then down the hair line of his stomach, and softly took him in her mouth, and soon it was over. He gathered her to him and kissed her and kissed her ever so lightly all over her eyes and nose and cheeks and mouth, and then they lay silently in each other's arms touching and just feeling. They clung to each other silently, basking in delicate joy, and then she spotted the watch on his wrist and cried, "My God—I must go," and hating to leave more than she thought possible, she got up and started to dress.

"I'm going to the bar to celebrate," he said and started to dress too. But they were magnets and kept coming together. Once he grabbed her and held her in front of him before the mirror, "We look pretty good together, don't you think?" and his strong muscular body outlined her small delicate one, and black eyes and golden eyes smiled at each other in the mirror, and then she turned to him and tried to memorize his face. He said, "You look at me with such candor—like a child," and he caressed her lips with his lips.

"Do you know what I feel with you?"

"What?" he asked, then sucked her tongue into his mouth so she couldn't answer.

At her car door he told her for the fifth time to drive carefully and to telephone him in the morning. Cupping her chin in his hands, he gave her a final kiss and she drove off in a euphoric daze.

How she got through dinner she never knew. The watermelon smell of Alexis was on her face and hands—she deliberately had not washed before dinner. She could hardly wait to be alone so that she could reconstruct everything that had happened.

Hallit left without having coffee, saying it was a school night and explaining that he had to begin filming at dawn. Since they had come in separate cars he whispered that perhaps she should stay awhile and be polite.

Driving home alone she had her first fears about Hallit—not guilt, for how could anything so beautiful be anything but beautiful? Nevertheless, she loved Hallit deeply and didn't want to hurt him . . . more than that, she wanted to make him happy. She needed his happiness. This doesn't seem to be the ideal way of making him happy though, she reprimanded herself. But she was unable to think another minute of Hallit—or of anything other than Alexis. Aloud she quoted his words, "I'm completely intoxicated with you," and relived the evening over and over again, making it a part of her forever.

Visualizing Alexis so clearly, feeling his lips still on hers, tasting him still, she climbed the stairs to Hallit's darkened room and kissed him good night in a very tender way. Then she went into her own room and got into bed still without taking her bath because she didn't want the smell of Alexis to be washed away, and with visions of him dancing in her head, she fell asleep.

Tingling all over, she awakened and reached for the phone to dial his voice.

"Dr. Otis' office."

"Is Dr. Otis in?"

"Who's calling?"

"Lady Lindsey."

"Just a minute please. I'll put you through."

His voice. "You left your cigarette case—I want to take it with me."

"You can't. I want it," she teased—she would have given him everything she owned.

"Then you'll have to come and get it right now."

"I'll be right there," she said and hung up.

Flying out of bed, dressing, singing, skipping with glee, she reached the hospital half an hour later. They sat in silence and smiled at each other, and smiled, and smiled, and grinned. They didn't even have to touch—their eyes did that and melted into one another—and still without a word they lit cigarettes and sat there just smiling. He spoke first. "You've been on my mind constantly since last night."

128

"Funny, that's just what I was going to say."

"Do you know I haven't even bathed because I wanted to keep you all over me—I can smell you and feel you."

"Funny, that's just what I was going to say," she said.

"I can't stand the thought of going today . . ."

"Funny, tha . . . no, I won't say it again. I can't stand it either. Can't you drive your car into a brick wall or something and have to stay here in traction? Will you write?"

"No, I never write. I just never do. Will you write to me anyway?"

She nodded. "Of course. Do you have an itinerary?"

He handed her a typed sheet from his desk drawer, glanced at his watch and said, "I've got to throw you out now because I have to leave for the airport. Come on, I'll walk you to the door."

As they walked down the corridor he lagged behind a few steps, then caught up with her again and said, "You move just like an Indian. Hell of a walk. You know I watched you coming down the hospital corridor one day last week and I thought to myself 'she doesn't belong to anybody,'" and with that he pulled her through the doors marked "Staircase" and kissed her and she clung to him and somewhere in the back of her mind she thought how stupid it was—anyone walking by outside or up or down the stairway could see them. She didn't care, though, so she nuzzled his ear and put her tongue in it and then he grabbed her harder still and finally in a last desperate kiss, he touched both her breasts with his finger tips and said, "Write," and was gone.

In a trance she drove home, took the phone off the hook so she wouldn't be disturbed, and lay by the pool the rest of the morning trying to relive every moment of the last two weeks. How had she gotten here, in this new world? It never occurred to her to wonder how she was going to get out.

She ordered lunch by the pool, and totally absorbed in Alexis she fell more and more in love with him as the time passed. While she was eating, a jet passed over and glancing at her watch, she knew it was his. She cried because he was leaving, because they had made a new world and lived in it only three hours, because the timing was so wrong—their love had just started, and now it had stopped—not finished but stopped—almost before it had begun. And she cried because she had so many things to ask him, to

129

tell him—she wanted to know every little detail about him—she wanted to study the hair on his arms and get to know his toenails. She cried because her only desire was to get on the next plane and follow him to West Africa and she couldn't, and how could she ever last three months? Time with him, time, time was what she wanted, and now he was gone. She thought again about flying after him. "Dear Hallit . . ." No, she couldn't do that, she really loved Hallit, she couldn't do that to him, besides Alexis hadn't asked her to join him. He had mentioned it but there hadn't been time—"time, the devourer of all things." She assumed of course that he wanted to be with her as much as she wanted to be with him. Reliving every embrace over and over again, she whispered to herself, "Last night, from a romantic point of view, was a form of perfection. Hindus have a goal of absolute perfection, and momentarily I reached it."

She wrote to Alexis:

"And so, Prince Charming, you rode your white horse right into my heart. I know just how Christopher Columbus felt when he discovered his new world, only he didn't have to give it up three hours after he found it. My new world is Ngong green and smells of watermelons and is filled with you. And here I sit and think of you, but it is 'impossible to envision your beloved'—so you must send me a picture of yourself. Isn't that juvenile? But ever since I found you, I've become a juvenile, I've grown younger, and magic affects adolescents of all ages. Yes, you must go into one of those little booths and take a picture of yourself and send it to me. You must feed me, and since you can't write, you may feed me with your picture. Send it to Jujubee's box:

> Baroness J. C. Boucher
> Box 24724
> Karen, Nairobi, Kenya

(Her name isn't really J.C. but she tells everyone it is.)

I sit here plotting ways of killing Captain Lambert. He is the pilot who took you away (why are all airline pilots named Captain Lambert?) and I hate him. That is, I would if I could hate, but right now I couldn't even hate Hitler because I am filled with such joy. Thank you, thank you for the beautiful orgasm of the heart which you have so gently given me.

Sleeping Beauty"

130

The days drifted on and she was full of him, and writing to him seemed the only moment she was content for it was a way for her to transcend time and distance. She wrote,

"You take me to emotional highs I have never reached before. You are my elevator. Come walk with me soon, soon, soon . . .

One day we must play in New York together. It is an electrifying city. I feel sensual about it. When we are in New York, you and I, we will genuflect to the skyscrapers which affect me as profoundly as paintings must affect others, and at night all the buildings get mixed up with the stars, and our necks will hurt from looking up. And during the day we will ride the Staten Island ferry and stand outside at the back of the boat in the cold and watch the sea gulls following the ferry. We will wave to the Statue of Liberty as we pass it, and we'll smile at the sky line—which looks just like the movies—as the two tallest buildings in the world fade from us. And on our return trip in the ferry we'll eat hot dogs as we zoom in on New York and again we'll wave to the Statue of Liberty, and this time she will wave back because she will know us now. And then we will ride the elevators to the top of those two tall buildings and walk down 110 floors and we will laugh and be tired and dizzy. Then we will go to Central Park and smile at the people in the horse-drawn hansoms, and we will stop for a while and listen to the rock groups playing guitars and singing—just because they want to—and some people will join in and sing too—just because they want to. Standing arm in arm we'll watch grown-up kids throw frisbees and we'll see how they sail through the sky, and we'll laugh at the ice skaters who fall down and wish we could skate as well as those who don't, and we'll pause to look at those men with gloves on playing chess outside in the cold and we'll wonder why they don't play in their own houses—don't they have houses? And then we—you and I—will eat roasted chestnuts and hot pretzels and walk across the stream on those little curved wood bridges and laugh at the ducks. And then we will walk up and down Fifth Avenue and look in all the shop windows and browse in some of the stores—especially in the one that has a sign on the door 'No Dogs, No Cats, No Elephants.'

And maybe our socks will even slide down into the heels of our shoes because we will feel like little children again. Why don't socks slide down in our shoes when we're big? Will our fingers shrivel up and get all wrinkly in the bathtub too?

131

And then we'll go back to Central Park because we forgot to ride the merry-go-round.

And so, Romeo, I long to see see you you soon, soon, soon.

Juliette"

Lysbeth calculated how many days before he would receive her letters and how long his answer would take to reach her, and the day before she thought she should receive a reply she went to the post office, and on the following day she went twice and the next day four times, but there was no letter. And during the days he spilled into everything she thought and did, and every night she dreamed of him and two weeks passed and she was still overflowing with him, but still there was no letter. Why don't I hear from him? Perhaps he didn't get my first letter, but by now he should have my fourth and fifth, and why isn't Jujubee here to tell me what to do? But why, why doesn't he write? Just because he says he doesn't write doesn't mean he doesn't write, not to me at any rate, for if he feels as I do, he would have to write, or call.

And then, for the first time it occurred to her that perhaps he didn't feel the same way she did. It struck her with great force, this very unbeautiful thought. Perhaps he wasn't intoxicated with her any more, perhaps he had sobered up, or perhaps she was nothing terribly special to him in the first place—not special at all. Maybe for him it wasn't "that moment when we reach perfection." If not, she felt sorry for him—look what he was missing. But also, at the same time, she felt sorrier for herself for she was not anxious to be made a fool of. She didn't mind going out on a limb if he did too, but she didn't want to go out there alone and then have him saw her off. Her letters to him continued but they were interlarded now with things like: "Perhaps you are a scalp collector. Perhaps everything that happened is one sided—my sided? It's a toss-up whether the reason that you haven't written is that you just don't care or that you've been run over by a truck. Naturally, I prefer to think that you have been run over by the truck. Why don't you telephone me next Monday?" But Monday passed and still she heard nothing.

If only she *knew*—what she hated more than anything was not knowing. If he would write and tell her he got married or that he loathed her—that at least would be definite and she could start to reverse her thinking.

And then, almost six weeks after he left, his letter came. Her fingers were actually trembling as she tore it open, and she did so with such haste that she ripped a large piece out of the letter and had to hold the pieces together. Scribbled in terrible prescription handwriting she deciphered:

"Dear Lysbeth,
This is the first personal letter I've written in a year. My silence may be interpreted as that I feel the same as when last we met. I hope this letter reaches you in three hours, for that is when you asked me to call you. I just don't believe in phone calls—for obvious reasons. I would really love to see you or hear your voice— I mean, I really would, but early each day I fly into the bush with another doctor from whichever hospital I'm organizing Flying Surgeon's in that day, and all day I operate with him, showing him how to cope with lack of equipment—we have only that which we brought with us in the plane. Then every evening we fly back and have endless meetings working out the logistics. And the next day the same thing.
Lysbeth, don't stop writing, your letters are simply lovely and charming—I really mean that, but for Christ's sake (and mine) don't be disappointed with this letter—it may seem bland, neutral, and impersonal, but you know and I know that is not how I feel. When I write seemingly trite sentences, it isn't so to me . . . I imbue the words with full meaning as I understand them, and since you have such a fertile imagination, you will be adept enough to be able to read between the lines.

Alexis"

She read the letter and reread it, and again, and once more wallowed in the magic—all doubts now erased. Thank you, thank you. . . . His letter kept her high all weekend, and she was still that way when she went to the airport on Monday to take Hallit, who was going to London to film for almost two weeks, and also to meet Jujubee, who was coming in on a flight half an hour later.

Glowing as Jujubee approached her she said, "I've fallen in love, Jujubee," instead of hello.

"Thank God—you've been such a bore these past few years."

"I really *am* in love Jujubee. It's Alexis Otis—that doctor William asked me to interview. I even got into his bed with him— we didn't actually make love, but I went down on him."

"That's the first normal thing you've done for two years."

On the way home from the airport Lysbeth did all the talking,

133

the words came rushing out and she covered every detail—from the minute she had walked into his office up until two days before when she received his letter. When they got home Lysbeth ordered lunch by the pool and continued her saga while they ate. Jujubee toyed with her food and listened. "And so, just yesterday, I was thinking why don't I go to Johannesburg? I know from his itinerary that he's going to be there for the next two weeks, and when he gets back here, which is not for two more months, I won't be able to see much of him—not alone anyway—Nairobi has got to be the worst city in the world for having an affair—it's such a tiny village filled with nosy gossipy people—all spies. So I was thinking if I could go to Jo'burg, I could do that story on the mine dancers—it would give us some time to be alone together. And I can't possibly wait two more months to see him anyway. What do you think?"

"As you say, 'You're only sorry for what you don't do,' and Christ, I can't stand the idea of your sitting around here talking to me about him all day everyday—you'd drive me nuts! What did you say his name was?"

"Alexis Otis. Speaking of the men in one's life, how's Louie?" asked Lys.

"Dull."

"Rest of your trip good?"

"Ummmm, but I don't want to talk about it now, I'm sleepy. I was up all night on the plane and you've talked to me all morning and all through lunch, and now I'm going to sleep." While Jujubee drifted off to sleep in the chaise longue in the sun, Lys booked a person-to-person call to the Johannesburg Memorial Hospital for six o'clock. Then she telephoned Washington and told *American Geographic* she would do the mine dancers story the following week, checked plane schedules, and awakened Jujubee.

"Wake up, I have to talk to you. Listen, I've put a call through to him to tell him *American Geographic* called *me* for this assignment and I'll be there next Wednesday. What do you think?"

"I don't know what makes you think I can think without a drink. How about a gin?"

The phone rang as Lys was pouring the drink, and her heart jumped—his voice? him? him? But it was only the operator saying there would be another hour delay on her call to Jo'burg. Handing Jujubee her drink she said, "Listen, I want to run to the post office to see if I got another letter from him—I'll be right back." And while she was gone the call came through. Jujubee took it, and when Lys drove in Jujubee was at the front door with her drink in her hand saying, "I just talked to what's-his-name—your doctor. I told the operator you weren't in and to call back in ten minutes, but she advised me to take the call while the connection was through—they're having trouble with the lines. So he says, 'Dr. Otis here,' and I told him I was your friend, that you were out, but I knew that you were calling him because you had to go to Johannesburg next week on an assignment—some business something or other—I should have told him monkey business . . ."

"Christ, Jujubee!" yelled Lysbeth, "does he want me to come or not?"

"Yes, yes—he even sounded very pleased—he must be dumb. He asked what time you were arriving and I told him I didn't know exactly what time but I knew it would be Wednesday night. He said he couldn't meet you because he had to operate, but I told him that didn't matter, *American Geographic* would have a car and driver to meet you there anyway. Then he asked me where you were staying so I told him the Fugitt—so you'd better stay there. That's all—oh, he said please tell you that he was looking forward to seeing you. I did suggest that he call you back, but he said that he was leaving that minute for Capetown and wouldn't be back until next Tuesday morning. That's it."

In the living room now, sitting on the sofa, Lysbeth said, "Christ, I am so nervous . . . I really am nervous. I don't know if I can go—I just don't know if I can cope. Perhaps I like the fantasy better than the reality."

"Well, if you have a lot of courage, you'll be faithful to your husband, and if you have even more courage, you'll be unfaithful to him," Jujubee told her, pouring another drink.

Lysbeth said, "Is it strength or weakness? I don't know. I guess you decide it's strength if you really want to be unfaithful, and weakness if you don't. I just don't know if I can cope," she repeated. "Now that I'm faced with the actuality of going there, for the first time I feel guilty."

"Then don't go."

"But I *want* to."

"Jesus. Well, as they say, 'A guilty conscience never kept anyone from doing anything, just from enjoying it!' And you know

135

what else they say, 'Always succumb to temptation lest it shall cease to assail thee!' Does that come from the Bible?"

"Why can't I be satisfied with what I have? Which is a hell of a lot. My cookie jar is full—Hallit pleases me both in and out of bed. What we have ranges from great to excellent, and I figure if you have fifty-one per cent of anything you win, and I've got ninety-six per cent. But this, this other dimension is crying to be satisfied too. Not going wouldn't stop me from wanting to go, or from wanting Alexis, and maybe by going I'll get it out of my system."

"Sure you will," said Jujubee sarcastically.

"Maybe it's just the two-year itch," suggested Lysbeth.

"That's the 'seven-year itch.' "

"I'm very advanced."

"Retarded, you mean," snorted Jujubee.

All that evening she didn't know what to do—one minute she was going, the next she was not—she vascillated back and forth feeling like a Yo-yo. It was a very small thing that finally swayed her to a final decision; walking by a card store in Nairobi the next morning there was a poster in the window which read, "If you don't scale the mountain, you won't see the view," and she knew she had to see the view.

She telephoned Hallit in London and told him that *American Geographic* wanted her to go to Jo'burg to do the mine dancers' story and that she was thinking of going on from there to Rhodesia and Swaziland to complete a piece she had started on migrant labor. He encouraged her, saying it was a good story and a good time to do it since he would be away for about another week.

Thus the plane arrived in Johannesburg with her on it—chasing her dream. Really expecting him to be at the airport to meet her, even though he had said he wouldn't, she was disappointed when only the *American Geographic* driver was waiting for her. She told herself she must try to understand his work. At the Fugitt a telephone message was waiting for her with his number for her to call him in the morning as he was not in Jo'burg but in the bush and would be back at 8 A.M. At 8:05 the next morning, her phone rang:

"I thought you were going to call me?" he said, and she could feel his smile over the phone.

"I'm still asleep—hello you, how are you?" she whispered joyously.

"When will I see you? I'm so excited you're here. How are you? When can you come in—I'm at the Memorial Hospital on State Street about twenty minutes from you. Do you know it?"

"No, but my driver will. How about in an hour?"

"That's too long—ask at the reception desk here and they'll show you where I am. Hurry up."

Although her heart was racing, she was also very ruffled because she knew what she must do. She would go to bed with him. After all, she wasn't a school girl, she was a woman and it was about time she started to act like one. For him she would. The only way for her to prove her total commitment to him was to give herself to him totally—she couldn't impose her psychosis on him; it wasn't fair. When she had gone to bed with Hallit on the ship there had been the gradual easing into it, patiently going step by step around the black monster, sneaking one more thing past it at a time, and although she certainly preferred that method, she knew with Alexis there just wasn't the time. She would have to solve that problem on her own, which she was not looking forward to but was nevertheless determined to do. If the monster descends, he'll slay it, she told herself. Parallel with the fear was the fact that never before had she had to overcome feelings of guilt. Ugly words like "unfaithfulness," "dishonesty," "adultery," kept arriving in her mind unbidden—so coming to Johannesburg and going to bed with him was consequently a major and significant thing to her. She was about to perform a most important act which was at the same time both the most selfish and the most selfless thing she had ever done. She assumed he recognized it for what it was.

Leading the way to Otis' office, the hospital receptionist was talking to her but she didn't hear a thing. Then she was introduced to a secretary in a small office from which a door led into a consulting room.

"Go right in, he's expecting you."

Waves of exhilaration consumed her as she opened the door and saw him. He is real, he *is* real. The same intimate grin was on his face, the same one as when she last saw him. The privacy in the room was even less than in the Nairobi Hospital, and they sat and faced one another across his desk without touching. Had they not been lovers he would have kissed her on the cheek, or they would have shaken hands, but it was with the familiarity of lovers that they abandoned greetings and merely sat and stared at each other—drinking each other in wordlessly—basking in the satisfaction of being together.

Because his secretary might think the silence peculiar, Alexis spoke first, "How long are you here?"

"It doesn't matter . . ."

"Your timing is perfect. It's the first time I've had a minute I can get away, much less a few free days. Why are you here?"

"If you don't scale the mountain, you won't see the view."

"Sorry?"

"To do a story on the mine dancers."

"Oh, yes . . . what about lunch? Can we have lunch together?"

"Oh, don't say it . . . oh dear, you see I really *must* photograph the mine dancers, since that's the only reason I'm here," she laughed, "and *American Geographic* have set it up to drive me there about noon, to have a luncheon interview with the man in charge, and then to photograph afterward . . . but after that, I'm entirely free. What about later on today?"

"At 5:30 then, in the Oak Room of the Fugitt," he said and stood to leave because he was scheduled to operate in fifteen minutes. Time, time, time—they had never yet had an unhurried moment, but that evening their time together would begin.

"I'll see you to the door."

Walking down the corridor, he was stopped twice by other doctors who asked him something briefly while she waited. He suddenly took her arm and led her through the double doors that once again read "Stairway" and there he pulled her to him and they just clung together, not saying anything but drowning in each other. Then words came bursting from both of them and got all mixed up in their kisses and fell on each others necks and hair and lips and noses, words of how they had missed each other, longed for one another, buried mouths in necks. If anyone walked up or down the stairway, neither of them noticed. Then over the loudspeaker: "Dr. Otis, Dr. Otis."

Holding her hair and gently pulling her head back so he could look into her eyes he said, "Dr. Otis is screwing someone on the stairway," and they both laughed, then dragged themselves apart and he went up the stairs three at a time, and she turned out of the double doors and went the wrong way down the corridor.

The clock in the lobby of the Fugitt read five-thirty as she rushed through to the Oak Room with her Nikon and Leica slung over each shoulder. He stood and beckoned to her from a corner table, and they sat down next to each other on the leather bench in the darkened cocktail room and stared at each other with such joy she felt as if they must be glowing visibly, lighting up their whole corner like a Christmas tree. She was the first to speak. "If you felt anything like I did after we left each other today, I feel sorry for your patient—it would have been utterly impossible for me to operate."

"Oh, it was for me too—that's why I took a sleeping pill and slept through the entire thing," he grinned.

"What do you drink?" The waiter was at their table.

"It seems impossible that you don't even know that about me. I don't drink, so I'll have whatever you have."

"I don't drink either," he said and turned to the waiter "so we'll have two double scotches and water." They laughed and he put his hand on hers. "Your letters, your letters were such . . . such succor to me. They really were you know. I was so disappointed that you weren't home when your phone call finally got through— who was that I talked to?"

"My good friend Jujubee."

He squeezed her hand tightly then said, very seriously, "Will you be my good friend?"

"I'm not sure—maybe—but I don't know you well enough to like or dislike you now. The idea doesn't really appeal to me much because I'm overpeopled already—there's standing room only in my life. I haven't got time enough now to see the friends I really like—no, I don't want any more friends."

"That's a very irritating thing for you to say. Friends are the most valuable asset anyone can have. Does Bebeju—"

"*Jujubee,* those little candies you buy in the movies . . ."

"I haven't the slightest idea what you're talking about . . ."

"She's the one whose mail box you use—or used *once.* You are terrible about writing . . ."

"Terrible!" he interrupted. "Do you know that yours is the first personal letter I've written for . . . over a year. Does Jujubee know about us then?"

Their drinks arrived. "Yes, but it's perfectly safe. She's practically me, we're so close."

"Is she the one you went to bed with?" he asked bluntly.

Slightly startled by his question, she managed to answer "yes" quite matter-of-factly, then asked him, "Have you been to bed with a man yet?"—not at all what she wanted to ask or talk about, but she said it in an effort to get him off the subject of her and Jujubee.

"No, I met a man about a month ago who appealed to me, but I could never hop in bed lightly with a man—it would have to be important. I'll see him again in Capetown in a few weeks and we'll see what happens."

She didn't like his honesty. After a pause she said, "You know I was thinking on the way down here on the plane how we all have many multiple selves, many conflicting selves. We're all more than one person, and I think it's terribly unfair that we have only one body. I need at least four bodies, don't you? Do you know what I'm talking about?"

"Of course I know, because I'm more intelligent than you," he grinned.

"Don't tease. I'm being serious. It's impossible to satisfy all our different selves—while we are satisfying one self we are automatically dissatisfying another because our different facets are in conflict with each other. I mean, I feel I should be a good and faithful wife to Hallit, and at the same time I feel as if I should have you because I want you—and I feel both these things equally strongly. Perhaps this is why we are never truly happy, never truly free—because there is just no way of satisfying every part of us. What I am trying to tell you is that I want you to know that I love Hallit very much—what he and I have together is truly great. I know, you're going to say if it's so great then what am I doing here? Well, don't think I haven't spent a long time trying to figure that one out, and of course I haven't done so, but the closest I can come to it is that what I feel for you is another dimension of me, an added dimension that is very powerful. But it doesn't change what I feel for Hallit. Do you understand?"

"Yes, of course. 'Be true to yourself.' But which self?"

"Exactly. When I checked in here yesterday and the desk clerk asked, 'Are you Lady Lindsey?' I wanted to answer truthfully and say, 'Most of the time, but not right now.'"

140

Brushing her hair with his lips and squeezing her hand he said into her ear, "I did tell you how much your letters meant to me, didn't I, and how happy I am that you're here?"

"You know, I am *so* happy right now. If I had one wish, it would be that I would be sitting and talking to you, alone, and here I am! The magic wand's been waved! Of course, *I* waved it, but that doesn't matter. All that matters is that the wish comes true. You know, happiness is usually a remembered emotion—you say, 'Oh, I was happy then' or 'that *was* a great party' or 'what a wonderful time we had' because usually you don't often stop to think, 'I am happy now.' I guess that's because happiness takes us away from ourselves, as pain never does. It's always, 'I am suffering now,' but, 'I was happy then.' This very moment I am *aware* of how happy I am—it's a rare thing. I wish I could bottle some of it and take it out during the next two months when I won't see you again." She gazed into his eyes and because the beauty was so great her eyes filled up, but she wondered if he understood that her tears were not of sadness but of intense happiness.

The waiter broke their spell and Alexis ordered another round of drinks. "Going back to the subject of multiple conflicting selves," he said, "I'm glad we agree on the complication of one's being. You know I always dislike women who say, 'Let's have an honest relationship—we must be truthful with each other.' What the hell does that mean? Which self should speak—and which truth? There are many truths. One strong truth"—and that Brandoesque grin appeared as he leaned close to her and whispered in her ear—"is that, right now, I'd like to screw you."

It went through her like a *panga*. What is he doing? she wondered, and stalling, she quipped, "What? And leave our drinks? First things first," and as he gave the waiter the second order, he rested his hand on her knee and said,

"I just can't keep my hands off you any longer. You're really driving me nuts. Lets go up to your room."

"After the drink," she promised. "Tell me what you've been doing this last month?" What she really meant was for him to tell her all the things he had been thinking about her this last month, this last century they had been apart. And so he told what he had been doing—things she didn't care about, at least not then, but she tried to listen and make the appropriate comments, gulping her

141

drink all the while, hoping it would give her the courage she needed for the next act, scene one, in her room.

"No, come on," he said when she suggested yet another drink. She was determined not to let him see how frightened she was, How can I be so happy and so miserable at the same time? she wondered. Once inside her room he walked directly to the window to draw the curtains, and she went up behind him and put her arms around him and rested her head on his back then pulled his shirt up and kissed his spine and ran her tongue along it. How could she ever explain to him that that was all she wanted to do? She wanted to run her tongue up his naked back, but just that and nothing more—her desire went no further. He turned and took her in his arms and she could feel him hard against her. Then he let her go and began undressing.

No black monster yet.

"Last one in bed's a rat fink," was all he said as he took off his clothes. What a puerile thing to say. That wasn't what she had wanted to hear at all. She started to pace, ready to run from the black monster which must be right around the corner now—could she hear the ominous black wings flapping in the distance? How she needed Alexis to tell her it would be all right, but he was just lying silent and naked on the bed, displaying himself like a teenage exhibitionist.

This wasn't how it was supposed to be—it didn't match her daydreams—it was so . . . sterile. She had often thought that theoretically a man and a woman attracted to each other and going out for an evening should go to bed first so that with the powerful distractor of sex out of the way they could appreciate dinner and conversation. But now she felt herself needing the mental foreplay, or at least some display of affection. Every instinct told her not to go to him. But standing there, faced with an immediate choice, she reasoned that since she had already reached what she took to be a logical decision *to* go to bed with him, to reverse it would be a cowardly act. Indeed, it occurred to her that in her desperation to justify her weakness and fear she might even have just invented her momentary disappointment in him as a kind of excuse. Such was her confusion when he said very gently, "Come here, I won't hurt you."

And so, with only those few soft words of encouragement, she stopped pacing, dropped her clothes to the floor, and in what she dramatized to herself as her most heroic sacrificial act, she walked naked to him. Please, please let me feel the joy, she begged silently, and the phrase "how little we own our bodies" flashed in her mind and she remembered thinking the same thought in Paris the night she had gone to bed with Jujubee when her body had led her where it wanted. That night her desire had simply drawn her into a situation her mind didn't wish but her physical self did, but with Alexis now it was just the reverse—she had no control over her body's lack of response to something her mind ardently wished . . .

He was making love to her now. She felt nothing and she knew why. As she had walked those few short steps to the bed she had blocked out all feeling—she had put up a barrier so the black monster couldn't get through—but of course nothing else could either. It was safer not to feel at all, not even pleasure—not at the risk of the pain. Thus, she was a tense zero and she recognized immediately that although she wasn't cured, she was better. Ending up with nothing was still better than being on the debit side of things.

Alexis was turning her sideways, upside down—almost standing her on her head—perhaps in an effort to get some reaction from her, but didn't he know that he should be elated simply because she was staying there on the bed with him? When she felt confident enough, safe enough, that the monster would not appear, her thoughts turned to Alexis. He looks like an overgrown Nureyev—I've never noticed that before—they have the same sculptured faces but it's more than that . . . it's their bodies . . . how similar they are . . . how easily they move . . . yes, that's it . . . it's the same powerfully graceful movements . . . why it's a ballet! . . . he's in an arabesque now, and now a jeté . . . and the crescendo built and then, with his head thrown back in agonizing bliss, in a perfect plié, he came.

She wanted to clap.

He collapsed beside her, then reached for his cigarettes and lit two, and as they lay in silence smoking that most enjoyable of all cigarettes and she realized why she had wanted to applaud. It had been a magnificent performance, but only a performance. He had not made love to *her*—she was merely the audience—it had had nothing to do with *her,* and then she realized it had had little to do with him either. He was showing her his talent, his skill—both of which were breathtaking—but where was *he?* Where was the man himself when the actor was performing? He had performed for her, but that was all, he had had no feeling *for her*—why, she had affected him no more than he had affected her! She knew that often men merely masturbate inside a woman, that the woman herself may have no importance for them, but when that was the case, at least the man was involved. But Alexis hadn't been there any more than she had. Why? "I've never been made love to like that," she said softly, breaking the silence in an effort to verbalize what had happened between them. She wanted to tell him how when she was confident of her safety she *would* begin to feel sexually. She wanted to tell him everything, every mixed up thing she was feeling—she couldn't just leave matters unspoken because it was the verbal interpretation of emotions that for her brought understanding. Hallit had grasped this immediately—this necessity for words so that she could comprehend what was happening to her—so that she could ask questions and unravel the disturbing tangle of her own sexual web. Now she wanted to talk to Alexis about his ballet and to ask him where *he* had been. Her need for understanding was great and she felt very confused. Talk to me, explain to me, please make me understand, she pleaded silently, for she had to be made to speak of these sexual things. It was too painful for her to tackle them by herself. He stubbed out their cigarettes and kissed her tenderly. She liked that. Now surely he would talk to her, but still he said nothing. He lay her on her back, kissed her breasts, and worked his way down her stomach. "No, no, no, please stop," she whispered and pushed him from her, for she could endure no more. She got up wanting to scream at him to talk to her, but instead she said very quietly, "Let's get something to eat," just as if she were hungry. She thought, anything, anything but another bout, I just can't cope again, and she got up and paced back and forth naked at the foot of the bed. Please tell me what is happening, she continued silently, please let me understand—explain to me what you feel—even if I won't like the answer, even if it hurts, I would rather hear it than know nothing. I must look like a question mark—can't you see? Won't you say something?

As if he had heard her thoughts, he said gently, "Come here," and she ran to him. Now he will talk to me. But instead he made love to her again. Here I lie, she thought, as he pounds me—my body jerks upward with every blow, then falls back again and I feel dead. Perhaps I am dead . . . why is my heart still beating when I know I'm dead? Maybe he isn't making love to me . . . maybe it's a type of artificial respiration he is giving me so I will come alive again . . . no, I'd rather be dead like this than alive to feel fear, bewilderment, confusion, shame, guilt, perplexity . . . whatever it was I felt five minutes ago when I was alive . . .

And suddenly he stopped his gyrations, withdrew himself and lay silently next to her. In a desperate effort to understand she asked, "What are you thinking?"

"I'm just trying to figure out what it's all about."

Her hopes soared. Perhaps he was as confused as she. Perhaps they would sort it out now together. Perhaps he would explain what was wrong between them. What he felt, or didn't feel, about her. Dazed, she waited, unable to help him by even asking a question, and looking back later she thought that possibly her biggest mistake of all was not to have pleaded, right then, for him to talk. Maybe she should have screamed and showed him what she was feeling, but she just continued to wait. Finally, he sat up and said, "Have you ever been to a bullfight?" and for the rest of the evening, which lasted two more hours, he spoke of nothing but the magnificence of bullfighting. About eleven o'clock, still lying on the bed talking of matadors and smoking, he said, "I wish I could spend the night."

But she was beyond that and answered, "No, you can't, you must go—we have all day tomorrow together."

"Oh, Christ, that reminds me—an old colleague of mine arrives tomorrow at seven in the evening and leaves early the following morning. I'm afraid he'll have to have dinner with us since it's the only time he's here—do you mind very much?"

Minding tremendously she said, "Not at all. What time do you operate in the morning?"

"Six-thirty."

"Then you'd better go—it's late."

So with a tender kiss and smile and saying he would call her in the morning he left her lying on the bed, paralyzed. She could not let the realization of what had happened sink in—he had said nothing about being intoxicated with her, much less being in love—he had treated her as if she were a casual date. It was all too painful, and she knew she would be unable to sleep. But equally to lie

145

there awake would be impossible—the feelings would start to flow, the questions would pound in her ears and there would be no answers, so she did something she had never done before, she took a sleeping pill. Jujubee had given her a small supply about a year before saying, "Carry them with you, you never know when you might need them—you might even be hijacked in your travels." Feeling emotionally hijacked, she swallowed a pill and it worked—it kept everything out, the pain, the questions, even the bullfighting.

It was daylight when the phone awakened her. "How are you? Are you all right?" he asked.

Waves of joy began to tumble her around and around and she came to. He cares; he *does* care—he said, how are you? Are you all right? . . . Jesus, Lys, get hold of yourself, anybody might ask if you are all right—even the desk clerk could have asked you that. "Fine," she replied automatically.

"Can you be ready in an hour? I got a picnic lunch from the cafeteria here at the hospital, so it promises to be uneatable, but I want to drive you out to the country—O.K.?"

The sleeping pills must still be fogging me, she thought, for she felt nothing—nothing whatsoever.

"O.K.," she said, having no idea what time it was. "See you then."

Room service told her it was nine A.M. and her coffee would be right up. By ten o'clock she was ready, but she felt as if she had dressed a wooden doll—a mannequin in a store window—for that was all she was—she had no feelings at all—no joy, no sadness, no bewilderment, no guilt—just numbness.

As she opened the door in answer to his knock he reached for her, and she recoiled, not so much against him—whom part of her wanted and needed—but against the thought of more confusion, more things she couldn't understand or cope with. He did not insist on holding her, nor did he seem to mind or even notice that she had drawn away from his touch. He said, "Look, I know this is crazy but the hot-water system in the doctor's quarters broke down this morning, and I'd love a shower. Can I use yours?"

"There's no shower—only a tub—is that all right?"

"Fine," he answered and disappeared into the bathroom. He left the door open and called to her from the tub, "Come on in and talk to me."

She sat sideways on the loo with her feet up on the basin, and faced him, trying to appear nonchalant. Scrubbing himself vigorously he said, "I feel a big change in you this morning; in fact, I sensed it last night after we made love the first time. I sensed you didn't want to make love again, yet somehow I felt instinctively I should persist—to get it out of your system or something—I'm not quite sure why . . ."

"Yes, there is a big change in me," she said so softly he didn't even hear.

"Oh, did I have an unpleasantness on the way out of here last night! There's this girl I've been seeing in England for about a year, and she's been in Jo'burg for a few months now, and I've seen her quite a lot over these last few weeks. We've had an affair —but for me it's over—there's just nothing there any more. Well, anyway, last night on my way out of here I saw her in the bar with her brother-in-law, and she insisted I join them for a drink, so I did, and then she asked him to leave, telling him she wanted to 'speak to me privately.' So when he had gone, she said to me, 'Our relationship is at the point of a decision . . .' and so forth, and then I had the unpleasant task of telling her that there isn't anything to decide, that I don't feel anything for her—other than friendship. She found this very hard to accept, especially since I told her there isn't anyone else—and there isn't."

And there isn't, and there isn't, and there isn't, echoed around the tiles and fell on Lysbeth's heart like cold stones. There—he's said it all, she said to herself. Then what the hell are you doing here? she screamed at herself. And what does this make him? And what does this make *me?* She wanted to push his head under the water and hold it down but she simply left the bathroom without saying anything and paced back and forth in the bedroom wishing she could revert to feeling nothing, for now anger was rushing in, and bitterness too. Pride kept her from telling him what she really felt—all the agonizing and conflicting things—and, besides, he didn't seem a bit interested in what she thought in any case.

Someone had told her a long time ago that if she couldn't think of anything worth saying not to say anything at all—a rule that had come in handy many times and one she now followed as they drove out for their picnic. Not that she was silent; she feigned reasonableness and chatted cheerfully about nothing, trying the whole time to decipher the indecipherable mess. Or at least to define questions—she knew she would never forgive herself later if she didn't find out something about what was happening to her, and to him—that only he could explain. But instead they embarked on a conversation about Bantustans, a subject in which she had a great political interest and concern, but which in the present circumstances she couldn't have cared less about. Eventually she managed to switch the topic and stammered, "Well, one thing I learned last night was how much Hallit means to me—how right we, he and I, are for each other. It's a relief, isn't it that you and I don't have to be all complicated and emotional about each other? Besides, you'd make a lousy lover." She figured that was about the worst thing she could say to him—to any man. She watched him closely as she said it and saw him flinch. Don't you see what I'm trying to do? Don't you see I'm trying to hurt you because you've hurt me? "I mean, you didn't even open the car door for me today—even small things like that are important to me. I require little thoughtful gestures—you're not in the slightest romantic. What would you have done if I had told you I was in love with you?"

"You never told me you were in love with me."

She looked him straight in the eyes and lied, "I know—because I'm not and never have been. But what if I had been?"

"It would have been very ugly. And what would you have done if I told you I was in love with you?"

"Well," she said flippantly, "we all have our problems, and that would have been yours." Then she asked in what she hoped was a very light hearted voice, "Aren't you glad we don't have to make love anymore?"

"I'll tell you something—I'd rather play the piano than screw. Really, I get so tired of it, I really do, but women just seem to have to have you screw them. I wish I weren't so indifferent to women—to sex—but I am."

Never had she felt worse—heartbroken, disillusioned, guilty, confused. So she smiled brightly and tried to think of something else to say to hurt him. It was so unlike her, she never felt an unkind thing for anyone, but it was a reaction, not an action; he hurt her, so she must hurt him back.

He was talking about the glory of friendship again, how marvelous it was that she was going to be his good friend. Your good enemy, she swore to herself. Then she said in the gayest yet derid-

148

ing tone she could manage, "Ah, so, the mystery unravels . . . I'm beginning to see what you're all about . . . you figured that since you are going to be living in Nairobi, the best way to get in with 'the right people' is through us—so you cultivated me. You said you were 'intoxicated' with me, wrote me the letter and all of that, just as a ploy—for my 'social contacts'—I see now. Right?"

For the first time she saw anger cross his face. "Did it ever occur to you that I finally realized, in just the past few weeks, how impossible our—yours and my—situation would be?" he scowled.

She remained silent and a minute later he stopped the car on what she supposed was a lovely hill overlooking a spectacular view had she been in the mood to appreciate it. They walked along the edge of the escarpment looking like two little dots in an otherwise empty space, and when they got to a huge flowing pepper tree, they spread a large blanket on the ground, opened a bottle of wine, and sprawled under the tree which hung over them like lace. As they ate and drank he talked. He spoke mostly about medicine. She tried to look as if she were listening, but she wasn't absorbing much—she lay on her back with a piece of long grass stuck between her two front teeth and studied him, thinking intensely, but not about medicine. She still felt the same longing for him, and as he talked she thought how stupid her emotions were—without logic, without reason. She was ashamed of them. But they wouldn't go away. As he droned on she thought, I certainly don't want a man who doesn't want me. It's no good if only one person feels something because a one-sided relationship is no relationship at all. How could I be so convinced that he was feeling the same thing I was feeling? Perhaps the magic was so strong I figured it had to come from both of us—that we were synergistic. Christ, I want him to be in love with me—but you're not in love with someone just because they want you to be, or because they're in love with you. I must face the facts and not be a burden to him. I hope my brain will be able to convince my emotions that I no longer desire what I don't want—but it's going to take a long time. The thoughts whirled around as she lay there listening to his voice. If I were a Catholic, I could go to the Pope and be exorcised; if I were a pagan I could go to a witch doctor—but I guess I got into this situation all by myself, so I suppose I must assume the responsibility alone. I just hope I'm stronger than my weaknesses.

He was on his stomach now, looking down into her face, and as they were about to leave he leaned down and touched her lips with his—ever so gently, and that was when she almost cried, for the moment revived her flagging dream of what South Africa was to have been. But it was only for that moment because on the drive to the hotel he never mentioned himself or her or their situation—he was totally impersonal. Christ, is it worth it? she asked herself. The organization it takes to have an affair—the arrangements, the lies—one has to be such an efficient and capable manager. Anyone who could run an affair properly could run IBM! I have invested all this planning, and what do I have?—torment and a burden of guilt—and what for?—for a casual fuck I hated and an afternoon picnic with a friend! So she asked, "Do you see many good films here?"

"I don't see many films—here or anyplace for that matter. I just don't seem to go to the flicks."

Well, that took care of that question. "Did you like Nixon before Watergate?"

"I have no views about politics, religion, or philosophy."

"What *do* you think about?"

"Medicine—no, not even medicine—just heart function. I dedicate my research to it—I'm a priest of heart function."

Christ, another priest, she thought, and asked, "Don't you ever wonder if merely keeping people alive for longer is always right? I mean, with the problems of the aged, and overpopulation and all that—don't you have to measure life against its *quality?* Couldn't you in some cases just be prolonging people's misery?"

"That's not my field. That belongs to the sociologists and the philosophers, and I told you—neither interest me."

"What do you do for pleasure—read electrocardiograms?"

"Well, I don't read much else—but as I said, for pleasure I play the piano—sometimes cricket."

How can I be in love with such an idiot? she thought.

"Let's see, it's seven—can I pick you up in an hour?" he asked, and although she wanted to get in bed and stay there and cry—something she had never felt like doing in her life—she got dressed and forced herself to be gay and frivolous throughout dinner with the other doctor, his friend whose name and face she promptly forgot. After they dropped him off, Alexis drove to her hotel, and as they turned into the driveway she said, "Just let me out at the entrance; please don't come up," which screamed to be interpreted as, "Please come up and tell me to stop playing this silly game, tell me you see through me, that you went along with me just to show me how stupid I am, but that you do really care as much as I do." And when he did drop her at the entrance with a casual, "Can you come to the hospital tomorrow morning at ten?" she took another sleeping pill, for if she started to feel again she might disintegrate all together and she had to get through the next day without going to pieces. In the morning she booked herself on the earliest flight to Swaziland.

At ten-thirty she was in his office. "I'm leaving at eleven."

Seemingly both surprised and disappointed he looked at her with dismay and said, "Eleven *tonight?* Can't you stay at least another day?"

"No. And no, not eleven tonight, eleven this morning. I have to be at the airport at eleven, the plane leaves at noon—my driver is picking me up in ten minutes. So I'll see you in a few months in Nairobi."

"Will you write?"

"No. I've lost interest," she heard herself saying, "but do come to dinner with us."

"I will if you invite me forty-seven times. It's the only way I'm convinced I'm wanted. I'll walk you to the door." He said it sadly, but without any other visible emotion.

At the stairway sign—something about these signs always seemed to trigger a reaction in him—he pulled her in through the double doors and looked hard at her, continuing to stare—as if he were struggling to get up courage to tell her something important.

If he takes me in his arms now, perhaps I can feel what he is feeling, perhaps I can see if he is playing the same game as I am, then we can stop all this nonsense and I'll stay and . . . The thoughts circled in her mind when she heard someone coming down the stairs, and as she turned she saw an old doctor friend of hers from Nairobi and heard him say, "Lysbeth Lindsey! What on earth are you doing here?"

"Hello, Esmond, I'm just leaving as a matter of fact . . . do you two know each other?"

"Yes, indeed, how are you Otis? Come on Lysbeth I'll show you the way . . ." and there was nothing she could do but walk back through the door with the older doctor to the front entrance where her car was waiting. She turned to Alexis, but all they said to each other was, "Good-by."

Pleased and surprised that she was back the same day he returned, Hallit was his usual loving self, and Lysbeth was glad to be with him again—it was so good, so safe, and fun. But the guilt . . . she was haunted by it, and the thing that she had never truly realized before was the truth of the adage that you are punished by your sins, not for them. It wasn't "immorality" which she considered her sin, it was dishonesty. Yet telling Hallit—making it an honest situation again to ease her own guilty conscience—would be even worse, for despite his insistence on truth, she knew he would never understand that she still loved him just as much. Because *he* would have been unable to do what she did and still love her, he would not believe she could—he would judge her by his standards, not hers. Hurting him would have meant even worse pain for herself. For consolation she kept telling herself that what Hallit didn't know, didn't exist. But I know it, she answered herself, and I also know that I've put a crack in the most perfect thing I've ever had. I've ruined its perfection, its purity. And now I don't have my virtue, and I don't have Alexis either. What a mess I've made in all directions but if I keep singing and dancing perhaps I won't hear the pain, she thought, and for the next few weeks she kept very busy with assignments and dinner parties, and soon she was on her way up the mountain again.

Or so she thought. But Alexis was more powerfully significant to her than she had imagined. After all, it was the first time she had ever committed adultery, and he was one of the very few men she had ever been to bed with. If she were but another woman to him, he was a long way from being just another man to her.

Thus, although she was resilient and seemingly had bounced back quickly, at night when she would finally collapse in bed her defenses collapsed too, and visions of Alexis would race through her heart and mind and not one night passed when she didn't dream about him.

There had been a note from Jujubee saying that an unexpected exhibition had come up for her and she wouldn't be back for another few days. By the time she returned, Lysbeth had recovered from despair and was eager to tell Jujubee all that had happened in South Africa, and once again they lunched by the pool while Lys gave her every detail and summarized: "So I guess he's a whore or a scalp collector—or both—or maybe his emotional background was so screwed up by Hitler and everything that he's incapable of love. He's like a child's drawing of a man, a round head with no body, just the arms and legs coming out of the head. Add a dingaling and there you have him—mind, extremities, and no heart. Maybe that explains his fascination for hearts." She smiled. "He has this thing about wanting to be my *friend*—I told you—he talked about it the minute we met. 'Will you be my friend?' he said."

"What was it then, fuck-a-friend week?" asked Jujubee.

"I tell you he's a real fuck freak! He as much as told me he was, but then the other day I called Doria and got the conversation around to him, and she told me that she'd heard through Nairobi gossip who he's screwed here in just the few weeks since he arrived, and adding it all together, I predict he'll have balled the whole city by October. Maybe he's trying to prove something, you know they say the need to project an 'image' can mean that you have just the opposite feelings . . . If you try to give the image of being a Don Juan, you could be doing it to cover up the fact that you're gay. . . ."

"That's right—that's what my image maker told me too. That's why I project the image of being an alcoholic atheist—just to cover up the fact that I'm really a deeply religious teetotaler."

Lunch was brought out on trays, and with a mouthful of salad Lys went on, "Christ, I wish he'd tell me what he feels. I wish he would just tell me he hates me because of the way I eat my soup, or that he's really in love with a . . . respirator. Anything—just to erase the doubt, the chance, that he still does care . . . or ever cared. I suppose I might have blown it. After all, I did spend a lot of time telling him how much I loved Hallit, and then I did tell him he'd make a lousy lover—I mean I wasn't exactly complimentary all the time. He keeps saying how indifferent he is, and we all know that the opposite of love is not hate but indifference. But then as someone said, 'pride and indifference look very much alike.' When he comes back next month, I'll have to have a long talk with him."

Jujubee said, "First you can tell him you're madly in love with him, then explain to him that he's madly in love with you."

"Nothing bothers me more than not knowing. I must get it

153

cleared up and either continue or finish. Alexis and I never finished, we just stopped—I'm not sure we even really started. I do feel he has some responsibility, and after all, he began it all by telling me how 'intoxicated' he was with me, and by grabbing me. . . . Oh sure, I responded to it, true, but if he hadn't started and it had been left up to me, we'd still only be exchanging glances and innuendos. Then he *did* write that letter confirming he felt something, so he is responsible to the extent that when you have a part in involving someone emotionally, you owe them something—at least an explanation."

"Have you convinced yourself? Can I go inside and take a bath now? May I be dismissed?"

"Look, if he doesn't feel anything—you can go in a minute—if he doesn't feel anything, I can cope with it. But now I am at that fork in the road and I must decide which one to take, but he's the only one who can tell me. He must talk to me."

"And if he says he does love you?" asked Jujubee.

"Then we can ride the waves together."

And then he was back.

Unable to wait to see how long it would have taken him to call her, she telephoned him the morning he arrived. He seemed pleased to hear her—how was she, when would he see her, all of that.

"How about lunch?" she suggested.

"Yes, where?"

"How about in your office—at least we'll have privacy—every restaurant in Nairobi will be full of people who will come up and talk to us. Can we have a picnic in your office? I'll bring the pepper tree . . ."

Otis' secretary had already gone to lunch when Lys walked in so they were alone and he looked at her with such hunger that she could say nothing at all, not even hello, and he kissed her and kissed her and without even stopping he said, "I hate you so much you drive me crazy, and I loathe you because I cannot get rid of you inside me. Why can't I be as indifferent to you as I am to all women? I could have killed you in South Africa, and I wish I had so I could be doing some work now instead of doing nothing but wanting you, and why didn't you write?" and he kissed her more. She was laughing and almost crying and talking and kissing and asking questions and not listening to the answers and she knew that he loved her and she was telling him how she loved him and they never ate their lunch but talked and kissed and clung, and their talk never made any sense but their kisses did and time was up again, and the secretary came back and Lys got up to leave promising to meet him outside the hospital at five. "I'll tell Olitipoti we'll be there at six," she said for the benefit of the secretary as she opened the door and left.

And still they never saw Olitipoti because they were in Alexis' bed and she was telling him how the black monster hadn't appeared in South Africa, and for him to be patient with her, that she would feel but that it would take a while and this was her problem and not his, and he was saying no, no it was his problem as much as hers and all the things she had wanted to hear him say in South Africa but hadn't. Suddenly everything was as she had hoped it would be—it was the whole movie version.

She asked him why he had acted as he had in South Africa, and he told her he had half hoped it wouldn't work with them because it was so complicated—with Hallit—and how hard he had tried to forget her, but couldn't, and he really didn't care how complicated it was, he had to have her, and the price was nothing when you really wanted something and he really wanted, needed her, and they kissed and clung and made love and more love and more, and he was careful never to be on top of her, and her fears gradually started to fade. When she asked him about his "performance" and why his behavior had been so anomalous, he didn't seem to know what she was talking about; so she let it go—she no longer cared.

Later on that night when Hallit made such beautiful love to her, she thought, Oh, Hallit, what am I doing to you, what am I doing to us? But please please don't blame me, I didn't ask for this. You taught me never to let any beauty pass—that life is too short and that it may never happen again. Could you advise anyone to let it pass? Even me?

At other times she would be swept by rough waves of guilt and she would look at Hallit and wonder how she could possibly deceive him this way. How *can* I do this? she would ask herself, but she knew she did it quite easily, with very little difficulty at all. During these bouts of anguish and self-recrimination she would make a rash promise to herself never to see Alexis again, and at the time she meant it, but in ten minutes the guilt would vanish

155

and she would feel so dead she would rush to the telephone for Alexis' voice to bring her back to life, and then she would be in his arms again for everyday she managed somehow to see him alone. During all of this time she felt even more tenderness for Hallit than ever, and she loved him no less. She adored him, in fact, and most of all she would have loved to talk to Hallit about her relationship with Alexis because Hallit would have seen it all too clearly, verbalized it so well, and advised her what to do. It was because she valued his opinions and insights that she longed to divulge everything to him. This gave her a small inverted satisfaction for she told herself she was depriving herself of something she really wanted—Hallit's advice—for his sake; that she was sacrificing her desire for Hallit's comfort, and at times she really believed it and allowed this distorted rationalization to console her—but only for a few minutes.

"When am I going to meet him?" Jujubee asked.

"I've told him all about you—I'll arrange something soon. I want him all to myself for now." And for the next few weeks she hardly had a chance to see Jujubee at all—when she was home she devoted herself to Hallit to help ease her guilt. She was also tired—she found the intensity of the affair exhausting—so she went to bed early every night. Then one day when Jujubee was sunbathing by the pool Lys went out to her and told her to come with her to meet Alexis. She did, but she didn't like him. Lysbeth said it wasn't fair because she hadn't had much time with him and that Jujubee must get to know him better, so she invited him for dinner and told Jujubee to pretend it was she who had invited him. "So I'm the beard, uh?" remarked Jujubee.

"That's what you are."

The dinner with just the four of them was a disaster—Hallit argued and insulted Alexis all through the meal. Lys had hoped it might become a foursome that could be repeated frequently, but with Hallit's evident dislike of Alexis, she abandoned that idea immediately—way before dessert. And Jujubee still didn't like him any better either.

"Why not?" Lys asked after he had gone.

"Because he's so stupid."

"Stupid—but you don't require that a person be intelligent to like them."

"No," answered Jujubee, "but not this stupid—he's a non-thinking, inarticulate, uncultured heart mechanic. Once he stops talking about coronaries he runs to the piano to hide there because he has nothing else to say."

"Might he not be the 'strong silent type'?"

"People are silent only because they have nothing to say. He's a witless, shallow, trivial, stupid, free-loading piano player who has a trade like a plumber—he fixes pipes and gets them flowing again," retorted Jujubee.

"How vivid," said Lys coldly.

"But look *I* don't care—you're the one having the affair with him—not me. You keep right on lying and I'll keep right on swearing to it—that's what friendship is for."

"I hate to admit it but you could be right about him," said Lys, her anger evaporated. "But he is . . . occupying me . . . don't you see?"

"I see you're talking from your ovaries."

Just a few weeks after Otis' return, the Reddys invited the Lindseys to the New Stanley Grill Room for dinner and dancing in honor of Doria's birthday. Doria invited Jujubee to come too and asked Lysbeth if she had any man in mind for Jujubee's partner? "Yes, how about Alexis Otis—you remember him?" Indeed she did, so there were to be the six of them and two other couples as well.

Late in the afternoon of the day of the party Lysbeth had planned to film Emperor Haile Selassie's arrival at the airport and later being greeted by Mzee Jomo Kenyatta—the two great African leaders. It would be marvelous footage for her African heads of state film. Since she didn't want to make the journey back to Langata afterward and then into town again, she decided to dress at the Reddys' in Muthaiga and to go on to the Grill Room with them. Before she left home she telephoned Hallit at his office and suggested that he drive to the Grill Room with Jujubee and she would meet them there at eight.

Then, with both her purse and movie camera bag slung over her shoulder, and with the long beige Halston sweater dress for that evening tossed over her arm, Lysbeth hopped in the car and told Mwangi to drive her to the airport.

Wanting to check and prepare her movie camera—she had not

used it since filming Amin—she opened the film bag and was fumbling in the bottom of it for a lens when she felt a bulge under the foam padding. She swore silently as she investigated and saw it was the revolver that she should have turned in to the Firearms Bureau months ago but had completely forgotten. Hallit would be livid when he heard, but she would hand it in first thing in the morning. Right now it was a problem. If a security man were to check her as she sought Press clearance at the airport she would certainly be arrested as a suspected assassin, especially as the thing was still loaded—she could see the little brass shell cases around the chamber but was frightened to take them out being uncertain how to do it. She finally slipped it into her purse which she was going to leave in the car with Mwangi.

When she had finished at the airport she went directly to the Reddys, and as she dressed she chatted with Doria who remarked how clever Lys had been to bring a dress that matched the brown Gucci shoes and bag that she had used during the day. They all met in the lobby at eight. Lysbeth greeted Jujubee and Alexis, kissed Hallit then told him about the gun, apologized and said that she hoped there would be no repercussions. Although he wasn't exactly pleased, he wasn't as angry as she had anticipated and said to keep it in her purse—he would take care of it himself in the morning.

Everyone was very gay and had several drinks before dinner, much wine at the meal, and then champagne. Lysbeth danced with all the men except Alexis. She could hardly look at him and did not display the same warmth to him that she showed everyone else—he was too important to her—but no one seemed to notice. The champagne flowed faster and faster, and Alexis, realizing it would be obvious if he didn't ask her to dance, waited for a slow quiet melody and finally they melted into one another on the dance floor. He whispered in her hair, "Do you think anyone would mind if I made love to you on the piano before we went back to our table?"

"I am loving you *so* much right now," she told him truthfully, for never had she been happier. She floated—on Alexis—on the music—on the champagne.

When they got back to the big round table Alexis casually changed his seat and sat next to Lysbeth. Jack toasted Doria, "Happy Birthday" on yet another bottle of Dom Pérignon, and then the other men toasted her too, Alexis included, and finally it was Hallit's turn. He gave an exquisitely witty birthday salutation and then continued very seriously, "And now, I'd like to propose another toast—this one to my wife, Lysbeth, and Otis. May their marriage be all that they wish." Then he turned and bowed slightly to both of them. Lysbeth could not believe what she had heard! She sat paralyzed, hearing only the awkward silence around the table. Everyone was staring at Hallit in disbelief, and he, still standing with his glass raised, said, "Did no one hear me? I propose a toast to my beautiful wife, Lysbeth, and to her lover, Alexis Otis, and may their marriage be all that they wish."

Lord Rufus Hallit Lindsey was still sitting in his Cheyne Walk, London, flat, which overlooked the Thames, idly fingering his shotgun. He realized he had been so absorbed in his thoughts that he had been sitting there for over two hours. Leaning the gun against the table beside his big leather chair, he poured himself another drink and thought, No one says you have to die sober. In fact, there aren't any rules at all for suicide. I should write "The Suicide Handbook" as my final contribution, but the idea of death, even my own, only bores me. However, the reflection of my life doesn't: should one be content with two perfect years? Is that more than most people ever have? Screw most people—I wanted more than two years. That first year Lysbeth and I were married was sublime, and the second year with Jujubee weaving in and out of our lives was superlative too. Yes, both those years were perfection—mountain-top joy—until . . . funny how I loathed him from the minute I saw him. Must have been a chemical reaction that made me chary of him from the beginning. An omen? But he certainly said nothing that was offensive, at least no more so than many other people, and he's certainly respectable looking—Lysbeth thinks he's the most gorgeous man she ever saw. But his face is too vacuous for the kind of looks I like in a man. Or liked. Jesus, I can't seem to realize he's dead. Even now.

Death often makes one forget the negative, or ugly side of a person—it usually erases the bad and leaves only the good. But even now I still feel nothing but distaste when I think of him. Of course that's not what I told the jury, but then the prosecutor didn't ask me what I felt about him—only what I thought about him. Let's see, exactly what did I say? I said, "I think he was an excellent surgeon who had contributed incalculably to medical

160

science." Yes, that's how I so cleverly and ambiguously stated it. I must admit I was brilliant throughout the trial. I thought I might obtain immortality from my films, but I know I shall from this case. People are still fascinated by it, and they'll be talking about it for years. If anyone knew the answer, if it were certain who had killed him, everyone would stop speculating about it—it's the curiosity that will keep it alive. "Who killed Dr. Otis?"—they'll be asking that forever.

But, back to the film of my life. Yes, I have the beginning—how I was born when I was forty-six years old, which was when I met Lysbeth on the ship, and I have shown my birth—my emotional birth—and how I grew for two years. I have introduced Jujubee who became part of our lives, and then, with ensuing danger music, enter Otis. Then I showed the three months he was on the scene—up to the dinner party at the Grill Room.

Now he'll be found murdered. I'll show him just as he was found the morning after the birthday party at the Grill Room—slumped dead in his car, shot through the head. No murder weapon. Who did it? Ummmmm . . . he took a gulp of his drink, then another, while he thought.

Christ, I know, I've got it! . . . I'll give them what they've created—a number of different solutions. I'll do the three most popular endings that everyone speculates about, and I'll let them decide which one is the true version. Of course, I'm the only one who really knows what happened, but I'll present the other possibilities with fully substantiating facts.

Yes, I'll draw from a hat which solution I'll present first, then the second, then the third—and I'll let everyone know I used this random method of selection so that no false importance can be attached to the order in which they are presented.

Hallit took three bits of paper and wrote a name on each. Then he went to the hall, got his bowler hat—which he wore only to family funerals—and dropped the scraps of paper into it. He poured himself another drink and sat back in the chair again, and reaching into the hat, which he had placed on the table next to the gun, he drew out the first slip of paper: "LYSBETH."

Lysbeth: Murderer?

Lysbeth sat paralyzed in the Grill Room, hearing only the awkward silence around the table. Everyone was staring at Hallit in disbelief, and he, still standing with his glass raised, said, "Did no one hear me? I propose a toast to my beautiful wife, Lysbeth, and to her lover, Alexis Otis, and may their marriage be all that they wish."

Lys felt Alexis' hand tighten on her knee under the table as she watched Hallit down his champagne, then turn to Jujubee and say, "Come on, Jujubee, take me home." He started out of the room, and Jujubee, jumping up to leave, broke the silence by pretending the episode was a joke. She laughed and said, "Hallit's always doing this kind of thing—you watch—this scene will be in his next film. He rehearses in real life to get people's true reactions, then he re-creates it for the screen. We've all just been used as emotional guinea pigs."

It worked. Everyone seemed relieved and the dancing started again. Lys sat, still frozen in her chair, and when Hallit, who had not looked at her since before his toast, turned to stare at her from the door she started to get up to run to him, but Alexis stopped her and softly but firmly said, "Let him go."

Jujubee had followed Hallit to the door, but then she came back to the table and whispered to Lys and Alexis, "He says for you not to be later than one—that you're tired. I'll go home with him and wait up for you," and glancing at her watch she said, "It's eleven-thirty now," and left with Hallit.

Stunned, Lysbeth just sat and looked at Alexis who said, "Go say good-by to the Reddys and then we'll leave."

Obeying, she found Doria and Jack dancing together and she muttered, "I don't know what Hallit is up to—he seems very drunk—I'd better go too. Call you tomorrow—" and left with Alexis.

Once outside, very nervous and upset, she said, "Do you think he knows, or do you think he was kidding?"

"He knows."

"No, he can't know," she said, twisting her necklace around and around, and as she got into his car she repeated, "No, he *can't* know."

"He knows," insisted Alexis.

Lys lit a cigarette and said tensely, "He *can't know*. He may suspect it . . . but I can't even believe that. I never dreamed he suspected, but then he's so very clever he *may* have been suspicious and is doing this just as a trap for us to see how we behave."

"He knows."

"Stop saying that!" she shouted.

"Lys, Hallit knows—because—I told him."

Eyes screaming, no sound, just eyes, big unbelieving eyes shrieking silently at him. Then, *"You told* Hallit about us?" she whispered.

"Yes."

"Why?"

He reached over with his arm to bring her close to him as he drove, but she pushed him away and sat sideways on the front seat of the car looking at him. With a wild expression on her face she asked, "Why were you talking to Hallit in the first place? Where? Why? *Tell me!"*

"He telephoned me just this afternoon and asked if I could see him at five-thirty. What could I say but 'of course'?"

"Why didn't you tell me?"

"I did telephone you right away, but you were out . . ."

"Oh, yes . . . the . . . go on . . ."

"And I was about to tell you at the Grill Room when I moved next to you, but just then he got up and gave the toast. Anyway, he came into my office and said right off, 'You are having an affair with my wife.' I couldn't deny it . . ."

"You couldn't deny it! Why not? *Why not?"*

"Because it's true—we are."

" 'Because it's true!' Jesus—that's no answer. Go on . . ." She was getting more and more distraught.

Alexis swung the car off the Langata Road onto a little track, stopped, and without even bothering to turn off the lights tried to hold her and comfort her, but she pushed him away and begged, "Please go on."

"Well, really there wasn't much more than his talking about you and me and saying how you are a person who is responsible for your actions; that I'm not, that . . ."

"Oh, God, he knows!" she interrupted, leaning back now against the car door with her head in her hands. "He knows. Hallit knows." Her mind was in a turmoil. What was it he had said? "I'd like to propose a toast . . . to my wife, Lysbeth, and her . . . lover"—was it "lover"? yes—"to her lover, Alexis Otis . . . and may their—" and her knuckles were in her mouth as she concentrated—"marriage," yes, their marriage . . . that's what he said. "May I propose a toast to my wife, Lysbeth, and to her lover, Alexis Otis, and may their marriage be . . ." Their *marriage!* . . . She felt fireworks within her, and she reached in her bag for another cigarette, then looked at Alexis as he lit it for her—both their hands were trembling, "Did you tell Hallit you wanted to marry me?" Her eyes looked like two amber question marks. She couldn't absorb it all. She was in love with Alexis but she had never thought about marrying him . . . about being with him always. He hadn't answered her, had he? "Did you tell Hallit you wanted to marry me?" she asked again. She was beginning to understand now. The importance of what had happened was starting to sink in; her whole world—her whole life—was about to change. Everything had been turned upside down—life without Hallit? . . . married to Alexis?

"Well . . . ," he started, but she interrupted him.

"Alexis, Hallit has just set me free—*free!* He has given me—us —his blessing—for our marriage! That is his gift to us—my freedom! And he did it publicly so everyone would know that he not only knows about us, but that he has consented. He must have recognized that if I could have an affair with you I could not be totally in love with him, and since he wants nothing less than perfection he has decided to let me go without a fuss. How many other husbands—oh, Alexis, can you believe it? Alexis, I had no idea you wanted to marry me . . ."

Dragging on his cigarette, he answered, "Well . . . I . . . as a matter of fact, Hallit asked me if I wanted to marry you, and I said, well, I had never thought about marriage with you, but that I do enjoy being with you . . ."

" 'Enjoy being with me!' Alexis, what are you talking about?"

"Well, Lysbeth, this is extremely difficult . . ."

He lit another cigarette, she took it from him, so he lit yet another and put his hand on hers and held it on the seat between them. He couldn't look at her, but he said, "Lysbeth, remember the girl I told you about—the one in South Africa? Well, I've promised her I'd marry her—when I'm there again . . . next month."

"You what?" she whispered.

She could not believe what she had heard him say. The pyrotechnics started inside her again, and they were bursting in her head and in her heart and pow-pow-pow, stop-stop-stop she screamed silently inside herself, but the explosions kept on going, and louder and louder, convulsing her with stupefying realizations: Hallit knew. Alexis had told him it was true. *Told him.* Hallit would never forgive her—she had destroyed the best thing she had ever known, she had ruined it, for she understood that it could never be the same between them again. With a sickening fear she knew that it would be the end. And Alexis had told him it was true *not* because he wanted her forever, *not* because he couldn't imagine life without her, *not* because he wanted to marry her . . .

"Alexis, what did you say about that girl in South Africa? Alexis, please look at me!" Still sitting sideways facing him with one leg crossed underneath her, she reached for his chin and turned his face toward her. "What did you say?" she asked trembling, her trapped animal eyes begging him not to repeat what she dreaded she had heard.

"Lys, I'm sorry—such a little word to say, I know, but I *am* sorry. But you see I did tell that girl in South Africa we would get married next month . . . I . . . I want to marry her."

Anger, pure ugly fury, had the effect of clearing her head and her thinking. Violence was replacing the confusion inside her now. Her face contorted with icy menace, she went on, "You mean you . . . you just said those things to me in your office when you got back, just . . . so you'd have a woman to go to bed with you?"

"Well, that's your way of putting it. I wouldn't express it that way . . ." he said lamely.

168

She fell back against the car door, silent, then she leaned toward him and hissed "Don't you know I would never leave Hallit for *you?* Don't you know that you're just a game to me? Perhaps an important game, but nevertheless, still a game. It was all make-believe for me with you. I never loved you—I only loved the way you made *me* feel. I was never interested in you—it was only my desire for you that interested me, not *you*—you don't exist. I didn't even play the game with *you*—I played it with myself—*I* created the challenge, the struggle, not to have *you* but to prove to myself that I *could,* to inflate my ego. *Don't you see?"* She was shouting now, "Don't you see—you were the . . . the . . . whipped cream on the sundae, but I wasn't about to sacrifice the ice cream. I wasn't about to give up my security, my comfort—and yes, even my material possessions, or my freedom which I have always valued tremendously and which I have with Hallit. And more important still, I wasn't about to give up the best friend I've ever had, which is Hallit, and most important of all—my *father* because that's what Hallit is to me—*all those things*—and *especially* my father for he not only takes care of me as my own father did, he worships me in exactly the same way. Hallit is my reality. You're only my fantasy." Shaking, she lit another cigarette from the one she already had and shouted at Alexis even louder, "To Hallit, I am his good little girl, his bad little boy, his Princess, his friend, his wife, his favorite toy, his mistress, his love, yes—his life! And what am I to you? Just *another piece of ass!* And do you think I'd give up all of that—for what? For some lousy fucking magic? Christ, I can always find another Prince Charming, they come and go all the time—they never last—because the magic never lasts—which is what *makes* it so special. They are always only temporary —both the magic and the person—for the person dies with the magic. It doesn't even matter *who* they are—it has nothing to do with them, it has only to do with me—not even me—it's a matter of the heart, *my* heart—which is fickle and so damned unimportant compared to the really important sides of me—like my mind, for instance. How about my mind, Alexis? How about my brain? Who else but Hallit can interest me for hours—for years—with talk, with ideas, with wit? He's intelligent, sophisticated, elegant, and verbal—and you don't even open a car door for me! I want to live in his cultured world of art—not your shallow personal little puddle nor your gloomy medical one! *So go marry your fucking South African!"*

A hysterical note had entered her voice and huge tears began to gush out as she broke into uncontrollable sobs. Her world had collapsed completely; her relationships with Hallit and with Alexis had ended within the space of a few minutes. She felt an implosion within her and her body was shaking violently as Alexis tried to reach for her. She screamed, *"Don't touch me!"* and her face was distorted and wet with tears as she groped hysterically in her bag for a handkerchief. And suddenly the tears stopped and her eyes glazed over at the feel of the heavy cold metal in the bottom of her bag. Amber eyes crazed, like an animal caught in a trap, she crouched down into herself and as she pulled the gun out and pointed it at Alexis he leaped at her and grabbed her wrist to keep her from pulling the trigger, and in the force of his lunge, she slipped under him, and he was on top of her now holding her down, holding her down, unable to get up, pinned, and she heard herself screaming, loud hysterical shrieks going into the trailer park, screams, and Alexis in an effort to snap her out of it was slapping her in the face, slapping her to quiet her, to stop her maniacal screaming, and was he going to put his cigarette out on her chin now, and pinned under the black drooling monster, Alexis, Alexis, the black monster of all time, and drowning, drowning, amber animal eyes more than trapped now, lost in the struggle for sanity—and then, mixed up in the sound of animal screams and deranged cries came a heavy deafening report in the closed space of the parked car, a thudding bang, and the monster jerked once, then twice, in a final ballet, and the black Gypsy monster eyes rolled intoxicated with death, and black ringlets of monster hair, red with blood and death fell on her, but would do so never again, never, no more, no more . . .

She struggled out from under the intoxicated dead monster, the dead black curly bat and pushed open the stairway door where he would take her in his arms and kiss her more, but when she got through the magic door, demented electric eyes-with-no-pupils of the monster were waiting and watching and she had to run and hide, and biting one arm to keep from screaming and the other arm dangling, the gun hanging from her finger, she ran and ran from the staring electric eyes-with-no-pupils which did not follow her, and she stumbled, ran, crawled, staggered, looking back always to watch for it moving toward her, so she could kill it with her gun dragging at the bottom of her arm, and falling and getting up and ankles bleeding from thorns, and her golden mane matted with blood, the black monster's blood, Alexis' blood clinging to her hair, clinging to her, blood kissing her hair, kissing her, intoxicated death, and hurry, hurry run, run from the monster with the electric ringlet eyes, hurry run home . . . home . . . home . . .

She stood in the doorway bloody, amber eyes unhinged and the gun hanging from her fingers still, and screamed wild animal screams and Hallit and Jujubee both came running from opposite directions upstairs, Hallit saying, "Oh, God, Oh, God," then, "Get your morphine, Jujubee," and walking down the stairs toward her saying softly, "Lysbeth, it's all right, Lysbeth, everything's all right, come, Lysbeth, let me take care of you, let me hold you safe, no one's going to get you or hold you down because you are going to let me hold you safe now." Hallit wondering if she would see him, Hallit, or if she would see in her blindness just a man coming at her for then she would surely raise her gun, but he was at the foot of the stairs now and had only to cross the hall to reach her, and her screams, reduced now to pathetic cries and wounded moans as she watched him coming closer, closer, and she backed away a few steps, an amber-eyed maniac, and bumped into the door behind her, and feeling cornered and trapped again, she screamed, *"Don't touch me!"* again and again, and so he stopped and said, "It's me, Lysbeth, Hallit. It's me and I love you, I love you—let me hold you safe," and he took two more small steps toward her slowly, and it was that final step that brought the gun up, pointing directly at him, very steady, and crazed eyes and frenzied voice wailing, "Don't touch me," still again and again. Lunatic Lysbeth, Lysbeth in lunacy, grotesque, her body twisted in madness, but steady gun still pointing death at Hallit. Jujubee frozen at the top of the stairs, waiting for the explosion of either Lysbeth or the gun—she knew not which—and surprised it was from Hallit the burst came, not the gun. Perfectly still, not moving, he bellowed in his strong commanding voice, "Put the gun down, Lolly. Put it down this instant and come here—to Pop. Do you hear me? At once!" and everyone and everything was immobile— a frozen frame as in the end of a movie—and then he repeated, "Lolly!" and her hand flew open like a white glove in a minstrel show, and clunk, clunk, the gun sounded on the marble floor and tap, tap, tap, the running feet, Lysbeth's little-girl feet running, with arms open wide and up, and a two-year-old Lysbeth looking up at Hallit with trusting, searching amber eyes screaming 'help me' silently, as she flew to him running, and he folded her in his arms and she buried her head in his chest and he held her tight and safe and patted her hair all bloody. Tears were now on his cheeks too, but he kept her head buried in his robe so she wouldn't see Jujubee coming up with the needle and he squeezed his arms around her tighter and kissed her cobweb hair all bloody as the needle went into the back of her arm and she didn't even notice because she was beyond feeling, beyond pain, and he was holding her now, holding her, safe now, and no more black monster, no more, no more . . .

Hallit and Jujubee leaned over her in bed, "Lysbeth, Lys, try to tell us where the car is. Wake up, Lysbeth, where *is* the car? You must tell us where the car is. Lysbeth, do you hear?"

Her eyes didn't even flutter, but she whispered, "At the track . . . opposite the . . . Langata junction . . ."

Another needle.

Then just before dawn the phone rang. It was the police saying an African policeman on his rounds had found what they thought to be the body of Dr. Alexis Otis on the Langata Road, and they had informed the hospital who suggested they call the Lindseys since there was no next of kin and they were known to be his closest friends. Hallit feigned unbelievable shock and was careful to ask how the *accident* had happened, and was told they could "disclose no details" at the time but would call him again in the morning. An hour later the police called back to confirm that the dead man was indeed Dr. Otis, and that he had been shot in the head.

"Lysbeth, wake up." It was morning and they were looking down at her and Jujubee had a towel and wash cloth and kept putting it to her hair and face and then wringing it out all red and bloody in the basin, and in a distant desolate recall Lys saw the black monster with curly black-and-red hair all intoxicated with death and she murmured, "I killed him, didn't I?"

"Who," asked Hallit, fearing from her answer she meant "the black monster" and all would be hopeless—forever lost in insanity. "Who did you kill, my baby?"

"I killed Alexis," she whispered.

172

He was relieved, for at least she was back in the world, albeit a grotesque one, but now at least there was a chance of escape.

He sat down and stroked her hair and forehead, squeezing her shoulder with his other hand and patting her quietly just as if he were soothing an overwrought child. "There, you'll feel better soon." Then, sitting on the bed as close as he could get to her, his hands caressing her face he said, "Now listen, my darling, I'm afraid the police are on their way here—you are to say you came home last night right from the Grill Room between 12:30 and 12:45 A.M. Alexis came into the hall with you and stayed about five minutes. Then you went upstairs and talked to Jujubee for a few minutes, and then you came in and talked to me. Right after you came into my room, Jujubee brought us drinks in my studio, then left immediately—this is an important point—it will establish that we were all here, that we all saw each other. You talked to Jujubee *only* about my reaction to your affair with Alexis and how marvelous it was that I understood, but you had not decided if you were going to marry him or not. Then you came in to me and thanked me for being so understanding, and you also told me you had not decided what you were going to do. You stayed with me for about fifteen minutes—just long enough to finish your drink—a brandy—then you said you were very tired and that we could continue talking in the morning. On your way to your own room you called good night to Jujubee because her light was still on—you could see it from under the door—she called good night back—this was about 1:45 or 2 A.M. They will establish that Alexis died at about 1:00 or 1:30—and we will establish that all three of us were here between 1:00 and 2:00 A.M. No one was upset about anything. None of us had cross words—I merely told you that if you wanted to marry Alexis Otis, it would be absurd for me to try to stop you. That what would I possibly want with a wife who was in love with someone else? That I understood these things could happen—that of course I was sad—but completely resigned."

Just then the phone rang, and telling Lysbeth he'd be back in a minute Hallit left to take the call in his room. It was William, who had only just heard the news, calling from the hospital. After a few words with him Hallit shouted to Jujubee to take it on her extension.

When he went back to Lys she watched him as he crossed the room, then she said weakly, "Why are you doing this?"

"Because I want to—because I love you—and because it will work."

"What about the gun?"

"It will never be found," replied Hallit. "I buried it. Now listen, the police will . . . understand why you are so upset. You will only have to say what I've just told you once, and then you can go with Jujubee to the farm—this afternoon. I'll stay here to sort this out."

"Why do you do this?"

"Why not?"

"Do you know that I love you?" she asked.

"I know that."

"They'll arrest you."

"Perhaps, but it could be most interesting—amusing even. If I'm charged with murder, you as my wife can't testify. So don't worry. I'll take care of it, you know I will. I might even enjoy it." He smiled at her, "It could be my greatest moment."

"No! I can't let you do it!" she was holding onto him now to pull herself up close to him and almost touching his face with hers, she said, "You may be able to get away with it, you may be able to live the lies that you are about to tell, but you won't be able to live *with* them afterward. Oh, no! Not you, Hallit—not with your integrity, you'll never be able to live with the lies or with my truth. I won't let you do it. I love you too much."

"You *must* let me, Lysbeth—I love you, I can cope. I want to do this. If you feel you owe me any debt—for Alexis—you can repay me by letting me do this. I feel responsible—I feel in a way it was my fault. You see, I've suspected you felt this for Otis for quite some time now. I knew he was a pathologically infantile and selfish lover, so I forced the situation tonight so you'd find out for yourself. But I didn't think you'd . . . go this far. I wanted you to come back to me. You thought I wouldn't understand about him—I understood too well. You shouldn't have underestimated me or how well I know you or how much I love you; and I want to spend the last years of my life with you . . ."

Before she could say anything, the doorbell rang. Jujubee answered it and they heard police voices downstairs. In a few minutes Jujubee called Hallit and he went down, and Lysbeth stayed in bed thinking, and then slowly got out of bed and put on a flowing white-satin robe and looking ghostlike, she started down the stairs clutching the bannister, then stopped.

The inspector looked up from the hall and said, "Lady Lindsey, sorry about the—death of Dr. Otis." And Lysbeth, still on the stairs, was silent and everyone waited for her to say something but she said nothing. Hallit's blue eyes pleaded with her and Jujubee's green eyes pleaded with her, and the inspector, already aware of the presence of a beautiful woman, asked, "Lady Lindsey, I know this is a dreadful time for you, but could I just have a few words with you? Would you care to sit in the drawing room—it won't take long?"

"If it won't take long I'd rather just stay here. What is it you'd like to know?" said Lysbeth in an unnatural voice as she continued down the stairs.

"Could you tell me what time you got home last night?" asked the inspector, but he was thinking that as she walked down the stairs so slowly, her white robe dragging behind her accentuating her grief, that she looked rather like a bride with no bridegroom. He felt sad. As well as lustful.

Hallit and Jujubee knew this next moment would determine the course of their lives. Lysbeth walked close enough to the inspector so she could look into his eyes, and at that moment Jujubee knew all was safe, for Lys had always said, "Look them right in the eyes and lie." Hallit also knew at that same moment, for he realized that Lysbeth was planning to use her eyes and would go through with the story.

They heard her saying, "It was just 12:30 A.M. when Dr. Otis and I arrived here from the Grill Room. I noticed the clock when we walked in. He came in with me and stayed for about five minutes, then he left."

"Did you see anyone else?" asked the inspector, trying to appear professional and hoping it wasn't obvious that he noticed that . . . that . . . quality about her which was making him want to take her in his arms and protect her from all of this.

"Yes. I saw my husband—and Baroness Boucher. First I went to her room and we talked for a few minutes—fifteen or so. Then I went to my husband's room and we talked."

"Do you remember for how long?"

"Another quarter hour or so. Juju . . . Baroness Boucher

175

brought us drinks—so it was enough time for us to drink them. Another ten minutes at least."

"May I ask what your conversation with Lord Lindsey was about?" asked the inspector gently.

"We were discussing the possibility of a divorce. He was being very co-operative, and I thanked him for it." Then turning to Hallit, but still speaking to the inspector, she said, "He's a much more astonishing man than you, or anyone but I and Baroness Boucher, will ever know."

The inspector paused a moment as if in respect to her tribute to Hallit, then asked, "Did Baroness Boucher stay and have a drink with you?"

Jujubee's heart quickened because she didn't know if Lys would remember that detail or not, and the inspector had already asked her and she had told him no, she had taken them a drink but had not stayed with them. Lysbeth didn't answer, she just stood there clutching the bannister and staring at the floor. The inspector coughed slightly, then said, "Lady Lindsey, did Baroness Boucher stay and have a drink with you and Lord Lindsey?"

Lysbeth looked up at him and still in a strangely soft voice said, "Oh, I'm sorry Inspector—my mind drifted . . . ummm . . . what was it?—oh, no, Baroness Boucher went right back to her room. She didn't stay with my husband and me, but when I left his room I saw the light was still on in her room, so we called good night to each other . . . it must have been at least 1:45 or 2 A.M. by then. Is there anything else? If not, would you excuse me, please?"

"Thank you, Lady Lindsey—that's all—sorry to have bothered you."

"We just heard about this a short while ago—it's very . . . shocking," said Lys.

"Yes, yes, terrible . . ." muttered the inspector, trying hard not to show how very much he wanted to gather this poor little delicate sparrow to him and kiss her—kiss away all her grief.

And she turned and glided up the stairs.

*H*allit was pleased with his scenario thus far. After topping up his drink again, he walked back to the table by his big leather wing chair, reached into the hat and pulled out the second slip of folded paper. Opening it he read: JUJUBEE. With his drink in his hand he went to the window and watched the Thames grow dark as the sun's disappearance deprived it of its sparkle. He thought, to show Jujubee as the murderer I'll have to start much further back than the Grill Room toast. Let's see . . . I'll begin with the first time she arrived in Kenya to stay with us. . . .

Jujubee: Murderer?

That first morning after Jujubee had arrived in Kenya to stay with the Lindseys, Lysbeth was sitting on her bed having coffee with her when Hallit poked his head around the door and reminded them that Sir William Fitzpatrick, head of the Flying Surgeons, was coming from up-country for their dinner party that evening, and that he would spend the night and might even arrive in time for lunch. Hallit had planned a surprise for both Lysbeth and Jujubee and he wanted to make sure they would both be there at lunch time. His surprise was a horse for Jujubee. He knew that both girls loved riding and although he had already given Lysbeth a horse, they had had to go to some trouble to borrow another mount in preparation for Jujubee's arrival, and it was then that the idea of the gift had occurred to him. He left to arrange the collection of the new mare, while Lysbeth on her Arabian and Jujubee on the borrowed horse rode off into the Ngong hills, the little range of rounded peaks lying to the west of Nairobi which take their name from the Maasai description of knuckles, for if you hold your clenched fist up at arms length ahead of you the four peaks will almost exactly coincide with the outline of your knuckles.

Cantering over the hills they soon saw a herd of buffalo, and after watching them for a while, they rode to the edge of the hill and gazed down at the spectacular view below them of the Great Rift Valley, the world's largest rift, which stretches five thousand miles from the Dead Sea to Mozambique. The two women just sat on their horses at the top of the hill, scanning the vastness of Africa below. Lysbeth broke the silence, "See that *manyatta* way down there? Remember our Maasai trip?"

"How could I ever forget?" answered Jujubee solemnly.

"You never told me you liked my article—did you?"

181

"Yes, it was excellent." Their Maasai trip had not reminded her of Lys's article.

"I guess we'd better head back, it's getting near lunch time."

On the ride back, two golden patterned giraffe loped by, then turned to stare at the visitors on horses. "Isak Dinesen called giraffe 'the giant speckled flowers of Africa'—they're my favorite—look at those eyelashes," Lysbeth called to Jujubee.

"This is where Dennis Finch-Hatton is buried," she shouted a little farther on as they passed a gravestone on the edge of the hill. "You know—Isak Dinesen's boy friend."

"I'd like to see her house."

"We can go there any time. Karen Blixen was her married name—Isak Dinesen is just a nom de plume—she is said to have lived with Dennis, but purely platonically, no sex."

"How are you making out in that department?"

"I'll tell you all about it sometime," said Lys as she flicked her horse with her rhino-hide whip and galloped the rest of the way home.

They gave their horses to the *syce* to stable, and when they reached the patio, Sir William was already there. He looked grave and sounded graver.

"How do you do, Lady Lindsey," he said formally.

"This is Baroness Boucher," said Hallit.

"How do you do, Baroness," said Sir William rigidly. Jujubee curtsied elaborately.

"Call us Lysbeth and Jujubee," said Lys gaily as she stretched out on a deck chair among the ferns and told Hallit yes she would have a tonic. But Sir William found it hard to use people's first names until he knew them well and compromised by studiously avoiding having to call them anything—although he was impeccably polite. When lunch was announced, he said to Lysbeth, "I do hope you won't be offended if I don't eat much, I haven't been frightfully well—stomach upset you know."

"Oh, I am sorry," said Lys. "Would you like something for it?"

Jujubee, whose taste in men could never be predicted—even by herself—had been eyeing him surreptitiously. She couldn't resist the chance to make him uncomfortable—he was so teasable.

"Got the good old squitters? I have these amazing pills for the runs, and if you take one now, you can plan your miraculous recovery by tea time." She went off and returned at once with two of the pills, and Sir William apologized again about not being able to eat such splendid food.

After the meal he excused himself and went to his room to sleep, and Jujubee muttered something about finishing unpacking.

"If you want any ironing done, Jujubee," said Lys, "there's no sense giving it to our servants now—they go off to eat. Every morning they come in at six-thirty, clean, do the laundry, cook, and so on. Then after we have lunched they go off, and return to serve tea, iron, and cook dinner. Finally they go home about ten or eleven."

"How long do they have off?" asked Jujubee.

"Lysbeth permits them about half an hour," answered Hallit, with a grin.

"Half an hour! Don't you think that's rather excessive?" exclaimed Jujubee.

"Lysbeth does indeed. She's a real Marie Antoinette—'give them cake,' she says every day—instead of giving them their time off."

Lys walked up to the chaise longue where he was sprawled and swiped him on the head with a rolled up magazine. He grabbed her and pulled her down on top of him, laughing and kissing her.

"You see," explained Lys, still sitting on his lap, "I am always saying how living here bothers me. It's pre-French Revolution. The rich masters in their opulence and the poor with nothing—and it doesn't even change as top Africans replace white people in the best jobs because they keep the system going too. I mean, look how we live in this house and how our servants live fifty yards from us in squalor—no hot water even—nine people counting kids and wives in three small rooms—rags for clothes—our cook earns thirty-five dollars a month. We have three cars for two people and they don't have a bicycle between them. They can barely afford to buy the meat we give our dog. Christ, it really gets to me at times."

"Of course it does," said Hallit, "but what should we do—fire our servants? Then they wouldn't even have thirty-five dollars a month, let alone electricity and running water which they enjoy here but don't have on their own *shambas*. They wouldn't be able to pay school fees . . ."

"What about education—how much are school fees?" interrupted Jujubee.

"About twenty dollars a year for a primary school. But you see, you are judging their lives by your standards, not theirs. Certainly it is all terribly wrong, but it is an inevitable part of the growth of a developing country. The average per capita income for twelve million people here is a hundred and forty dollars a year, so if you measure our cook against that, he is earning three times the average *and* is being housed and clothed and provided with basic amenities. More than 90 per cent of the population of these countries are unemployed in the sense of not receiving a monthly pay packet for a job. They live a subsistence life, eating what they grow, building their houses out of sticks and mud and thatch and getting their water from the river. A few break out into a cash-economy life—half a million right here in Nairobi—and of those a few do very well indeed, just like their Western counterparts. The poverty is dreadful, but what is the alternative until the economy, generated by the vision and energy of a few, can provide more jobs—sustain more people? But even as the jobs increase so does the population—at a terrifying rate." Hallit lifted Lys from his knee, got up from the chair, and took a bow, saying "Thank you, ladies and gentlemen of the press. I now have an errand to do. I'll be back in half an hour."

When he returned he came into the entrance hall and called excitedly for Jujubee and Lys. Both girls came running and even William appeared to see what all the fuss was about. Hallit told them all to come outside. There, standing in the gravel driveway, was an Arabian horse. "Happy Birthday, Jujubee," said Hallit. "Now you two can ride together whenever you want without having to borrow a horse." Jujubee and Lys were ecstatic. They jumped up and down and hugged Hallit and kissed him and thanked him over and over, and finally Jujubee said, "But it's not my birthday."

"That doesn't matter—I might not remember your birthday."

"Would you like the first ride on her, Hallit?" Jujubee offered.

"I despise horses," said Hallit, "they're too high, uncomfortable in the middle, and dangerous at both ends."

Lys appeared with their riding hats, and off they rode together, while William went back to bed.

Hallit went into town to meet his film crew, and Lysbeth left later to film Amin. Neither of them got back until dark, and as Jujubee was mixing them a quick drink, William joined them asking, "Are we wearing a black tie this evening?"

184

"Afraid so. How do you feel now, William—any better?" asked Hallit.

"Oh, yes, thank you," he said in a very proper way. "Yes, much better, much better, thank you," and with a sidelong glance at Jujubee he showed that he could give as good as he got, "I can now fart with confidence."

Jujubee and Hallit and Lys all roared with laughter and looked at William from that moment on with new eyes.

Everyone at the dinner party had a stimulating time with much laughter. They all adored Jujubee, especially William, whom Jujubee knew was about to have the biggest treat of his life. "This night is just for you, Billy Baby," she told him.

At breakfast next morning William looked nervous and sheepish, and when Jujubee appeared in the doorway and announced, "I'm going to let the cat out of the bag," he looked as if he would die of embarrassment. Then Jujubee took a large paper bag from behind her back and dumped the Lindseys' cat on the floor. William laughed so hard—with relief mostly—that he could hardly speak.

The girls rode again after breakfast, and at lunch Jujubee announced with her huge grin, "I'm not going to have that dirty weekend with my friend from Philadelphia everybody, but with someone else—can anyone guess with whom?"

So Jujubee and William left, leaving Lysbeth and Hallit alone, which they really appreciated since it was to be their last few days together before their first separation. "I really like Jujubee," said Hallit as they stood in the driveway and waved them off.

"It was so nice of you to give her the horse. It's such a super present for me too," said Lys looking up at him. "I'll miss you. I hate to think of your going," and tears filled her eyes.

"Come on now," said Hallit, though he was touched and secretly pleased that she cared so much about his leaving. "I'll only be gone three and a half weeks."

On Monday he left and on Tuesday Lys decided she and Jujubee should go to Lamu since she wanted to do an article on the people of this ancient and isolated community on their tiny island in the Indian Ocean just off the Kenya coast.

Lamu is both the name of the four-mile-long island and of the town, and time seems to have stopped there in the middle of the eighteenth century, leaving an organized Muslim society of eight

185

thousand people whose daily functions have not altered with the passage of time, and whose surroundings are the same as when it was an Arab Sultanate. The *dhows* still sail from Zanzibar to Mombasa to Lamu to Aden and the Persian Gulf—then back again in a never-ending cycle, carrying mangrove poles and charcoal and spices, oblivious of the 100,000-ton oil tankers and giant cargo ships whose wakes they must cross. Lamu is as much an anachronism as the *dhows* themselves. The ancient gray stone houses all face Mecca, and there are twenty-one mosques, all in daily use.

To get to Lamu you must fly in a chartered plane from Mombasa and land on a grass strip on another island (there is no landing strip on Lamu) or alternatively you can drive to the end of the mainland. Either way means crossing to Lamu in a boat, and as Lys and Jujubee sailed in a most unseaworthy looking craft toward the sea wall they fell silent, overcome, like many before them, by a kind of *déja-vu*-induced awe, as if a time machine had transported them back through the years to a place that was both familiar yet strange.

The moment the boat stopped, an eager African grabbed their bags and led them toward an Arab hotel on one side of the town square. A town crier was in the square shouting his public announcements, and many men—all in long white robes and embroidered white Muslim caps—milled around like nuns in a convent. There were no women to be seen and no dogs. Dogs are "unclean," and women, swathed in the black *buibuis* which make them look like giant bats, come out only at night to hurry through the narrow busy streets as they make their purchases. There are no bicycles, indeed no wheeled vehicles at all on the island—only sweating porters or donkeys. But two laden donkeys cannot pass because the "streets," often no wider than three feet, are merely tiny crooked paths between the ancient stone-built two- and three-story houses.

Their hotel was a clean, whitewashed building and they were shown to a clean whitewashed little room on the second floor containing two iron beds without bedspreads but with fresh white sheets. A single naked light bulb hung from the ceiling, a single wooden table separated the beds, and three hooks on the wall synonymously completed both decor and utilities.

They were greeted with great courtesy and dignity by the proprietor and having paid for the room in advance—a dollar each—they were given a key. Then Lys took her camera and Jujubee her sketch pad and they wandered out into the square dominated by a whitewashed fort which serves as the jail. They sat on the steps and absorbed the feeling of Lamu, and in a few minutes Jujubee began swift but unerring sketches of the black-and-white Lamu scene—of the Swahili men in their long, loose robes which matched the fort in their whiteness. Lys claimed that even she could have sketched a woman—it would just be a long black blob like a Rorschach blotch.

They went to a "restaurant" on the waterfront and had a hot vegetable curry with *popadoms* and *japatis*. Jujubee selected an old man with a wonderfully gnarled face and pirate eyes who claimed to have been a *dhow* captain, and she arranged to meet him the next day so that she could sketch him. Lys was appalled to learn that as a woman she would not be allowed to enter any of the mosques to photograph the interiors for her article. However, the restaurant owner knew of a young Arab who was a keen amateur photographer and would help her out on this part of the assignment.

After dinner the girls strolled up and down the narrow dimly lit streets, peering into the stores and admiring the massive elaborately carved doors for which Lamu and Zanzibar are justly famous. Snatches of Middle Eastern music served only to heighten the sensation of being immersed in a real live Ali Baba land.

"This place reminds me of New York," said Jujubee. "There's not much difference between stepping in donkey shit or dog shit every ten paces."

"Yeah, but I don't remember seeing open sewers filled with chicken heads in New York, nor the bath water just running down the outside walls of the Plaza Hotel."

It was almost midnight when they turned into their lodging, and tired from all the walking, they both fell asleep very quickly. However, at five A.M. the Muezzin called from the balcony of the mosque, summoning the faithful, and in a few minutes Lamu's town square was as busy with bustling figures as New York's Time Square on a Saturday evening. Jujubee, who could not accept that five A.M. even existed, was awakened by the racket and concluded that Lamu was the noisiest place she had ever been in. Then she lay there thinking how happy she was just to be with Lys again, how they looked at everything through the same end of the telescope, how they laughed, and always at the same things. It was good to share her dreams, her fears, her hopes—her life, indeed—with Lys once again. She realized how empty this last year had been without her, how poverty-stricken her existence was in that elegant, expensive suite at the Ritz in Spain, and at Claridges in London, and how in this grungy little hole in Lamu, she was rich. The wealthy patrons of art she knew, her famous international friends, the skipping around the globe to her various cocktail party openings at major galleries—all that was nothing compared to what she had here in Kenya. It was not the Lindseys' beautiful house in Nairobi or the hideaway on the farm or even the game parks or the scenery or the atmosphere of Africa; what made life for Jujubee was continuous days to spend with Lys. She could ride with her in Rousseau-like scenery or lounge in the sun with her, and to be sentenced for life to share this room with her, to have it a prison cell just for the two of them—that would be ultimate bliss. Just let me lie here, she thought. Just let me feel the joy, just let it seep in—this precious feeling.

Suddenly Lys got up from her bed and without saying a word she crossed the small space to Jujubee's bed and just stood there, looking at her. Still without a word, she slid one shoulder strap from her shoulder, then the other, dropped her nightgown to the floor, and stepping over it, climbed into the bed with her.

Happening as it did, unexpectedly, without preamble, and at the precise moment when Jujubee was in that half state between waking and sleeping and was engrossed in her daydream of Lys, it produced for Jujubee a peak of sublime ecstasy that until that moment she had only been able vaguely to conceive.

Half an hour later the first words were spoken. Lys, getting out of bed and starting to get dressed, asked, "Can you understand that I love Hallit very much? That I like him, that I enjoy being with him, that I love being married to him—that he is my friend, my companion, my husband, my father, that he takes care of me and worships me—that I love him deeply and that I would not be able to cope if he stopped loving me? Can you understand that, and at the same time understand that although sex with him is all right—I have an orgasm—it lacks the . . . the fire I feel with you? Sex with Hallit is satisfactory, but there is no *desire*. Part of me is dead and only comes alive with you, and to ignore that would be allowing a part of me to commit suicide. But if I had to make a choice, if I had to choose between you and Hallit, I'd choose Hallit because he is more important to me. You are important to me, but not serious. Do you know what I mean, Jujubee?"

Lys sat on the edge of the bed now, looking at her and begging her to understand, but not waiting for an answer she continued, "Oh, Jujubee, you know I love you—I love you as a friend, I love being with you. I like you. I love sex with you—I want it, in fact—but I don't *need* it to survive. But I do need Hallit to survive. More than that, I need his happiness, and I need it more than I need yours. I *want* you to be happy, but your unhappiness would not destroy me. His would. What I want is both Hallit *and* you, and I don't want to have to choose. But there is no real conflict for me because I am not giving you something that Hallit has in any case—my sexual desire—so I don't feel guilty. Having both of you fills me completely, but if I were forced, I *would* choose Hallit—with no hesitation. If this—with you and me—is to continue, you must know exactly what it is, what it means to me, and where you stand."

Responding to Lys's seriousness, appreciating her honesty, and also overjoyed to learn she was so important to Lys both as a friend and sexually, Jujubee answered gently, "I understand. I've always understood that I am not as important to you as you are to me. I am not disappointed, Lys. On the contrary, I am happy to know that I am 'spring' if not all four seasons to you. To have a part of you no one else has is more than enough for me. To be with you every day, to ride, to swim, to laugh with you, to share your life, and to have you physically, is more than I ever hoped for. Your loving Hallit, and even lying in his arms and making love to him doesn't bother me at all because it is something different from what we—you and I—have. One relationship should not interfere with the other, and we are both clever enough never to let them get mixed up, and above all, never to let Hallit know. We both know it's wrong to tell someone more than they're capable of understanding, and Hallit could never understand our relationship, nor the fact that it isn't eroding your love for him. To tell him about us would cause him unnecessary hurt. I'll make a point of seeing lots of William—he's a nice enough old goat—I like him—and he'll make the perfect decoy."

"Oh, Jujubee, you're so—so *everything!*" squealed Lys like a small child. Running a comb through her golden hair and flinging her camera bag over one shoulder she raced out saying, "Meet you at Petley's for lunch at one, O.K.?"

And so the next year of their lives continued in Kenya, Hallit's and Jujubee's and Lys's. All three of them would readily have described it as a perfect year. Hallit was busy with his films and was sometimes away for weeks at a time. Jujubee preferred these absences, naturally, but when he was home she saw a great deal of William and in a way enjoyed that too. With Hallit home, Jujubee and Lys would often ride for an hour or so in the afternoons and they would dismount in a glade near a little stream where they would . . . not make love, exactly, for it was not really a question of love, but they would enjoy exquisite sex—they reveled in raw sexuality. For Lys it was merely an extension to her life, a pleasant sideline—like someone who is happily married but goes off to play tennis three times a week for physical joy. It was no more to Lys than that.

To Jujubee it was everything.

And to Hallit, it did not exist.

Toward the end of that year at a dinner party the Lindseys gave one night, William asked if anyone remembered seeing a cover story in *Time* six months earlier about a Dr. Otis in South Africa who had made a major break-through in overcoming rejection problems following heart transplants, and who had attracted world-wide attention to his techniques in a series of operations performed in Russia. His latest project was the development of a treadmill machine that accurately measured and recorded the strain imposed on the heart as the subject "walked" on it. Some of the dinner guests remembered, others didn't, so William described the experiment and told them how Dr. Otis was going to join him and the Flying Surgeons in Nairobi for a year to operate and to do heart research on the Maasai.

Lysbeth said it might make a good story and William confessed with a wry smile that that was why he had brought up the subject—so she would do an article. Why didn't she make an appointment to talk to Dr. Otis about it? She agreed, and two days later when Jujubee went off to Paris she had made an appointment to see him.

190

When Jujubee returned to Kenya from Paris, she found Lys a different person. She was waiting for Jujubee at the airport, and even before she spoke, Jujubee knew something about her had changed—she glowed, but in a different way from anything Jujubee had seen before. "I've fallen in love, Jujubee," said Lys instead of saying hello. The knife went through Jujubee's heart and her stomach and her mind all at the same time, but even so she managed to crack, "Thank God for that, you've been such a bore these last few years."

"I really *am* in love, Jujubee. It's Alexis Otis—that heart specialist William asked me to interview. I even got into his bed with him—we didn't actually make love, but I went down on him."

"That's the first normal thing you've done for two years," Jujubee was able to say. She hoped it sounded casual enough.

All the way home Lys told Jujubee about Alexis—she talked and talked and smoked one cigarette after the other, a sure sign that she was nervous or excited because usually she only smoked at night. They got home and lay by the pool before lunch and Lys continued to tell Jujubee how much she was in love. Jujubee felt like a waterfall. Everything was spilling, falling, tumbling, crashing, and now, sitting in the chaise longue by the pool with lunch which had been brought to them on trays, Lys was telling her about how she was going off to meet—what was his name—Alexis —in Johannesburg. I must think, Jujubee told herself. After lunch, which she couldn't eat, with the excuse she had eaten too much on the plane, she pretended to sleep, but in fact her mind raced, seeking a solution to keep from losing Lys, and the fear of that prospect made her almost physically ill. Afraid her reaction might be apparent to Lys, she kept her eyes closed, feigning sleep, but she could hear Lys telephoning Washington and Johannesburg and then calling to her that she was off to the post office to see if there was a letter from him and that she'd be back in about fifteen minutes. No sooner had she driven out of the driveway than the phone rang and it was "Dr. Otis calling from Johannesburg." Jujubee talked to him—a formal conversation about Lys's arrival —and when she hung up she wondered again how she would be able to cope with this situation. She knew there was nothing to do but let Lys go, to let her have her affair, and to hope she got over it soon, but never had she seen Lys like this before—not with

191

Frank, not with Hallit—never. It was obvious this man was important to Lys—she really must be in love with him. Jujubee was frantic. How would she even get through the evening without Lys seeing her despair? She knew only one way—and she also knew she shouldn't take it: she went for her morphine—something she had secretly indulged in since her kidney operation. The white liquid worked quickly and she was just hiding the syringe in her bureau drawer as Lys drove into the driveway. She ran down the stairs, grabbed her drink, and reached the door as Lys got out of the car. "I just talked to whatshisname . . . he said he was glad you're coming to see him."

The morphine made Jujubee's evening an endurable haze, and Lys, fully preoccupied on her own private cloud, noticed nothing unusual about her friend.

All through dinner and coffee and brandy she listened to Lys telling her about Alexis and her magical night with him. Although Jujubee swore to herself, she managed to smile in the right places and make her usual caustic-cum-affectionate remarks. But even they were wasted—Lys wasn't hearing or absorbing anything. There's nothing I can do, I'm not reaching her at all, thought Jujubee. Lys just rattled on—now she was saying she didn't know if she should go to Johannesburg or not. She thinks she can't decide, thought Jujubee, but I know she's going. She'll go. My only hope is that she goes and gets him out of her system, forgets him, and comes back to me—and Hallit.

With Hallit there were justifications for Jujubee's sharing their lives, but with Alexis she would be excluded, for Lys would always be with him, she'd never be alone. Aware that the morphine was wearing off and that she might no longer be able to control her despair, she said, "Let's get some sleep. I was up all night on the plane—remember?" Her physical longing for Lys was enormous—the drug had done nothing to dull that—and she had waited so long for this night—savoring it in anticipation—but she knew that Lysbeth was not now interested in anything but Alexis. But I'll try, thought Jujubee, on the one chance in a thousand that I'm wrong, so when Lys was in the bathroom brushing her teeth she walked in, stood at the doorway, and said, "Maybe what you need is something to get your mind off Alexis and whether you should go to Jo'burg or not. If you forget all that for a bit, you might have clearer vision when you return to it. Nothing like some sex to erase everything else from your mind."

"Christ, Jujubee! Are you crazy?" said Lys, turning to her with her toothbrush still in her mouth. "As if I could do anything but think of Alexis now. Can't you see he has me almost insane?"

"Yes, I can see. Good night, Lys."

" 'Night."

And the next day Lys left for Johannesburg. It scooped a great hollow inside Jujubee. She felt almost as if she had died. Unable to stand being so close to the lack of Lys—in her house, near her possessions, her perfume, unable to bear even riding her horse alone—she decided she had to get away. Hallit was coming back soon, and she didn't want to have to make the effort to act normally around him, so she left a note saying an unexpected exhibit had come up for her and she'd be back in a week or so. Then she packed a bag, flew to Ethiopia and sat in a hotel room in Addis Ababa for a week thinking, planning, reaching no conclusions, and wondering what to do.

When eventually she telephoned and learned that Lys was back in Nairobi, she got herself together enough to return too—she had to find out what had happened in South Africa, what Lys was feeling, what she was planning to do, for whatever it was would determine her own future. It was incredible, she pondered, to have one's life and happiness in the hands of someone who wasn't even aware of it.

Lys was pleased to see Jujubee and anxious to regale her with all that had taken place in South Africa. They lunched, as usual, by the pool while Lys detailed everything that had happened with Alexis. Jujubee realized quickly that Lys was desperately in love with him but that it was uncertain whether or not he was in love with her, and from that standpoint the trip had not been altogether satisfying. Otis and Lys had gone to bed, of course, but evidently that had not been a great success either. I'm still the winner of *that* battle, thought Jujubee.

From all that Lys had told her she surmised that Alexis Otis did not sound too intelligent or too much in love—or even as if he were endowed with a great deal of character. He seemed to have left her confused and had not assumed any responsibility for his actions—not even in the way of an explanation of what he did or did not feel for her.

Lys pointed out that she hadn't actually started the romance—Alexis had, and she had responded, but she felt that the onus was upon him to tell her what he now felt and that when he returned to Nairobi she would insist that he do so. He had told her at the outset that he was "intoxicated" with her, and now she was saying he would just have to tell her if he was still intoxicated.

Jujubee asked, "Can I go inside now and take a bath? May I be dismissed?" She felt if she didn't get away she would scream because the main thing she feared had been confirmed—Lys was still deeply in love and Alexis had by no means been relegated to what Jujubee had hoped he would be—part of a distant fairytale in South Africa. It was equally obvious to her that he would thus be a part of their lives—at least for the forseeable future.

"You can go in a minute," answered Lys before launching into a description of how she had "touched perfection" with Alexis, asking Jujubee if she knew what she meant, did she understand, had she, Jujubee, ever touched perfection? Jujubee had touched it that night in Paris with Lys and every time they had been together since. That joy, that perfection, was her motivation for living—in fact it was her life. Lys didn't wait for an answer, not that she expected Jujubee to reply in any case, but gabbled on about her own future being in Alexis' hands and that he was going to have to verbalize his emotions.

"And if he says he does love you?" Jujubee asked seriously.

"Then we can ride the waves together."

Then he was back.

Although the weeks before had been torture for Jujubee because it was devoid of anything physical between her and Lys, she was in still greater agony the morning Lys went off to meet Alexis. And when she came back at seven that evening, Hallit was already home and Jujubee was unable to talk to Lysbeth alone. But she didn't have to—Jujubee knew what had happened. Lys radiated. Why hadn't Hallit noticed the change in her? He seemed perfectly normal through dinner, Jujubee thought, but she had had so many martinis to ease the pain she admitted to herself that she was not able to judge very well. After coffee Jujubee couldn't stand the casual conversation between the three of them any longer, so she said she had some letters to write and excused herself. She was sitting on her bed with a bottle of gin trying to annihilate herself without the aid of morphine—the amount of it she had taken recently and her growing dependence upon it was beginning to scare her—when Lys came in and said in a soft voice, "Alexis does love me, Jujubee. He *loves* me. *He* loves *me*. I think I am going to burst with happiness," and she hugged herself and did a little spin in the room and continued, "I'll tell you all about it tomorrow. I wish Hallit weren't here so I could tell you now, but he wants to show me his script. I feel so guilty about Hallit, but I love him even more now—I really do." Jujubee had never seen her so radiant. "Hallit's waiting for me—see you in the morning— get up early so I can tell you all about it!" And she was gone.

The next morning Lys sat on Jujubee's bed and gave her a full description of what had happened when she saw Alexis, how he had told her the minute they had met in his office that he wasn't indifferent to her, how they went to his hotel room, and how they had made love over and over again.

"Was it enjoyable?" asked Jujubee, trying to sound light.

"It was the most beautiful thing I have ever known," answered Lys almost reverently. "Oh, the sex wasn't as good as with you but better than with any man before," she added. "But everything else was . . . there's just no word to describe it."

Hope flickered inside Jujubee—if the sex wasn't as good, and if a strong mind wasn't there—if what Lys felt was just a matter of the heart—romance—then wasn't there a chance that it might pass and life could return to what it had been? "When am I going to meet him?"

"I've told him about you . . . I'll arrange something soon. I want him all to myself for now. Got to run . . . I'm meeting him in a half hour . . ."

During the next few weeks Jujubee caught only glimpses of Lys, for when she was home she lavished all her attention upon Hallit and never even came into Jujubee's room to talk to her. At dinner the three of them would be together and Jujubee would ask, "How about riding with me tomorrow?"

"Oh, Jujubee, I'd love to, but I have so much work to do on that article," she would answer with a knowing glance so that Jujubee would not press the subject, and then soon after coffee every night, Lys would say she was tired and off she'd go to bed. Night after night, morning after morning, Jujubee would sit in her room waiting, waiting for Lys, but not once did she come in. Not that she was avoiding Jujubee in any way, it was just that she was so absorbed in her world of Alexis that she wasn't really aware that Jujubee existed.

Then one morning when Jujubee was sunbathing by the pool Lys went out and sat next to her.

"How goes it?" asked Jujubee.

"It's tearing me in two, Jujubee. . . . I've got two people living inside of me—one who loves Hallit and now another one who loves Alexis. I need another body to satisfy both my selves. I don't want to hurt Hallit, but you know Alexis' charm . . . hey! that's right —you haven't even met him yet. Come with me after lunch—we'll go see him."

The fact that Jujubee had not met him was an afterthought to Lys. It was not that she had purposely not introduced her to him, as if she had been keeping them apart for a reason, it was simply that it had not even occurred to her, and this was yet another fact that was hurtful to Jujubee—it was a measure of her insignificance, her lack of importance in Lys's current life. But Jujubee did want to meet him. She wanted to study the enemy because in the last few days she had decided to fight, not just to surrender feebly without a battle. She wanted to plan both strategy and tactics.

Walking down the hospital corridor with Lys she realized she loathed him more than she thought it was possible to loathe anyone she had never met. They turned into an office, and there stood a giant of a man with black curly hair and black gypsy eyes. Even if she hadn't despised him in advance, she would have done so the moment she saw him. An instant revulsion struck her because of . . . what was that quality, or lack of quality, she sensed? His conversation only strengthened this conviction, and after a few minutes of inane small talk, Lys said, "Well, Jujubee, we'd better not keep Alexis from his work any longer," and they all stood and said good-by. In the corridor Lys could hardly wait. "Well? Do you like him?"

"No."

"Why not?"

"I don't know. But I don't know *why* I don't like spiders either, I just know I don't like them. He seems inane, inarticulate, and superficial—to name a few of his better qualities."

"Oh, Jujubee, that isn't fair—you really have to give him a

chance. Look, I'll bring him home for dinner tonight and pretend you invited him—O.K.? Then you can get to know him. Don't you think he's good looking?"

"No. He looks . . . dirty to me."

"I thought you'd call it animal, but I'm glad you don't find him attractive—I'd be livid if you went after him. See you tonight."

Both women went their separate ways, and when Jujubee got back to the house that evening about seven, Lys was walking around the garden with Hallit, who called to her affectionately, "Hear you're having a new boy friend out to dinner. Where's William? I'm going to tell him. I feel sorry for this new one—poor bastard—doesn't he know you'll destroy him?"

At seven o'clock, Lys was fussing over a flower arrangement in the drawing room, and wondering what she was going to wear, while Jujubee sat and watched her. "I'm so nervous, Jujubee," said Lys.

"Have some calm balm," suggested Jujubee, gesturing to her martini. Then apropos of nothing, she said, "You know, it's a good thing Hallit's second name isn't Otis, or Otis' first name isn't Hallit, because when you made an introduction it would sound like 'Halitosis.' "

"You're crazy," said Lys. "Fix me a drink. That is a good idea. Where is Hallit?"

Pouring Lys a drink, Jujubee recited:

"The King is in the counting room, counting out his money,
The Queen is in the parlor, drinking gin and honey,
The Maid Jujubee is in the garden, hanging out the clothes,
When along comes Alexis and fucks up everything."

Lys smiled, took the drink and went up to her room to dress. At eight Alexis arrived and Hallit pretended to remember him from before, though he didn't really, and then proceeded to argue with him all through dinner. After dinner, Alexis played the piano, then Hallit excused himself, and Jujubee talked to Alexis about his work. Then she got the nod from Lys, so she excused herself too, and went to her room, and about half an hour later she heard Alexis' car drive off and Lys came into her room. "He was too nervous to stay alone with me when Hallit thought he was here for you. Do you like him any better?"

"No."

"Why not?"

197

"Same reason—because he's stupid."

"But you don't require a person to be intelligent to *like* him."

"True, but not this stupid—he's a non-thinking, uncultured, inelegant idiot. Once he stops talking about coronaries, he runs to the piano and hides there because he has nothing else to say."

"Might he not be the 'strong silent type'?"

"People are only silent because they have nothing to say. Look, Lys, *I* don't care—you're the one having the affair with him, not me."

"I must admit that next to Hallit, he does pale, but then everyone does. Also, I looked up the name 'Otis' and it means a 'nothingness of being' . . . but that's just silly. Sex is O.K., but it could be better . . ."

Jujubee grasped the opportunity—"Would you be interested in some that is?"

"I sure would. But not with you, dear one—my life is complicated enough right now. I don't need that to feel guilty about too."

"Guilty? Whatever for? You've never felt guilty with me before."

"I know, but now I'd feel as if I'd have to tell Alexis. So thanks . . . but no thanks," and Lys said good night, almost sadly, and left.

Although she had been rejected sexually, Jujubee felt encouraged that night because Lys had admitted some negative aspects of her relationship with Alexis. She also thought she had succeeded in introducing some further seeds of doubt, and hopefully they would take root and grow.

However, after a couple of weeks Jujubee was more disillusioned than ever before, for not once since that night had Lys even spoken to her alone. In fact, she had barely seen Lys—except at dinner with Hallit. She grew more despondent each day, not being able to know if she were winning or losing—or even if there was a battle. One evening, when Lys had gone to bed early as she always did now—exhausted from making love to Alexis all afternoon, Jujubee suspected—she knocked on her door, Lys called to come in, and Jujubee found her just lying on her bed, fully clothed, and smoking. "What are you doing?"

"Thinking."

Jujubee wished Lys would talk to her as she used to—she decided she would rather hear all the dreadful details and suffer that way than not know what was going on. She recognized that her imagination was probably more lurid than Lys's actual escapades, and speculating about what she was up to probably caused her more anguish than the actual knowledge of the facts would have done.

"Thinking good or bad things?"

"Both, I guess. Oh, Jujubee, I don't want to involve you in this, to make you take sides . . ."

"I don't mind being involved—perhaps I could help . . ."

"It's just that I am so much in love with Alexis—I really cannot imagine life without him. But I can't imagine life without Hallit either. I don't know—I am getting more deeply enmeshed with Alexis each day—I didn't expect this to happen. He says . . . but you see, I really also feel disloyal talking to you about it. It is a private thing between Alexis and me, not something I really want to share. I don't think you could help anyway—no one can. Please understand, Jujubee. You do, don't you?"

"Sure."

"Having an affair is exhausting. I don't know how Alexis does it—he works every night in his laboratory now, since he takes the afternoons off to be with me. Being in love is such a motivating force, but I find it so tiring—perhaps because I put so much into it. I'm going to have a bath and get some sleep now, Jujubee—see you in the morning," she said with a dismissing smile.

As Jujubee left the room she thought, I've been dismissed from her room, and from her life. This is it. She has chosen him over me—romance over sex. Or maybe sex with Alexis has improved. At any rate, he has won. With Hallit, she chose him *and* me—but not this time. So face it, Jujubee, she told herself. "I don't have to," she answered herself aloud as she closed the door to her bathroom and went for the morphine.

No one noticed Jujubee's odd behavior, or at least they accepted her explanation that she had a touch of malaria, and attributed her not coming to meals—her almost total withdrawal from them for almost a week—to not feeling well. Hallit was so preoccupied with his film's completion that he was in his office all day and in his study almost all night. Once or twice a day both Lys and Hallit would stick their heads in Jujubee's room and ask how she was and if she wanted anything. Then Lys would say, "See you later," but Jujubee knew she never would.

After a week, Lysbeth finally did come into Jujubee's room and sat on her bed. "Jack Reddy has invited Hallit and me and you to the Grill Room on Thursday for dinner and dancing for Doria's birthday—do you think you'll be well enough to go?"

"Yes, I'll be fine by then," answered Jujubee, knowing she'd have to pull herself together soon—she couldn't just keep on morphine forever—and also she didn't want to miss the opportunity of being with Lys for an evening.

"Jack asked if I had any man in mind for you—so I suggested Alexis since William's away—hope you don't mind—would you rather have someone else?"

"No, that's fine. William gets back that night, but not until late, so he couldn't come anyway. How goes it with you and Alexis?"

"Oh—it goes fine."

Jujubee sensed her reluctance to talk about it, so she changed the subject just in order to keep Lys there talking to her for a few more minutes.

Thursday afternoon Lys was out and Hallit telephoned Jujubee from his office saying he wouldn't be back in time to take her to the Grill Room, so for her to get Mwangi, who would be back from taking Lys to the Reddys', to drive her there, then to let him go—she could drive home with them. As Jujubee got out of the car, Hallit was waiting in the New Stanley lobby and Alexis was arriving from one direction and Lysbeth and the Reddys from another, so they all went into the Grill Room together. There were two more couples, and the ten of them sat at a large round table and everyone was very gay through drinks and dinner—everyone, that is, but Jujubee. Hallit seemed a bit despondent, too, she thought —most unusual for him. Lysbeth sparkled more than ever . . . "Sparkle Plenty over there is beckoning to you," said Jujubee to Hallit, who was sitting next to her.

"Dance with me?" mouthed Lys to Hallit.

They got up to dance and Jack Reddy invited Jujubee, "Shall we?"

"No," answered Jujubee, with no further explanation, which made him uneasy, so he turned quickly and asked one of the other women. Jujubee watched Alexis and Doria on the floor, and Lys and Hallit, and then everyone was back and then Lys was dancing with Alexis. Seeing the look of exultation on Lys's face, she knew definitely that she had lost her forever. She felt as if she were witnessing her own death. She had drunk too much gin, then wine, now champagne, but none of it was numbing the torment. It was just making her morose. Perhaps it was that without morphine life seemed as terrible as it really was. What if he took Lys off to South Africa and she never saw her again?

Everyone had returned to the table from the dance floor and Jack opened yet another bottle of champagne to toast Doria a "Happy Birthday." The other men toasted her as well, Alexis included, and then it was Hallit's turn. He did so exquisitely, but when he finished he didn't sit down, he remained standing with the glass in his hand and announced very solemnly, "And now, I'd like to propose another toast—this one to my wife, Lysbeth, and Otis. May their marriage be all that they wish." He turned and bowed slightly to both of them. Jujubee could not believe what she had heard. Everyone sat paralyzed, staring at Hallit in disbelief. Still standing, and with his glass raised, he said, "Did no one hear me? I propose a toast to my beautiful wife, Lysbeth, and to her lover, Alexis Otis—may their marriage be all that they wish." He drained his champagne glass in one gulp, turned to Jujubee and said, "Come on, Jujubee, take me home," and started for the door.

Christ Almighty! thought Jujubee, and even sodden with drink and despair as she was, an automatic reflex impelled her to try and dissipate the awful tension and embarrassment that had transfixed all those present. Standing up to leave she turned to them and said, "Hallit's always doing this kind of thing—you watch—this scene will be in his next film. He rehearses in real life to get people's true reactions, then he re-creates it for the screen. We've all just been used as emotional guinea pigs."

She rushed to Hallit who had turned and was standing in the doorway staring at Lys. Jujubee glanced back at Lys who looked as if she were about to run to Hallit, but she didn't, she just sat frozen next to Alexis, staring at Hallit. "Tell her to be home by one, Jujubee. She's tired."

Jujubee quickly went back to the table and whispered, "He says for you not to be later than one—that you're tired. I'll go home with him and I'll wait up for you—it's eleven-thirty now," and then she left with Hallit.

They got into the car and Jujubee asked, "How did you know?"

"Isn't that a stupid question?"

201

"Yes. Have you known all along?"

"From the night she brought him to dinner with you. I thought at first it might just be a flirtatious thing that would pass, but I saw her getting more and more entangled every day, so this afternoon I telephoned Otis and went to see him. I asked him if he were having an affair with Lys and whether he wanted to marry her, and he said yes, he was having an affair with her but that he had never considered marrying her—though he did 'enjoy being with her.' . . . He is such a prick—I just can't believe Lysbeth could be serious about him. I don't really think she is. I think she is only interested in the romance of it all. I stayed just long enough to let him know I knew. It was all very genteel and civilized—I wouldn't want him or Lysbeth to think their sorry little affair was important enough to upset me—and actually it isn't—it's almost challenging in a way."

"Why did you go to him, why didn't you talk to Lys about it?"

"I didn't want to hurt her."

"You didn't want to hurt her! Christ, what kind of saint are you?"

"None at all. Don't you see . . ."

"Don't you think what you've just done will hurt her?"

"No, hardly at all. It will shock her, but she has Otis there to comfort her—she'll enjoy the drama, as a matter of fact. I told her when we first met that life, for her, is to be lived at the peak of one's spirit and that she might come to need another peak, and that when a new pleasure did present itself, she would react to it with her usual merriment and commitment. Don't you see that Lysbeth is an incurable romantic and she loves play acting? I thought that I'd join the game now too, so she'll know who can provide the most drama. It's my fault in many ways that this has happened because I have not given her the perpetual attention and excitement she must have—I've been so busy on my film that I've neglected spoiling her every five minutes, which is what she needs. So she is feeding her ego with Otis, playing love games with him. But this little performance of mine tonight will shock her out of it and she'll come back to me because now he will tell her I talked to him today. He may even ask her to marry him, and then she'll just be faced with the reality of him instead of the intrigue. She doesn't love him, she loves the intrigue—the challenge of leading two lives—the game of trying to keep me from finding out—the drama of a doomed love affair. All those things Lysbeth adores. But it is utterly impossible for her to adore *him.* If he asks her to marry him, she'll have *won* the game with him, there'll be no more challenge, so it will end. She doesn't want *him,* she just wants to win. So now, with all the intrigue wiped out, he will just stand there naked before her, exposing himself with nothing but his stupidity showing. She will see him for what he is, and the game will be thrown back into my court because suddenly I will be the one she will fear losing."

"But she's in love with him," said Jujubee cautiously, not wanting to hurt Hallit, but believing Lys's feelings for Alexis were more serious than he evidently thought.

"She's in love with being in love—not with him. If he doesn't want to marry her, she'll suffer from broken pride, which she'll pretend is a broken heart. But it will soon mend, and meanwhile all will be dramatic and wonderful for the two of us—Lysbeth and me—because, as I said, now she'll be afraid she'll lose me, and this will renew her interest in me—for another year or so, and then she'll find someone else to play with."

"You understand all this about her, yet you still love her?"

"Of course—don't you?"

"Yes, but I . . . but it's a little different with me . . . I just didn't know you could understand this about her and accept it," answered Jujubee, alarmed now and wondering what else he knew about Lys and whether he would be able to understand and cope with *that.*

"She's always been in love," he went on. "Why, she told me once she fell in love the first time when she was eleven years old, the second time when she was eleven, and the third time too . . . and it's never stopped; and it never will. She collects romances as others collect stamps. The person doesn't matter—just the hobby. Can you understand that? She does it because she wants to hear music through her heart not her ears, or because she wants to lose weight—or any of those absurd but charming theories of hers. It has only to do with her, not him . . . whoever 'him' may be. It won't affect what she feels for me—that is real and important. As long as it is only romance she feels—which is really falling in love with herself because she feels she is so attractive—as long as it is no more lasting than romance—which never lasts—as long as it is only a romantic sideline—which after all is only froth—then I

203

don't mind. But if sex were part of it, or love, I couldn't take it. If it's only being *in love,* then I'll give her a long leash, but I'll always hold and control it . . ."

"But don't tell me you don't think she has been to bed with Alexis?"

"Of course she has, but she hasn't enjoyed it."

"Oh, I see," said Jujubee sarcastically. "If she has sex with someone it's O.K. as long as she doesn't enjoy it?"

"That's exactly it. Don't be cynical—face the truth. No one is jealous of someone who's going out with another person if he doesn't have a good time. What one resents is the enjoyment he receives from that other person. Right?"

"I see your point," answered Jujubee, "but I'm not completely sold on its validity." The turn of the conversation was making her nervous and she wondered if he was leading up to saying something about her and Lys. He went on, "As long as Lysbeth loves me more than anyone else and enjoys sex only with me, as long as I'm more important to her than anyone else—in every department except romance, because that is impossible for any two human beings who have been together over a year—then I'll accept it. Don't think I like it. I don't. Nor do I think it's right, but it *is* understandable. I can understand why she is having this affair. She was caged in that preposterous marriage for years. What does she really know of love?" What Hallit didn't tell Jujubee was that he also had accepted, even before he married Lysbeth, that sooner or later she would have to find out if she were "cured," as she called it—cured sexually with any man other than himself. She would have to know if he, Hallit, had finally made her into a normal woman. He had known all along that she would be unable to resist the experiment forever.

As they drove in silence, Jujubee was thinking that Hallit thought Lys was just having a romantic fling. What he didn't know—did he?—was that Lys only truly enjoyed sex with her, Jujubee—not even totally with Hallit—and also that what Lys felt for Alexis was much more important than Hallit thought. Jujubee was shocked that he had known about Alexis all along, and she was still wondering nervously if he had any inkling about Lys and herself. As if he had heard her thoughts, he said, "I know you've known about Lysbeth and Otis, and I've known you were upset, and I understand why you've been upset"—Jujubee drew her breath in—"you have been upset for my sake. Well, don't be. It's under control now. You know, I never cared at all about you and Lysbeth having your little sexual escapades because that was before I knew her. But if it hadn't stopped, I would never have been able to accept it even though it was only sex . . . because, you see, I can offer her sex. But as I said, I can't offer her romance—we know each other too well." She let her breath out. He didn't know. "But I think it will be all right now . . . nothing to worry about."

"I hope you're right," answered Jujubee quietly as they turned into the driveway. If Hallit were right, she thought, then everything would be the same again with Lys and her—but he obviously didn't know all there was to know about Lys, so he could be wrong.

They both went to their own rooms to think their own thoughts—for both their futures would be determined by what Lys said when she got home. An hour later they heard Alexis' car drive in, Lys and Alexis come into the house, then Lys running up the stairs. Jujubee thought she would go into Hallit's room, but the door to Jujubee's room flew open and Lys leaned against the chest of drawers and looked at her. Very seriously and determinedly she said, "I am going to marry him."

"*Marry* him?" exclaimed Jujubee, the panic sounding in her voice.

"Yes, marry him. I'm leaving with him now."

"*Now? Christ!*"

Lysbeth walked to the bed and sat down. "Listen, Jujubee, this is going to destroy Hallit, but I can't help it—I am just so much in love with Alexis—he's everything to me—even sex is good. Jujubee . . ."

"Got a cigarette?" Jujubee interrupted, tossing away her own empty pack on the floor in despair. Lysbeth fumbled in her purse for a second, then dumped the contents on the bed and handed the pack to her, asking, "Jujubee, would you tell Hallit for me? If I just go now, will you explain it to him?"

"Jesus, Lys, you owe him an explanation at least." Her hand shook as she lit the cigarette.

"I guess I do. But I can't go through with it now. I hate to hurt Hallit, and you could tell him so much better than I. Don't you

205

see, there is no way I can give up Alexis—he's my life now—why are you looking at me that way? What's wrong, Jujubee?"

"What's wrong?"

"Oh, Jujubee, you've just got to understand. And you've got to tell Hallit. He's so articulate he'll confuse me and make me feel guilty and make me wonder if I should marry Alexis. If you tell him . . ."

"No."

"Please, Jujubee—don't dilute the joy I feel—Alexis has asked me to *marry* him—it's so wonderful—don't ruin it for me . . ."

"Don't ruin it for *you?* How about what you're ruining for Hallit? For me? Oh, no, you're going to tell Hallit yourself. I'm not!"

"But, Jujubee, it'll take hours—you know Hallit—he won't accept any short summary of things—we'll have to talk for ages, go over everything twenty times. And he won't talk to me with Alexis downstairs waiting—I won't be able to leave tonight. You know how long he . . ."

"Then leave tomorrow," Jujubee declared firmly.

In a fury Lys got off the bed and ran toward the door which stood ajar. She flung it open and Hallit was standing there. Both women looked at him but neither spoke. Finally, after what seemed an age, Hallit said, "Get rid of him. Tell him he can call you in the morning if you wish, but get him out of here now and come to my room." Finding herself actually confronted by Hallit, Lys's defiance evaporated as she had feared it would were she to see him.

"All right, but . . . I'm going to marry him, Hallit," said Lysbeth quietly, standing in front of him, but with her eyes lowered. "Alexis said that he told you he hadn't thought of marrying me, but that was because he . . . he never thought you would give me up. But now that you not only gave me up publicly, but added your blessing, he wants very much to marry me. And I want to marry him." Her last sentence was said with her eyes raised to his. Then she ran past him down the stairs to ask Alexis to leave.

Jujubee stared at Hallit who was just standing there, and she saw a look in his eyes that appalled her—it was the look of a man destroyed, of greatness broken, of nothing but pain that would never end, and a life condemned to it. Seeing this in Hallit, she knew that he too was engulfed in the same despair as she. She knew with crystal clarity that she was witnessing the disintegration of a fine and noble man, and she could not stand to see it so she turned her head away. In that small movement she glanced unconsciously at the purse Lys had emptied on the bed, and sprawled amidst a comb, a wallet, a lipstick, she saw the revolver. In that same second she knew what she was going to do. No one should be allowed to ruin three people's lives—hers, Hallit's, and yes, even Lys's own, because one day Lys would recognize her mistake and be unhappy. Hallit had returned to his room and closed the door. Jujubee ran to the stairs and heard the muffled voices of Lys and Alexis and ice tinkling in a glass in the drawing room below. Calculating that she had only a few minutes, she raced back into her room, opened her bottom bureau drawer, took out her syringe and the vial of clear liquid, filled the syringe expertly and stuck it into her arm. Soon her emotions would be numb enough to do what she had to do. She grabbed the gun, thrust it into her bathrobe pocket, and tip-toed to the top of the stairs—voices, ice. She crept down and past the living room, out of the front door— pushing the unlock button as she went out—and slid into the back seat of Alexis' car. She crouched on the floor feeling horror and pity and shock and revulsion and despair at what she was about to do. The morphine wasn't working . . . her mind knew the only way to save herself and Hallit and Lys was to kill Alexis, but her emotions were reacting against murdering him. When he is gone, her mind told her, our lives will continue as before. Lys and I will ride in the yellow fields which will come alive and tremble with love and butterflies . . . Just then Alexis came out—alone— and climbed into the car and started up. She glanced at her watch —five minutes she had waited in the car. The morphine was working now. She was numb. She stayed huddled on the floor, feeling nothing at all, and when the car slowed down she knew they had reached the Langata junction where Alexis would have to come almost to a stop. She straightened up from behind his seat, put the gun to his head, and pulled the trigger. Just like that.

The noise seemed deafening and he jerked forward and sideways, half slumped over the wheel. The car stalled. She got out, and carefully using her bathrobe for everything she touched—to conceal her fingerprints—she closed the door behind her, walked around to the driver's door, and opened it. She still felt nothing—no fear, no joy, no relief—not even the awareness of feeling nothing. She didn't even wonder if Alexis had known what had happened to him at the last second.

Still clutching the long skirt of her bathrobe she shoved him over—he toppled sideways quite easily—and climbed into the driver's seat. She started the car and drove it a little way down the dirt track opposite the Langata junction. Then she walked, neither slowly nor quickly, across an empty field. She glanced back once and saw the car lights glowing—she had forgotten to turn them off—but the fact did not worry her, and still she felt nothing at all. Halfway home she buried the gun.

When she reached the house and let herself in she saw by the clock in the hall that just over half an hour had elapsed since she had left and realized that probably neither Lys nor Hallit were aware that she had been gone. As she climbed the stairs she heard voices in Hallit's room, so she opened his door and said dully, "I killed him."

Both Lysbeth and Hallit whirled around and looked at her as if they had not properly heard what she had said. Without any emotion she stared at them vapidly and repeated, "I killed him. Now we three can continue where we left off."

There was silence.

More silence.

No one said anything. Both Hallit and Lysbeth continued to stare at her—that was all. Then they noticed the great streak of blood on her bathrobe and the earth on her hands, and when she repeated, for the third time, "I killed him . . ." Lysbeth screamed, and Hallit rushed to Jujubee, took her by the shoulders, and shook her, shouting, "What are you talking about?"

Very calmly, Jujubee answered, "I took the gun from your purse, Lys—you left it on my bed. I hid in the back seat of his car, and when he stopped at the Langata Road turn-off, I killed him. Now you won't marry him, Lys. You'll stay with us—won't she, Hallit?"

"Oh, God!" said Hallit, aghast.

Lysbeth raced at Jujubee, screaming, "You killed him? *You killed him!*" and started tearing at Jujubee's face with her hands. Hallit pulled Lys away and forced her into the big wing chair; she put her head in her hands and began to weep. Jujubee was still just standing there. Mechanically, like a wound-up doll, she recited

208

to Hallit, "The war is over, the conqueror is vanquished, your kingdom is restored."

"Come, Jujubee, come to your room with me." As he led her down the passage, he asked gently, "Where's the gun, Jujubee?"

"I buried it."

Hallit saw the syringe on the bed, confirming what he had suspected for some months. "Give yourself some more now, so you can sleep." She obeyed as if she were a robot. She filled the syringe and put the needle into her other arm this time. "Get into bed now, Jujubee," Hallit said, still gently, but impatient to get back to Lysbeth, and without taking off her robe, but slipping her shoes off, Jujubee got into bed and lay down quietly, but her eyes were still staring blankly. "I'll be back in a few minutes. Just stay there and rest."

In his own room, Lysbeth was crumpled into the chair, sobbing loudly now. "Jesus," was all he was able to say. He picked up the bottle he had brought upstairs with him when he had come in and poured two stiff brandies. Handing one to Lys, he told her to drink it, and threw his own back in one gulp. Pulling up a straight-back chair, he sat facing her and watched her hands tremble as she drank her drink.

"What are we going to do?" she whispered.

"I don't know yet. Hopefully we have a few hours before the police . . ."

"Oh, God," wailed Lys, and got up and started to pace back and forth, wringing her hands and sobbing. "I can't believe it. I just can't believe it . . . he's dead, he's dead . . ."

Then she broke down completely, crying hysterically, moaning into Hallit's shoulder as he held her. It was more than half an hour before he had soothed her sufficiently for her even to be able to understand anything he said. "I'll give you something to calm you down. You've got to rest—and I've got to think." From the medicine cabinet in the bathroom, he took two strong sleeping pills. "Come, I'll sit with you until you sleep." She leaned against him sobbing as they went into her bedroom. He pulled her sweater dress over her head, undressed her, and covered her when she lay down. He sat on the bed stroking her hair and saying, "Ssssshhh, don't talk now, don't talk now, my love," until finally she drifted off into a drugged sleep. On the way back to his study he looked in at Jujubee, who lay there with her eyes still wide open, but she

209

hadn't looked at him when he had entered, nor now as he went to- ward her. At first he wondered if she were dead too, but then he realized she was just in a morphine daze. Back in his room he poured himself another drink and sat down with it in the leather chair.

Jujubee killed him. Christ! Well, she did—so go on—*think!* he told himself. Forcing thoughts, he continued, Why did she kill him? Why? Because she didn't want to see her life here end, and it would have had Lysbeth gone off to South Africa with him? But it was more than that. She must have been so upset for me. She must have killed him for me and for Lysbeth—to keep us together. Yes, that must be it—that's why she did it. Remarkable. I could protect her. . . . No one would know it was my gun that is miss- ing because no one knows I had that gun here—it has never been licensed. No one would suspect the weapon came from here, and if it comes to that, no one could prove it. Why would anyone suspect Jujubee of killing Otis anyway? Christ, even *I* don't know why she did, except she's slightly mad anyway, emotional at times, and drugged tonight on top of it. On our way home I told her I wouldn't be able to cope if this thing with Lysbeth was any more than romance. When Lysbeth came in and said she was going to marry him, Jujubee panicked—for me. I looked distraught pur- posefully—more so than I actually was—because I was going to make my "attack" when Lysbeth got rid of Otis. That was part of it—to capture Lysbeth's sympathy. I must admit I was surprised when she said she was going to marry him, but I had anticipated the possibility—her almost thinking she should marry him—as a re- action to the evening. But she wasn't serious—I know that. Even if she had gone off with him, having persuaded Jujubee to tell me, she would have been back by morning—when the drama had evaporated and only the facts were left to deal with. Why, when I was talking to her in here just now, right after Otis left she was . . . but I must think of what to do *now*. His thoughts whirled around and around, but with a conscious effort, he forced himself to apply logic: Jujubee killed Otis for my sake—she was fighting for me from the beginning tonight, refusing to tell me Lysbeth was going off with him, insisting that Lysbeth tell me herself. But no one would ever suspect Jujubee killed him, or that she did it for me. Yes, I must protect her. I must . . . Let's see, Alexis' car will be found with him in it, dead. Then the police will discover

210

he has been shot. There will be no murder weapon. They will look for a motive and will learn that Lysbeth and Alexis had an affair, and that I knew about it. Christ, *I* will be their suspect! I, they will say, am the only one with a motive. But they will then learn that I not only knew about it, but approved because I toasted them at the Grill Room—"May your marriage be all that you wish." I said it in front of nine other people—eight now—Jesus. But eight people did hear it—funny how people turn into witnesses through no doing of their own. So, I have eight witnesses—seven, if one's wife can't testify—to say that I not only accepted the fact of Lysbeth's affair with Otis, but that I gave them my blessing . . . that's it! No one, especially the police, would ever believe that the real reason I toasted Lysbeth and Otis was just a bit of histrionics to bring this ridiculous situation to a head and get it over with, so I must say I knew they were going to be married, but that I didn't mind. Oh, I cared, certainly, but I had accepted the fact, for alas, what else could I do? After all, I will tell them, I am quite a bit older than she. I am a man absorbed in my work—which often separated my wife and me. Otis was young and could be with Lys all the time—could give her children—I'll even throw that in . . . all those things. Yes, that toast is my perfect alibi—it will demonstrate my innocence because it will prove that I had no motive for murdering him. I could convince any police officer, any judge and jury that I am innocent—because I am.

Yes, this is what will be done: we—Lysbeth, Jujubee, and I—will all say we cannot imagine who murdered Otis. The three of us are . . . staggered . . . shocked. Jujubee and I came right home after the Grill Room and went to our rooms. An hour later, we both heard Otis' car come up the drive, and we will both say—individually—that we heard Lys and Otis come into the house together and about five minutes afterward, we heard Otis leave and the car drive off. Lys came upstairs and spoke to each of us for a few minutes, which will prove we were all here. Alexis drove away and was murdered. We are shocked. Who could have murdered him? A jealous girl friend? An Arab? An Afrikaner? None of *us* certainly had a motive. Lys was in love with him and about to marry him, I had known it for quite a long time and was reconciled to it—had, in fact, even toasted their happiness that very evening. And Jujubee would have no motive at all—Jujubee as the murderer would not even occur to anyone. When she is ques-

211

tioned routinely this morning she will say, "Of course Lys and Otis were lovers—they've been having an affair for months—yes, of course Lord Lindsey knew . . ."

Hallit realized he had been sitting there for two hours. He got up and poured himself another drink, walked to the door and stepped out onto the upstairs terrace into the African night. His thoughts continued, I will probably be arrested—not at first, but they will come to it sooner or later for they will find no other motives or clues. I will also be acquitted because they will never be able to prove I killed him, especially since I did not. He went over it and over it, and just before dawn the phone rang. It was the police saying an African policeman on his rounds had found what they thought to be the body of Dr. Alexis Otis by the Langata Road, and they had informed the hospital who suggested they call the Lindseys since there was no next of kin and they were known to be his closest friends. Hallit feigned disbelieving shock and was careful to ask how the *accident* had happened. He was told they could "disclose no details" at the time but would call him again in the morning.

A few minutes later there was a knock on his door. "Come in," he said.

Jujubee stood by the door, in a clean robe, and said, "Call the police and tell them I killed him." She was totally "sober" now.

"I'll do no such thing. Nor will you. You killed him, but you did it for me. I will not let you go to jail for my sake. He's dead— nothing can be done for him. But there's no need for the law to punish you—you'll punish yourself enough. I have it all worked out"—he raised a hand—"no, don't interrupt. Sit down. This is how it's going to be: You have no idea who killed Otis. You are as shocked as everyone else. You came home with me last night, we went to our separate rooms and an hour later Lysbeth came in with Otis. He stayed about five minutes, then you heard him drive off. Lysbeth came upstairs and talked first to you, then to me. I'll go over with you both what was said . . . what do you mean you're no actress? You act all the time. Now don't ask questions—just listen and answer carefully. Is the gun truly buried and did you touch the body or steering wheel—could they pick up from your fingerprints?"

"Hallit—this is outrageous . . ."

"Of course it is—the whole situation is outrageous, but your going to jail isn't going to make it any better, is it? Or bring Otis back to life—not that I'd even suggest it if it were possible. Look, Lysbeth will get over this, and our lives will go on as before. You couldn't be with Lysbeth if you're doing a murder rap in jail, could you?"

Suddenly Jujubee looked hopeful, as if perhaps there was a chance, "No," she answered, thinking hard, "I left no fingerprints. When I opened the car door to get both in and out I wrapped my bathrobe around the handles. I touched nothing, and the gun will never be found."

"Good girl. Now, is there anything that you can think of that could incriminate you? Any clues? Did you leave your cigarette butt or any of that movie stuff? No one will suspect you, so they won't be looking for . . ."

"They'll suspect *you*. . . . Christ, Hallit, this is ridiculous—I can't get away with it."

"Of course *you* couldn't get away with it, but with my help and with my direction you'll get away with it." He poured her a drink, handed it to her, and with a smile said, "Will you deprive me of this great challenge?"

"They'll arrest you . . . they'll say you're the only one with a motive."

"How marvelous. Innocent and jailed! It gets better by the moment. Look, Jujubee, some people *should* be dead, and Otis is one of them. There is no loss really—some other doctor will get his monkey's hearts to work in people, and if they don't, it will be better for the world's population problem anyway—so there's no loss in any direction. So be it. But for you to go to jail is absurd."

"But it's not absurd for you to go to jail?" asked Jujubee sarcastically.

"But I am innocent! How could they prove I did it? They must acquit me. They may not even arrest me—I have eight witnesses who heard me give that toast. I will say . . ." and he went on to explain again to her what he, what all of them were going to say and why.

"I can see one problem," said Jujubee, interrupting him. "What makes you think Lys is going to go along with all of this? She'll want my neck—after all, I did kill someone she . . ."

". . . *thought* she was in love with. I'll convince her. In fact, I'll go and talk to her now. The problem is not so much getting her to

213

agree, as being able to get her to do it convincingly. I'll carry it off stunningly, and you'll be all right, but I'm not so sure Lysbeth won't break down . . . let me see if she's still sleeping."

Jujubee poured herself another drink, and in a few seconds Hallit was back saying Lys was still asleep, and before he awakened her he wanted to go over everything with Jujubee just one more time. There were no flaws, he said, and Jujubee had to agree. She must wash her blood-stained bathrobe and her shoes. She asked, "What if they don't acquit you, but find you guilty for some wrong reason. It could happen, you know."

"Then you can confess."

"They might not believe me."

"Then you can dig up the gun," he answered logically.

Realizing that was a perfect insurance, she asked, "Why are you doing this for me?"

"Why not? I am feeling generous today—much better than yesterday. Otis is no longer an issue, and I have nothing to lose. And it may be interesting. I will appear to be a hero in Lysbeth's eyes—and in yours—and in my own. And—it may make a great film . . . my next film may be a murder case. . . ."

He tried to cheer her up, but Jujubee had never felt worse. Here was Hallit, whom she had betrayed every instant she had been in his house, not just by wanting his wife but by having her—protecting her because he thought she had killed Alexis for his sake.

But Lys knew better—Lys knew the truth. What if *she* told Hallit? A few hours earlier Jujubee hadn't cared about anything because she had anticipated the end of her own life—the possibility of being hanged for murder. But now Hallit had given her a chance—not simply to live, but to live with him and Lys as before, and without Otis; and the idea was more than attractive to her.

"Hallit, don't you think it would be a good idea if I took Lys up to the farm today—to get her out of this, so she won't go to pieces —to let her get a hold of herself?" Jesus, I am a bitch, she thought.

Hallit said, "We'll all have to go through some sort of questioning first, I suppose—then you can go."

"You'll join us as soon as you can, won't you?"

"Of course. I'll . . ." and the phone rang. Hallit picked it up, noticing as he did so that dawn was breaking, and nodded at Jujubee that it was the police again.

While he was talking Jujubee seized her chance to go into Lys's

214

room to talk to her. Jujubee sat on the bed and called her name and Lys opened her eyes but closed them again immediately.

"Listen," said Jujubee. "You must listen very carefully and very quickly. Hallit is not going to leave you because he isn't convinced you were going to marry Alexis. I must say, I thought he would quit, but he won't—not now, at any rate. He is going to stay with you, and he is also going to protect me."

Jujubee saw a frown of agony cross Lys's face, but she continued, "I know you don't want me protected, I know that you hate me now, but you will come to understand why I did it. However, we haven't time for that now. What you *must* listen to is the fact that Hallit does *not* know about you and me. I thought maybe he knew that too, since he knew about you and Alexis—which we thought he didn't—but he does *not* know about us. If he finds that out it *will* be the end—he would leave you because although he might be able to tolerate a few months of silly romantic aberration, he'd never tolerate something that has gone on for over a year right in his own house. That's something he could never understand. Oh, he'd understand our relationship, but he'd not be able to accept our dishonesty, and you know he would leave you if he finds out. And he would divorce you without your getting anything—without money, without this house, and without your reputation, for he would tell everyone about us and it wouldn't miss a newspaper in any country. So, if you tell Hallit you won't protect me because I killed Alexis, then I'll tell him *why* I killed Alexis, and destroy both of us—because Hallit would turn me in, then ruin you. I'd be in jail and unable to help you and no one else would sympathize. So, if you won't protect me, you'll go down with me. I'll make sure of that. Hallit thinks now that my motive for killing Alexis was for his—Hallit's—sake, so that you two could stay together. If you tell him anything different, then I'll tell him the truth, and it will be the end for both of us."

"Do you really hate me enough to do that?" Lys asked, opening her eyes for the first time.

"No, I love you enough. So much so that it has driven me almost insane. I want to be with you at any cost—I am capable of anything now. If you just keep quiet, everything will work out. Keep quiet until you are sure you know what you want. Keep quiet until you have time to think out the consequences. We can go to the farm this afternoon, and there you can hate me and

215

scream and throw things at me, and if you decide I still must go to jail, you can always come back to Nairobi and turn me in. But for God's sake, don't say anything now—not just for me—for yourself . . . here comes Hallit . . ."

Jujubee told Hallit she had peeked in the room just as Lys was awakening, and she had suggested to Lys they go to the farm. Giving Hallit her place by Lys, Jujubee left—or pretended to leave. She stayed outside the door to hear what was said.

"My darling, my poor darling. Lysbeth, you must listen carefully—we haven't much time, I'm afraid, because the police are on their way here. Do as I say, exactly as I say, and we can talk it out later. We must protect Jujubee. It will be painful for you to do so right now, but you would never forgive yourself later on if you betrayed her. I know, you will say that it is she who has betrayed you, that yours is a reaction not an action, but you must consider, my love, *why* she betrayed you—she did it for me, and for you— for both of us. Her going to jail isn't any answer—it won't bring Otis back, and if you decide later on that you still want to punish her, you can do it much more effectively if she isn't in jail. Or you can turn her in later—you will still have that choice. But right now you must say that when you returned from the Grill Room last night Alexis came in with you for about ten minutes, left, and then you talked to both Jujubee and me for a few more minutes, and then we all went to bed. None of us can imagine who killed him. All right?"

Jujubee's future hung suspended in that moment of silence which followed. Standing right behind the door, Jujubee actually held her breath until she heard Lysbeth mutter, "All right."

"Did anyone—Doria, Mwangi, anyone—know you had that gun with you yesterday? No? Good. Now listen carefully, you must get these details . . . you will say you came home at 12:30 . . ."

Jujubee turned and went quietly toward her room to begin the job of washing her bathrobe and shoes.

Hallit sat on the bed and looking down into Lysbeth's swollen eyes, he continued, ". . . Alexis came into the hall with you and stayed about five minutes and then you went upstairs and talked to Jujubee for approximately fifteen minutes. Then you came in and talked to me. Right after you came into my room, Jujubee brought us drinks, then left immediately—this is an important point. It will do two things. First, it will establish that the three of us were here, and secondly it will account for the glasses and ice bucket down-stairs this morning if they question Mwangi—Jujubee got the drinks. This will save you from having to say what you were talk-ing to Alexis about—he was only here for five minutes. You talked to Jujubee about my reaction to your affair with Alexis and how marvelous it was that I understood. Then you came into my room and thanked me for being so understanding. You stayed with me for about fifteen minutes too—just long enough to finish your drink—a brandy—then you said you were tired and that we would continue talking in the morning. On your way to your room you called good night to Jujubee because her light was on—you could see it from under the door."

Just then the phone rang again. "I'll take it in my room," said Hallit, leaving.

It was William who had just heard the news. Hallit talked to him briefly and then called to Jujubee who took it on another ex-tension. Hallit returned to Lys. "Listen, my love, this part will all be over in a short while . . . if you can just get through this morn-ing. You must say you called good night to Jujubee and she to you—this was about 1:45 or 2 A.M. They will establish that Alexis died around 1 or 1:30 A.M.—so this will cover all three of us. Remember, no one was upset about anything. None of us had cross words—I merely told you that if you wanted to marry Alexis Otis, it would be absurd for me to try to stop you. That what would I possibly want with a wife who was in love with somebody else? That I understood these things could happen—of course I was sad, but completely resigned."

"What if they find the gun?" asked Lysbeth weakly.

"It'll never be found. Jujubee buried it. Now listen, the police will understand why you are so upset. You will only have to say what I have told you once, and then you can go with Jujubee to the farm . . . this afternoon."

"Where will you be?"

"I'll stay here to sort this out."

"Why are you doing this?"

"Why not?"

"Do you know that I love you?"

"I know that."

"They'll arrest you."

"Perhaps, but it could be most interesting—amusing, even. If I'm

217

charged with murder, you as my wife can't testify, so don't worry. I'll take care of it, you know I will. I might even enjoy it." He smiled at her. "It could be my greatest moment."

"No! I can't let you do it!" Lysbeth flung her arms around Hallit, clinging to him.

Just then the doorbell rang. Jujubee answered it, and they heard police voices downstairs.

"You *must* let me, Lysbeth. I love you. I can cope—I want to do this. If you feel you owe me any debt—for Alexis—you can repay me by letting me do this."

Jujubee called Hallit and he went downstairs while Lysbeth stayed in bed, thinking. Then, slowly, very slowly, she got out of bed and put on a flowing white-satin robe, and looking ghostlike, she started down the stairs clutching the bannister, then stopped. The inspector looked up from the hall and said, "Lady Lindsey, sorry about the—death of Dr. Otis." Lysbeth, still standing on the stairs, was silent, and everyone waited for her to say something, but she said nothing. Hallit's blue eyes pleaded with her, and Jujubee's green eyes pleaded with her, and the inspector, already aware of the presence of a beautiful woman, asked, "Lady Lindsey, I know this is a dreadful time for you, but could I just have a few words with you? Would you care to sit in the drawing room—it won't take long?"

"If it won't take long, I'd rather just stay here. What is it you'd like to know?" asked Lysbeth in an unnatural voice as she continued down the stairs.

"Could you tell me what time you got home last night?" asked the inspector, but he was thinking as she walked down the stairs so slowly, her white robe dragging behind her accentuating her grief, that she looked rather like a bride without a bridegroom. He felt sad. As well as lustful.

Hallit and Jujubee knew this next moment would determine the course of their lives. Lysbeth walked close enough to the inspector so she could look into his eyes, and at that moment Jujubee knew all was safe, for Lys always said, "Look them right in the eyes and lie." Hallit also knew at that same moment for he realized that Lysbeth was planning to use her eyes on the inspector and would go through with the story.

They heard her saying, "It was just 12:30 A.M. when Dr. Otis and I arrived here from the Grill Room. I noticed the clock when we walked in. He came in with me and stayed for about five minutes, then he left."

"Did you see anyone else?" asked the inspector, trying to appear professional and hoping it wasn't obvious that he noticed that . . . that . . . quality about her which was making him want to take her in his arms and protect her from all of this.

"Yes. I saw my husband—and Baroness Boucher. First I went to her room and we talked for a few minutes—fifteen or so. Then I went to my husband's room and we talked."

"Do you remember for how long?"

"Another quarter hour or so. Juju . . . Baroness Boucher brought us drinks—so it was enough time for us to drink them. Another ten minutes at least."

"May I ask what your conversation with Lord Lindsey was about?" asked the inspector gently.

"We were discussing the possibility of a divorce. He was being very co-operative, and I thanked him for it." Then turning to Hallit, but still speaking to the inspector, she said, "He's a much more astonishing man than you, or anyone but I and Baroness Boucher, will ever know."

The inspector paused a moment as if in respect to her tribute to Hallit, then asked, "Did Baroness Boucher stay and have a drink with you?"

Jujubee's heart quickened because Lys had dropped her eyes and obviously was thinking of something—was she trying to decide if she should . . . Jujubee recognized that expression and knew that Lys knew this was her last chance of telling the truth—that if she concealed the knowledge about Jujubee now, she would be committed to it forever that no one would ever know. Lys didn't answer. She just stood there clutching the bannister and staring at the floor. The inspector coughed slightly, then said, "Lady Lindsey, did Baroness Boucher stay and have a drink with you and Lord Lindsey?"

Lys looked up at him and still in a strangely soft voice said, "Oh, I'm sorry, Inspector—my mind drifted . . . ummmm . . . what was it?—oh, no, Baroness Boucher went right back to her room. She didn't stay with my husband and me, but when I left his room I saw the light was still on in Jujubee's room, so we called good night to each other . . . it must have been at least 1:45 or

2 A.M. by then. Is there anything else? If not, would you excuse me, please?"

"Thank you, Lady Lindsey—that's all—sorry to have bothered you."

"We just heard about this a short while ago—it's very . . . shocking," said Lys.

"Yes, yes, terrible . . ." muttered the inspector, trying hard not to show how very much he wanted to gather this poor little delicate sparrow to him and kiss her—kiss away all her grief.

And she turned and glided up the stairs.

So immersed in thought that he didn't even realize he was sitting in the dark, Hallit reflected, yes, that's how it would be if Jujubee were the murderer. Leaning across the table to switch on the light he said to himself, "Well, now to the last name in the hat—Hallit—me. Let's see, where to begin?" He got up and opened a new bottle of gin for he had finished the first one, and while mixing himself a fresh martini he decided he'd start the version of his being the murderer at that fatal dinner party when William first introduced Otis into their lives.

Hallit: Murderer?

At the dinner party the Lindseys gave that night, William asked if anyone at the table remembered seeing a cover story in *Time* about a Dr. Otis of South Africa who had made a major break-through in overcoming rejection problems following heart transplants and who had received much publicity for his technique in a series of operations performed in Russia. He further explained how Otis was joining the Flying Surgeons in Kenya to work with the Maasai for a year to do heart research. Lysbeth said it might make a good story, and William confessed that was why he had told her—he wanted the publicity for the Flying Surgeons—would she make an appointment with Dr. Otis?

She promised to do so when Jujubee left for Paris few days later.

During the next three months Hallit grew aware that he and Lysbeth had developed a different pattern of living from their former existence, not out of choice, but dictated by the fact that Lysbeth had had to go to Ethiopia, then he had had to go London and Lysbeth to South Africa; and even when they were home together he saw little of her because he was so busy. Although he worked best under pressure, he was torn because much as he loved his work, he was nevertheless saddened by not having enough time to spend with Lys. But she knew that his work was his passion and had accepted this from the beginning—in fact she seemed not to mind at all and she didn't complain about his preoccupation saying she was taking advantage of the situation to get caught up on her rest by going to bed early almost every night. How nice it was, he reflected, to have a wife who didn't depend on him every minute for her happiness. She depended on him for her state of well being, but with the knowledge that he loved her she could motivate her own happiness without him for a few weeks at a time, and she had always been able to enjoy her own company. "Our two minds met, respected, and loved each other—became one yet remained two—the perfect situation," Hallit was fond of telling anyone who was interested, and even those who weren't. Sometimes late at night he would go into Lysbeth's room and sit on her bed. She would awaken and he would tell her how sorry he was he had not been with her more and she would say, "But just think how we're going to enjoy life when your film is finished," smiling sleepily at him. "You act as if you have duped me. You haven't, you know—I knew you were a film maker when I married you. As long as I know you're in the house, or in Nairobi even, then I feel as if everything's all right. You have enough to worry about with your film—you don't have to worry about me—it's needless. I love you, Hallit."

And he would take her in his arms and make beautiful love to her.

One day he learned he had a free evening sandwiched between two weeks of work so he telephoned Lysbeth from his office and said, "Hey, may I have a date with my wife tonight?"

"What do you mean?" asked Lysbeth gaily.

"I mean I have the whole night off and would like to be with you alone."

"Oh, darling, Jujubee's invited Alexis Otis here for dinner tonight . . ."

"So, let her have—whoever it is—and we'll go out. Where would you like to . . ."

"Oh, Hallit, I promised Jujubee I'd be here. Listen, you and I like being home more than anywhere, so come on home now—it's five o'clock—come now instead of at seven. We'll be alone here for two whole hours, we can walk in the garden in the sunset, and then you can make the time up by working two hours after dinner while I talk to them."

"Fine—be right there."

That walk around their garden with Lysbeth was the last happy thing Lord Hallit Lindsey ever did in his life.

Jujubee drove in while they were still in the garden and Hallit called to her and teased her about having a new boy friend and how he was going to tell William. Just before eight Hallit went into the living room and found Jujubee there but Lysbeth had not yet come downstairs. The two of them had a drink and Hallit asked where William was. "He's not in Nairobi until tomorrow—but this doctor is someone I just met—nothing serious at all."

"Is William serious?"

"Yes," answered Jujubee. "In fact, I've never taken anyone so seriously before—and who would ever have thought . . ."

Just then the doorbell rang, Lysbeth rushed down the stairs and then came into the drawing room with Alexis. Hallit had planned to pretend he remembered him because Lysbeth had told him he had been at their house to dinner once before, but the minute Otis walked in Hallit felt an instant wave of dislike and recalled how he had been gun shy of him on that earlier occasion. This was an unusual reaction for Hallit—not that he liked most people but usually they affected him not at all. He felt the same indifference toward the majority of those he met that he felt for a nondescript lampshade. But this dislike reappeared the moment he saw Otis again and persisted for no reason at all. Hallit thought to himself, how terribly unfair—poor bloke hasn't said one word and already I want to kick him out. Maybe certain people give off chemicals that attract or repel others.

"Tell me about Hollywood," said Otis, sitting down and accepting a drink from Lysbeth. "I've always wanted to go there—what's it like?"

"Revolting."

"I have heard they even have topless weddings now."

"Soon they'll be having topless funerals . . ."

"Wow—I'm such a . . . tit man . . . that I'll admit I might even like that. Are you a leg man or a tit man, Hallit?"

"I'm a crotch man," answered Hallit lightly without pause for thought, and by having gone straight to the heart of the matter, so to speak, made Otis appear even more puerile by contrast. Then he added, "I could never get excited, as some men do, about bosoms—I equate big bosoms with stupidity and small ones with intelligence. In the Playboy Clubs I hear the only requirement to be a bunny is that your IQ doesn't exceed your bosom size."

"Have you ever been in the Playboy Club in Johannesburg?"

"I can think of no worse combination than a Playboy Club and Johannesburg. . . ."

"I beg your pardon?"

"Nothing—no, I have never been to a Playboy Club, nor to

South Africa. And I never shall. I would rather spend a week in the Mayo Clinic than a weekend in South Africa. What are your views on apartheid?"

"I don't have any political views . . ."

"How can anyone *not* have political views?"

"I stick to medicine . . ."

"If you are going to dedicate your life to one thing, you must not spread yourself about, but concentrate in that one area . . ." said Lysbeth, trying to make up for what she considered to be Hallit's rudeness.

Then, not wishing to embarrass her, Hallit made an effort, not so much out of kindness but rather through an innate sense of justice, in trying to offset his negative feelings, and said, "Yes, I suppose that's what's good about being in the film business—it encompasses all the arts, politics, philosophy—everything. You certainly have made a name for yourself in the field of medicine, Otis. It must be very rewarding for you—it must give you a great deal of happiness . . ."

"No more, I suppose, than anyone else. Why should I be any happier than a . . . street cleaner, for example?" asked Otis with what Hallit was sure he thought was his charming smile.

"*Why?* Are you joking?" asked an astonished Hallit.

"No. None of us can help what we are . . . looking at it in the socio-psychological sense, no one can help what he or she is. We are all victims of society. Even if someone steals, it isn't his fault—there is always a reason. Perhaps he is underprivileged. If someone takes heroin how can you blame *him*—he may have been rejected by his mother and have such a sense of inferiority that he is unable to cope with . . ."

"What are you a victim of?" interrupted Hallit.

"I am a victim of success," answered Alexis, quoting a remark he had heard.

"What rubbish," said Hallit adamantly. "You worked for that medical degree—for how long—ten years? You've earned your success. You should enjoy it." He was becoming angry now. "'Victims of society'—the all-time alibi. Jesus, it makes me sick. I don't care what happened to anyone as a child, there comes a time when a person must make something of *himself*. By his own convictions and strength he must transcend his background, whether that may be the ghetto where his dope addict mother throws the garbage out the window of the fourth floor walk-up while her half-wit brother screws her, or whether it's a background of indolent aristocracy. There comes a time when a youth must say to himself, 'My father's a homosexual junkie and my mother beats me every day before she goes off to shoplift at the corner store, but I am going to be great—I am going to rise above it all because I am alive and life is a gift to be enjoyed, and I am going to seek and find that joy.' Equally, someone born in a palace with a silver spoon in his mouth may say, 'My family and surroundings are decadent and so on, and I must rise above it.' And even if his family aren't decadent, he must use the advantages of affluence and education and insulation from hardship as a springboard to meaningful work of his own—and I don't just mean making money. Many unimaginative idiots can do that. I see that man's happiness stems from his ability to live up to what is the best in himself, not the worst. I see that the junkies and the uneducated peasants are not the people who form the world or contribute to it in any way.

"I want to leave the world a better place than when I came into it by contributing something—an idea, some laughter, a discovery . . . Why? For the sake of humanity? No! For my own sake, for my own pleasure, because it would give *me* the greatest pleasure I can imagine. If it also happens to be a contribution for everyone else too, fine—all the better—but to do something only for the sake of someone else is not my motivation. Nor is it yours."

Refilling his martini glass, he held up his hand to stop Lysbeth interrupting and continued, "All of us here and most people in our immediate circle are lucky enough to have been born into the less than one per cent of the world's fortunate people. We weren't born a low caste in India or an African in South Africa—our birth is a precious gift, and it is also a responsibility. We have the freedom, health, education, and opportunity to do something with our lives. Hell—even a prostitute from the New York slums has a better chance at joy than an Indian in the squalor of Bombay or a Bantu in Johannesburg. Every person born in the Western world should be in love with his life, yet so many people who have been given this opportunity fuck it up with booze or drugs or a weakness of a worse kind—opting out, doing nothing, and claiming they are victims of society because they don't have everything—even the luxuries—given to them. What they forget is that they have the opportunity, which thousands never do, to earn

229

whatever it is they want. But they don't want to *earn* anything. They wallow in self-pity and say, 'Don't blame me—it isn't my fault I'm an unhappy failure. I'm a victim of society.' And so they blow their lives. When I look at these people—the young drug addict, the older alcoholic—it's all I can do to keep from screaming at them, 'How did you let yourself come to this? Why did you throw your life away? What else do you think you have?'"

"Can't it be that you are a victim of geography and time?" asked Lys timidly, finding herself thrown off by Hallit's burst of unaccustomed vehemence. "I mean, can't it be that because you are in a certain place at a certain time you meet someone who . . . changes your whole life—which would not have happened if you hadn't been there? For example, you and I met on the ship . . ."

"Yes, but if I had not liked you do you think I would have said, 'Because we've met, we must marry'? Victims of fate and geography only exist if you want to pretend they do. That kind of thing is fine for bad theater or poetry, but it isn't valid. You have a mind with which to make your own decisions."

Lysbeth asked, "But what if we *hadn't* met on the ship? What does that make you think?"

"That has nothing to do with thinking. That has to do with contemplating the unknown which is an utter waste of time. Being a victim of society works both ways—it excuses us from ever being wrong, but it also robs us of ever being good. If I do something right, or when I achieve excellence, I want the credit and the praise I've earned, and I want it from myself and from others whose opinion I value. But looking at it in your socio-psychological way, Otis, if I save a man from drowning, I am told I did it to ease my guilt complex or to satisfy my ego or because that person is important to my state of well being. I am told I did it to satisfy my psychological needs. What crap! I did it because I am generous and courageous, and that makes me an admirable hero."

"So therefore what you are saying is that good and bad no longer exist," stated Alexis uncomfortably.

"That is what *you* are saying! You will also tell me there is no such thing as free will and that man is nothing more than an animal driven by psychological and physical needs and that we must respect his needs." Then turning to Lys, he went on, "This is why Alexis is no happier than his street cleaner—because he doesn't accept the joy of his own achievements." Glaring at Alexis, he continued, "Why don't you acknowledge you have worked hard and well and earned your right to be happy? I think it's a sin to be great—which you are in your field—and not to exult in it. I hate creative or brilliant people who lack a proper self-esteem."

"I've never hated anyone."

"Then I feel sorry for you."

"*Sorry* for me?"

"Yes, sorry for you, because if you've never hated, then you've never loved. If you can tolerate the intolerable, it is only because you don't expect anything from anybody—that you'll accept any form of unacceptable behavior, any lack of integrity, any hideosity—anything. Therefore, you do not risk being disappointed when people fail to respond nobly—you feel only indifference. And the person who is indifferent and has no passions either way is the most unhappy man."

"But all of us—Christians, Jews, Moslems, Buddhists—are taught that God wants us to love—not to hate."

"To say that is to assume there is—forgive the expression—a God."

"You don't believe in any form of superior being?"

"Oh, yes, very definitely. I believe in men who have superior intelligence and ability. I've never heard of any unknown superior being writing a great book, composing a great score of music, discovering how to transmit sound waves, building a great airplane . . . but when it happens, I'll pay attention. Until then it's a waste of time."

Jujubee, who hadn't said a word, commented, "Every time I look for God, I find myself."

"Why," exclaimed Hallit, "would you not say, Jujubee, you are deeply involved in religion?"

"Dinner's ready," said Lysbeth with relief at the sound of the bell, hoping the break would change the conversation, but the minute they were seated, much to Lysbeth's distress—didn't he know he would never win with Hallit?—Alexis said, "Hallit, getting back to the 'victims of society,' have you no pity for anyone?"

"I hope not—pity is an ugly emotion."

"Don't you feel sorry—say—even for some of your friends because their lives may not be so full or significant as yours?

231

Don't you go to them to give them some joy, to share some of your good fortune—to make them happy—because they need you?"

"No, not for the sake of their need. I may do it because *I* want to but never because *they need me*—what kind of reason is that? The only relationships that are any good are the ones stemming from mutual consent and mutual benefits."

"The law of mutual consent and goosepimples," said Lys, "is a good code to live by."

Hallit went on, "The only relationships I have with people are when I am seeking my own pleasure and they are seeking their own pleasure. Anything else is false. Everything I do is for my own pleasure, but I must never impinge upon the rights of others. I make movies for my own pleasure. Why do you do whatever it is you do—transplant hearts?"

"I know why I'd do it," interrupted Lysbeth, "I'd do it so that *I'd* be able to live longer myself. Just one more day . . ."

"Isn't that a selfish motive?" Alexis asked her.

"Of course. But selfish motives *are* the only ones that ever . . . work," Lys said.

Jujubee added, "I can't experience your joy. The only greatness that has ever existed stems from selfishness. You must learn not to think of it as an ugly word—it's a beautiful word, really."

Feeling everyone had ganged up on him, Lysbeth said, "Alexis, tell them about the new idea you have about the heart not rejecting the . . . what is it?" and Alexis spoke about his work throughout the rest of dinner.

As they walked into the drawing room for coffee, Hallit whispered to Jujubee, "Jesus, Jujubee, this one wins the asinine award—how can you like him." He expected Jujubee's reply to be something like, "He has two pricks: one of his own and one he has transplanted from an elephant?" But her answer seemed oddly out of character for all she said was, "I don't really know," and walked toward the others. Following her he said quietly, "How unJujubeeish," and as they approached Lysbeth and Otis who were sitting by the fire, he announced with a grin, "I have come to be offensive." He caught the smile that crossed Jujubee's face, and the look of disapproval on Lysbeth's, and in that instant Hallit knew something was wrong—something didn't fit. It was a fleeting feeling, not yet formed into words, but it was definitely there and it made him uneasy. No one else, of course, noticed anything, but Hallit couldn't ignore it. He ignored nothing—though frequently he dismissed things, but only after he had reasoned them out and found them to be unnoteworthy. He asked himself what it was that was bothering him. He knew it was more than his dislike of Otis—what was it? He had no answer—yet.

Lysbeth felt the uneasiness that was building through Hallit's silence, for tension is contagious, yet she was afraid that if he did speak it would only be to abuse Alexis further. In an effort to break out of the uncomfortable moment, she asked Alexis to play the piano. He was masterful at the keys but Hallit heard nothing. While Alexis played, Hallit watched Jujubee; then Lysbeth.

Then it was only Lysbeth he watched.

And then he knew.

Lysbeth . . . his Lysbeth. Every part of him responded in agony. His mind, his emotions, his body—it was total pain—much worse than any physical beating. Since he had never been in love before, he had never known jealousy, but he realized instantly it could corrupt every decent thing about him. Unable to sit there a minute longer, he excused himself and went to his study, but he did no work at all. He remembered the way he had felt when he first met Lysbeth on board the S.S. *Victoria*—he felt possessed just like a Giriama tribesman. He was still possessed—perhaps more used to it now, but nevertheless still under a spell. Suppose Otis felt this way for Lysbeth? Worse, suppose Lysbeth felt this way for Otis? How could she?—he was such a dreadful person. But he did remember her telling him once that she had been in love with men she had actually loathed—"dreadful people" had been her actual words ". . . dreadful person, yet there I was in love with him." Hallit wondered, if that was how she felt about Otis or if she was completely in love with him? Was he in love with her?

All night he tortured himself with questions and thoughts, and still awake at seven A.M. he telephoned William at the club, saying he was the only other person he knew who would be ready to leave for work at such an early hour and suggested they lunch together. Then Hallit casually asked William how long he had been in Nairobi. "Why, I came down two days ago—I wanted to come out to Ol Olua with Jujubee last night, but she said she had to have dinner with some friend of Lysbeth's—rather annoyed me,

233

but I'll see her tonight—and you at one?" Hallit's fears were confirmed.

At lunch he soon got around to asking, "What do you think of Alexis Otis?"

"Excellent man," answered William.

"Excellent man or excellent doctor?"

"Oh—excellent doctor—I don't know anything about him as a man. I hear he's quite a ladies' man, but then I never see him socially—don't know anyone here who does—just Sugar in New York. Why do you ask?"

"No reason, really . . ." answered Hallit and changed the subject.

For the next few days Hallit said nothing about it, pretended to be normal and to work, but watched Lysbeth instead. Every afternoon after lunch, Lysbeth would leave the house and every afternoon Hallit would call the hospital, and with a different voice would ask to speak to Dr. Otis. He was never there. Each night he studied Lysbeth at dinner, asked her questions, watched her responses but never let on that he knew or even suspected everything was not as it should be.

William was away now, and Jujubee sick with malaria, so Hallit hadn't seen her either. He considered talking it over with Jujubee—he knew she knew—but he also knew she would deny that Lysbeth was having an affair with Otis. She would say, "If Lysbeth lies, I'll swear to it—what else is friendship all about?" Then he would ask, "What about your friendship for me?" and Jujubee would say, "Yeah, but it was with her first. I'll do the same for you with anyone but Lys though." So, anticipating the futility of such a conversation, he dismissed discussing the subject with Jujubee.

Hallit was almost physically sick from the torture he had gone through in the past few days—how he wished he had a broken body, bubonic plague, leprosy. Anything would be less painful than this, he thought. And I am the man who used to say, "It is only pain." But that was when I knew only of physical pain, which is nothing to bear compared to this. This anguish stems from the very core of me, and I feel I cannot get away from it. He thought of nothing else all day, and all night he would lie awake thinking the same dreaded thoughts over and over again, brooding endlessly. Never before in his life had he felt or acted this way, but

234

then never had he been in love before. He didn't know what to do about it. Making decisions did not usually pose any difficulty for him, but he didn't know how to fight this. He wasn't certain of what he was up against. "Certainly not Otis—he is no competition for *me*. I am a champion, he is a weak amateur—yet I feel he is winning. Why?" he asked himself. He would toss in bed, and then, having broken out in a cold sweat, he would get up and smoke and pace back and forth as if he were trying to get away from the horror of losing her. Each night he went into her room and just stood at the foot of her bed and watched her asleep and tears filled his eyes. Then he would go back to his bed and at dawn he would drift off for a few minutes of restless sleep, and then awaken with a start and lie there agonizing again.

Mornings brought more rational thoughts and he tried to analyze what it was that made Lysbeth have an affair with Otis. If she were drawn to him at first as "superman doctor," he could understand it—there was Otis, handsome on the cover of *Time,* and fame is a powerful aphrodisiac. Hallit could concede that fame in a white coat and stethoscope might be irresistible. At first. But what happened when Lysbeth *talked* to Otis? She could admire his skill, but what about his mind?—or in his case, lack of mind? But rationalizing didn't ease the agony. His jealousy grew like a cancer inside him, but instead of destroying him cell by cell, it was as if it was turning every cell into a nucleus of violence. Anger set in at the realization that even his work had ceased to matter to him. He was also annoyed at himself for having nothing else to fall back on, no other distractions—nothing positive to counteract the negative of pain. He realized that Lysbeth was everything to him, everything, and without her nothing mattered. And Otis was trying to take her away. It was much more than losing Lysbeth, it was losing his life, for that was what she was to him; and what was as important to him as Lysbeth herself was his *desire* for her. Never before had he felt this tremendous desire, and he knew he would never experience it or find it again. He knew, too, that nothing less was worth experiencing. She made him feel alive, she gave him life by creating this superlative longing in him, and now Otis was taking that away too. He wasn't fighting against a despicable man—he was fighting for his own life. He said aloud, "I will win."

"Lord Lindsey to see you, doctor," said Otis' secretary when

Hallit walked into his office. They shook hands and nodded at each other. Hallit was the first to speak, "You are having an affair with my wife," he stated calmly but firmly, looking right into Alexis' eyes.

Otis gestured nervously at Hallit to sit down while he lit a cigarette and sat too, murmuring something that sounded like, "Are you joking?"

Hallit said nothing, but by the expression on his face and the tone of his voice Alexis knew he was not joking. Hallit just sat there and stared at Otis. Finally Otis answered, "Why ask me—why not ask Lys?"

"If you have to ask that question, then you won't understand the answer. However, make an effort—try. You see, you are not taking anything away from my *wife,* you are not doing an injustice to *her,* you are doing it to *me.* It is from me you are stealing, not her; it is to me you are being unjust, unfair, dishonest—not to her."

"But . . . she's doing the same thing I am—"

"But she is a responsible person—I know she must be struggling with herself and punishing herself. She has moral integrity and will be responsible for her actions. Even though she may claim she is a 'victim of fate' she *will* be responsible for the consequences, but you will simply claim you are a victim of circumstances and exonerate yourself. I will not allow you the luxury of this deceptive evasion. You see, integrity, honesty, faithfulness—all these things are important to me. Do they mean anything to you?"

Trying his charming smile, Otis answered nervously, and with a slight chuckle, "Aren't those things a little old-fashioned? People don't think in those terms today."

"People I value do. Lysbeth thinks in those terms—she is very much aware of them. She has standards and values."

"Well, we'll see if we can get her over them," said Otis, trying to be light-hearted and casual, hoping his attitude would defuse this dangerous situation.

Hallit glared at him and said, "You represent everything I loathe. You were born with a talent, you acquired a skill—you have a tremendous potential but you ignore your mind. You don't *think* at all. How can you separate yourself from your mind? Have you never acquired any set of convictions? Have you even given thought to serious questions? How can you determine what you value when every decision you make in life must be based on

236

some code of your own—some ethic at which you have arrived after conscious thought?" And then, while searching his face, he stopped as if he had discovered something. "Looking at you reminds me of what Paddy Chayefsky once told me: that a friend of his almost committed suicide one morning because he said he looked at himself in the mirror and 'saw no one there.' I think that's the best reason for committing suicide I have ever heard, don't you?"

". . . Are you suggesting . . . I commit suicide?"

"As a matter of fact, I wasn't. But come to think of it, it's not a bad idea. Do you want to marry her?"

"Marry her! Why . . . why . . . I hadn't thought—I enjoy her—she's whimsical . . . she's . . ."

"What do you think this is—some fucking cocktail party? This is my *wife* and my *life* you're interfering with—you who have no idea what life is all about. Christ! Why don't you want to marry her? You do love her, don't you?"

Otis put his head in his hands and didn't answer. Hallit looked at him with fury and asked in a louder voice, *"Do* you love her?"

Otis, looking defeated now, the charming smile gone completely, said softly, "I don't know what love is—you just said I don't know what life is all about—how can I know what love is? There are no absolutes."

"That is an absolute." Then came a command, phrased as a question, but demanding a response, "Do you tell her you love her?"

"Of course, but . . . only . . . casually . . ."

"Love *has* no casual side," said Hallit. "Jesus, you are doing an injustice to her too—I thought it was only me you were cheating. I assumed you loved her. . . . If not, then why Lysbeth? There are plenty of unattached women, if all you're looking for is a good lay. . . . What are you looking for? What? Why her?" and suddenly he shouted at Otis, *"Why?"*

Otis put his head back in his hands—he was coming apart—and Hallit continued, "Listen, Otis. I love Lysbeth. I want her. But just having her physical presence is no good at all, is it? I want Lysbeth, but it has to be because Lysbeth wants to be with me. Anything else would be a farce. Can you understand that? But if you love her and she loves you, then *you* two must be together. I assumed you loved her and wanted to marry her, and I came here today to tell you I was going to fight—fight to keep Lysbeth—and I would have done so by proving to her that she loved me and not you. But it would have to be *her* choice. It hadn't occurred to me that you didn't love her. But that is what you are trying to tell me, isn't it—that you are not sure if you love her or not, and that you don't want to marry her? Is that right? *Is that right?*"

"I . . . yes . . . I guess so . . . I don't want to marry her—I don't want to marry any woman."

"Why?" Hallit whispered.

"I can't tell you."

Hallit leaped out of his chair, smashed his fist on the desk and put his face close to Otis'. "Yes, you will," he hissed. "I demand to know."

Hallit stood there and looked at Otis, and Otis looked at the desk and whimpered, "I'm . . . I'm a . . . homosexual—I'm so ashamed . . ."

"Jesus," was all Hallit said. Then he sank into his chair. "There's nothing wrong with being a homosexual, but there's a hell of a lot wrong with being ashamed of it."

"I can't help it . . ."

"That's right—you can't help anything. Christ, I should have known when William said you were such a ladies' man—having to demonstrate that you're virile is proof that you're not. I don't dislike homosexuals, but I hate the ones who spend their lives trying to prove they aren't. It's all such a waste of time and effort—of everything—of life." But the feeling of relief showed in Hallit's voice, for he *was* relieved at least to the extent that he was now sure there was a good chance of getting Lysbeth back. He decided to temper his thoughts and line of action accordingly.

"Do you know what I think?" asked Otis.

"I'm astonished that you think," muttered Hallit.

"That isn't nice."

"I am *not* nice. Well, go ahead—tell me—I'm riveted."

"I think we all should forget the whole thing—I won't see Lys again . . ."

Hallit laughed cruelly. "Don't confuse my wife's standards with mine. I don't care personally that you're an insincere homosexual shit, but she may."

Otis looked horrified and said, "You wouldn't tell her, would you?"

"You're counting on my integrity, aren't you? Most bastards like you usually do—the dishonest always count on the honesty of others. No, I won't tell her. But you will. Tonight." Hallit spoke as a man accustomed to giving orders and having them obeyed. He continued. "I will help you. I will force the issue. After dinner at the Grill Room I will bring things to a head in some way—and then I will leave with Jujubee. You will drive Lysbeth home and tell her you do not want to marry her *and* the reason why."

"But . . . but . . . you can't force me to tell her . . . you can't force your ideas on me . . ."

"Neither I, nor anyone else, can force ideas on you or anyone else—be they stupid or intelligent. I can only present them to you—and it is up to you whether you accept them. You have"—Hallit stood and glanced at his watch—"two hours to decide; and I would advise you to accept them."

"But . . . I can't tell her—I can't stand the thought of her knowing. I can—perform with a woman . . . I can please her . . . she doesn't have to know . . . I . . ."

"You will tell her the truth."

As if Hallit's dignity had inspired him to try to emulate such behavior, Otis replied, " 'I will die for her, but I can't live for her.' " But his stab at honor was too little and too late.

Hallit's voice was very low and very controlled when he answered, "Yes, you will." Then he walked out of Otis' office.

Hallit had a few hours before they were all to meet in the Grill Room and he wanted to be alone, so he drove to the Nairobi Game Park and sat by the hippo pool. There were many hippos, monkeys, several giraffe, and even a lion in view, but Hallit saw none of them. He was rethinking what he had quickly decided in Otis' office: My forcing the issue of their affair with a toast to them and to their marriage will accomplish two things: One, it will let Lysbeth know I know about them, and if the method is theatrical, it will not only appeal to Lysbeth, it is more likely to produce a definite response than some gloomy confrontation where there is an opportunity for denials or excuses. Two, it will force the question of marriage with Alexis, thus leading to his confession of homosexuality. If *I* tell her he is gay, she'll be inclined to disbelieve it or think I've made it up to discredit him, and even if she does believe me, she'll resent me for being the bearer of bad news. Isn't it odd the way people hold unpleasant facts against those who have told them—"Your son has failed," says the teacher, and the mother never likes the teacher again, quite forgetting that it is the boy who has failed. No, Alexis will have to tell her himself—might as well give him a lesson in responsibility while we're about it. A Vervet monkey jumped onto the front of Hallit's parked car and pounded impatiently at the windshield, hoping for a scrap of cake or candy, and though the sight would normally have made Hallit chuckle, he didn't even see the little creature, so immersed was he in his thoughts.

When Otis tells Lysbeth he is a homosexual, she will naturally be upset, but it will solve the problem because she is too rational to ever want the impossible, and she will know how weak the foundations of their continuing relationship would be. Lysbeth desires a strong man—not a homosexual.

Right now she thinks she is *in love* with Otis, and being in love, by her own definition, is flimsy and unreliable and never lasts long, so she couldn't base her decision just on being in love—she would know it would not be enough reason by itself to marry someone. I don't think she *loves* him—that takes so much time; but she does love me. She can't admire him—she can admire his work, but she can't admire *him* as a person—he doesn't exist as a person; but she does admire me. When she learns he is a homosexual, that will destroy the chances of her enjoying sex with him—she could never cope with the knowledge that all the time he really desired someone else, especially a man, because she would not know how to fight that. She will also dislike and mistrust him for not telling her before . . . yes, this unexpected homosexual factor really is a stroke of luck—this should be the end of the problem.

Again Hallit felt a surge of relief. He could feel some of the pent-up anxiety of the past week actually flowing out of him, trickling down the slope before him to be lost in the hippo pool. But then he checked himself. What if he doesn't tell her—what if he tells her something other than the truth? What then? Well, it would depend on what it was he did tell her . . . and by the time Hallit left the game park he had decided what he would do in the case of each alternative of what Otis told Lysbeth.

On the way into the Grill Room, Lysbeth told him about the gun and he took it as an omen. Although one of his alternatives disturbed him, he nevertheless knew it was the only thing to do, but it was the one thing he wasn't actually equipped to do, and he wanted to be fully prepared for whatever Otis might do or say. Now he was.

The Grill Room was crowded and too noisy for intimate conversation, and Hallit was glad—it isolated him with his thoughts. The stage was set, all props were in place, all actors and actresses had arrived in the theater, and the show was about to begin. He drank too much champagne, but it didn't affect his clarity at all. He danced with Lysbeth and then as he watched her dance with Otis—for the last time, he thought—he reached surreptitiously into her purse and transferred the gun to his pocket. Then he gave his dramatic toast as planned and left at once with Jujubee. On the way home he told her he was confident Lys would now return to him, and that faced with reality—a choice between him and Otis—Lys would quickly drop Otis, who was no more to her than a romantic playmate, even though an important one.

When they reached the house Jujubee and Hallit went to their respective rooms and he waited in his study until he heard Otis' car drive in. Then he locked the door of his study from the inside, turned on the shower in his bathroom, locked that door from the outside and went out onto his upstairs terrace. Carefully, and with an ease which surprised him, he stepped over the balustrade surrounding the open terrace, and using the ledge of a ground floor window as a foothold, he lowered himself to the grass. Staying in the shadows and keeping always on the grass, he made his way to the end of the driveway. He looked back at the house and estimated that no one would be able to hear their voices when he spoke to Otis. He had to wait about three minutes, and it seemed much longer, before he heard Otis' car start up and saw the lights come on. As it approached the entrance gates Hallit stepped into the gravel driveway in front of the car. Otis came to a halt, left the motor running, and got out. Hallit walked up to him and asked, "Did you tell her?"

There was no answer.

"Did you tell her?" Again it was a command, not a question.

"Well," answered Otis timidly, "I got thinking after you left my office about how you had intimidated me, and I realized I should never have told you . . . the truth. However, it made me face the fact that I will never be able to live openly as a homosexual; not only would it ruin my career, but I personally wouldn't be able to cope with it. I have the reputation of being a ladies' man, so no

241

one suspects it—except you, and a few men who would never reveal it for obvious reasons. Therefore, the only person who could . . . destroy me is you. But it would be your word against mine. I'm thirty-five years old, I should remarry soon for appearances' sake. Lys would be a very good wife for me—I'm fond of her, she is beautiful, well known, and if I do marry her, your saying I am a homosexual would just seem ridiculous—it would be interpreted by anyone you told as simply being motivated by jealousy. You can't *force* me to say anything to . . ."

"Shut up. What did you tell her?" insisted Hallit in a powerful but controlled voice.

"I told her," continued Otis, the words spilling out too fast and revealing how frightened he was, "that I wanted to marry her and that your toast was only a hoax and that you would probably go to any extreme to prevent our marriage . . . that you might even make up something outrageous such as my being a . . . homosexual. I told you . . . you can't force me . . ."

"What did she say?" asked Hallit in a voice that didn't sound like his own.

"She said," answered Otis feebly, "she said, yes, she wants to marry me."

Hallit's whole body shook with anger. His hand flew up and slapped Otis across the face.

"Did I hurt you that much?" asked Otis, scrambling back into his car.

"If you understand that, then you'll understand why I must kill you. . . ." and while Hallit was saying those words he pulled the gun out of his pocket, put it to Otis' head and pulled the trigger.

Then very calmly, he took from his pocket a pair of soft white cotton gloves, which he used for handling film when working in the editing room, and put them on. The force of the bullet, combined with a last second attempt by Otis to duck, had thrown his body sideways across the passenger seat and all Hallit had to do was lift his legs over a bit so that he could slide behind the wheel. He then drove to the Langata junction where there was a little dirt track leading off into the bushes, and stopped the car. He climbed out hurriedly and started to run home before he realized he had left the lights on—but he hesitated only a moment and decided not to go back. Farther on he stopped to bury the gun. When he reached the house he climbed back up thinking how, by all his

242

standards and values, he should be appalled at what he had just done. But he wasn't. He felt as if he had carried out an act of justice. It had been Otis' choice, not his.

As he let himself into his room he looked at his watch. Twenty-five minutes had passed since he left. Had Lysbeth or Jujubee tried to talk to him? Did either of them know he hadn't been in his room? He took the key to his bathroom out of his pocket, unlocked the door and rushed into the steaming room, threw off his clothes and got under the shower, staying just long enough to drench himself and his hair. Quickly he put on a robe, unlocked his study door, and walking into the hall he saw a light from under Jujubee's door and heard voices coming from the room. Knocking on the door, he called, "Hey, Lysbeth, Jujubee?" and they answered, "Come in."

"I'd like to speak to you, Lysbeth," said Hallit quietly as he walked in drying his hair. Jujubee was sitting on her bed smoking a cigarette and Lysbeth was sitting in the chaise longue. He knew at once that Lysbeth was very upset.

"Why didn't you answer me when I called to you a few minutes ago?" she asked, her voice high and tense. "You locked me out and wouldn't answer. I thought you weren't speaking to me."

"Did you call me? I didn't hear you. I was having a long think in the shower. I didn't even realize I had locked the door. I suppose a lot of us aren't realizing what we are doing right now. . . . Come, Lysbeth, I do want to talk to you. Jujubee, would you be good enough to bring us all a drink?"

Lysbeth went into Hallit's room with him and as she sat on the edge of the leather wing-back chair she said, "This is all so terrible. I feel so dreadful, Hallit, I really am sorry—what an empty thing to say—I'm so confused . . ."

"Wait a minute, Lysbeth," Hallit said gently, as he pulled up a small chair and sat facing her, "you know me well enough to know I don't want you to stay married to me for any other reason than that you want to. To have only your physical presence would be absurd, wouldn't it? You must stay married to me only because that is what you want. You must not consider me. If you stayed with me for my sake it would be only out of pity, and I couldn't stand that. Nor could you. You must consider no one's desires other than your own. You must not substitute my judgment or Otis' for yours."

"But I'm not sure I even have any judgment any more . . . I . . . oh, why did this have to happen?"

Jujubee brought drinks, then slipped out quietly. Witnessing their pain was not something she wanted to do. She understood how tragic and tortured they both felt.

"But it has happened," said Hallit. "If the three of us were given a choice, we might all wish it hadn't, but that doesn't alter the situation. I certainly wish it were otherwise, but I am capable of understanding how it did happen . . . people fall in love. . . . If you want a divorce, of course I won't fight it."

"You won't?" said Lys puzzled.

"What would be the use, my love? I am desolate, naturally, but what can I do but accept it if you want to marry him? I would then just . . . try to recover."

Lysbeth was stunned at his attitude, for knowing Hallit as she did, she had expected him to tear into Alexis with a withering verbal attack, and with devastating, searing remarks, to attempt to destroy her chances of happiness with him. She expected Hallit at least to try to convince her that she should stay with him and to offer compelling reasons for doing so. She knew he meant it when he said she must be the one who wanted to stay married, but she also knew, or at least thought she knew, that he would try to make her want to stay married to him. She had felt sure that he would fight for what he believed was right. It was odd—even Alexis had been suspicious and had said that Hallit's toast at the Grill Room was a hoax—a ploy of some kind—and that he would probably go to all extremes to fight to keep her. Alexis had even said something—what was it?—oh, yes, that Hallit might even say that Alexis was a homosexual . . . Confusion swirled in her head and the drink wasn't helping her thoughts to become any more orderly. Hallit was saying that she must decide but not consider him, and that he would co-operate with whatever her decision was. Stunned, she couldn't think of much to say, so she answered, "Thank you, Hallit. I must admit I didn't expect this—I expected a lot of questioning and interrogation to satisfy your important sense of truth, and I do want to tell you about it. I want you to know that I *am* responsible, and that I know that I not only owe you an explanation, but I want to give one to you." Then Lysbeth put her head in her hands and confessed, "Perhaps what I am try-

244

ing to say is that I will tell you the facts and then you can explain it all to me."

"Not now. You sleep now—you'll be able to think better in the morning. Come," he said looking at his watch, "it's nearly two o'clock, it's late."

He put his arm around her shoulder and as he walked her to her room they passed Jujubee's door and the light was still on, so Lysbeth called, "Good night, Jujubee," and Jujubee answered. When they reached Lysbeth's bedroom she turned and looked at Hallit and he looked at her longingly and said, "I love you, Lysbeth." She said, "I love you too, Hallit," but her eyes were downcast and she turned immediately and closed the door after her.

She drew a deep hot bath and lay soaking in it, feeling alternate joy and sorrow. Both extremes. I feel just like the hot and cold water, she thought, bliss that Alexis has asked me to marry him, and sorrow at the thought of hurting Hallit. Why does joy so often have to be at someone else's expense? To leave Alexis is impossible, but to leave Hallit, though difficult and painful, is not impossible. True, she reflected, Alexis wasn't as smart as Hallit or as creative, but then who was? She certainly wasn't, and when she wanted intellectual stimulation she would read a book or talk to an intelligent friend. She didn't need Alexis to be anything more than he was because whatever he was, he made her life sing. He provided that quality that sets life apart from itself—that turns the heavy chore of mundane routines into happy yellow butterflies dancing in the sunshine. She felt she had to follow that flow of being in love for without it, *she* didn't exist. Falling in love with someone was, after all, just falling in love with yourself—you became a brighter person—brighter not only in the sense of being more alert, but bright in that you actually glowed more with—life. Would it end one day with Alexis? she wondered. Probably so. If, as they say, your past is your future—that even personal history repeats itself, that you follow a pattern—then yes, Alexis would one day no longer be the source of her lifespring. Then she would go on to a new source—as a heroin addict would go on to a new pusher if his old one no longer supplied what was needed.

As she got out of the tub she caressed herself in a giant terry cloth towel, and she realized how, if she weren't in love, she would simply be drying herself. She could not choose to do the lesser of the two. Hallit would be able to understand this. He would be hurt, of course. She would explain all of it to him in the morning—how she dreaded morning.

In the midst of a deep sleep she heard the phone ring—one of Hallit's film units arriving probably—they were always calling in the middle of the night from the airport—why didn't planes ever land in civilized hours? She drifted back to sleep and then half an hour later the phone rang again. Lysbeth scrinched at the clock on her bedside table—7:30 A.M.—why am I awake? Then she realized Hallit was calling her name and she turned and saw him standing at the foot of her bed and by his face she knew something was wrong. "What is it?" she asked, sitting up in bed.

"I have some bad news, Lysbeth. Really bad," he said as he walked toward her and sat on the bed. "Otis has been in an accident. He is dead."

There was no answer, just silence and big eyes looking at him screaming, two screaming eyes which made no sound, so he said it again, for what else could he say? "Alexis is dead." The amber eyes stayed on his and her voice whispered slowly, too slowly,

"What do you mean?" and the next time it was the same slow words, only louder. The third time she screamed, "What do you mean?" but the scream was still not as loud as the scream of her eyes.

The noise brought Jujubee hurrying into the room. Hallit was saying, "The police called before to say there had been an accident near the Langata junction and they thought it was Otis who had been found dead in the car. They called again to confirm it . . ."

"Christ—a car crash," said Jujubee.

"Well, no . . . when the police telephoned the second time I thought it was going to be to confirm whether or not it *was* Otis, but they said it . . . it wasn't an accident . . . that he has been found . . . shot."

"Suicide?" asked Jujubee unbelievingly.

Lysbeth sat in the bed, poised, as actors sometimes are at the end of a film—with the frame frozen in time—that's how she looked sitting there . . . not as if she were in slow motion, but as if she had stopped forever.

"No," said Hallit very slowly, as if he, too, were trying to understand, "they say he was shot—that it must be . . . murder."

246

Lysbeth came unfrozen and melted into the bed. Hallit and Jujubee both ran to her. Hallit loathed seeing her so tortured, but he knew it was far less now than it would have been if she had married Otis. What she was suffering now was like an operation—dreadful to go through but much better when it was over. Married to Otis she would have been in constant pain for years, but she would be over this present agony in a few weeks and over Otis forever in a few months. Hallit had his arms around her and kept repeating, "Oh, my love, I'm sorry," and Lysbeth kept moaning, "I can't believe it, I can't believe it," and Jujubee left the room and came back with some brandy. She handed her a glass and Lysbeth sobbed, "Who would want to kill Alexis—who? Who?"

Hallit noticed a strange look cross Jujubee's face, and then she turned and stared at him, but she said nothing.

Fifteen minutes passed while both Hallit and Jujubee tried to calm Lysbeth, and when Jujubee handed her a second glass of brandy and a tranquilizer, Lysbeth asked for a cigarette. Jujubee didn't have hers with her, and when Hallit reached into his bathrobe pocket for his, he saw the pack was empty, so Lysbeth reached for her purse which was right by the bed, and fumbled for her cigarettes. Unable to find them immediately, she dumped the contents on the bed, and as she lit her cigarette, her hands trembling, she suddenly said, "Where's that gun? The one I had in my bag last night? The one . . ."

"I buried it," answered Hallit quietly.

"You buried it?—buried it? Why? When?"—her voice was a plea of confusion.

"I didn't want it to become an issue—that gun was unlicensed. I don't want any complications. It's just easier this way . . ."

Jujubee turned and stood looking out the window.

Lysbeth said, "But that gun has nothing to do with Alexis—his death has nothing to do with us . . ."

"Exactly. That's why I buried it. That gun is completely unimportant—but it is bad timing to have a gun and a . . . someone being shot. I just wanted to save you a lot of unnecessary questioning and complications . . ."

"When did you take it?" asked Lysbeth, not in a tone of interrogation or accusation, but rather of bewilderment.

"When the police called back and said it wasn't an accident but

247

that Alexis had been shot—it reminded me of the gun and I just didn't want you to be associated with a gun in any way—it would invite all kinds of ghastly probing and cross-examination if they knew you had had an unlicensed firearm in your bag all the time you were with Alexis yesterday and on the way home last night, so I came in here while you were sleeping and got it, then buried it . . . in the middle of Africa."

Jujubee turned and said, "Hallit, don't you think it would be better if I took Lys up to the farm today—to get her out of this—so she won't have to endure . . . to let her get a hold of herself?"

"Good idea. I'm afraid the police are on their way out here now—they will ask you a few questions, my darling. Just tell them the truth—but don't mention the gun, and if they ask you about 'a' gun—say you know nothing about any gun. They'll probably ask you such things as what you and I were talking about last night. Just tell them the truth—that we were having an amicable discussion about the possibility of a divorce, that . . ."

The telephone rang. "I'll take it in my room," said Hallit, leaving.

Lysbeth grabbed Jujubee's arm and whispered frantically, "Jujubee, do you think . . . do you think . . . Hallit . . . don't you think it's strange about the gun? His attitude last night was very unlike Hallit—do you think . . ."

Just then Hallit reappeared and said it was William calling from the hospital—he had just heard of the tragedy, so Jujubee rushed out to talk to him and Hallit sat on the bed and gathered Lysbeth into his arms again, but this time he felt her stiffen. Something had changed . . . had she suspected? He had anticipated this, and had mentally directed the scene many times before dawn. On cue now he said, "It's all so confusing, and it is impossible to think that anyone would want to kill Alexis, but darling, I do have a clue. Yesterday afternoon when I talked to him in his office—perhaps he has mentioned this to you himself—he told me how unpopular he was in South Africa with the Afrikaners—that because he is so well known throughout the world *and* has a voice, they were afraid he would use it against apartheid, and with world opinion mounting against them, they don't want anyone who lives there speaking out against them—especially him. He was telling me he was afraid he may not be able to go back to South Africa, that he had even been threatened . . . perhaps it was a political murder . . ."

248

"But Alexis wasn't political in any way, you know that, you got angry with him about it, he . . ."

"You never know, do you? Perhaps he had us all fooled—it would be a good cover. Perhaps he was actually working for the . . ."

Just then the doorbell rang and Jujubee answered it and they heard police voices downstairs, and in a few minutes Jujubee called Hallit and he went downstairs while Lysbeth stayed in bed thinking. Then, slowly, very slowly, she got out of bed and put on a flowing white-satin robe, and looking ghostlike, she started down the stairs clutching the bannister, then stopped. The inspector looked up from the hall and said, "Lady Lindsey, sorry about the—death of Dr. Otis." Lysbeth, still standing on the stairs was silent, and everyone waited for her to say something, but she said nothing. Hallit's blue eyes pleaded with her, and Jujubee's green eyes pleaded with her, and the inspector, already aware of the presence of a beautiful woman, asked, "Lady Lindsey, I know this is a dreadful time for you, but could I just have a few words with you? Would you care to sit in the drawing room—it won't take long?"

"If it won't take long, I'd rather just stay here. What is it you'd like to know?" asked Lysbeth in an unnatural voice as she continued down the stairs.

"Could you tell me what time you got home last night?" asked the inspector, but he was thinking as she walked down the stairs so slowly, her white robe dragging behind her accentuating her grief, that she looked rather like a bride with no bridegroom. He felt sad. As well as lustful.

Hallit and Jujubee knew this next moment would determine the course of their lives. Lysbeth walked close enough to the inspector so she could look into his eyes, and at that moment Jujubee knew all was safe, for Lys always said, "Look them right in the eyes and lie." Hallit also knew at that same moment for he realized that Lysbeth was planning to use her eyes on the inspector and would go through with the story.

They heard her saying, "It was just 12:30 A.M. when Dr. Otis and I arrived here from the Grill Room. I noticed the clock when we walked in. He came in with me and stayed for about five minutes, then he left."

"Did you see anyone else?" asked the inspector, trying to ap-

pear professional and hoping it wasn't obvious that he noticed that
. . . that . . . quality about her which was making him want to
take her in his arms and protect her from all of this.

"Yes. I saw my husband—and Baroness Boucher. First I went to
her room and we talked for a few minutes—fifteen or so. Then I
went to my husband's room and we talked."

"Do you remember for how long?"

"Another quarter hour or so. Juju . . . Baroness Boucher
brought us drinks—so it was enough time for us to drink them.
Another ten minutes at least."

"May I ask what your conversation with Lord Lindsey was
about?" asked the inspector gently.

"We were discussing the possibility of a divorce. He was being
very co-operative, and I thanked him for it." Then, turning to
Hallit, but still speaking to the inspector, she said, "He's a much
more astonishing man than you, or anyone but I and Baroness
Boucher, will ever know."

The inspector paused a moment as if in respect to her tribute to
Hallit, then asked, "Did Baroness Boucher stay and have a drink
with you?"

Hallit's heart quickened because Lysbeth dropped her eyes and
obviously was thinking of something else—trying to decide if she
should . . . he recognized that expression and knew that Lysbeth
knew this was her last chance of telling the truth—that if she concealed the knowledge about the gun she would be committed to it
forever, that no one would ever know. Lysbeth didn't answer. She
just stood there clutching the bannister and staring at the floor.
The inspector coughed slightly then said, "Lady Lindsey, did
Baroness Boucher stay and have a drink with you and Lord Lindsey?"

Lysbeth looked up at him and still in a strangely soft voice said,
"Oh, I'm sorry, Inspector—my mind drifted . . . ummmm . . .
what was it?—oh, no, Baroness Boucher went right back to her
room. She didn't stay with my husband and me, but when I left his
room I saw the light was still on in Jujubee's room, so we called
good night to each other . . . it must have been at least 1:45 or
2 A.M. by then. Is there anything else? If not, would you excuse
me, please?"

"Thank you, Lady Lindsey—that's all—sorry to have bothered
you."

"We just heard about this a short while ago—it's very . . . shocking," said Lys.

"Yes, yes, terrible . . ." muttered the inspector, trying hard not to show how very much he wanted to gather this poor little delicate sparrow to him and kiss her—kiss away all her grief.

And she turned and glided up the stairs.

W*ell, thought Hallit, there are my three versions. Each one is entirely possible, but only one is entirely true. Let the world decide.*

He got up from his chair, refilled his glass, and stood by the window looking out. He thought, there, then, is the end of my . . . film. I don't have anything more to say. Everyone knows I was arrested and accused—as I knew I would be—and if anyone didn't follow the headlines and stories they can look it up easily enough to find out how I was acquitted on "insufficient evidence." Because the murder weapon was never found it didn't take the jury long to reach their verdict.

I must say Hobson was spectacularly clever as my defense lawyer. I'll never get over what he said when he was told of the verdict. Hallit took a large gulp of his drink, picked up the shotgun and swung it back and forth as he envisioned the scene at Kennedy Airport when Hobson had returned to New York after the trial: Hobson had been unable to wait for the verdict due to another urgent case in the States, and judgment on me was passed when he was flying over the Atlantic. The news that I was acquitted was telexed through, and two of Hobson's partners as well as a number of reporters met him as he stepped off the plane. "Lord Lindsey was acquitted," they shouted. "Of course," said Hobson, with that devastating arrogance of his—oh, I can just picture him now. "Well," asked the reporters, "if Lindsey didn't kill Otis, then who did?" Hobson looked at them coldly, and as he turned to walk away he answered, "I forgot to ask."

is cha...

with policing the state's medical profession, have generally

ities,
Medic
gents.
overse
pline

/onge-
Shel-
were
t the
gedly
lviser

MILESTONES

Died. Lord Rufus Hallit Lindsey, England's five-time award-winning film maker — "Sound of Silence," "Lollipops Make Me Cry" and many others, recently acquitted in notorious murder trial in Africa, of suicide, in London. See feature story, page 1.

The
on evi
eral ag
sixties
port
in De
cobs
ulant
man

March
,est ar-
of the
igation
of the
Com-
iously
: Shel-
n the

cians earlier this year. The report contains 235 findings of fact against Dr. Jacobson

If
shc

tion by the P